The Begum and the Dastan

TARANA HUSAIN KHAN

Happy reading!
Tarana

hachette
INDIA

First published in 2021 by Tranquebar, an imprint of Westland Publications Private Limited

This edition published in India in 2023 by Hachette India
(Registered name: Hachette Book Publishing India Pvt. Ltd)
An Hachette UK company
www.hachetteindia.com

SRD

ISBN 978-93-93701-62-6

For sale in all territories excluding Pakistan.

Hachette Book Publishing India Pvt. Ltd
4th & 5th Floors, Corporate Centre
Plot No. 94, Sector 44, Gurugram – 122003, India

Typeset in Minion Pro 11.5/13.8
by Manmohan Kumar, Delhi

Printed and bound in India
by Manipal Technologies Limited

FSC
www.fsc.org
MIX
Paper | Supporting responsible forestry
FSC™ C104740

For Mamola Begum
and the women of Rampur

This world is but a tale we hear,
Men's evil and glory disappear.

Shahnameh
Abolqasem Ferdowsi

◆

Chahiye naam usi ka ae khama,
Zeenat-e-naam zeb sar nama,
Falak uski namoona qudrat ka;
Ek qalamdaan hazaar sanat ka
Rukh-e-qartaas ko safai di
Aur siyahi ko roshanai di.

I invoke His exalted name as my cup-bearer of inspiration,
The beauteous name of the Creator of miraculous heavens,
Who imbued the humble ink stand with artistic inspiration;
Who granted whiteness and purity to the face of the page,
And illuminated the darkness of black ink.

Tilism-e-Hoshruba
Sayed Muhammad Husain Jah

Cast of Characters

In Sherpur

1. Nawab Shams Ali Khan: Nawab of Sherpur. Sherpur was a north Indian princely state under the British colonial rule.
2. Feroza Begum: The second wife of Nawab Shams Ali Khan. She was given the title of Sarkar Aliya.

Feroza Begum's family:

1. Miya Jaan Khan: Feroza Begum's father.
2. Phul Begum: Feroza's mother.
3. Gauhar: Feroza's sister.
4. Zubeida Begum: Miya Jaan's second wife and Feroza's stepmother.
5. Ruqayya: Feroza's stepsister.
6. Nausha: Feroza's stepbrother.
7. Murtaza Ali Khan: Feroza's husband.
8. Azmat Khan: Feroza's father-in-law.
9. Tabu (Tabassum): Feroza's milk-sister and friend.
10. Bua (Akbari Bua): Tabu's mother and Feroza's wet nurse.
11. Asiya: Feroza's first cousin.
12. Amina Khala: Feroza's aunt and Asiya's mother.
13. Nanhi Begum: Feroza's daughter.
14. Mehdi Raza Khan: Nanhi's husband.

15. Husain Raza and Sumayya Begum: Mehdi's parents.
16. Mohsin: Mehdi's brother.
17. Farhat: Mohsin's wife and Nanhi's sister-in-law.
18. Dadi: Feroza's granddaughter.
19. Ameera: Feroza's great-granddaughter.
20. Jugnu: Ameera's brother and Feroza's great-grandson.
21. Meel and Chanda Bua: House servants at Ameera's house.

At the Palace:

1. Sultanat Ara Begum: Nawab Shams's first wife. Also called Basodeywali Begum.
2. Huzur Aliya: Nawab Shams Ali Khan's great-grandmother-in-law.
3. Babbo Jaan AKA Shahana Dulhan: Nawab Shams Ali Khan's third wife.
4. Daroghan Chhamman: In charge of the harems of the Nawab.
5. Diwani Begum: A mutah wife of Nawab Shams Ali Khan.
6. Azeezan and Mahabat Khan: Servants at the harem.
7. Sara Small: Wife of Colonel Small, who was posted at Sherpur.
8. Hasan Ali Khan: The Crown prince of Sherpur.
9. Achhi Begum: Hasan's mother.
10. Rafi Ali Khan and Zafar Ali Khan: Sons of Shams Ali Khan.

Characters in Dastan

1. Ameeruddin Haya AKA Mirza Kallan: A dastango and Tabu's husband.
2. Mirza Waliuddin: Kallan Mirza's brother.

3. Saad bin Ameer Hamza: Son of Ameer Hamza and a great warrior.
4. Princess Lalarukh: Saad's wife.
5. Amar ayyar: A trickster and friend of Ameer Hamza.
6. King Sheez: Lalarukh's father and ruler of Koh Kaaf.
7. Asman Pari: Ex-wife of Ameer Hamza and Lalarukh's paternal aunt.
8. Tareek Jaan: A powerful sorcerer and son of Afrasiyab, the creator of *Tilism-e-Hoshruba* and opponent of Ameer Hamza.
9. Afreet, Aaseb and Tez Chashm: Djinns under the command of Tareek Jaan.
10. Chalak bin Amar: Amar ayyar's son.
11. Sarsar: Wife of Amar ayyar.
12. Huzur Afat Char Chashm: The four-eyed great-grandmother of Tareek Jaan.
13. Malika Husnara Jadu: Chief queen of Tareek Jaan.
14. Begum Mahpara: Second wife of Tareek Jaan.
15. Princess Sadaf: Husnara's cousin and a sorceress.
16. Gulistan Jadu: A powerful sorceress.
17. Rohu Mahipusht: A fish man living in the River of Silver Hues.
18. Zaroon and Rafey: Powerful magicians imprisoned in the Zulmat Dungeons by Tareek Jaan.
19. Goshtkhor: A powerful sorcerer sequestered in a hujra for forty years.
20. Prince Bemisal: Tareek Jaan's crown prince.

Prologue

The Nawab was gone, leaving a gaping cavity in the weed-ridden grass.

Ameera pressed her face close to the school-bus window and peered out at the empty space. The school buses had stopped in a clamorous yellow line and the students jostled around the windows. A few senior students jumped down, ignoring the dire threats of the teachers. Crowds had gathered around the little unkempt garden and some men had climbed over the iron grill to examine the hollow, keeping a safe distance from the officious policemen.

Ameera was accustomed to looking at the familiar marble statue on the way to school. Dadi had told her that the Nawab was their ancestor. He had been married to Dadi's great-grandmother – a scandalous family history which Dadi loved to narrate.

Towering over scattered bougainvillea and wild cannabis bushes in the triangular garden, the statue of Nawab Shams Ali Khan had stood in full court attire, rows of pearls covering his chest and forearms, the legs slightly apart, one hand holding the sword at his side. It was magnificent despite the black fungus patches. A few years ago, the Nawab's nose had been broken and the sword by his side taken away by vandals, prompting the district administration to enclose the garden with an iron grill and secure it with a gate. That morning, the gate was found locked, as usual, but the statue had vanished.

She must tell Dadi.

That was the first disappearance. Soon, the three ancient *topkhana* gateways, with their scalloped arches leading into the city, were almost magically wiped out. The old became a memory as the new gates forced themselves into their consciousness. In time, fewer people would know the gates had ever existed.

Photograph, 1885 (approximate year)

In a formal official picture taken probably at the British Agent's office at Bareilly, a ten-year-old Shams Ali Khan stands wearing a black *achkan*, a gold watch chain dangling from his breast pocket, a black *topi* on his head and a confident, smug half-smile.[1] His complexion, costume and age are a stark contrast to the white skinned, distinguished, thick-moustached and clean-shaven British officials towering over him. Even as a child he looks sure of himself and his position among the British officials. He was, after all, the crown prince of Sherpur State. The officials shook his hand and British ladies fawned over him, offering cakes as he spoke his tutored English lines.

He stands behind an important-looking official, probably the British Agent, seated on an armchair, stiff, in control; his wife next to him, smiles primly at the camera; a thoroughbred Jack Russell at her feet looks away, alert. Three other ladies in their fashionable, prudish gowns and the gentlemen in their formal suits with medals pinned on their coats, lounge on dissimilar chairs.

Notes

1. The princely state of Sherpur came under the administrative supervision of the British Agent stationed at Bareilly.

I

Feroza Begum

Sherpur, 1896

> The Nawab was not happy with Feroza Begum for she was the cause of his ill-repute. It was because of her that he got the reputation of preying on newly married women and forcing them into his harem.
>
> *Darbar-e-Sherpur* (An unpublished memoir),
> Bilquis Begum[1]

Ameera buried her face into the attar-scented embroidered cushion on Dadi's bed. Right at that moment, she wanted to dissolve into another, less complicated world. Dadi's room had the most comforting and tranquil smells – the earthiness of the molasses-dipped tobacco scent of her hookah, the cardamom smell of her paan and the musk fragrance of attar. Dadi's face floated above the puffs of white smoke from her hookah, smiling down at her. The windowless room was enveloped in a cool darkness, the walls slightly moist to the touch, a single ventilator window near the roof bringing in a slice of the blue-heated afternoon sky. Ameera unfolded herself and drew in the stillness.

Dadi's huge four-poster bed dominated the room with the intricately carved royal monogram and hand-painted inlay of peacocks that Ameera loved to trace her fingers over; a gauzy mosquito net draped over the carved framework was tied back for the day. The room itself seemed to exist in an alternate dimension with its antique dressing table, the original Belgian glass showing age spots, a line of coloured glass bottles of attar perfumes that Dadi insisted on using and a silver *surmadani* with the famous Bareilly kohl that kept her beautiful eyes free of glasses. China figurines from pastoral Britain sat on the wooden mantel of a defunct fireplace alongside the books of Urdu and Persian poetry Dadi enjoyed reading and quoting from. There was a lumpy sofa set upholstered with faded red brocade that had seen more glorious days, low stools for the servants and a table with her silver *pandan* and *khasdan* to prepare and serve her betel leaf concoction. Most days, Dadi would listen to her old gramophone records – ghazals and *thumri*s in voices from far beyond captured on ancient black discs moving slowly on a hand-wound gramophone. Ameera laughed when the singer announced, 'I'm Gauhar Jaan' or 'I'm Babbo Jaan.'

'Ah, there are such stories in these voices. I remember listening to the great Gauhar Jaan as a child. You know, this Babbo Jaan became Her Highness Shahana Begum, Queen of Sherpur, and ruled over us,' Dadi would cackle, her eyes closing with mirth and the wrinkles deepening over her cheeks.

'Dadi, tell me a story,' Ameera murmured into the pillow.

'*Aap beeti ki jag beeti*, my story or a story of the world?' This was the choice she always gave her. Ameera knew the answer.

'Aap beeti, tell me about the night great-grandma was kidnapped by the Nawab.' This was always her demand. Ameera cupped her cheek and curled up before Dadi's ancient armchair.

'Hush, that's the end of the story. So let me begin with the *sawani* that changed the course of our destinies.'

'What's a "sawani"?' She knew the answer, but that was her cue.

'*Beti*, sawani celebrates the coming of the monsoon, the first rains of the month of Sawan. There are swings in orchards, fried puris and pakodis,' Dadi's voice echoed, whispering in the cool darkness. Ameera sighed, closing her eyes, letting the cadence of the familiar story lull her mind.

'So, this is the story of Feroza Begum, my grandmother and your great-grandmother. May Allah forgive my tongue for any transgressions. The year was 1896 or 1897, the reign of Nawab Shams Ali Khan had just begun, and Feroza Begum desperately wanted to attend the sawani hosted by the Nawab at Benazir Palace to commemorate his twenty-first birthday. Now, Feroza was a very wilful and headstrong girl, indulged by her father, Miya Jaan Khan, who loved and despaired at her familial stubborn streak and her temper, so very like his own. She was his firstborn and the only one with his blue eyes. He had named her 'Feroza' for her blue Feroza gemstone eyes. So, if Feroza wanted something, there could be no peace until she got her way. Miya Jaan Khan had hoped that her marriage two years ago to Murtaza Raza Khan, the son of his dearest friend and kinsman, would calm her down; but the sweet-tempered Murtaza, wonderstruck by her beauty, was completely dominated by her.

Now I must tell you, just to make things clear, that Feroza and Gauhar were Miya Jaan Khan's daughters by his first marriage to his cousin, the formidable Phul Begum.

At that time, in every household and in Miya Jaan Khan's *haveli*, two parallel lives existed in tandem – the *mardana* and the *zenana*, the male and female sections, connected by a single door. Only the master of the house, his sons and very close male relatives could access the zenana.

As she was about a year older than her husband, Phul Begum found it fit to call him by his formal name – a practice unheard of at that time. 'Altaf Khan!' she would bellow from the zenana and he had become a figure of ridicule among friends and elders sitting in the mardana *baithak*, the 'males only' sitting room. 'Go, your *bulawa* has come,' they would snigger. He had to abandon the conversation, hookah and chess to attend to her or she would go on calling. Despite many warnings, she, with the same obstinacy, continued to take his name. Miya Jaan Khan divorced her in a fit of rage and forbade the daughters to ever meet their mother.

I don't know what happened to Phul Begum after that, but the girls, about six and five at that time, were completely cut off from their mother. Feroza and Gauhar sat on the takht, their arms touching each other, watching the inglorious departure of their mother in petrified silence. Miya Jaan Khan then married a biddable, down-to-earth woman, Zubeida Begum, who produced two sons, Nausha and Pyarey, and a daughter, Ruqayya, in quick succession. Zubeida Begum walked the edges of Miya Jaan Khan's mercurial temper, soothing his rages and trying to ensure a peaceful household. Nausha's antics also contributed to her constant stress.

Nausha was a precocious thirteen-year-old who loved to dabble in medicines and alchemy and found a mentor in his maternal grandfather, a *hakim*. Nausha would often make concoctions to play pranks on hapless servants and even experiment on himself, with disastrous results. Feroza loved him for his ability to make everything fun and laughable.

He would pander to her cravings for street food, running off to the bazaar to get her chaat and sweets. She in turn would shield him from parental wrath and help him out of scrapes. Only Nausha dared to smuggle out Miya Jaan's treasured books of romantic poetry from the mardana for her and she would sit reading the ghazals and setting them to simple tunes.

The *dai* had recently diagnosed Feroza's pregnancy after two years of Unani medicines and rustic cures. It was a cause of great happiness but Zubeida Begum was worried that some calamity might befall the unborn child during Feroza's Sawan visit.

'If I had known that she was with child, I would never have called her,' Zubeida Begum sighed. The girl was quite a handful and never took heed of the warnings constantly thrown at her throughout the day by Zubeida Begum and Akbari Bua, Feroza's wet nurse.

Even today in Sherpur there is a tradition of married daughters spending the month of Sawan at their parents' place. So Zubeida had invited both her stepdaughters home. If she didn't, there would be much criticism from relatives. Gauhar, married to a rich nobleman, was to arrive a few days later and the girls would celebrate the monsoon in their paternal home. Zubeida, whose existence revolved around pre-empting and dodging unprovoked, fault-finding remarks by her in-laws, had sent Nausha to fetch Feroza in the new buggy, laden with fruits, sweets, pattey,[2] puris, and a light green monsoon ensemble for Feroza.

'Begum, you don't worry. I have prayed at Baghdadi Sahib's *dargah*. All will be well for Feroza,' said Akbari Bua adding extra tobacco to Zubeida's paan to soothe her nerves. Zubeida handled the troubles at home – the bitter edge of tongues and frayed tempers – with an extra pinch of tobacco.

It was customary for girls to take their personal servants with them when they got married and shifted into their husband's home. So, when Feroza got married, Akbari Bua and her daughter Tabassum, 'Tabu' for short, had settled down with Feroza at her in-laws' place. Bua took charge of everything relating to Feroza. Bua and Tabu, Feroza's milk-sister and confidante, were the two pillars of her domestic life.

'When will this girl show some maturity? Since yesterday she has been arguing with her father to send her to the Nawab's sawani,' said Zubeida Begum, ruminating her paan. It was Nausha's fault. He had attended the sawani with his father a year ago and spoken endlessly about the singers, poets and dancers who came to perform from Lucknow and Delhi, the mind-boggling dishes served and the fun ladies had had on the swings.

Feroza was fanatic about music and poetry. She enjoyed attending ladies singing events and writing ghazals. Her voice, though untrained, was sweet and tuneful and she often led the chorus. She particularly loved singing Dagh Dehlvi's passionate love compositions though they were considered a bit bold for a woman singer.

'*Ooi* Begum, doesn't Feroza Bibi know that Pathan women from good families don't go to the Nawab's palace? He gets after all kinds of women and our Feroza's beauty is such that all the royal Begums will fall at her feet!' Akbari Bua carefully covered the paan leaves with a wet rag to keep them fresh.

Zubeida Begum sighed again, fanning herself rapidly, anxiety and extra tobacco inducing a tide of sweat to drip down her back. She couldn't imagine how Feroza could challenge her father's towering rage.

'You are as stubborn as your mother and… and shameless. How dare you throw your marriage at my face!' Miya Jaan had roared.

'But *Abba*, Murtaza doesn't have any problem with my going there. Women from his family are allowed to attend the zenana durbar,' Feroza had retorted.

'Ya Allah, don't take the name of your husband. It will reduce his life!' Zubeida Begum had warned, touching her cheeks alternately, begging forgiveness from the all-listening God ready to shower misfortune because of a single unthoughtful utterance.

'Beti, your Abba is right. Pathan women don't go there because of the Nawab's misdemeanours. It is for our own safety...'

Feroza ignored her and continued, 'Abba, you never let us go to the durbar. What would the Nawab do to a married woman?'

'Go when you are old and toothless! This Nawab is already showing his true colours. He is a debauch drunk on power. He takes away women from their homes!'

'I promise I shall keep away. He won't see me.'

'How will you stop him from coming into the zenana? I'm from the family of Nawab Nasrullah Khan and I won't parade my women at the court!'[3]

He stormed out of the zenana to his peaceful male quarters, sending for his friends to rant about Feroza's latest tantrum.

Miya Jaan had not attended the grand *taajposhi*, the crowning ceremony of Nawab Shams Ali Khan, in 1895 when the British had granted him full rights over the state, ending a rather controversial regency period. Miya Jaan and several Pathans secretly blamed the young Nawab and his great grandmother, Huzur Aliya, for engineering the dastardly murder of the regent, General Ameerullah Khan. Miya Jaan was distantly related to the young General and had been fond of him even though he hadn't approved of his attempts to modernise and anglicise the state. However, on the advice of Feroza's father-in-law, Miya Jaan had attended the sawani at Benazir Palace and offered *nazar* (tribute) to the Nawab last year to stay on the right side of the powers. The grudging acceptance veiled a deep mistrust.

Feroza cried in petulant anger, refused to eat and threatened to return to her in-laws where everyone loved her.

'Send her back!' Miya Jaan Khan said when he was told of her threats. He refused to enter the zenana and had all his meals in the mardana. Miya Jaan Khan's mardana baithak was well-equipped with large takhts and two bedrooms to rest in during the day and to accommodate male guests. The male section was completely inaccessible to the women folk and a refuge for men in times of domestic crises.

Miya Jaan Khan would stand at the connecting door between the zenana and mardana and say to a quivering Zubeida, 'Tell your daughter…' he would begin and proceed to rain insults. Zubeida Begum was in a quandary. She couldn't send Feroza back till her husband came to fetch her – it would be a breach of protocol. Besides, Zubeida's in-laws and extended family might accuse her of making Feroza feel unwelcome in her own house.

Caught between father and daughter for two days, Zubeida sent for Gauhar to broker peace. Gauhar was supposed to come after a week for her sawan stay. Zubeida Begum sent Akbari Bua with gifts to have a quiet word with Gauhar about the current crisis and ask her to come earlier. Gauhar was younger but the more sensible of the two and marriage had further matured her into a self-possessed young lady. However, things didn't turn out the way she had hoped. Gauhar was Feroza's soulmate so Feroza bullied and cajoled Gauhar into supporting her case. Gauhar acquiesced much against her better judgement. After several more angry scenes and threats to cut off all ties, Gauhar was able to persuade her father to let Feroza go to the sawani for the day, escorted by Zubeida Begum and Akbari Bua.

Miya Jaan's pleasure at Feroza's visit was marred by the discord and his lingering anxiety. Still furious, he told Zubeida, 'You women always do what you want. Just bring her back safely and send her back to her *sasural*.'

Notes

1. Bilquis Begum's aunt, Daroghan Chhamman, was a female guard in the harems of Nawab Shams Ali Khan. The unpublished memoir based on oral history is the only written account of the royal harems.

2. A colocasia leaf (*arbi ke pattey*) preparation made during Sawan.

3. Nawab Nasrullah Khan was a famous Rohilla chieftain and one of the founders of the Rohilkhand empire of north India in the eighteenth century. The Rohillas were Pathan tribes from the Roh highlands in Afghanistan.

2

Jashn-e-Benazir

Sherpur, 1896

Nauroz Holi kijiye is jashn par nisaar,
Saqqey bharey hain, rangon ki mashqey kai hazaar.

(Nauroz and Holi pale before the celebrations at the Benazir,
Thousands of water-skins are filled with colours for the play.)[1]

Musaddas-e-Tahniyat-e-Jashn-e-Benazir,
Meer Yar Ali Jaan Sahib Rekhtigo

On the day of the sawani, Feroza took a long, luxurious bath and dressed up in a green brocade churidar pyjamas, a red velvet half-sleeved blouse with a sequinned neckline which dared go deeper than the diktats of modesty. The semi-transparent muslin *jama* she wore over the blouse, gathered under her breasts and flared out to mid-calf length; her exposed waist and cleavage was a tantalising suggestion under the soft folds. Feroza loved to design her own dresses, choosing and combining fabrics, favouring flamboyance over subtlety and diligently supervising the *mughlani* seamstress. Maybe you don't know this, Ameera, at that time the noble households employed a mughlani who would stitch dresses for the ladies at home. The *bajaj*, cloth merchant, would come bearing swathes of silks, *jamdanis* and mulmuls before every occasion, for it was inconceivable that the ladies walk in the bazaars. I myself never visited the shops till much later.

As always, once her demands were met, Feroza was in high spirits, moving ahead, shrugging off the vexation she had caused. She knew Abba would forgive her; she would be extra-loving towards him once she got back, teasing and laughing with him the way only she could dare. She would hug him tight, burying her face in his chest, refusing to let go till he forgave her, call her *churail*, *pagli*, and kiss the top of her head, his rough beard brushing her forehead. The intensity of their love always flowed out in dramatic scenes. None of the other children dared defy him or hug him. If he was really happy with them, he would put his hand on their heads in blessing.

The children had all played with Miya Jaan's beard as babies but outgrew it when they began to recognise his volatile, disciplinarian side. Feroza had carried on stroking his beard to adulthood, running her fingers through it and teasing out the knots. He enjoyed the caress, laughing and saying, 'What do you want, churail?' He ultimately gave in to all her demands out of the tremendous love that only a firstborn can command. After their mother left, while Gauhar had retreated into a precocious silence, Feroza had dealt with the loss by throwing tantrums, banging her head on the floor and breaking things till they gave in to the motherless child. This was one of those rare occasions that Miya Jaan had been adamant in his refusal.

'*Apa*, I can see your tummy, haw, haw!' screamed Ruqayya, her little stepsister, clasping her hands over her mouth.

'Just wait till I wear the dupatta. See, now you can't see a thing.' Feroza wrapped the leheriya, crinkled muslin dupatta around herself and twirled in front of the mirror. She loved the new dress, a present from Murtaza, and her own blossoming curves highlighted by the tight-fitting blouse. How thrilled he would be to hear the news of her pregnancy! Her kind mother-in-law had never remarked on her childless state. Now she wouldn't let Feroza's feet even touch the floor!

She had been engaged to Murtaza when she was seven and he, eleven years old. Murtaza's father, Azmat Khan, was a close friend and a distant cousin of Miya Jaan Khan. For Miya Jaan Khan, the chief merit of the match was that his beloved daughter would continue to live in Sherpur, close at hand. He often requested Azmat to send Feroza over. The house was livelier with her whooping laughter, her songs and demand for special dishes, which, she swore, tasted much better than at her in-laws' place. Feroza would team up with Nausha to play pranks on her siblings and the servants. Miya Jaan pretended anger, threatening to send the pagli back. He adored Feroza's outspoken nature and often provoked her to verbal sparring, enjoying her witty repartees. It was as though the focus of the household turned towards her as she encompassed everyone with her energy and generous love.

Since strict purdah was observed in the families, Murtaza had not seen Feroza before the wedding. He had only heard of her beauty from the maidservants who visited her bearing Eid and sawan gifts. Her blue eyes coloured his adolescent dreams and he had made sure that most of the wedding dresses were in shades of blue, much to the consternation of the seamstresses.

Feroza had an advantage over him because she could tiptoe into the mardana and peer from behind the curtain when he came with his father to say his formal salams on various occasions. Over many Eids and visits she had watched him mature into a striking young man with dreamy eyes and vulnerable lips that moved her to tears of tenderness. Her awareness of him was mingled with her consciousness of her own self transforming into womanhood.

'This looks like a nautch girl's dress. Beti, wear a *farshi* skirt instead; you're a married lady now going to attend a durbar.' Zubeida Begum came into the room, her voluminous farshi trailing on the carpet.

'Ammi, please let me wear this. Besides, I don't have a green farshi. We are supposed to wear green for the sawani, right?'

Zubeida Begum pursed her lips and bit back the pointless argument.

'Tabu, get my small ruby *teeka*. I won't wear these heavy *magars*; my ears will ache.'

'Apa, you're so beautiful!' sighed Ruqayya, watching Tabu tie the ruby teeka on Feroza's forehead.

'You will be beautiful too, my doll, just wait and see. I'll bring sugar toys from the *mela* for you, I promise,' Feroza smiled and hugged Ruqayya.

She put on her lipstick – a daring thing even for a married lady, and jumped up as Zubeida Begum called out to her from the gallery.

'Why can't I go, Ammi?' Ruqayya whined, clutching Zubeida Begum's *burqa* wrap.

'Because Abba will get angry at you too. You stay here, and look after him.'

'Feroza, be careful. The Nawab should not see you,' said Gauhar coming into the room as Feroza flung off the dupatta and put on her burqa, fastening the veil under her chin. Tabu folded the dupatta and put it in a small bag, which also contained a change of dress for Feroza – a farshi, just in case she changed her mind. Generally, women carried a change of dress, for churidars were wont to tear at the wrong places – they were always too tight!

'Yes, yes. I will. Tabu, my bangles!'

She quickly slid on the traditional sawan green and red bangles, shattering quite a few in her haste.

'Wait, you'll injure yourself!' Gauhar helped her ease the rest of the bangles and cleaned the drop of blood on a scratch with her dupatta.

'I wish you could come too! I'll have such stories for you,' Feroza gave her a hug, kissing both her cheeks to soften her disapproval.

Zubeida Begum folded the trailing hem of her farshi *gharara* and held it under her corpulent stomach as she walked out of the door whispering prayers. Tucking a paan in her fleshy cheek, she heaved herself into the buggy, taking up the whole seat. Tabu and Feroza sat opposite her. Bua was forced to sit next to the driver, grumbling at the shamelessness of sitting out in the open with a man. She was sure somebody would recognise her even though she was completely covered.

'Bua, you look like a bride going to her sasural,' laughed Feroza, watching Bua's half-crouching form. The door was closed, Tabu drew the curtains on the side windows and the buggy rolled out of the gateway.

Nausha was going to ride with them to the palace. It was the first grown-up assignment for the young boy and he sat with a solemn look on his horse. Miya Jaan Khan had strictly forbidden him from going inside the palace because he would have to offer nazar to the Nawab and the sharp-eyed Nawab was then sure to ask him about his father.

Feroza threw back her veil, ignoring Zubeida Begum's warning 'hmm' in the middle of her prayers. She hated the headgear of the burqa with its narrow eye slit criss-crossed with tiny crocheted squares which only allowed a blinkered, sliced view of the world. Zubeida Begum completed her prayer and secured Feroza's safety by blowing several prayer breaths on her face and her stomach. Her household routine revolved around prayer timings, the men frequenting the mohalla mosque several times a day. Feroza had a youthful indifference towards religious practices and had to be prompted to pray. Gauhar often pulled Feroza to pray alongside her to shield her from reprimands. Her in-laws were more relaxed about prayers and she would sometimes join her mother-in-law on the prayer mat to please her.

Feroza was excited riding the plush, new two-horse buggy. She must ask Murtaza to get one too. Theirs was a small, one-horse open buggy, with the curtain fastened on the hood if she rode. Her radius of movement was narrow enough to be negotiated by a covered palanquin but she loved the clip-clop energy of a buggy.

The Benazir Palace was on the outskirts of the city. They drove through the gateway to the bazaar set up in the early nineteenth century by Nawab Nasrullah Khan. Nasrullah Khan Bazaar was famous for *chaku* and molasses-dipped hookah tobacco. Shops with colourful awnings selling all kinds of wares – spices, grains, utensils, cloth, jewellery lined the streets. Traversing the bazaar square, they turned right and the buggy went through the three identical arches of the cannon-mounted topkhana gates. The scalloped arches, stationed at a distance of about half a kilometre from each other, were the impressive entrance into the town and the royal fort.

The city fell away as they exited the gates for the encircling outer ring road. Sherpur was situated in the fertile terai region of the Himalayan foothills, cupped between the Ramganga and Gagan rivers. The vast greenery of mango orchards, paddy fields and bamboo forest flanked the road to Benazir Palace. They could discern the dark grey silhouette of the mountains merging into the purple clouds.

'It'll rain today. How will we have our picnic?'

'Bibi, they have tents as big as cities,' said Tabu.

'I want to go to the swings,' Feroza slid open the glass window and inhaled the humid air, the breeze whipping her hair. Zubeida Begum pulled her back.

'Beti, you can't do all that. You're now with child,' she said, smoothing Feroza's hair and straightening her teeka. Bua opened the tiny window behind the driver's seat, her mummified face peeping in to catch the conversation.

'*Uffo*, I wish I didn't have this child. You can't do this; you can't do that...'

'*Tauba*, *tauba*! Don't say it again. Say *astaghfar*!' Bua screeched, almost causing the driver to swerve.

Feroza muttered the prayer superstitiously under her breath. Akbari Bua was always so melodramatic.

'Poor child, what does she know about being a mother? Akbari, you have to take care of her.'

'We'll go to the swings,' Feroza cupped her hand and whispered in Tabu's ear. Tabu raised her eyebrows.

'We'll go out when Ammi sleeps after lunch,' Feroza winked.

I must tell you of this magnificent Sawan Mela held at Benazir Palace – no one remembers the Benazir mela now, and very soon Benazir Palace will also crumble to dust. The Nawab's father had started the tradition, inspired by the legendary Jashn-e-Benazir of Rampur State, described in Jaan Sahib's poetic work, *Musaddas-e-Tahniyat-e-Jashn-e-Benazir*. The account spoke of famous poets, *dastangos* (storytellers), *tawaifs*, *randis*[2] and singers invited by the Nawab from Delhi, Agra, Lucknow and Calcutta. There were sketches of renowned dastangos of the time – Amba Prasad, Ghulam Mehdi and Meer Nawab sitting in the classic storyteller style. They were the creators and narrators of the immortal tale, *Tilism-e-Hoshruba*. I'll narrate that story to you some other time.

Nausha had smuggled an illustrated copy of Jaan Sahib's work from the mardana. Feroza had pored over the evocative paintings and read the couplets describing the scenes of the mela. She had murmured the forbidden names of the courtesans – Lazzat Baksh and Nauratan from Agra, Hingan Bai, the great singer of Lucknow and Ali Jaan, the male tawaif. Of course, they wouldn't meet the tawaifs; they never came into the zenana, but there would be other forms of entertainment for them.

'Look Bibi, the stalls!'

Feroza and Tabu drank in the astonishing sights, their faces pressed to the gap between the curtains, ignoring Zubeida Begum's warnings. They were outside the walls of the palace and the Benazir fair for the commoners was splayed out gaily on both sides of the road leading to the palace. There were canopied rows of makeshift shops along the roads selling clothes, sweets and glistening green bangles. The Hindu shopkeepers in their colourful, round turbans and Muslim shopkeepers in their topis called out their wares to men and women milling around. Feroza could smell the crisp samosas and puris. Two men turned the spokes of a crude four-armed wooden wheel while the children, seated in the cot-like seats, squealed away. Tabu laughed, pointing at the bare-bodied wrestlers showing off their rippling muscles in different poses, getting ready for the fight.

'Ashfaq! Ashfaq! Slow down, we want to see,' Feroza commanded the driver.

'This is for the common people. The real show is inside the palace,' said Zubeida Begum.

'Look Bibi, a snake and mongoose fight!' exclaimed Tabu.

They watched the mongoose sink its teeth into the black silvery neck of a cobra as the snake struggled to free itself. Suddenly, their eyes were drawn to two women laughing and talking to a man on horseback. They looked like the women in Jaan Sahib's sketches with their trailing farshi skirts, revealing blouses, bareheaded, their hair dressed in high coiffeurs – brazen and free. The taller one caught hold of the horse's rein, her dupatta slipping from her chest. She turned and, seeing Feroza, pulled out a red, paan-stained tongue and winked. Feroza dropped the curtain and pulled away from the window, her heart thudding. She had heard of such women selling their bodies.

'Randis,' Tabu's awestruck whisper tickled Feroza's ear.

Bua put her hand through the window and slapped Tabu's back.

'You get back! Or I will send you packing! What will people say? Everyone knows Miya's carriage.'

They were finally at the grand gates of the Benazir Palace, crowned with the royal insignia of two lions. Carriages of kings, zamindars and British officers were moving almost in a procession into the driveway edged by dark mango trees, some bearing mangoes, others shorn of their fruit. The palace orchards were famous for over a hundred varieties of mangoes, including the local varieties, the *aamans*, developed by the *Nawabs* – *samar bahisht*, *majnu*, *tota pari*, etc.

The girls now put their faces to the front window, begging Bua to move aside, so they could watch the graceful arches and domes of the palace draw closer. From afar, it seemed to rise out of a silvery rivulet curving around it – an artificial stream sourced from the Ramganga River by the innovative French architect, Mr DuPont. Benazir was the monsoon retreat of the Nawabs and a favourite venue for hosting musical soirees by renowned artists.

Feroza's gaze tumbled over the fountains playing in the oblong tank in front of the two-storeyed building, the carriages, the bowing uniformed guards and the British officials walking up the sweeping staircase to the durbar hall. The front entrance was for the male guests and English ladies; their buggy swung off to a side lane towards the zenana palace – the Badr-e-Muneer.

Feroza flung open the door, her torso bending out and looked around. Walls of tenting canvas enclosed the ladies' section so that the women could enjoy themselves away from male eyes. A *khwajasara*, eunuch guard lowered the steps, bowing deeply and touching his forehead, uttering the traditional words of welcome. Feroza sprang down the steps.

'Bibi, we have to first go to our room and take off our burqas,' Tabu whispered.

A gaily dressed *kahari* (maidservant) ushered them into a plush room in the zenana palace. Since Miya Jaan Khan's lineage belonged to that of Nawab Nasrullah Khan, his family would occupy the best rooms. The tents were for the lesser Begums.

'I don't have to cover my head. There are no men here.'

'You're a married woman, not a girl. Cover her head, Tabu. Besides, Her Highness, Begum Sherpur would be there too. Say your salam properly, bend down and salam thrice,' Zubeida Begum was flapping around her and struggling out of her burqa.

Two young maids entered the room bearing trays. On one tray were glasses of mango and *khus* sherbet along with sweets. The other girl presented several colourful *chunris* for the Begum and her daughter from Her Highness. A large basket of samar bahisht mangoes was kept in the room – a present from the Nawab. Feroza was feeling a bit queasy after the ride and gulped down the tangy, sour green mango sherbet. Begum Zubeida allowed Feroza to go outside after issuing several strict instructions and collapsed on the plump cushions.

'Uff! I hope I won't become as fat as Ammi,' muttered Feroza.

'Bibi, you are going to have a huge stomach and walk like this,' Tabu bent backwards, balancing an imaginary protuberance and walked comically with her legs apart. Feroza laughed as they walked out to the veranda and surveyed the ostentatious sights of the sawani. Her in-laws had hosted one for her after her marriage but it was nothing compared to the opulence that met her eyes. Several green and red awnings with takhts dotted the orchard where the sedate older women sat leaning against bolsters chatting, eating paan and smoking hookahs; tens of gaily coloured swings bore young girls, their green gharara skirts billowing and the bells on the ropes tinkling. Some girls were strolling down the pathways, drunk on the whole aspect of the vast openness and the feel of the earth beneath their feet.

Feroza descended the steps as if walking into a romantic dream. She had heard that it was here that the poet Dagh Dehlvi had met the great love of his life, Munni Bai Hijab.

'You are the only married woman wearing the churidar. Everyone is looking so good in their ghararas.'

'Shh Tabu, be quiet. Come, someone is singing,' she pulled at Tabu's hand and started walking quickly along a path edged with mango trees and heady with the scents of jasmine and mogra flowers. A small crowd had gathered around a swing on which sat a charming woman in the most resplendent gharara. A hefty woman stood singing an Amir Khusrau sawan song accompanied by a group of musicians with their instruments strapped around their waists.

'That must be Her Highness, Begum Sherpur. The sawani is in her honour,' whispered Feroza. Her eyes caught the Begum's embroidered shoes with golden bells clinking as she swung up. Feroza didn't want to be a face in the court crowd bending thrice to say her salam. She turned to move away.

'Feroza!' Asiya, her cousin, appeared out of nowhere and hugged her. Feroza responded warmly to the hug, glad to see her, especially now that she was all dressed-up and a notch above the still-unmarried and nearly-on-the-shelf Asiya. Asiya was Zubeida Begum's niece and around the same age as Feroza. As is common among cousins, there was always an underlying rivalry between them, fuelled by thoughtless comparisons made by elders.

'Are you staying for Moonga Jaan's recital in the evening? You know she is half-*angrez* but trained in Hindustani music and kathak.'

'Yes, of course,' Feroza immediately decided to persuade and coerce the hapless Zubeida Begum to stay longer. They were supposed to be back by *maghreb*, the evening prayers, but all the fun would begin after sunset. She wanted to stay till the next day and watch the fair culminate with a fireworks display and the procession to the Qadam Sharif shrine. It was said that the shrine housed the foot impression of the Prophet brought from Mecca by the heaven-residing Nawab Rehmat Ali Khan. Miya Jaan scoffed at the claim. His puritanical religious view forbade visiting shrines.

'Tonight the Nawab will recite his new ghazal.' Asiya established her superiority with the piece of information gleaned from her brothers. Feroza knew that the Nawab wrote poetry and some tawaifs who sang at the court were renowned poetesses. She had once asked her father to appoint a tutor to correct her poetry and was rebuffed with, 'Tawaifs write poetry, not Pathan women.' She had shrunk away from the harsh word – tawaif.

'Let's go to the stream and ride the boat!' Asiya led them down a path going to the stream. Shikara-style boats pulled by eunuchs and festooned with streamers and golden tassels were sailing in the rippling waters. They stood at the rose-entwined archway awaiting their turn, watching the other shikaras against the backdrop of the glowering clouds.

'I hope we get a ride before it starts raining,' said Feroza.

'Say your salam. It's Her Highness going to her boat,' hissed Asiya and the girls bowed a low courtly salam, swinging their arms back and forth, touching their foreheads thrice. Feroza straightened up as Begum Sherpur acknowledged them by lightly touching her forehead. It was said that she could not have children; some even said that the Nawab had never lain with her. She stepped into the royal shikara with a red velvet canopy, followed by a tall, elaborately hatted English lady.

'Look at the *angrezan*. She has feathers in her hat – like a bird,' giggled Feroza as the boat slid away. But the lady must have heard her for she turned to look at her with a stern and haughty expression.

'Shh, she heard you. She is the British Agent's wife and knows Urdu.'

'Really? How do you know that? You're just teasing me.' Feroza reddened.

'No, ask your father. Our Nawab speaks English and the angrez have learnt Urdu.'

'If she wanted to understand us, she should have worn our dress and not that strange gown.'

'That's their dress.'

'But they are here in our country.' Feroza's eyes lit up with the argument.

She got into the shikara and sat down on the bench, feeling irritable and hungry. Tabu whispered something to Asiya.

'*Hai*, Feroza, you didn't tell me,' Asiya hugged her. Feroza smiled.

'He'll call me *Khala*! Can you imagine! Does Murtaza know?' Aliya laughed and kissed her cheeks.

'Shh, everyone will hear you, silly. No, I'll tell him when I go back. They are organising a sawani for me too!'

She would sit with Murtaza on the swing and *domnis* would sing for them.[3] Murtaza wanted her to wear purple and green for the occasion and had himself chosen the fabric.

'Then there will be *godh bharai*. You'll sit with your huge tummy and women will come and put coconut and dry fruits in your lap and pray that you bear a son as white as the coconut!' Asiya said.

Feroza laughed. She had waited so long for all this – the world revolving around her.

'Oh, I wish Murtaza were here.' Feroza trailed her hand in the soft blue water. She wanted to share these glorious sights with him.

'*Arre*, you will go back to your beloved soon. Enjoy the ride with us,' said Asiya.

'I'm so hungry,' said Feroza, watching the cooks frying puris and kababs in huge *kadhais*. She had suddenly developed an enormous appetite, especially for sour mangoes and tamarind.

They cut their ride short, in spite of Feroza's protests, and Asiya took them to the picnic spot where food was laid out on thick carpets. The *dastarkhwan* was a long strip of white cloth with plates piled with puris, kababs, different types of halwas and glistening round jalebis. Zubeida Begum was already seated on the carpet and called the girls.

'Where have you been, girls? Eat quickly! It's going to rain.'

Suddenly, Feroza felt that she couldn't eat the oily puri and the too-sweet jalebi – she would definitely throw up. She was feeling hungry and nauseous at the same time. Bua, squatting behind Zubeida Begum and fanning off the flies, immediately handed Feroza a sour mango preserve.

'Have this, you 'll feel better. Then eat the chickpeas – they are very tart,' she whispered.

Zubeida Begum, busy encasing her kabab with a puri, nodded. Two ladies seated nearby noticed her eating sour mango, smiled and started congratulating Zubeida Begum.

'Arre Zubeida, don't be so careless! You are going to be a grandmother soon. You should keep her away from the evil eye. This is not the place for her,' said an old, toothless woman chewing with meticulous ardour.

Feroza felt so embarrassed and annoyed at the old crone that she could barely eat. Her pregnancy became the topic of conversation, the ladies recalling food fetishes from during their own pregnancies. She excused herself and got up.

'She feels shy. After all, she is so young,' said Zubeida Begum, munching on a crunchy jalebi.

'Ooi, not so young! I was only fourteen when I had my first one,' said a lady, crooking a brow.

'Tabu, give her some fruits and make her rest,' Zubeida Begum said.

Feroza was grumbling and still hungry. It had started drizzling and the ladies were getting up; the servants were clearing the dishes and rolling up the carpets before the downpour.

'Come to my tent or we shall get wet,' said Asiya.

'You go. I'm going to my room,' said Feroza, spreading her palms to catch the drops. Asiya was already off, running down a lane towards her tent, her gharara gathered in her hands, not daring to spoil the only decent dress she had.

The ladies gathered in the verandas, taking wistful pleasure in Rajeshwari Bai's sawani song as the clouds gathered momentum:

'*Apney mahalwa mein jhoola jhoolat thi sayyan ney bheje kahar*
Ae ri sakhi jhoola jhooley na payi sayyan ney bheje kahaar...

(I was at my father's house playing on the swings
My husband sent palanquin-bearers to fetch me
Dear friend, I couldn't play on the swings...)'

Feroza stood under the mango tree, listening to the longing notes rising above the clatter of the rain, the clamour of the servants and the chattering women.

'Tabu, I want to swing in the rain. Let's hide behind the mango tree!'

'Bibi, your Ammi will kill me if anything happens.'

'Fine, you go! I'm going to the swings,' Feroza turned away, knowing Tabu would never leave her alone. Tabu followed her as usual, shielding her face from the raindrops with her dupatta.

'Bibi, do it quickly.'

Hopefully, no one would miss them. A turn in the path shielded them from public view.

'We'll go to the other side. No one will see us there.'

'You'll get wet!'

'Never mind, I'll wear the other dress. The farshi you brought,' Feroza smiled, took Tabu's hand and they started running towards a distant swing. Tabu giggled, ignited by the live wire of Feroza's emotional upswing.

They reached a swing overlooking the canal. There was no one around, just a deserted guard room nearby with its rough wooden door shut. Feroza caught hold of the swing ropes and sat down on the seat.

'Here, take my dupatta and push.'

She wriggled her feet out of her silken, wet *jootis*. Tabu stepped back and pulled at the swing, letting it go with a shove. Feroza laughed, leaning back, her toes pointing up to the sky.

'Higher, Tabu!' she shouted closing her eyes, turning her face to the raindrops, tasting their metallic tang and pushing the ground away with her bare feet. She looked down at the concentric circles of raindrops on the purple-hued canal and started singing a playful barsati. Tabu joined in, missing the notes with the effort of pushing the swing.

It was raining heavily now and the ground beneath the massive tree was slushy and dotted with little puddles. Feroza's kurta was dripping wet and her toes were slaked with mud.

'Bibi, let's go now. Your Ammi will be frantic,' Tabu looked around and noticed that the door of the guard room was slightly ajar. She was being paranoid but she could swear that the door was shut when they came. She caught the rope and killed the speed of the swing. Feroza made a face and got up. Her feet splashed in the little pool under the swing and she slipped a little.

'Careful, Bibi,' screamed Tabu, coming around to hold her. Feroza skidded and landed with a thump. She had held on to the rope, staggering her fall.

'Allah!' Tabu tried to move forward. Feroza sat stunned for an instant, and then found herself pulled up by her forearms. Her hands rested on a hirsute chest and a white shirt steadily getting wet. An arm snaked around her waist and bemused eyes lingered over her red bodice. She steadied herself and tried to pull away, the slime making her slip a little.

'Pick 'er up, fella,' said a voice in English, and Feroza found herself swung up with an intake of breath and cradled close against a drumming chest. Tabu snapped out of her shock, came forward and covered Feroza with her dupatta. An Englishman with tiny eyes and blond whiskers stood laughing at the scene, a glass in his hand. They had probably been enjoying a drink in the guard room.

Her rescuer was wearing English clothes but his darkish complexion and Indian-style clipped moustache indicated that he must be an Indian nobleman. Up close he had large pores from old acne and a bulbous nose with cavernous nostrils. There was a strange decaying smell on his breath, invading her face, probably alcohol. She could feel the throb of his heart and the warmth of his skin against her body through the thin, wet fabric between them.

Feroza was taken to the little veranda of the guard room in casual, slow strides and set down with another swing; but not before a daring hand had caressed her nearly bare waist. She felt violated, not rescued.

'You have lovely nautch girls. Can I have the other one?' the Englishman leered.

Feroza's face burned with rage as she caught the word 'nautch' and its implications dawned on her. In her protected life, she had never encountered strange, drunken men and could only imagine where the situation might lead to.

'Tell your esteemed angrez friend that I belong to the house of Miya Jaan Khan of Sherpur. Your friend's mother is not fit to draw water for my toilet!' she said in Urdu, her voice rising and her eyes glittering with imperious rage. Everybody knew her father and her grandfather, the late Hadi Hasan Khan, Chief Magistrate of Sherpur.

She turned her back to the Englishman and said to the Indian with slow deliberation, 'You emulate these filthy Englishmen, wear their clothes, become their slaves and sell off your mothers to their harems!'

Tabu caught her arms, turned her around and said, 'Let's go, Bibi.'

The Indian's brow darkened with anger as Feroza continued to glower at him. They wouldn't dare touch her. She was protected by her father's name and her haughty rage. Turning sharply, she stomped down the veranda steps.

'Drunken bastards!' she muttered loud enough for the men to hear.

Hot, angry tears coursed down her cheeks and the mud squelched under her bare feet as she walked back to the zenana. Tabu hurried behind her, with Feroza's dripping shoes in her hands, glancing back.

'Don't look back. Those *haramzadey* will know you're afraid.'

She wished she had slapped that Indian's insolent face. How dare they call her a nautch girl!

Seething, Feroza returned to her room to a hyperventilating Zubeida Begum. Bua caught hold of Tabu and started slapping her.

'Bua, stop! I wanted to go. Tabu was telling me not to. Then I fell and…'

'Ya Allah *khair*! May Allah have mercy,' shrieked Bua, abandoning Tabu and rushing to Feroza.

Zubeida Begum made her lie down, muddying the sheets. By tacit agreement, the girls did not mention the encounter with the men.

Feroza bathed, rubbing herself clean; the warm water calmed her but the humiliation lingered. Changed and fresh, she relaxed with a hot cup of tea in bed, nibbling cookies from the Nawab's English kitchen. Tabu's eyes were swollen from crying. Feroza gave her a cookie.

'I'll find out who those men were and tell Abba.'

'Bibi, let it be. Why make things tough? And you were wearing that dress, so maybe they made a mistake.'

Were the nautch girls and ordinary girls treated like this? Felt all over, used or raped? What if she were a common girl or if Tabu was alone there?

'Tell Ammi we'll go after the soiree.'

'She won't agree.'

'Then call Asiya.'

Zubeida Begum had gone out for tea on the veranda, her head throbbing with anxiety.

Feroza knew that Asiya would be able to persuade Zubeida Begum. Asiya and her mother, Amina Begum, were also staying back and Zubeida Begum would enjoy herself.

Asiya found Zubeida Begum pouring out her worries into the sympathetic ears of her sister, Amina Begum.

The *andarsey*, sweet rice flour fritters, prepared with rain water, and crunchy *pakodis* had somewhat mollified Zubeida Begum.

'What to hide from you, Amina Apa, we were so apprehensive of her temper and beauty that we married her off as soon as we could. Now she is with child, but not a shred of maturity. The way she runs off without care! I'm just waiting for Murtaza to come and relieve me of this burden.'

'Khala, Feroza is still not feeling well. Let her rest and watch the musical programme. Moonga Jaan from Kalkatta will be performing kathak and the orchestra will be playing under the great Wazir Khan. Nawab Sahib himself has arranged the orchestra. You cannot miss it,' pleaded Asiya.

'Miya Sahib wants us to reach before the maghreb prayers.'

'Maybe you can send word that Feroza needs to rest? Besides, music will calm Feroza down. She is very upset after the fall. If, God forbid...'

Zubeida Begum's plump frame trembled – this was an even greater trouble than Miya Khan's annoyance. Finally, pressed by Amina, she agreed to go back the next morning. Asiya assured her that she would send word through someone about the change of plans. Miya Jaan would surely understand.

Feroza wore her elaborate blue farshi for the evening soiree, thanking Tabu for having brought it along. Zubeida Begum gave a silver coin to Bua as *sadqa* to ward off the evil eye and troubles for Feroza.

'I'll have a goat sacrificed once we reach home,' she said. Zubeida Begum believed that goat sacrifices were the ultimate way to ward off all afflictions. She routinely got the sacrifice done if any of her children so much as had a cough. It was good to see Feroza happy and lively again – well worth Miya Jaan's caustic anger that she was bound to face.

Notes

1. All translations in the book are by Tarana Husain Khan.

2. Tawaifs or courtesans were at the top of the social hierarchy among singers. They were singers and dancers, well-educated in literature and classical singing, often penning their own compositions. Randis were prostitutes at the lowest strata of the hierarchy. Some of them danced and sang as well.

3. Domnis sang in the zenanas of genteel households on celebratory occasions. They were not as educated or well-read as the tawaifs but were practitioners of folk and regional songs.

3

Feroza Begum

Benazir Palace, Sherpur, 1896

> When Feroza Begum laid eyes on the Nawab, she was struck dumb with awe at his wondrous persona. When the time came for her to depart, she fell at the Begum's feet, imploring her to let her stay for some more time. It became obvious to all that she was unhappy with her husband and in love with the Nawab. Feroza Begum promised to spend her life as the Nawab's servant girl. She even threatened to take her life if she was sent back. The elders of her family and her in-laws' family came to the Nawab asking for a solution. The Nawab said, 'This is your household matter and the solution should also come from you.' They conferred and persuaded her husband to give talaq to Feroza. It is possible that at the time of the divorce some amount was made over to the groom by the Nawab.
>
> *Darbar-e-Sherpur*, Bilquis Begum

There are stories, whispers and then there is the truth. My story can draw from any of these or from all of these. That evening, Feroza Begum and her family entered through the ladies' entrance to the durbar hall of the Benazir Palace. It led to a gallery that ran around the hall, shuttered with split bamboo curtains hanging on elaborate arches to shield the ladies from male eyes.

A eunuch ushered them to their seats to the right of the royal throne where they had a good view of the proceedings. The lights in the viewing gallery were low, such that only the silhouettes of the ladies with a gleam of colour could be discerned by an attentive male eye.

Feroza sat close to the frieze, peering at the hall resplendent with glittering chandeliers, turbanned kings, bejewelled in their long jama-kurtas, the noblemen and British officers in their smart trousers and red coats with badges and insignia. The musicians were seated at the centre on a platform with Moonga Jaan, glamorous in her red and gold dancing costume, lithe and ready, her tinkling feet beating a rhythm.

The *chobdars* (mace-bearers) entered the hall and announced the arrival of the Nawab, reciting his high-sounding titles – *Ameer-ul-Umara, Farzand-e-Aala, Daulat-i-Inglishiya*. Everybody rose from their seats and the British officers tucked their black hats under their arms. Moonga Jaan bent double with her salam. Zubeida Begum asked Feroza to get back to her seat.

'Ammi, no one can see us from outside. Let me just look at the Nawab once.'

The Nawab entered with quick, impatient steps, his head surging ahead of his body, flanked by the British Agent and the chief minister. The British and Pathan officers followed. By any standards, his frame was unimpressive and puny, but clothed in a cleverly padded, flesh-coloured brocade shervani. The ruby gleaming in his *sarpech* (aigrette) and the pearl and diamond strings covering the pigeon chest created a dazzling aura of royalty.

The Nawab turned to speak to his chief minister, the immaculately clipped moustaches quivering with his smile.

It was an unremarkable face, imprinted with an arrogance that befitted all the tales of despotism she had heard whispered about him.

'Bibi, it's him!' Tabu clutched her hand and whispered.

He knew her. She had insulted the Nawab and identified herself as the daughter of Miya Jaan Khan.

She watched as he sat down on his brocade takht with a swish of his coat and motioned the gathering to take their seats with a whisk of his hand. He was vindictive, Abba often said, and he never forgot or forgave a rebuff. Fear pricked at the roots of her hair and dripped down her back.

Moonga Jaan stood up and began her recital, her feet synchronising with the *thaap* of the *tabla*, commanding the orchestra with a beat of her hand and the twirl of her skirts. The Nawab leaned forward as though his whole being depended on the words of the *todi*. 'Moonga Jaan sold off all her jewellery and came to Sherpur to learn from the great Ameer Khan, from the family of Tansen,' Asiya whispered.

Feroza barely listened to her. The Nawab was known for his lechery but maybe she had gone overboard in her anger. But if she hadn't resisted, he would have molested her.

He could destroy their lives and condemn even their future generations.

She had to tell Abba everything. Miya Jaan would be in a towering rage and blame Zubeida – all that had to be endured. The only way out was for Abba to apologise on her behalf. Knowing his loathing for the Nawab, she felt sure that he would never do so – not even out of his love for her. She would cause the downfall of her family.

Maybe she was making too much out of a small incident of mistaken identity. The Nawab might already be embarrassed about flirting with a Pathan Sardar's daughter.

The recital ended and the Nawab took off a long string of pearls and gave it to a salaming Moonga Jaan. A flickering red-glass lamp was placed before the Nawab, indicating that he would now recite his ghazal.

The Nawab began with salutations to his teachers and then paused, his gaze concentrated on the quivering red shadow of the lamp, looked up and said, 'This afternoon I composed a ghazal in honour of a chance meeting that left me yearning:

'*Kiya us ne qatl aur mai ney muaaf,*
Abas ahl-e-shahar uska charcha karein.

(She slew me and I forgave her,
Needlessly the townfolk talk of us.)'

The Nawab touched his forehead, acknowledging the appreciative '*wah, wah*', and turned towards the enclosure where Feroza sat and continued reciting his ghazal.

'*Wo jab aap se apna parda karein,*
To band-e-qaba kis tara vaa karein.

(When she keeps herself veiled from me
How can I unknot her tunic.)'

He finally stood up, the eyelids half-closed and said, 'These last lines in honour of her anger:

'*Unhein kyon ho "Nazim" qayamat ka dar,*
Jo har roz ik fitna barpa karein.[1]

(She fears not the apocalypse, O Nazim,
For she construes anarchy every day.)'

The listeners broke out into cries of '*wah, wah, kya khoob*' requesting an encore.

With a bashful boyish smile, he touched his forehead and turned his face slightly towards Feroza's enclosure.

Feroza walked out of the enclosure to the veranda.

'What happened? Are you all right?' Asiya had followed her.

'Asiya, help me!' Feroza pulled Asiya into a side room and briefly narrated the whole episode.

'Asiya, tell me what should I do? Tell Abba? Apologise?'

'The ghazal was for you, Feroza? The Nawab is besotted...'

All the frightening possibilities lay unsaid between them.

'But I'm married. Maybe he doesn't know...'

Of course, the Nawab knew of her marriage. He had even attended the function and given a gift. There was little that escaped his notice in the lives of his prominent subjects. Some said he even paid the house servants to spy on the families.

'Abba knows him so well. Oh, what a fool I have been! I can't stay here. I'm scared... Tabu, go, call Ammi. We'll leave right now.'

They had all heard tales of the so-called *bashata*[2] women who lured young girls into the harem with false promises. Even Miya Jaan Khan would be powerless if the Nawab trapped her in his harem.

'No, wait, I will go back with Tabu in your tonga, Asiya. You explain to Ammi. Tabu, quickly get our burqa from the zenana.'

The Nawab must have sensed that she had left the gathering and if he intended to stop her, he would act fast. Ammi was always so slow and they would have to explain everything to her first. Asiya went off to summon the tonga.

Within minutes, Feroza and Tabu were out on the side veranda waiting for the tonga. The stables were right under the high plinth of the palace and the tongas were lining up for the ladies as the programme drew to a close. A dilapidated tonga with a scrawny horse came up to them. No one was approaching it – that must be the one. She and Tabu settled into it and the driver pulled down the thick curtains attached to the hatch. He probably had no idea that the veiled women were not his mistresses. The path to the gate was alive with spasmodic fireflies under the grim mango trees. The driver got down at the gates reporting to the guards who logged the departure in the register.

Finally, they were out of the gates of Benazir Palace and Feroza relaxed as the tonga clip-clopped back to the town.

A twinge in her abdomen reminded her of her baby. She longed for her bed at home and for Murtaza's arms around her. She would go back to Murtaza tomorrow. But how would she explain her sudden departure from her father's place? Should she tell him everything?

The buggy came to a halt. Tabu peeped out.

'Bibi, we're at the *qila* gates. Where is he taking us?'

The driver was talking to a soldier on horseback.

'Give him the address. Maybe he's mistaken.'

The buggy pulled into the fort gates and the huge wooden gates closed behind them.

'O tonga driver, stop! Where are you taking us? We have to go to Nasrullah Khan Bazaar, to the *kothi* of Miya Jaan Khan,' yelled Tabu, leaning out of the curtain.

A soldier rode up to them and said, 'It is the order of the Nawab that the daughter of Miya Jaan Khan shall be escorted to the *mehman khana* (guest house) near the Durbar Hall.'

'Stop this minute! I'm not going to the mehman khana. Take me home!' screamed Feroza, leaning forward, trying to catch the shirt of the driver. The driver, ignoring her shouts, sped the vehicle through a driveway and stopped outside an ornate building with its archways lit up with tiny diyas.

'Begum, you can speak to Daroghan Chhamman at the mehman khana,' said the guard. The driver jumped down and ran off, disregarding Tabu's calls. A *khwajasara* (eunuch guard), dressed in a maroon angarkha and turban took the reins and salamed deeply.

'Call the Daroghan now! Why was I brought here?' Feroza tossed the curtain aside.

'Begum, you must be tired, please come inside.'

'I'm the daughter of Miya Jaan Khan. Send this tonga to my house immediately!'

A tall lady of indeterminate age with a swiftness of manner despite her girth emerged from the guest house and bent in salam.

'Begum, I'm the Daroghan of the *mahalsara*.' The Daroghans were the female administrators of the Nawab's harem or mahalsaras, as they were called then.

'Daroghan bibi, I think there has been a mistake. I'm the daughter of Miya Jaan Khan. Kindly escort me back home.'

'Begum, be our guest. You are safe here.'

'I don't desire to be a guest of the Nawab. Your Nawab has insulted a married Pathan lady of the family of Nawab Nasrullah Khan. Take heed, this will not be overlooked. Send me home now!' Feroza convulsed with rage.

'Begum, we cannot defy the orders of the Nawab. Take my word, you're safe here. I'm a *sayyidani*.[3] You rest now and let tomorrow take care of itself.'

'My parents will be worried sick!'

'I have already sent word that you are at the mehman khana attending a dinner party. I give you my word as a true sayyidani that no harm will befall you.' Daroghan Chhamman smiled a reassurance and held out her hand to help Feroza down from the tonga.

The tonga was not going to take her back and Feroza felt ridiculous standing practically on the road. She snubbed Daroghan's hand and climbed down.

The Nawab only targeted poor and vulnerable women. He wouldn't dare insult an honourable woman from such a prominent Pathan clan. There would be an open rebellion! The Pathans would give up their lives and defend her honour.

Feroza was escorted through huge oakwood doors to a high-ceilinged guest room with a massive four-poster spring bed, gilt sofa sets and a chandelier with tens of shining candles. Even in her state, she felt overawed.

'Daroghan bibi, speak to the Nawab. Surely he cannot humiliate me thus? My husband and my father will be at his door, ready to fight!'

'I understand, but the Nawab is busy with his guests tonight. We'll see what we can do tomorrow. Don't worry. You may rest here. Here, take these keys. You can lock yourself in after dinner.' Daroghan Chhamman handed the keys with a reassuring smile.

'I don't want any dinner,' Feroza dismissed the Daroghan with a wave of her hand.

She collapsed on the bed as soon as the Daroghan left. She was spending a night outside the protective ambit of her family – an unforgivable act. There had never been such an incident in her family. What if they abandoned her? What would become of her child?

Surely, they would plead with the Nawab tomorrow. Murtaza would be there. He would never forsake her even if Abba was too proud. It would be shameful if they didn't even try to rescue their daughter – their *izzat*, their honour. They couldn't live with the disgrace.

Tabu rushed around, securing the windows and locking the doors.

'Bibi, your father will definitely come to take you back tomorrow. Now rest. I have locked up everything. Here, have some fruits.'

A simple set of mulmul kurta and pajama lay on the bed. Feroza changed for the night, helped by Tabu.

'Don't leave my hand, Tabu. If you hear anything, wake me up.'

Tabu, who had never dared to sit on Feroza's bed – she was slapped by Bua if she even sat on a chair while playing – lay with Feroza on the grand bed, holding her hand.

It rained throughout that restless night as she kept watching the shadows thrown up by the burning lamps. Sometimes she would lapse into a fitful sleep only to wake up with a start, convinced that the Nawab was lurking behind the curtains and wake up Tabu to check.

The next morning, she was served a rather elaborate breakfast which she barely touched. She requested Daroghan Chhamman to send her home or at least allow her to meet her father.

'The Nawab gets up by the afternoon and then attends to matters of the state. Only then will he be available. He has called Miya Jaan Khan to the durbar.'

'Why has he called my father? To hand me over?'

'Only the Nawab knows his will.'

'Daroghan bibi, maybe His Highness doesn't know that I'm married and with child.'

Daroghan Chhamman had attended to many frightened women and girls, counselled and prepared them for the Nawab but Feroza's predicament and her genteel background filled her with pity. She sat with her, spoke a few calming words, that sounded heartfelt, made her eat some halwa and left.

It is important to tell you a little more about Sherpur or you'll get confused, Ameera. When Sherpur was established in the eighteenth century, a covenant was drawn up between Nawab Faizullah Khan and the Rohilla sardars. The heads or sardars of the Rohilla Pathan tribes, who helped to establish the state, considered themselves as *shareek* or partners in the kingship as opposed to other *rayyat* or citizens. So the *Nawabi* was traditionally an agreement between the Nawab and the sardars by which the latter had given him the right to rule, under the condition that the Nawab would look after their interests. At the time of ascension, Nawab Shams Ali Khan, as all the Nawabs before him, had signed the covenant.

So Feroza rightfully believed, and hoped, that all the Rohilla clans would stand up against the Nawab to preserve her honour. No Nawab had ever kidnapped a married lady from the Rohilla chieftain clan – it was a great insult. Her family and in-laws could go to other Rohilla families and plead the case together. The Nawab had to relent. He could not defy all the Pathan sardars.

If that failed, Abba or Murtaza could appeal to the British Agent at Bareilly who looked after the affairs of Sherpur State. Abba always said the Nawab had to obey the British because Sherpur was under British rule. She had hope still.

'Tabu, they allow the kaharis to go out of the qila gates. You can leave with them. First, go to my husband and tell him everything. Ask him to meet the Nawab and get me out of here. Then go to Nausha and ask him to persuade Abba to plead with the Nawab.'

Tabu managed to slip out of the back gate of the guest house and left the qila with a few other maids. Feroza waited out that interminable day. She tried to walk out of the building but was politely led back. It was pointless throwing a tantrum – her dignity would not allow her to be handled roughly. There was no escape. She tried to will herself to murmur the comforting rhythm of Quranic verses, but all she wanted to do was scream and shatter the silence. What decision had been made at the court? What if Abba refused to answer the Nawab's summons?

Lunch was brought in by a kahari. Feroza sent it away untouched, telling the kahari not to disturb her.

In the evening, Daroghan Chhamman came into the room. 'Begum, your palanquin is here.'

Feroza sat up with a start. She must have dozed off.

'You are going to my house for safekeeping.'

'Why? Why can't I go home?'

'You have been divorced by Murtaza Khan. Your *iddat*[4] period begins from today. You will stay with me for your iddat, after which you can formally receive the Nawab's offer of marriage.'

'Divorce? I don't want to be divorced. I'm with child!' Feroza's whole being jolted and she burst out crying, 'Murtaza will never divorce me. He doesn't know I'm with child! Ya Allah, have mercy on me!'

Would her child be brought up in the harem of the Nawab, or as a motherless child at Murtaza's place with a stepmother? Murtaza would surely remarry and have more children.

'Begum, we are pawns in the hands of fate...'

'I beg of you Daroghan bibi, send me to my husband's house. All will be well. He cannot divorce me. He'll accept me back.' Feroza clutched and kissed the Daroghan's hands.

This never happened to women of her background.

'Forgive me, Begum, this is beyond my powers. I'm but a slave. A greater and more illustrious fate awaits you as the second Begum of the Nawab!'

Daroghan Chhamman knew that the only practical option for Feroza was to accept her fate with dignity and make the best of the situation. The Nawab was known to be a generous husband and master to those who submitted to him and pleased him. But if he were thwarted, his rage was beyond all reason.

'Curse your Nawab! May he become a leper and his body be riddled with worms!' Feroza screamed, standing up, flinging Daroghan's hands away.

To her utter shock, Daroghan Chhamman bowed deeply and touched her forehead thrice in salam – a salutation to royalty. She then walked backwards and left the room, locking the door behind her. Feroza threw herself at the door, banging her hands on the carved wood, screaming curses and pleas, shattering her red-green bangles.

Maybe Tabu would come with some news.

Tabu sneaked back to the mehman khana that evening. Feroza clasped Tabu, sobbing.

'Is it true that Murtaza has given me *talaq*? Did you meet him? And Abba?'

'Bibi, what can I tell you! Miya Jaan Khan has left the city with the whole family for Bareilly! Only my mother and a guard were in the house. Amma was waiting for news from us. She said when they returned without you, Miya Jaan Khan was furious and called his sons and told them that he had disowned you. He has willed that no member of his family should ever meet you!'

Miya Jaan had said that Feroza had discarded the honour of her ancestors. He could not live with the shame and fled to Bareilly that very night. At that time, Bareilly was a British-ruled town about fifty kilometres from Sherpur; it was a haven for disgruntled members of the royal family and those who wished to escape the wrath of the despotic Nawabs. So Miya Jaan and his family were now refugees from Sherpur, the place where all his ancestors lay buried, where every person knew his glorious bloodline and respected him. Her family had abandoned her.

'And Murtaza?'

'I did not dare go there, so I sent the guard. He said Murtaza Miya's father met him and said that they had severed the relationship between you and Murtaza Miya. Murtaza Miya has given talaq. The Nawab had called them to court saying that you wanted to marry him and had refused to go home; that *you* had asked for talaq!'

'How can Murtaza believe that? What will become of me, Tabu? Where will I go?'

'The kothi was so quiet, Bibi, like someone had died. My mother was crying like at a funeral.'

'Yes, it was my funeral. They have declared me dead. Now hear this, I will also never set my eyes on my father or see his dead face. This is my promise. I'm his daughter!'

How could Abba or Murtaza believe that she had chosen to stay with the Nawab? Abba's rage was just a pretence to cover his cowardly flight. In fact, he had left the night before Murtaza went to court. He had given up, and decided not to stand up for her. It was clear that the Rohilla Pathan families, fanatic about their pride and protecting their women, would not come to demand their daughter back.

Daroghan Chhamman had instinctively known that the death of hope was the only way that this unholy alliance could take place. She had, meanwhile, set off rumours in all circles that Feroza, overawed by the glamour of the court and enraptured by the grand persona of the Nawab, wanted to marry him and had demanded a divorce from her husband.

So the beautiful Feroza Begum, loved and treasured by her family, who had known only happiness and love, followed her fate into the Nawab's mahalsara.

Notes

1. Nawab Yususf Ali Khan 'Nazim'.
2. Smooth-talking, manipulative women.
3. From the lineage of Prophet Muhammad.
4. Iddat is a period of waiting of about three months to be observed by a divorced or widowed woman. During this period, she cannot remarry. Its purpose is to establish the paternity of a child born after the divorce or death of the prior husband. In case a woman is already pregnant at that time, she has to observe iddat till the birth of the child.

4

Mehfil-e-Dastangoi

Sherpur, 1896

Ustaad khushnavees hain ek dastango
Nassar be-badal koi shayar hain dekh lo,
Ye char fun baney isi ustaad ke liye
Zeba ye fun hain Amba Prasad ke liye.

(Ustad is a master calligrapher, dastango, poet and an incomparable writer of prose.
These four arts are created and beautified by the master – Amba Prasad.)

Musaddas-e-Tahniyat-Jashn-e-Benazir,
Meer Yar Ali Jaan Sahib Rekhtigo

Mirza Ameeruddin Dastango, nicknamed 'Kallan Mirza' for his dark complexion, wrapped the thin cotton wool quilt around his shoulders, shivering a little as he trudged through the uneven brick lane from his house towards Gher Mardan Khan for the dastan session. The dust from the sweeper's brooms had increased the opacity of the misty evening. He raised his hand intermittently, greeting his neighbours, acquaintances and distant relatives on their way back from work, or sitting in tea shops by the road.

On such days, he could almost believe that he had left his Nigar cooking his invariably late dinner, throwing a warning at him to return on time. He used to laugh at her sarcastic remarks when he slept over at his host's house, curled up on a takht, too high on *afeem* to walk back. Life was a secret joke that the two of them could cheat with complicit trickery. When his stories got muddled up beyond solution, Nigar would come up with surprising ideas to resolve the cliffhanger of the night before.

'Salam, people of the grave,' he muttered, touching his forehead with habitual reverence as he passed by the family graveyard. His father, Mirza Raheemuddin Haya Dastango lay buried there, his name etched on a marble tombstone. Mirza Haya, a dastango at the court of the Mughal emperor, Bahadur Shah Zafar, and his cousin, had fled the destruction of Delhi in 1857. He had settled in Sherpur as the court dastango, under Nawab Yunus Ali Khan.

Nigar, lying next to Mirza Haya, was a mound of earth with no headstone but Kallan made sure that her grave would always bear fresh flowers and the smouldering, rose-scented incense sticks that she had loved.

Kallan traversed the gullies of his childhood and reached Gher Mardan Khan. He touched his forehead in greeting, smiled and took his seat on the takht, facing his all-male audience. Mandated by age and social standing, some were seated on takhts like him and some on the white *chandni* sheets spread on the ground. Their hookahs were primed for the long dastan session. Kallan's most remarkable features were his expressive eyes and thick, mobile eyebrows on a forehead that could be classified as noble if it wasn't so dark – light complexion being an indicator of nobility and good breeding in the eyes of the locals. He wore his hair long, thick and curling on his shoulders and was clean-shaven, except for his clipped moustache under an unremarkable nose. His bearing and stylised Urdu were the only indicators of his Mughal lineage.

The courtyard of Gher Mardan Khan was a brick-laid, rectangular area, large enough to seat a hundred people. All around the *gher*[1] were the grand houses of the descendants of Mardan Khan, commander of the Rohilla army, who had been martyred defending Sherpur against the British. Like most dastangos, Kallan narrated his dastan every Thursday or Friday evening till late night, ending with a cliffhanger to pull the audience to the next session. Most dastans continued for months, even years.

Kallan took out a silver box from his pocket, opened it to extract a tiny black ball of afeem, wrapped it in a muslin cloth and put it in a silver bowl. He then filled the bowl with water from his *lota*, slowly rotating the muslin to ensure that the afeem dissolved. He preferred to make his own mixture, its potency dictated by his mood and the scene he was going to narrate – a war scene required a higher plane of intoxication than a romantic one or an *ayyari* (trickery) narration. It was well known that Mirza Kallan's memory, imagination and *kalaam* heightened with afeem. Even with a high dose he never appeared intoxicated or muddled up. His grip on his dastan and its characters were legendary as was his encyclopedic knowledge of food, dress, armaments and other matters crucial to the tale.

The bitter liquid coursed down his throat and opened up his veins to a tender flame. The members of the audience were also sipping afeem and priming hookahs with deep puffs; the tea was on the boil, ready to be served to warm up the session along with bits of sugarcane.

Kallan's narrative style, drawing on the witticism and idioms of the Sherpur gullies, had endeared him to his audience who came from all classes, cared little for the Persianised Urdu couplets of his contemporaries, loved his passionate romancing, his tongue-in-cheek humour and somewhat oblique irony. His narrative was the *tilism*, the magic. While his famous brother, Mirza Aleemuddin, had succeeded his father as the court dastango, Kallan, unlettered, was of the masses. Most listeners paid any amount depending on their station in life, keeping the *annas* and *paisas* at a predetermined place, generally in a *taaq* or alcove in the wall. The nobleman-host paid much more.

The women folk, prohibited from attending the opium-riddled mehfils, were his invisible audience, peering from behind half-opened doors of darkened rooms, their eyes fixed on the expressions and gestures of the dastango, stifling giggles and sighs. Sometimes, Kallan would imagine his Nigar leaning forward, listening to his story, smiling in the half-light; he exaggerated the act, yearning for her throaty laughter.

Kallan sat up on the takht, his legs folded under him in the classic dastango style. Next to him sat his brother and scribe, Mirza Waliuddin, a less successful dastango. In spite of all the efforts by his father, Kallan was illiterate and relied on Waliuddin to pen down a rough copy of the dastan during the session.[2]

'Huzur Mirza Sahib, *shuru kijiye*, let us begin,' said Hasan Khan, the host, sipping his afeem.

'*Bahut munasib*, as you say. I begin with a *saqinama*[3] by Sayed Muhammad Jah Sahib,' Kallan took another sip of afeem, feeling a flame fan his body, the light from lanterns suddenly burnt with greater intensity and he could glimpse Nigar's profile from the half-opened window to his right. He touched his forehead and began:

'*Ae saqi-e-gulrukh o gulandam,*
Dey phool ka aaj phir wahi jaam;

Haan zor-e-khumar past kar dey,
Saghar o pyaley sey mast kar dey.[4]

(My muse, my flower-faced cup-bearer,
Give me your floral wine once more;
To dispel my half-drunken stupor,
And intoxicate me with inspiration.)'

My salutations to the great master dastango, Mir Ahmad Ali and his pupils Amba Prasad and Asghar Ali who brought forth the immortal dastan of Ameer Hamza and created the tale of *Tilism-e-Hoshruba*. My humble tale can never hope to emulate their great dastan, but attempts to dispel the darkness of our enslaved hearts.

The first *daftar* (sequence) of the dastan of Saad bin Ameer Hamza, the son of Ameer Hamza *Sahib-e-Qiran* – the Lord born on the most fortunate stars, the great warrior of Islam, has been narrated. In the first daftar, Saad falls in love with Princess Lalarukh and sets off to Koh Kaaf, the land of *paries* to win her. Amar ayyar, the trickster and the most loyal friend of Ameer Hamza, accompanies him to Koh Kaaf. He tries to dissuade Saad from marrying a pari, reminding him of his father, Ameer Hamza's disastrous marriage to Asman Pari, resulting in eighteen years of suffering for Ameer Hamza. But Saad, smitten like his father, wins the heart of Lalarukh, who turns out to be half-pari and half-human, and proposes marriage.

King Sheez, Lalarukh's father, and her aunt, Asman Pari, the ex-wife of Ameer Hamza, also try vainly to discourage Lalarukh, but the princess is too enamoured to heed their advice. The astrologers have warned Sheez of the disasters the marriage would inevitably face. Finally, King Sheez accepts the proposal, and Saad promises to live his life in Koh Kaaf and succeed King Sheez.

Aunt Asman Pari takes off the egg-sized *teeka-e-yaqut*, the ruby teeka, from her own forehead and presses it on Lalarukh's forehead saying, 'Use it to know! Though truth never gives happiness.'

The two lovers are united in marriage and by the conjunction of fortunate stars, Lalarukh conceives on the glorious *shab-e-shadi*, the wedding night. Every day the young couple pray for the long life and health of their child, of whom the astrologers say nothing.

So, we shall now continue our tale to the second daftar.

Fate lies in wait for the beautiful couple – Saad and Lalarukh, its snares tightening each day. At the edge of the realm of Koh Kaaf, a grand magical illusion, a tilism, is being created by the most powerful *sahir* (sorcerer) of the time, Tareek Jaan. He is the son of the greatest sahir who ever lived – Afrasiyab Jadu. As you all know, Afrasiyab had created the grand *Tilism-e-Hoshruba*, the enchantment of senses, the most epic magical kingdom ever made. The kingdom was destroyed by the warrior of Islam, Ameer Hamza, and Afrasiyab was killed. But before the final battle, where Afrasiyab knew his death was fated, he had entrusted his treasures to his son and disciple, Tareek Jaan, who ran away from the destruction of Tilism-e-Hoshruba. Tareek Jaan thus inherited *Kitab-e-Sifi*, the original book of magic written by King Sulaiman, the flying *takht-e-Sulaimani*, King Sulaiman's throne and the *sheesha-e-Samri*, the oracular mirror of Samri, the first magician.

O listeners, what words can describe the vile Tareek Jaan, his face as dark as his heart. Those who worked under Afrasiyab find him more terrifyingly powerful than Afrasiyab. Tareek Jaan had practised magic tirelessly for several years and had at his command the greatest djinn – Afreet Tilismi, his son Aaseb and his diabolical daughter Tez Chashm, along with thousands of other djinns and djinnis.

So, Tareek Jaan is creating the *Tilism-e-Azam*, the grand illusion to rival Tilism-e-Hoshruba in its magnificence, right at the edge of the peaceful kingdom of Koh Kaaf.

Tilism-e-Azam is a city of illusion created by Tareek Jaan from ordinary things like lentil flour, dust, ashes and paper imbued with cosmic powers. He hypnotises men and djinns to see what he wants them to see. For example, he takes a paper sun and hangs it up with magic and we ordinary people believe that the sun is shining when it's pitch dark, stones are made into jewels and an army of lentil-flour people makes us secure and creates fear. We feel happy, satisfied, our bellies feel full with food – which is actually ashes made to look like food.

Tareek Jaan completes his illusion of Tilism-e-Azam, and euphoric, declares himself (tauba, tauba, *nauzobillah*) Khudawand, King of Samris, and commands all the *sahir*s, *sahira*s, paries and *parizad*s to prostrate before him or he would unleash terrible perils on their kingdoms. He erects a magnificent statue of himself, which floats over the magical city.

Arre bhai, have you seen the statue of our Nawab? Wah, the sculptor Mehboob Khan has created such an image – and he looks so fair in marble!' Kallan winks and the audience titters.

'Now, King Sheez of Koh Kaaf, because of his loyalty to Ameer Hamza, hadn't attended the Grand Durbar to pay obeisance to the King of Samris. Tareek Jaan wreaks terror on the borders of Koh Kaaf. Since Ameer Hamza had set a *hisar*, a magic circle of the Great Name, around Koh Kaaf, the greatest of sorcerers cannot breach the bounds of Koh Kaaf. But the gentle paries weep for the innocent people who are tortured by Tareek's minions. King Sheez fears that Tareek Jaan might learn the Great Name of Allah or some magic to destroy the hisar. So, after consulting his chief astrologer, he sends his son-in-law, Prince Saad bin Ameer Hamza, to vanquish the giant devs.

Saad, armed with the sword of Prophet Daud and the shield of the vanquished Afrasiyab, bids adieu to a weeping Princess Lalarukh and goes to battle with six lakh human soldiers and twenty lakh paries and parizads. Marching with him is the unscrupulous trickster Amar ayyar.

Now King Sheez had given Princess Lalarukh a *pariru*, a golden peacock with the face of a girl, because she couldn't fly like the other paries. Lalarukh, against the express orders of King Sheez, secretly flies to the Koh Kaaf border on her pariru peacock, accompanied by several pari maids to watch the battle from a safe distance above and pray. When she sees Saad's army being killed by devs, she is filled with apprehension for her husband and Koh Kaaf.

Overseeing the battle from the other side, is Tez Chashm, the daughter of Afreet djinn, who could capture images in her eyes. Tez Chashm was exceedingly vicious and when her eyes capture the beautiful Princess Lalarukh, a vile scheme enters her heart. She sends down a terrible rain of burning coals and stones on Saad's army, forcing a hasty retreat. A typhoon whirls around Princess Lalarukh and the accompanying paries. Princess Lalarukh cries out, flying forward to find her Saad.

'Princess, don't go beyond the hisar!' shouts Shabnam. No one is allowed to go beyond the magic circle, the hisar, but Princess Lalarukh is heedless, plunging down, looking for Saad. The pariru is helplessly borne with the wind to another place by Tez Chashm's magic. Then, the wind drops, the rain becomes a pleasant drizzle, the princess sits up and looks down to see a mango orchard around a glittering palace of sun-yellow topaz.

'Ya Allah, where am I? Is this Koh Kaaf?' She sees several girls dressed in green, singing and playing on the swings in the orchard, their voices melodious, their youthful laughter floating up. The pariru's wings are wet and she is shivering from the cold. Princess Lalarukh decides to fly down into the orchard.

'*Khushamdeed*! Welcome to my humble abode. I'm honoured to receive the Princess of Koh Kaaf.' Tez Chashm comes forward, bowing her head in salam. She has transformed herself into her favourite form of a white-haired pari with mystical eyes.

'Is this Koh Kaaf? Where are my paries?' asks Princess Lalarukh, getting down from the pariru and touching her forehead in response.

'No, this is outside Koh Kaaf. Your paries cannot come outside the hisar; their wings will get burnt. I'm a pari too,' Tez Chashm's kind smile puts the princess at ease.

'Please help me get back to my husband! I have to rescue him.'

'Don't worry, Prince Saad is safe and the armies have retreated. You rest here for a while and let your pariru dry its wings.' Tez Chashm takes Princess Lalarukh by her hand and escorts her into the Topaz Palace. A change of clothes, verdant green to celebrate the monsoons, are laid out for the princess. Several maids spring into action drying her, changing her clothes and serving her magic apple juice. The princess drinks the juice and falls down in a dead faint.

Meanwhile, Tez Chashm reaches Tareek Jaan in a *lamha*[5] and narrates the routing of Saad's army.

'King of Samris, I have the most beautiful gift for you. Look into my eyes!'

Tareek sees the lovely Princess Lalarukh with her wet tresses and is filled with great lust. Tareek Jaan loves women, paries and sorceresses and has several palaces in which he has trapped innocent females. Tez Chashm has performed her most important duty – to swell the ranks of her master's sex slaves; and Princess Lalarukh, the beloved wife of the Prince of Islam, lies captured in the harem hell of the dastardly Tareek Jaan.

Doston, har urooj ko zawaal hai, har urooj ko zawaal hai.

(Friends, for every rise there is fall.)

Kallan sighs, wraps his loi and touches his forehead in a farewell salam. Wali gathers the coins from the taaq and follows him.

Notes

1. A gher, literally meaning a round area, was the settlement where the members of an extended family or *khail* built their almost conjoined houses around a common courtyard which became the scene of celebrations, marriages, funeral prayers and social gatherings over the centuries. The village of Sherpur was segmented into settlements for the different tribal chiefs by the first Nawab in 1775.

2. The dastans were oral narratives, but after 1857, the Nawabs started encouraging the dastangos to pen down their stories. These were purchased by the Nawabs and preserved in the State Library.

3. Dastans begin with a saqinama – a poem in praise of the person who serves wine. The *saqi* or the muse inspires the storyteller.

4. Sayed Muhammad Husain Jah, *Tilism-e-Hoshruba*, vol. 7.

5. An instant or a second.

5

Feroza Begum

Qila-e-Mualla, Sherpur, 1896[1]

'Get up, Tabu! Tabu!' Feroza shook Tabu awake. Tabu rubbed her eyes and sat up on the divan. Feroza was sitting on the floor beside her, wisps of hair that had escaped her braid, framing her face.

'What happened, Bibi?' Tabu sat up, wiping the innocent dribble from her cheek.

It was still dark and the hurricane lamp that Feroza had kept lit throughout the night, was flickering on the last dregs of oil.

'How can I be divorced, Tabu? I never asked for divorce. And if he wants to divorce, it has to be face to face!'

'Bibi, he has divorced you. Azmat Khan told the guard…'

'I cannot be divorced like this. He has to utter the words to my face! What was my fault? Does he believe that I came here to marry the Nawab? Can he believe that, when I'm carrying his child? But he doesn't know of the child. If I tell him… Get up, call the Daroghan! I want to speak to her now!'

'Bibi, you rest. In the morning...'

'Go now! Tabu, my sister, please do this for me,' Feroza pulled up Tabu and handed her her dupatta, pushing her out of the room with pleas and instructions.

It was the last part of the night. Tabu walked towards the Daroghan's room at the other end of the common veranda. They were now housed in the Daroghan's house until the birth of the child.

The room lay in complete darkness and Tabu raised her hand to knock when a hefty woman guard appeared and asked, '*Ae ladki*, what are you doing?'

'Feroza Begum is calling for Daroghan bibi now.'

'You go back! I'll send her.'

Daroghan Chhamman in her crushed night clothes salamed and stood before an excitedly pacing Feroza.

'Daroghan bibi, I'm not divorced. I never asked for a divorce, and if my husband wants to divorce me he has to face me!'

'Begum, I know it's difficult for you to accept the reality. I can arrange for Murtaza Khan to give you talaq, but...'

'Then do it! He has to utter "talaq, talaq, talaq" to my face or at least to my father's face. Only then shall I be divorced.'

Feroza continued to argue, citing the Quran and Hadith till Daroghan Chhamman promised to speak to the Nawab about it. Miya Jaan was a *Sheikh ul-Hadith*, a master of Hadith, the sayings of the Prophet, and would often give Friday sermons at their mohalla mosque. All the children were well-instructed in the intricacies of Hadith and Islamic law.

The Nawab was informed by Daroghan Chhamman of Feroza's demand. He smiled.

'Miya Jaan Khan left Sherpur like a rat in the darkness. She has no one. Azmat Khan will not take her back and bring on his ruin. Get her the divorce she wants.'

Daroghan Chhamman dithered for a brief while, lowered her eyes and reminded the Nawab of Feroza's pregnancy.

'You go, and do what I order. I can feed many bastards!'

That evening, Feroza sat waiting for the gentle Murtaza in the mehman khana drawing room. She had dressed herself in a simple white churidar kurta and taken off all her jewellery to look like a widow or an abandoned woman.

She wanted to see the shame on his face.

Feroza's father-in-law, Azmat Khan, was ushered into the room followed by Murtaza.

'*Adab*, Baba,' she touched her forehead, the way she had greeted him every morning since her marriage.

'May you have a long life, beti,' Azmat Khan raised his hand in blessing. His pious white beard spread on his chest and his turban towered over his head, proclaiming his position as a zamindar. Murtaza's turban, subdued and flat, clung to his head.

'Baba, I want to speak to Murtaza Khan alone.'

'He's no longer your husband. You cannot be alone with a *namehram* (stranger).'

'He's my husband till he gives me talaq face to face!' Feroza straightened her back, readying herself.

'Feroza Begum, I married you to my son and kept you in my house with full honour. Today, I relieve you...'

'Baba, forgive your unworthy daughter. I bear your grandchild!' Feroza walked towards Murtaza, her eyes fixed on his lowered head.

'Do you hear, Murtaza Khan? You want your son to grow up a fatherless orphan in this harem?'

Murtaza stood immobile next to his father, his face barely registering the outburst.

'Murtaza, you said you loved me a hundred times. Is this your love? You know I didn't come here to wed the Nawab with your son in my womb! How can you, so-called proud Pathan, abandon me to the vile Nawab?'

Feroza stepped even closer to Murtaza, ignoring Azmat Khan's shocked face at her daring. Murtaza turned red, embarrassed at his ex-wife talking directly to him in the presence of his father.

'I take the responsibility of my grandson. He shall not want for anything. Murtaza has decided to divorce you. I wish to hand over your bride money of fifty gold coins and your jewellery,' Azmat Khan picked up a tin box which he had kept on the table, holding it like a talisman to ward off Feroza.

Feroza closed in on Murtaza, her face a hand's breadth away from him. She wanted to slap him, shake him, anything to break his lowered gaze.

'Say it to my face, you imbecile!'

'Feroza Begum, I, Murtaza Raza Khan divorce you – Talaq! Talaq! Talaq!' Murtaza's voice quivered at the end, or maybe she imagined it. He could never defy his father.

Azmat Khan handed over the box to Daroghan Chhamman and touched his forehead thrice to Feroza. Murtaza, his part in the play over, mimicked the salute to a sovereign. They moved towards the door, not turning their back to her – the future Begum of the Nawab.

'*Mubarak*, Murtaza Raza Khan, you have given your pregnant wife as a concubine to the Nawab! A thousand curses on your family. May you perish childless! And Azmat Khan, what a friend you have been to my father! I'll pray every day for the ruination of your *khandan*.'[2]

Azmat Khan's eyes sparked with impotent rage as Feroza's tongue lashed out the vilest curses on their heads.

'Feroza Begum, you shall observe iddat here till you have delivered your child. The maulvi has so ordained.'

'Which maulvi – Shia or Sunni? What does he say about a woman taken against her will? My religion says that such a man should be stoned to death!'

It is important here to explain the Shia-Sunni conflict in Sherpur. You, dear child, are probably unaware of the religious differences between Shias and Sunnis, but it played a great role in our family history. So the Pathans of Sherpur were Sunnis but at the beginning of the nineteenth century, the Nawabs of Sherpur converted to Shiaism. The Nawabs were deeply influenced by the powerful, culturally rich Shia kingdom of Awadh. They also added the prefix 'Sayed' to their name, claiming descent from the family of Prophet Muhammad, thus buffering their crown with exalted status. It was both faith and a reflection of the political climate of the time. There was an age-old schism between Shias and Sunnis which came to play in Sherpur. The earlier Nawabs did not make any announcements but followed their faith. However, Nawab Shams, a devout Shia, declared his faith publicly and performed all the rituals of his religion. This had become the cause of tension between him and the Sunni Pathan populace of Sherpur. In fact, the British Agent was unhappy over Nawab Shams's declaration as he feared rebellion.

So Feroza Begum was housed in Daroghan Chhamman's house till the birth of her child – the end of her iddat period. It was a typical Sherpuri house in the mahalsara with two spacious bedrooms opening into a veranda with takhts and chairs to entertain guests, several windowless side rooms, and a large brick-laid open courtyard culminating in a washroom to one side and a large kitchen on the other. There was no mardana baithak, for no males would be entertained in the harem. Daroghan Chhamman, a childless widow, occupied one room and made Feroza comfortable in the other bedroom for her long stay.

Miya Jaan used to speak about *barzaq*, the place in between heaven and hell, where the souls dwelled till the day of judgement. This was Feroza's barzaq, where she awaited her ultimate fate in hell.

Feroza thought of her mother, divorced and unceremoniously rubbed out of her life in a fit of rage. The mangoes had rotted that year, baskets of them from the orchard; maggots burying in their soft, sweet flesh. No one bothered about them, not even Bua who loved to sit with a pile of the slightly soft ones that Miya Jaan rejected, tearing them apart, burying her teeth into them, the juice dribbling down her chin. Then, there were many years of eating perfectly ripened mangoes in buckets of cool water, the girls squishing juices at each other. Their new mother, entering their life, carefully affectionate, the boys getting born, their own mother soon a lost memory. Feroza dimly remembered the tumultuous household when her mother lived with them, the guests, the impromptu singing, even the fights.

Bua said that their mother, Phul Begum, often sent word asking to meet her daughters. After a few years, she was married off somewhere outside Sherpur by her brothers. Gauhar and Feroza had each other and they had Bua to cling to at nights when stories of djinns and witches excited and scared them.

Once again, the rotten stench of mangoes must be permeating their home. Bua would tell the sweeper to throw them on the garbage heap outside the house – surrender them to the buzzing black flies.

Feroza stopped eating, bathing, even praying. God had abandoned her. She lay in bed watching the rains recede and the *pachadia*, the western wind, bring in the dry frigidity of winters that even the towering walls of the harem could not hold back. Something stirred within her – a whisper of quickening in her belly.

'Tabu, feel this! It's moving!' Feroza put Tabu's hand on her stomach.

'Yes, Bibi.' And they clung together in laughing grief.

There was still time for the birth. Her daughter, she was sure it was a girl, would be born in spring, the dai said. The mango blossoms would perfume the air with promise. A lot could happen in five months. She would grow fat and ugly. Maybe the Nawab would lose interest in her. But where would she go, if she was allowed to leave? Back to her father's haveli, of course. Bua and Tabu were enough for her. Life with its promptings pulled her back and Feroza started eating, deciding to give God another chance. She prayed only for her daughter growing with tenacity inside her.

'Begum, what is the need for this child? If she's a girl, she will be brought up in the harem; a boy would be separated from you after four years. He would be humiliated at every turn,' said Daroghan Chhamman, finding her in a good mood.

'There are hundreds of girls in the harem. What does one more matter? I know it's a girl and I shall look after her.'

'Begum, I speak for your own good – abort this child!'

'What? Have you gone mad? Didn't your maulvi tell you that it's *haram*, forbidden, to abort a child!'

'The Nawab doesn't want this child…'

'How much more will that bastard make me suffer? Now he'll murder my child! Go away, right now!' Feroza pushed a surprised Daroghan out of the room, shutting the door behind her but not before she had called her a female pimp and cursed the Nawab and his family.

'You can't do anything to my child. My Allah will protect it. You just see!'

The Nawab's foster great-grandmother, the imperious Huzur Aliya, had decided that abortion followed by the *nikah* nuptials was the only way to appease the Pathan families linked to each other by a complex network of marriages. Shams's blatant flouting of the basic norms of decency towards a Rohilla Sardar family was causing much anger. Rebellious words were being spoken behind closed doors in mardanas and whispered anxieties trembled in the zenanas. Miya Jaan Khan's flight and his status as a refugee had further infuriated the Pathans. If his daughter was forced into the harem, how could they ensure their own honour?

Nawab Shams saw the merit in the counsel, especially now that he didn't have to wait for six months to bed Feroza. The abortion would be kept a secret – a whisper with limited believability. A nikah in the most honourable style with invitations to all Pathan families would calm things down. It might prompt Feroza's family to return from Bareilly. He would give them some more land and promise jobs to the sons.

Abortion in the fourth month of pregnancy was risky and no local dai would dare touch Feroza. She was already hysterical, tearing her hair and beating her head against the walls, crying for Gauhar, and shouting profanities at the Nawab's family. The Daroghan sent for Hakim Ajmal Khan's medicines to calm her nerves. But Feroza threw them away, the bottles shattering, bleeding red and black on the brick courtyard, the packets of *majun* medicines littering around them. She had become paranoid, not allowing the Daroghan to enter the room, retreating into its recesses as soon as she saw her coming, sharp-tongued curses her only weapon.

Tabu became the informer, listening at doors and reporting faithfully. Daroghan Chhamman had to handle the daily tantrums on the one hand and the growing impatience of the Nawab on the other. Then Huzur Aliya gave the unheard-of verdict – the male English doctor would abort the baby under *behoshi* (anaesthesia).

Dr Wilson was a florid, balding old physician with a warm manner; but his manner was not given the occasion to exercise itself for as soon as he entered the room, Feroza coiled up on the bed, screaming.

'Tabu, save me! This butcher will kill my child!'

Feroza clung to Tabu. She had been dreading the visit since Tabu had told her about it.

'Relax, Begum. It won't hurt,' the nurse said, trying to prise Feroza's fingers away from Tabu. Finally, two strongly built maids pinned her down to the bed, holding her on each side. Feroza looked at Tabu with wild eyes.

'Call Bua! They will kill me!'

The English nurse busied herself by setting the cold chrome box on the table, taking out the instruments and laying them on the enamel tray – strange, shining, grotesque, all lined up in a neat row. Feroza watched with fascinated horror as the doctor pulled up his sleeves and the nurse held the sterile rubber gloves with a twisted scissor-like instrument for him.

'What will you do? What will happen, Tabu? Daroghan bibi, please save me. I'm like your daughter!'

The Daroghan held her hand and wiped her brow, murmuring reassurances. Tabu stood petrified in the corner. One of the maids roughly pulled off Feroza's pyjamas, while the other bent her legs to her stomach, putting the weight of her own body to bend Feroza's knees. Feroza unsuccessfully tried to kick off the maid and twist away her body. She could feel the doctor's cold fingers prodding inside her painfully. She screamed louder, her voice cracking, spit congealing on the side of her lips.

'Relax Begum, or it will pain,' said Dr Wilson in Urdu.

'She won't let me examine her,' he said to the Daroghan, shaking his head.

'Ether, sister!'

Feroza could smell something pungent and knew she couldn't do anything to stop them.

'Listen, Daroghan bibi. Call the Nawab. I want to speak to him.'

She gave a last cry as a white cloth was held to her face, obliterating the painful reality.

She woke up after what seemed like hours, a hollow ache inside her where her child used to live – torn out of her and thrown away like scum. Tabu said she had kept screaming and crying throughout the procedure.

Days after the abortion, Feroza felt a deadness descend upon her. There were no tears, no anger, even her womb stopped weeping. She lay quietly in her room watching the patch of sky turn brilliant blue with the onset of winter. Tabu asked the Daroghan to send for Bua and Gauhar. Bua came immediately but Gauhar would not dare defy her father's ban.

Bua sat muttering prayers, coaxing her to eat. She lay with her head in Bua's lap, inhaling her earthy paan and cardamom scent while Bua absentmindedly probed her hair for nits as she used to when Feroza was a child, talking all the while, simple aphorisms, family stories and loud prayers to the all-merciful Allah. Allah and all his valiant subjects had deserted her and her unborn child.

She slept poorly with vivid dreams of swimming in a pool of blood towards a dark shadow of her child and woke up with the sound of a wailing baby ringing in her ears.

Feroza sensed a change in the rhythm of the household, an enhanced activity, and peeped out at the veranda. A host of mughlani seamstresses sat on the durries amid bolts of glistening silks, measuring, sorting and cutting. The Daroghan was giving instructions in a low voice, feeling the textures, and devising colour combinations.

'Bibi, they're getting your trousseau made. Daroghan was saying that your iddat is over because you lost the child; you are now free to marry the Nawab!' Tabu informed her.

'Ask them to prepare a shroud for my funeral.' Feroza lay back on her bed.

'Hai, hai! May my years be added to your life! Don't say such words,' Bua covered her ears.

'I won't marry that killer!'

'What other way is there, Begum?' Daroghan Chhamman came into the room.

'I'm like a mother to you. There shall be a brilliant future for you as the second Begum of Sherpur, the mother of the heir!' Daroghan sat on her bed and held her hand.

Feroza closed her eyes; a single tear buried itself in her hair.

'What will happen to my Bua and Tabu?' she said finally.

'They can live with you, if you want, or they can go back to your house.'

'I want them with me.'

'Oh, if you could see the beautiful palace that the Nawab is decorating for you! And he has got a *nath* (nose ring) specially made with diamond beads because pearls, he said, would pale before your complexion.[3] Why, only today he told me to get dresses made in all colours of the rainbow.'

'I won't wear blue.' Murtaza's obsession in dressing her in blue – all that was over now.

'All right, no blue. And here's the key to the jewellery box that Azmat Raza Khan gave…'

'I don't want it.'

'Daroghan bibi, since you are going to officiate as the mother of the bride, give it then,' Bua said quickly. Jewellery was the only insurance that women had in a world where men's affections wavered with the wind. Feroza turned away and closed her eyes.

'Akbari Bua, you are her foster mother. Why hide this from you – the first Begum from Basoda cannot bear children. Our Feroza will wear the crown as the mother of the heir. The people of Sherpur want an heir from the oldest Rohilla Sardar family!' Daroghan's beady, kohled eyes swallowed Bua.

She spoke of the great power and riches of the court of Sherpur and the glamorous life Feroza would live. Bua was thrilled – her own child might rule Sherpur as Her Highness, Begum of Sherpur.

Feroza remembered the Begum of Sherpur on the swing at the sawani – it seemed a lifetime ago. The Begum was probably younger than her and was already condemned to childlessness after three years of marriage. What if she too never bore children? She would live out her life on the fringes of the harem.

'Listen to me, Bibi. The Nawab is giving you an honourable position. He could have made you his concubine. You just wait, Miya Jaan Khan will return when he hears of your good fortune. All your brothers and sisters will come back and your house will be *abad* again,' Akbari Bua whispered later.

'Bua, Miya Jaan Khan is dead to me. I won't even spit on his grave!'

Her only condition was that the nikah be conducted in the manner of Sunnis and that she should not be forced to change her religion. The Nawab agreed, adding that a Shia maulvi would also be present at the nikah. Nawab Shams never forced his religion on his Sunni wives and mistresses, though some converted to the Shia faith to win his approval and affection.

Notes

1. The Grand Qila.
2. Murtaza Khan never remarried. Oral history claims he took a mistress, probably a dancing girl. They didn't have any children.
3. Oral accounts say that the nose ring was specially made for Feroza with diamond beads instead of the traditional pearls.

6

Feroza Begum

Mahalsara, Sherpur, 1896

> All the citizens of Harampur are under great stress – fear is writ large on their faces. Brides go missing on the way to their new homes. People have started guarding the bride's palki with armed guards. There is always some chaos en route and the palki vanishes. Even if the palki reaches the bridegroom's house, it's found occupied by a prostitute tied up and gagged! There is an air of suspicion and the citizens now mistrust their fellowmen.
>
> *Husn Ka Daku*,
> Maulana Abdul Haleem 'Sharar'[1]

Feroza dressed herself up as the Nawab's bride with cold brutality. She wore the red and gold dress, strung the teeka-jhoomar on her head and studded jewels into her thin braid that Gauhar always teased her about. She used to envy Gauhar's thick long braid that came down to her knees, playfully tugging at it. Gauhar would shout, 'Ya Allah, make her bald.' Feroza pulled the chain of the nose ring covering her cheek with the blood-coloured ruby nestled between two large diamond beads, and pinned it into her hair. The jerk caused her nose to bleed, the blood congealing around the sharp gold wire of the ring. She weighed down her arms with bangles – gold, glass and diamond, covered her chest with necklaces, the ropes of pearls reaching down to her navel. Finally, she covered her head with the heavy gold work dupatta. Her face was without any makeup. She brushed aside Tabu's suggestion to put on some surma and lipstick.

The women, festive and garrulous, entered her room. She didn't touch her forehead in greeting as Daroghan Chhamman wheezed out the introductions, enumerating their levels of closeness to the royal family. Undeterred by her stony look, they bore her out into the veranda with a wave of teasings and compliments. Tabu walked behind her, holding the skirt of her voluminous farshi. She was seated on a red silk-covered takht. A formidable, grey-haired woman, probably some relative of the Nawab, eased herself next to her on the takht and assumed charge of her. She replied to the greetings, extolled Feroza's bloodline, showed off her jewellery – see this belonged to so and so, the magars are so heavy, especially brought from Lucknow; she went on touching her jewellery and chatting till Feroza felt like screaming at her. She could hear the women whispering behind their fans, gossiping about her. Tabu told her later that they believed Feroza insisted on the marriage because she had fallen in love with the Nawab and the glamour of the court. They all knew about the abortion, tut-tutting over Feroza's heartlessness in killing her child, some even going on to wonder what punishments awaited such women in hell.

Feroza looked at the red and yellow awnings covering the courtyard strung with flowers in the September sun; the corpulent Begums from various Pathan families, resplendent in jewels and brocades; seated around, masticating paan, sweating in spite of the large cloth ceiling fans pulled by kaharis, and the swishing handheld fans of their personal maids. Gauhar and Amina Khala didn't come, probably apprehensive about Miya Jaan Khan's displeasure. Her trousseau was displayed in silver trays set on the carpet. Daroghan Chhamman and the seamstresses had worked on it through the long afternoons, their continuous humming talk, as they snipped and sewed, driving her mad.

The domni singers sat on the carpet, their full-throated singing set to the rhythm of the *dhol.*

Khwaja jee sun le hamari jiya ki peerh, ankhiyan se bahe hai neer,
Kahey ko byahin bides arey lakhiyan babul mohey?
Hum to babul torey angney ki churiyan, arey chug piye udh jayen;
Hum to babul torey khoontey ki gayyan…

(Khwaja-ji listen to the pain of my heart, my eyes are filled with tears,
O my wealthy father, why did you marry me off to a foreign land?
We are just birds from your courtyard, pecking at food, we fly away;
We are just your tethered cows; we go where you send us…)

The Begums sighed, sniffed and wiped their tears as Amir Khusrau's ancient lament sent them back to their own *rukhsati* with tearful embraces, their fathers and brothers handing over 'their' woman to another set of males – the culmination of the wedding. Feroza had heard the song many times, had cried clinging to Gauhar at her rukhsati with her siblings hugging her, Ammi's stomach shaking with her crying and Abba kissing her forehead. Her three young brothers had self-importantly tied a piece of turmeric, a silver coin and green grass to the corners of her dupatta, repeating the customary Pathan blessing, '*Behen main ṭujhe neki deta hoon*. Sister, I give you goodness.'

There were no males from Feroza's family to hand her over, as her *wali*, the male in-charge of her body. Since there could be no nikah without a wali, Zaamin Khan, the *Haakim Mahal*, the administrator of the mahals, agreed to be her wali. He would pledge her into matrimony.

Someone said, 'Maulvi Sahib is here!' Feroza's face was covered by the *sargah*, a gauzy white scarf.

'Bibi, lower your eyes!' whispered Tabu.

Everyone straightened up, the domnis stopped their poignant songs, the khwajasaras sprang up to hold a long curtain across the veranda to shield the Begums from the lusty stare of the two maulvis (a Shia and a Sunni) and two male witnesses. Feroza became aware of her damp sweaty back and the suffocating tight blouse in the humid September heat. What if she said 'no'? Nikah was after all based on the free will of both the parties. Would they let her go? Or would she be forced still?

The maulvi was chanting some prayers in Arabic.

'Feroza Begum, daughter of Altaf Khan *urf* Miya Jaan Khan, your wedding has been arranged to Nawab Shams Ali Khan Bahadur, son of Nawab Murad Ali Khan Bahadur for a sum of two lakh rupees as *mehr*.[2] Do you agree?'

What if she just didn't say anything?

'She says "yes"!' A middle-aged woman dressed in her bridal dress, suddenly shouted towards the curtains. Feroza turned towards the woman. The old lady in charge of her elbowed her ribs.

'Uh?' she turned sharply towards the offending lady.

'I heard it too. She said "yes"!' said the old lady, then another woman joined in bearing witness to her acquiesce and then another. They closed down around her, hugging, touching her chin, showering blessings and praise. '*Mubarak!*

Mubarak!' they echoed, embracing and congratulating each other. The domnis started singing the *shadiyana* – the congratulatory wedding song.

Their duty done, the maulvis left and the curtain was taken away.

'Arre, she didn't even wait for maulvi to ask thrice,' giggled someone. The crush of bodies around Feroza intensified, the younger girls joining in. She felt dizzy and breathless.

'Oho, move away girls. The bride is fainting.' The old lady pushed away a young girl bending to see the bride's face. All brides fainted, overwhelmed with sorrow at leaving their parents' house and the finality of change in their lives. She had pretended to faint at her first marriage. Feroza stood up and walked back steadily to her room.

'Let the *dulhan* rest!' said Daroghan Chhamman as Bua and Tabu rushed to escort Feroza.

Soon they were back again, the women bristling with renewed energy after the lavish lunch in the courtyard, bringing with them nauseous, curry smells. Feroza had refused food, feeling sure that she would throw up.

'Tabu, don't leave me!' she held Tabu's hand as they rustled around her, covering her with more veils till everything became opaque. She was led out, near-blind, to a silver palanquin in the courtyard. Where was Bua? She could only see coloured shapes.

Daroghan Chhamman salamed her thrice, begged her forgiveness for any misdemeanours during her stay. Feroza sat in a daze in the plush palanquin with Tabu, the silk curtains were drawn and they were borne away.

'*At least you are going with honour*,' *Gauhar would say*.

The first night after her nikah, Feroza had been taken directly to the Sher Mahal, the Nawab's residence. She was received by a crowd of loudly dressed Begums, braying with laughter at sexual innuendoes, and somewhat derisively blessed by Huzur Aliya. After a host of ceremonies that only her body attended, she was taken to the royal chamber. She sat for hours waiting for her new husband, sick with apprehension. The Nawab was busy watching the dance performance celebrating his wedding. Finally, the emotional exhaustion overcame her anxiety and she dozed off.

He came in the early morning hours, drunk with happiness and alcohol, ravaged her with the zeal of a conqueror and stumbled out of the room. She tried to fight him, but it only excited him, so she closed her eyes and turned away from his alcohol breath, submitting her soulless body and riding the brutal pain. After he had left, she lay staring at the powder blue and gold patterns on the ceiling, her body an aching mass, the humiliation seeping into her bones.

A maid had come after some time, helped her to get dressed to go to her mahalsara. Like a violated woman she had worn her crushed dress, her jewels were counted and loaded back on her body, a little askew. She walked the wood-panelled gallery with its grand paintings and stubbed-out chandeliers, trying not to stumble from the pain. She avoided the interested gaze of the maids and the khwajasaras as she was escorted to a palanquin in the courtyard.

'I'll not go there like a common randi! Go, tell your Nawab!' Feroza told the Daroghan waiting to usher her into her new mahal.

'Begum, every house has its own rules. This is not your earlier house. It is the way of the Mahal. The Nawab calls the Begum to his house when he desires…' began Daroghan Chhamman in the soft, patient voice she employed with Feroza.

'So, one day he desires the nautch girl and calls her. Then he calls me, does his business on the same bed and sends me back! Enough, if he wants, he can visit me here – in my mahal. I'm not a bazaar girl! I'm Miya Jaan Khan's daughter. Maybe the Nawab forgets because he only lies with prostitutes, whores and poor kidnapped girls!' Feroza's voice was steel though her body felt battered and violated to its core.

'If I live here, it will be on my own terms. The Nawab owes his crown to the Rohilla sardars and he has to respect their daughters.'

The Nawab liked women who could sing well, skilled in the art of coquetry, often giving the honoured status of *mutahi* bibi or temporary wife to the tawaifs who pleased him. He often plucked them from the *Arbab-e-Nishat*, the music department of the qila. The women who got pregnant after such encounters also became mutah wives.

Now you would want to know what a mutah wife is. The mutah wives were the so-called temporary wives. They were a rung lower than the nikah wives, though the offspring had the same privileges. The distinguishing factor between the nikah and mutah wives was one of status rather than permanence. No mutah wife was ever sent away. You were a Nawab's woman – wife or concubine – forever. The earlier Nawabs had also married courtesans and given them high titles and positions.

Daroghan Chhamman had to make peace between Feroza and the Nawab and make sure they lay together often because Huzur Aliya wanted an heir for Sherpur. Feroza had refused to go to the Nawab's palace after the first night.

Feroza's continued refusal had enraged Nawab Shams. He was a hot-tempered young man known for his earth-shaking furies. Huzur Aliya had to hold him back from forcing the girl into his rooms. This would never do. There was still a simmering discontent and a sense of insecurity, barely appeased by the grand wedding. News of any ill treatment would filter out. He had to impregnate her and then the woman would settle down.

'Feroza is beautiful and obstinate. You have to win her over, son.' Huzur Aliya took the dish with the shredded paan leaves, sprinkled them with a generous amount of local black tobacco, and took a mouthful. Her molars had decayed and blackened with age and tobacco, forcing her to have her paan without betel nut. Her strong front teeth resisting the decay had coalesced together and rested on her lower lip. She looked predatory.

'She'll settle down once she has a child. You have to go to her often. If she gets you an heir, which that Basodeywali couldn't manage, all the Pathans will rally behind you.' Shams's first wife from the princely state of Basoda in central India was called 'Basodeywali', enhancing her foreignness in the eyes of the clannish Pathans.

Huzur Aliya herself had engineered the match with Sultanat Ara, daughter of Nawab Ibrahim of Basoda. The British-ruled princely state of Basoda was much smaller than Sherpur and of less political significance; but the Nawabs, educated at Mayo College and universities in London, considered themselves politically enlightened. Sultanat Ara, educated by an English governess, had a supercilious attitude towards the less-educated women at the Sherpur royal court. Shams had never taken to his proud first wife and barely visited her before she was pronounced infertile.

'Hah! Sherpur Pathans are selfish brutes. Give them power and money and they are yours,' Shams spat out. The Pathans constituted a prosperous majority in Sherpur State and he had to cater to their opinion, at least for some time.

'True, they can be bought. But their damn pride surges up suddenly. Have you forgotten how they nearly rebelled after the regent's murder? Bloodline is all they respect and this girl is from the regent's family. Woo her, give her a title and position. She will come around.'

Shams could never forget the anxious years after the regent's death. The British saw the murder as an affront to their authority and could have easily given the crown to Shams's younger stepbrother, Prince Nadir, who was attending college in England. The case of the regent's murder and its investigations had dragged on for two years. Finally, Shams was absolved of all charges. Abdullah Khan, an eminent courtier, and his sons were pronounced guilty. Abdullah Khan committed suicide and his sons were hanged. However, most Pathans (including Miya Jaan) still secretly blamed Nawab Shams and Huzur Aliya for the murder.

The British government abolished the regency and crowned Nawab Shams with full rights in 1895. This was a major victory for Shams and Huzur Aliya. Highly ambitious and intelligent, the young Nawab had thrown himself into modernising Sherpur. He perfected the administrative framework laid down by the slain regent, connected Sherpur to the railway network, introduced telephones and undertook electrification. By the end of the nineteenth century, he had created a 'model state'. Lord Reading had been impressed by Nawab Shams's hospitality, his command over the English language, and had described him to his successor, Lord Irwin, as 'a man of extraordinary intelligence, great accomplishments and a proponent of eastern culture.'

Feroza stepped out of her bedroom into the long veranda with its colourful mosaic floor and the wide arches. The split bamboo curtains on the arches were rolled up for the day. Two women, sitting on their haunches, were sweeping the floor; their colourful sarees bunched up under their knees. They stood up and salamed. Feroza nodded and walked out to the brick-laid courtyard, twice the size of the courtyard at home, edged with verandas leading to rooms on all sides. Three steps led down to a small garden with two guava trees laden with light green fruit.

'Ammi used to say monsoon guavas have worms.' She longed to climb up, pluck and dissect the fruit, eating the good parts. At home, they had a long, hooked stick to pluck guavas. Tabu and Gauhar would make raw guava chutney, sprinkling salt and chilli powder – their secret afternoon snack while Amma and Bua slept.

Two kaharis sat at the end of the garden outside the kitchen area, grinding flour in a stone *chakki*, their legs spread out on either side of the stone implement.

'This is for their own meal, Begum. Your food will come from the royal kitchens,' said Laila, her designated personal maid, walking behind her.

'Who's that man?' asked Feroza as a tall man standing at the courtyard door bowed and touched his forehead.

'Not a man, he is the khwajasara guard, Mahabat Khan,' whispered Laila.

Feroza looked at Mahabat Khan's hairless, aquiline face. He wore a flat turban different from Abba's turban, a long maroon tunic and white churidar; a curved dagger tucked into the black sash. They walked out of the courtyard door, around the house to the lavish front lawns with a marble fountain at the centre. A cherub smiled with carved delight at the drops raining on its head. The dark-leaved mango trees, which, Laila said, had been planted by the Nawab's late grandfather nearly fifty years ago, skirted the edges of the garden, their ominous stillness punctuated by the cursing babbler birds. Feroza looked at the towering walls surrounding the mahal. The only way out was through an iron gate to the right.

'Where does that lead to?'

'The quarters of the eunuch guards and female guards. Your palanquin came through this gate.'

Feroza turned around, facing the frontage of her elegant palace with its arches and columns. The mahalsara set up for Feroza was second only to the Sher Palace in grandeur. This was her home now. The banality of the years stretching ahead sickened her.

'That's Khursheed Manzil, the royal durbar,' Laila pointed at a marble dome which she had earlier seen from the rooftop of her father's house.[3] She felt trapped from all sides.

Her mahalsara had a British-style furnished drawing room, a dining room with a long ornate table and chairs, and two bedrooms with beautifully carved masahri beds. Feroza felt suffocated in the drawing room with its maroon, heavy velvet curtains and dark wood furniture. The idea of eating alone at the dining table was foreign to her. She spent most of her time in her bedroom and the veranda. All her meals were laid out on the veranda takht.

Feroza was left alone for the next few days. Daroghan Chhamman came every day to enquire politely about her health, her sharp eyes noting the settling down of the new occupants in the mahalsara. Feroza was still getting used to her new life, the shadows of her old life lurking in her mind, the red blood dream returning every few days, jolting her back to her grief.

Bua regarded the barren Basodeywali as the main rival to her Feroza who should, with her lineage and looks, rule Sherpur as Her Highness. Feroza disregarded her advice to be more amenable towards the Nawab. She was determined to never suffer humiliation at the hands of the Nawab, even if it meant giving up her life. For Feroza, every emotion dwelt on the extreme and she took up challenging positions. There was no midway. She knew Gauhar would not approve.

Tabu got all the inside secrets from the kaharis and the almond-eyed Badamiya, the scavenging sweeper who carried the night soil from the mahalsara in a wicker basket on her head. Tabu exaggerated the gossipy bits, narrated funny incidents, intrigues and wrangles in the zenana. Their household, managed by Bua, consisted of Mahabat Khan, two kahari maids who cleaned and cooked and Badamiya. Food came from the kitchens in huge *nashteydans* – a feast big enough to feed ten people. Fruits, paan and other groceries were provided as per demand. If only Gauhar could see her grand palace and her servants.

'Arre Bibi, all these female guards have slept with the Nawab. He doesn't even leave the kaharis,' Tabu whispered behind the Daroghan's massive receding back as Feroza refused to go to the Nawab's bedroom yet again.

Notes

1. *Durbar-e-Harampur* and *Husn ka Daku* were penned by the famous Urdu writer, Maulana Abdul Haleem Sharar Lucknowi in the 1920s. Both the wildly popular books write of a debauched ruler of the fictitious town of Harampur, who kidnapped young brides.
2. The obligation in the form of money or possession which is to be paid to the bride by the bridegroom at the time of the nikah. If it is not paid at that time, it should be paid later.
3. Khursheed Manzil, built by Nawab Ahmad Ali Khan in the 1840s, functioned as the royal durbar. It was demolished by Nawab Shams Ali Khan in 1905. Shams Manzil, designed and constructed by the French architect A.C. DuPont, replaced Khursheed Manzil as the durbar hall.

7

Ameera

Sherpur, 2016

Dadi's story had continued till late into the night and still hummed in my semi-awake mind. I had curled up next to Dadi on her massive four-poster bed, pestering her to complete the story.

'Wake up, my doll,' Dadi's ancient eyes smile at me.

'I dreamt about Benazir Palace. I want to go there.'

'Like your great-grandmother Feroza Begum, you won't rest till you go,' Dadi chuckles. 'It's now in ruins and they tell me the roof has fallen in. But we shall go one day. Now get dressed for school.'

I kiss Dadi's soft, withered cheek and get out of bed.

Ammi is sleeping in my room again and I have to tiptoe around, not daring to switch on the dressing-room light. Ammi barely sleeps, her rosary beads click softly through the night. I keep stroking her arm till I fall asleep.

I drape my scarf, rehearsing the YouTube instructions, swishing the edges and settling the perfect pleats. The cute little fringe that was supposed to peep out of the scarf edge, refuses to flatten. If only I had a straightener. I pin back the rebellious lock and now my prominent forehead sticks out. Maybe Sonia will magically settle the fringe. I pull up my socks to cover my knees. The skirt is too long but non-negotiable. The scarf and long socks are my passport to my new co-ed school – Scholars' Academy.

It was a tough battle won after several arguments and promises. When Sonia decided to leave St. Mary's, our all-girls school, after Class X to attend the more 'happening' Scholars' Academy, I had to follow her. Ammi was totally against the idea. She believes that co-ed schools are dens of vice and unsuitable for young girls. My brother Jugnu, being a boy, could of course be trusted to attend Scholars' Academy. Finally, Abba agreed to send me there only after Dadi ruled, 'They have better teachers and my Ameera will be a doctor*ni*. Send her there, Jugnu will look after her.'

Jugnu, my brother, had sparkled momentarily like his namesake – the fireflies – he loved to catch. He is just a year older than me and used to lord over me with all his alpha-male superiority.

I sneak out of my room, haul the school bag on my shoulder, waving away Chanda Bua with the waiting milk. We used to gulp it down before racing to the gate. Getting there first was a matter of pride, especially because Jugnu teased me for being fat and slow. I resist the wave of despair always lurking to overwhelm me and walk out with quick steps.

The house looks ridiculous now that Naved Chacha and Samiya Chachi decided to wall off the garden – 'their portion'. The courtyard and garden were always open spaces. We played there, sunned ourselves in the winters and slept there through summer night power cuts. 'Theirs' and 'ours' was a hazy concept. The lower rooms at the end of the garden, which earlier functioned as the male drawing room and pantry were occupied by Naved Chacha after he got married. Later, two rooms were constructed on the first floor for the boys – Hammad and Zahid.

It was about two months after Jugnu was taken away that I realised that the courtyard belonged to us and the garden was Naved Chacha's. The garden and the mango trees are now cordoned off by an ugly L-shaped wall, sparkling white against the lichen-streaked walls of our home. I walk through a passage flanked by the wall to the vestibule of a shared garage, enclosed by the main gate which still serves as an entrance to both the households. The garage houses the immobile 1930s navy blue Fiat, its doors opening the wrong way, and two (functional) scooters. We have to go through the garage now for our rare visits to Naved Chacha's. Samiya Chachi is just a presence in the upstairs window. Sometimes she creeps in gingerly to see Dadi, avoiding Ammi, as if the very air in our house is a corrupting influence. Naved Chacha comes over quite often. Dadi says Hammad and Zahid have been forbidden by Samiya Chachi to visit us. It's hard on Ammi because she practically brought them up. At least, I can catch up with them on the school bus.

Meel, our old retainer, stuck with the childish name I had given him, is standing at the gate.

'Your rickshaw is here. Come quickly, child.' Meel removes the iron latch and drags open our monumental twelve-feet-high gate. I hate bumping along in the creaking rickshaw, pulled by the super-thin Jumman, to the school bus stop which is barely half-a-kilometre away. But walking down the street is not an option – Abba won't allow it.

'*Chalo*, *chalo*, let's go!' Meel croaks with his eternal smile as I sit in the rickshaw clutching the bag to my chest. The bumps really shake things up. I don't know why every male on the street has to ogle at every passing female. Size, shape and age don't matter. Meel gets on to his bicycle, another relic that suffers from frequent breakdowns, to perform his special duty of escorting me. For the rest of the day he sits at the gate in his toothless, wrinkled glory to announce visitors, smokes his hookah, gets provisions from the nearby shops and battles Bua over the food portions she hands out to him thrice a day. Meel has an abusive parrot who shouts at all passers-by and dances on Meel's hookah pipe when he sings old *charbait* songs.[1]

The rickshaw trundles through the brick lane with its windowless houses packed together, often with common walls because they belonged to members of a family or they had been portioned off from the main kothi. The rich people with money from Gulf jobs have built two or three floors with jutting out balconies claiming spaces over the lane. These are interspersed with ramshackle, old houses announcing the dire straits of the owners. Soon they shall be sold off and disappear into the Gulf people's houses – I have seen it happen in our mohalla. The smelly, busy drains running on both sides of the gully are clogged with plastic wrappers and are dark with old moss and slime. When there is a dengue or malaria scare, the drains are cleaned out and the town fogged with asthma-inducing and mosquito-destroying sprays. The minister punishes the administration for epidemics and the doctors for deaths.

Dadi is very upset at the (still unexplained) disappearance of the Nawab's statue and the destruction of the topkhana gates. They used to look so grand. You drove into the city through the topkhana gates and the marble cupola of the durbar hall, positioned right at the centre of the gates, would draw closer. There were ten gates all around Sherpur leading out to different cities – Bareilly Gate, Bilaspur Gate and so on.

There were protests after the topkhana gates were broken. Then the others started to disappear overnight as well. The disappearances are almost magical. Rumours are going around that the drivers of the demolition cranes are dying of mysterious illnesses. Some say the djinns living in the ancient gates are trying to save the gates. The humans have given up, anyway. Maybe the minister has recruited evil djinns for the demolitions. I feel terrible looking at the blank spaces where the gates stood.

I shut my eyes and try to imagine our gully in Feroza Begum's time. Dadi says Mardan Khan's palatial kothi had an archway high enough to walk an elephant through. Mardan Khan was the sardar or head of one of the tribes who founded Sherpur. His kothi was right next to our mansion – it used to be a mansion then. All around the gher were the kothis of courtiers and zamindars from Mardan Khan's tribe – my forefathers were his kinsmen. The kothis were partitioned between children and then sold off one after another as the occupants lost their vast lands after the abolition of the zamindari and became poor overnight. The grand gateways were broken down and shops appeared, edging the gully with their colourful wares and hoardings. Some kothis were divided up between brothers and cousins and broken down to make tiny, unimaginative houses.

Dadi had to sell off the zenana portion after Dada passed away. We are now living in what used to be the mardana portion. At least our gateway with its floral engravings, fitted with the wooden *phatak* still stands.

It's disgusting that people still pee by the roadside like babies who can't hold on. I count the wet patches like I used to with Jugnu. He once told me that the high curves are from Hindu pees and low ones from Muslims because Muslims have to sit and do it. Jugnu was seriously disgusting. But there are less of Hindu pees because most Hindus are shifting out from the Muslim-dominated city area to Civil Lines. Maybe they are scared of living with Muslims now or maybe it has just become too congested. Sonia will also shift to her new house in Civil Lines soon. She'll have to take another bus and we won't have that blissful, undisturbed one hour before and after school.

Meel cycles slowly beside me on his misbalancing contraption, chatting with Jumman, waving a cheery salam to everyone till I feel like melting away. I focus my thoughts on Sonia who had promised to bring all three *Fifty Shades of Grey* movies on pen drives. I can watch one tonight, that is, if Ammi falls asleep. They'll see me through the weekend.

My cell phone buzzes. We are not allowed to take it to school but everyone does so anyway. It's a message from Sonia:

'*Hey, don't come to school today. Sami is saying they will punish the fee defaulters again.*'

'Stop, Stop the rickshaw!' I scream. We are just a turn away from the bus stop and they will see me. Meel nearly falls down from his cycle.

'I have to go back now.'

'Why, Bibi?

'Uffo, just turn back! I'm not feeling well!' I practically scream at Jumman who is ready to take the turn.

We return home and I stomp into Dadi's room. I'm so angry, I could burst. I had asked Abba to pay my fees and all he said was, 'Of course, I'll pay. Tell your teacher we won't run off with the fees. I have to pay my lawyer first, and then it's your turn.'

Abba is fighting a case against the government. The minister wants to acquire his shops along with other lands around the Gandhi Memorial for the 'Mahatma Mall' project.

'Why doesn't Abba sell off his stupid shops to the minister?' I wail.

'Ah, it's always the *ana*, ego of us stupid Pathans. The minister cannot snatch away what is ours!'

'But he'll get money and my fees will be paid.'

'Huh, tell your father this,' Ammi comes in with Dadi's medicines. Ammi's eyes look so watery these days, like she's crying all the time.

'What is the point of this fight with the minister? Naved sold off his shops and got a lot of money,' Ammi sniffs.

'I'm not going to school till my fees are paid!'

I ready myself for Ammi's scoldings, protests, orders – anything. But she says nothing, like I had decided not to go to a birthday party. She seriously doesn't care anymore.

Abba-Ammi aren't even bothered that I was punished last week for non-payment of fees. It was so humiliating. I was made to stand outside on the playground for the whole day with other fee defaulters. The girls kept sniggering and calling me 'princess'. I was the only girl from my class who was punished.

Sami was there too, though I'm sure his fee was paid. Sonia says he has a crush on me and I didn't hear his name being called out in the assembly. So, we had a really long chat because there was nothing else to do.

Actually, I barely ever speak to the guys in my class. Strangely, guys don't pester scarf-wearing girls with 'I want to be your friend' proposals. So us scarfed girls choose to talk to guys we like and make boyfriends on our own. It's pretty cool that way, though I long to throw away the scarf and open up my hair like I used to at St. Mary's.

If I needed to be rescued like Feroza Begum, I'm sure Abba would never come for me. If his measly shops are more important than my education, I can't expect anything from him. Anyway, he only cared about Jugnu. I remember his hand on Jugnu's shoulder, the pride in his voice as he introduced Jugnu as 'my son, Javed Raza Khan'. He always took his full name, the whole weight of it. They don't have a Nawabi inheritance to give but their male heir is all they care about. Even Ammi is thrilled to have produced a male to bear their name and their lineage. Dadi says the Prophet Muhammad had no sons and his lineage was through his one daughter, Bibi Fatima.

It must be lunchtime at school and I Whatsapp Sonia.

'Thanks for saving my life.'

'Ask Uncle to pay the fees. They are saying they won't allow the defaulters to sit for the exams next week. You can borrow from my Dad. It's cool.'

'No thanks. Abba will manage by next week. Missing you.'

I do believe that in this day and age nobody should bully you into selling your property – these are not the Nawab's times; but if it was Jugnu's fees and his exams, Abba would sell off the shops and chuck the case in a heartbeat. We females always depend on our fathers or males to rescue us – our default response to a crisis. Imagine, poor Feroza Begum's father dumped her in the harem and ran away!

Notes

1. Popular folk songs sung by the Pathans. It owes its name to the quartet arrangement of the verses.

8

Feroza Begum

Sheesh Mahal, Sherpur, 1896

> The libertine practices of the Nawabs, which would ultimately result in their destruction, harboured a small miracle – Bandi Jaan Tawaif. She, with her disreputable birth, her scandalous life and ignoble education, became the Begum of Nawab Yunus Ali Khan and was honoured with the title of 'Mehtaab Mahal'. Later, Nawab Shams gave her the title of 'Huzur Aliya'. She ruled the harem till her death and the Nawabs were greatly influenced by her.
>
> From the private papers of Zaamin Khan,
> Haakim Mahal, Sherpur State

At the Sheesh Mahal, a zenana durbar was held to welcome the new Begum. Huzur Aliya personally supervised the arrangements. Invitations were sent to Miya Jaan Khan's family at Bareilly and to all the nobility. Badamiya would sit talking of the preparations for the durbar. In spite of everything, Feroza was excited. She sent an invitation to Gauhar and Asiya hoping they would come to witness her glory. They, and all her family, should know that she was being received with honour. She wanted Gauhar to witness her elevation as a queen of Sherpur and tell Abba – it still mattered.

She longed for Gauhar to listen to her feelings, catching them in her voice and expressions – the lightness of unburdening. They had always discussed their married lives, confessed their feelings, buried their hurts and found courage in each other.

'*You are a queen now, Feroza, be happy!' she would say.*

Daroghan Chhamman came with a box of crown jewels from the *toshakhana*, the royal treasury, and a heavily embroidered dark pink farshi dress that belonged to Shams's mother, the heaven-residing Begum Sherpur. The Daroghan pronounced it a rare honour.

'Huh, they call her "heaven-residing Begum Sherpur"...' mocked Tabu later and received a resounding slap from Bua.

'You're such a useless girl! All idle talk! Go and get that Laila. She'll get Bibi ready,' Bua banished Tabu from the room with a push.

Bua bustled around, commanding the kaharis to get the water slightly heated for the bath and laying out Feroza's durbar dress.

'Tabu, get ready. Wear your pink churidar that you wore for the wedding. You and Bua will come with me,' Feroza called out, some of her old spirit returning. Tabu grinned and executed an impish *thumka*.

Laila, tutored by Daroghan Chhamman, spoke incessantly of the grandeur of Sheesh Mahal, while dressing up Feroza.

'Such pink feet, they don't require henna,' she said.

'Our Feroza was always fit to be a queen.' Bua brought a handful of red chillies and circled her fist around Feroza – head to toe, seven times to ward off the evil eye. She burnt the chillies in the mud chulha with a bout of satisfied coughs. The acrid smell indicated that the evil eye had been decimated.

'All the Begums will attend the durbar in your honour and a male durbar will be held at Shams Manzil,' said Laila, easing the gold anklets on her hennaed feet. Bua came into the room still rasping. She mistrusted Laila, calling her a spy for Daroghan Chhamman, but today she settled down on a low stool to listen to her speak of the durbar.

'Bua, get dressed. I won't go without you and Tabu,' smiled Feroza.

'Hai Bibi, how can I go?'

'Wear the suit Daroghan Chhamman gave you at my wedding.'

Tabu was preening in her pink churidar and holding Feroza's farshi skirt as they walked out of the drawing room to the front veranda. The Sheesh Mahal was a short walk from Feroza's mahalsara but an open buggy was sent to fetch the bride.

'Begum, this buggy was sent from angrez country. The angrez queen, what's-her-name I forget, sent it for the personal use of our Nawab Sahib. After all, he is called the "Farzand-e-Aala" – the most exalted son of Queen Victoria – yes that's her name,' Laila informed her audience. She opened the buggy door and let down the steps.

'Nawab Sahib rides it, but today he has sent it for you!'

Feroza walked down the veranda steps to the dark wood open buggy with two thoroughbreds and a khwajasara on the driver's seat holding the reins, raising his hand in salute.

'Tabu, come!'

Tabu jumped in. They were excited little girls again as the victoria swayed and clopped out of the iron gates to the Sheesh Mahal. Feroza had never been in an open carriage before. It felt liberating to look around unconstrained by curtains and a burqa. A pleasant chill presaged the beginning of winters that Sherpuris called *gulabi jaada*. The last rays of the setting sun brightened the high wall flanking the lane.

Tabu pointed at the wall to their left. 'That's the wall of Sher Mahal. Can you see the door? That's the *lal purdah*.' That was the door she had crossed after the night at the palace.

She had heard of the lal purdah – the red curtain beyond which no male over the age of five could ever be allowed. There used to be a red curtain to mark the limits of the harem earlier. The Nawab's women almost never walked out to the other side. Feroza's throat constricted with suffocation.

The narrow alley gave way to a pebbled driveway and Feroza could see an imposing marble pavilion – the Sheesh Mahal. Begums from the Nawab's family stood to receive her at the arched entrance. She straightened up, waiting for the door to be opened, settling her teeka and composing her features. They were the same women, introduced by Daroghan Chhamman at the nikah, less loquacious, bending to touch their foreheads in formal salam.

Feroza stepped down, assailed by the overpowering attar and rose water scents that the maids were spraying all around her. Tabu walked behind her, picking up her skirts, as she was escorted by the salaming women through a veranda arch into a thickly carpeted hall with glistening red and green chandeliers hanging from a domed ceiling. The light from the chandeliers reflected on the intricate mirror-work on the walls and the ceiling, casting an ethereal glow. Feroza stopped – almost gasped in awe – then started walking slowly to the end of the hall towards the Nawab's throne. The gold-plated throne was overhung with deep red velvet awnings supported by four silver poles. On either side of the Nawab's throne were his Begums' takhts covered with silk and made comfortable with bolsters.

Huzur Aliya sat to the right of the throne and Feroza met her keen stare boldly, walking towards her. Daroghan Chhamman joined her in her march towards the royal takhts, propelling her towards Huzur Aliya. She had to pay her respects to the old matriarch first.

Scrawny and flint-faced, Huzur Aliya sat with one leg drawn towards herself on which she circled her arm, her chin working on her paan, her white silk gharara spread around her. The lobes of her ears hung nearly to her shoulders, weighed down with large *kundan* diamond earrings supported by golden chains over the ears. Withered folds overhung the dark eyes, razor-sharp in spite of the grey cataract. She motioned to a young girl standing by her side who picked up the silver spittoon. Her gaze not wavering for a second, she spat red paan juice into the spittoon, the ropes of Basra pearls clinking on the silver rim.

Feroza stiffened with anger as she deciphered the gesture. Abba had told her that Huzur Aliya, who had brought up Shams, was a *nat* – a performing gymnast.

Her story is very interesting; I heard this from my grandmother, so it must be true. She was Bandi Jaan Tawaif, a concubine in the harem of Nawab Wajid Ali Shah, the last Nawab of Awadh or what you call 'Lucknow' now. During the revolt of 1857, she had saved the lives of British ladies and children; she dressed them in Indian clothes and smuggled them out of Awadh to her village. She had been instructed to kill them, but moved by pity and having little faith in the rebels, she housed them safely. After the revolt was suppressed and Awadh was annexed by the British, she had been richly rewarded by them.

Then Shams's great-grandfather, Nawab Yunus Ali Khan, who had supported the British during the revolt, married Huzur Aliya. Nawab Yunus was bent on pleasing the British and safeguarding his princely state. She must have been a unique person and she was said to be close to the British. So though she was childless, the harem was her stronghold. Nawab Shams consulted her in all matters.

So Feroza Begum stood before Huzur Aliya, her head pulsating with anger. Her eyes were unblinking steel as she merely brushed the tips of her fingers to her forehead and moved away almost immediately. Daroghan Chhamman had asked her to bend low and salam thrice to the old lady.

'Did you see that? The hussy threw her salam at my face and didn't even wait for my response!' Huzur Aliya glared at Daroghan Chhamman. Feroza moved on towards the takht of Begum Sherpur to the left of the Nawab's seat.

The zenana durbar was presided over by Her Highness Sultanat Ara, Begum of Sherpur. Feroza was meeting her for the first time. She smiled at the charming Begum, bent low, touching her forehead thrice in the elaborate courtly salam. Daroghan Chhamman handed Feroza the nazar – a gold coin on a velvet kerchief which she proffered on her palms to Her Highness. Sultanat Ara touched her forehead, smiled slightly and accepted the nazar. The Daroghan ushered Feroza to her seat next to Her Highness; her takht was clothed in red brocade befitting a bride. Tabu arranged her farshi skirt to cover the takht almost completely. Bua, who had walked with Laila to the durbar, stood behind her takht with Tabu. She would report every detail to Gauhar on her next visit.

Begum Sultanat's cold response irked Feroza. Shouldn't the Begum have congratulated, or at least, welcomed her? Maybe she was jealous of a new nikah wife. Feroza refused the paan offered by a maid and looked around. All the Begums were chewing cow-like, flashing red-teethed smiles and flicking reddened tongues. Feroza vowed she would never be like them. She searched in vain for a familiar face, half-expecting Gauhar or Asiya. *Look Gauhar, I'm a queen!*

The relatives and members of the family were seated along the sides. Right behind her were the mutah wives of the Nawab wearing only teekas on their central parting. Only the two nikah wives – Sultanat Ara and Feroza were allowed to wear the jhoomar and nath ornaments. At that time, there were six mutah wives. The number would increase to over twenty by the end of Shams's reign in 1930. The numerous concubines sequestered in barrack-like airless hovels were considered too lowly to attend the durbar. They were the women Feroza could never meet, their shadowy presence and stories gossiped about in whispers. They awaited summons from the Nawab, most of them forgotten and condemned to live in the harem after a brief encounter.

The arrival of the Nawab was announced by a khwajasara bearing a long, silver mace, reciting the full length of his inherited titles. By the end of his reign, more titles and honours would be bestowed upon him as he became a spokesperson for the British and an indispensable part of the empire. The British, in turn, turned a blind eye to his excesses.

The Nawab entered quick-footed, his eyes scanning everything; all the Begums rose to their feet and bowed low in salam – all except Huzur Aliya. Shams bowed before Huzur Aliya, touching his forehead and she put her palms on his head in blessing.

Feroza regarded the man she was married to. Without the royal paraphernalia he was quite ordinary – of below average height with the arrogant ego that often accompanies a short man in power. He was narrow-shouldered which made his stomach look like a protuberance when he sat relaxed. But he carried no extra fat there or on any part of his person. An unremarkable face imprinted with the undeniable aura of royalty. His moustache always remained immaculate and thin, even when it was dyed, and his full lips withered with his prematurely ageing body.

'Respected Begums, today's special durbar is in honour of Feroza Begum, daughter of Miya Jaan Khan. We welcome Feroza Begum as the nikah wife of Nawab Shams Ali Khan Bahadur. The Nawab bestows upon his new Begum the title of "Sarkar Aliya",' Daroghan Chhamman announced.

Feroza half-turned towards the Nawab and lightly touched her forehead in acceptance, her gaze skimming the envious faces. She knew that they would take away her name from her and call her by a strange new name. The high-sounding title overwhelmed her. She flushed with reluctant pleasure wishing, yet again, that at least some member of her family could witness the rare distinction. Her father should know that the daughter he abandoned was being received with such honour. 'Sarkar Aliya' was even more high-sounding than 'Huzur Aliya'. Feroza looked under her lashes at Her Highness sitting stiffly, almost as if she had sent a statue of herself to grace the occasion.

The festivities began and a moon-faced singer entered the hall followed by her accompanists, and arranged her troupe on the carpet facing the Nawab. The accompanists started tuning their instruments and the singer cleared her throat, touched her forehead and said, 'Nawab Sahib, on this momentous occasion, your lowly servant has taken the liberty to present your ghazal set to music. I fall down on huzur's feet and beg a thousand pardons if this wayward tongue commits any errors.'

The Nawab looked at an evasive Feroza, smiled and whispered something to the Daroghan.

'Our beloved Nawab Shams Ali Khan has composed this ghazal in honour of his new Begum, Sarkar Aliya Feroza Begum Sahiba,' Daroghan Chhamman said.

'*Wo tadap jaye ishaara koi aisa dena*
Usko khat likhna to mera bhi havala dena

(When you write to her, write of me
In a subtle way to heighten her ardour.)

Is qayamat ki jab us shakhs ko aankhein di hain
Ae Khuda khwab bhi dena to sunehra dena[1]

(The Creator who has bestowed her with ethereal eyes,
I pray, shall grant her golden dreams.)'

The tune was melodious, the words filled with desire. Shams gazed at Feroza with a lazy, sidelong glance.

Notes

1. Azhar Inayati, *Jhonka Naye Mausam Ka.*

Photograph 1919

A photograph of Nawab Shams Ali Khan taken on the occasion of his birthday in 1919 against the backdrop of the grand durbar, Shams Manzil, shows a trim figure in full military regalia, the British awarded medals arrayed on his chest; one hand on his dress sword and the other arm at his waist; the legs, sheathed in high riding boots, are casually apart – the controlling stance of an authoritarian ruler.

9

Princess Lalarukh in the Crystal Palace and Amar Braves the Zulmat

Kallan Mirza stirs his afeem, pouring another dash of water from his lota, inherited from his late father, used by the noble gentleman for his *wudu* ablutions before namaz. He takes the first sip from his silver-plated bowl with the special Quran inscriptions for curative properties – *shifa*. Shifa from the forbidden afeem and Quranic text – the combative irony always amused him. His feet are warm in hand-knitted socks pulled over the lower edge of the crushed cotton pyjamas. A quilted *bandi*, sleeveless coat, over his angarkha protects his asthmatic chest from the cold. He wears a bottle green velvet Rampuri cap, its edges stained dark with sweat and oil. Hidden under the cap sits a miniature woollen cap which Nigar had knitted for him from leftover wool from the many sweaters she used to knit through the winters. Ah, he mourned for his Nigar from the very core of his being.

He notices many new faces in the audience, some on the takhts and durries while others hesitate on the fringes. The talk of his bold dastan has spread through the bazaars of Sherpur. People are intrigued and whisper that he tells of the excesses of the Nawab in the garb of dastan. Waliuddin purses his lips, unsure whether to be happy at Kallan bhai's popularity or censure his increasing notoriety.

Kallan takes permission from the host and begins with a saqinama by Muhammad Husain Jah:

'Mae tu be shikan dey saaqi, abhi fasl-e-bahar hai baaqi;
Abhi baaqi hain din jawani ke, aish o ishrat ke kaamrani ke;
To utho aao maekadey ko chalo, bazm-e-rindan ko chal ke raunaq do;
Rooh-e-Jamshed ki qasam tumko, apni ummeed ki qasam tumko;
Lab-e-saaghar ke phir lo bosey, phir surahi ke galey se milo;
Apne saaqi ko meherban paaya, waqt afsana goi ka phir aaya.[1]

(O cup-bearer, give me your oath-breaking drink of wine for the spring blossoms still;
Youth spreads before me with the promise of happiness and success;
So let's go to the tavern and illuminate the gathering of wine lovers;
For the sake of the soul of King Jamshed, for the promise of hope,
We kiss the long-necked goblet and embrace our intoxication,
And finding my bibber of wine in a benign mood, I'm inspired to tell my tale.)'

Razm, ishq, ayyari aur tilism – war, love, trickery and magic – these are the strands of my humble narrative. May the cup-bearers of this infinite tale of Ameer Hamza pour their tilism on my lips!

So, dear listeners, Princess Lalarukh opens her eyes. And what does she see? Her bed is crystal, the chairs of crystal with red silk cushions, and the roof is studded with shining stars. She is astounded that the floor is of flowing water with rainbow-coloured fishes. She puts her foot on the water and it immediately solidifies. She walks on water, the walls cascade down, with windows overlooking snow-capped mountains, green valleys and blossoming gardens. She is mesmerised and walks out of the Palace of Crystal as if in a dream to the *Bagh-e-Panj-Hiss*, the Garden of Five Senses, which is bathed in the fragrance of thousands of flowers; gold and silver birds trill melodious choruses on trees laden with several kinds of jewel-like fruits.

Why is she so lost, so oblivious? It's the magic invading her senses. Her forehead is heavy and aching; she touches it and finds the teeka-e-yaqut – Aunt Asman Pari's gift.

'You shall know,' she had said. Suddenly, the magic falls away and she knows that she is trapped in Tilism-e-Azam, the creation of the despicable Tareek Jaan. She collapses on the grass, crying and beating her chest. Ah! Why had she defied her father and come out of the hisar?

'A thousand salams to Princess Lalarukh, the betrothed of the King of Samris,' Tez Chashm bends low, her grey hair touching the grass. Lalarukh looks up, brushing away her tears.

'It shall never be so! Tell that *khanakharab*, Tareek Jaan, that he has abducted the wife of the Prince of Islam, Saad bin Ameer Hamza. He shall be destroyed like Afrasiyab! How can a married woman be betrothed to another? Has your master lost his mind?'

'Ah Princess, forgive me, but that was a contract of marriage in Koh Kaaf, another world, and the rules of Koh Kaaf don't apply here. Besides, a pari who leaves Koh Kaaf without the permission of the King cannot go back. Your father can't take you back even if he wanted to.' Tez Chashm's fiendish smile enrages Lalarukh.

Suddenly, everything turns red, the singers and the birds quieten. Princess Lalarukh looks up to see a crimson cloud bearing Tareek Jaan seated on a throne, descend in front of her. Sitting on the throne, leaning forward, his eyes red with lust, topped with a thick, single eyebrow, nose with large dark cave-like nostrils, moustaches like swollen leeches on red, blood-smeared thick lips, is Tareek Jaan.

Princess Lalarukh masters her heartbeat and says, 'I'm Princess Lalarukh of Koh Kaaf, the wife of the Prince of Islam, Saad bin Ameer Hamza, and the daughter of King Sheez of Koh Kaaf.'

'Who is Saad? Who is Ameer Hamza compared to my power? Leave Saad and be my queen. I'm Khudawand, the great God, the commander of djinns, sahirs and men, the ruler of Tilism-e-Azam.'

'You dare challenge God! Ah, you will be reduced to dust like your predecessor, Afrasiyab. I can never be yours for I bear the child of the Prince of Islam, who shall be the successor of Ameer Hamza.'

'Saad bin Ameer Hamza is a craven coward. He couldn't stand in front of my army of devs. How can he conquer my tilism? He'll forget you!'

'Hear this then, Tareek Jaan – if Saad bin Ameer Hamza does not come for me in a year, I'm yours!'

'Agreed!' Tareek Jaan descends from his crimson cloud and stands towering above the haughty princess, his eyes feasting on her form.

'You can never compare to Prince Saad. Look at you!'

Tareek laughs and claps, 'Aaseb, Afreet! Enter this woman!'

And before Princess Lalarukh could take the Great Name she feels a tingling in her head, a squeeze of pain in her womb, blood spurts down her legs and she falls screaming in agony. She has lost her child! Aaseb and Afreet, the djinn brothers, have been appeased by what they love the most – blood from a woman's womb.

Tareek Jaan smiles as the maids carry the princess into her chamber. Of the many women and paries he had snatched from their homes, from the hearts of their families, torn away from suckling babies, none enraptured him as much as Lalarukh. A year would go past and Lalarukh would fall in love with his Tilism-e-Azam and get used to its constant wonder; everything outside would seem dull.

Now hear the state of the devastated Prince Saad:

Prince Saad, disheartened, leading a bleeding, defeated army back, hears the shocking news from the paries – his Lalarukh is in Tilism-e-Azam.

'I'll mount the largest army, double the size of the army that destroyed Afrasiyab,' says Saad with great passion while King Sheez sits with his head bowed.

'Ah, Lalarukh, why did you disobey me!' King Sheez laments.

'Do not despair, O King. I have penetrated many tilisms with my ayyari and I will find out the secrets of Tilism-e-Azam. But for that I require ten sacks of gold, four of diamonds and precious stones…' Amar counts on his fingers. Saad smiles. Uncle Amar is as greedy as ever.

'You shall have all the treasures my kingdom possesses, but get my Lalarukh back,' says King Sheez. In his heart he knows his astrologer's prediction that Lalarukh would marry a sorcerer would come true; but he clings to the desperate hope that the writing of fate could somehow be erased.

Ummeed, hope in the face of fate – if we didn't have that, we would die every day, stop breathing with the death of our beloved. Amar ayyar gets ready with the *zambeel* pouch, which can contain several kingdoms, tied to his stomach;

the invisibility cloak, *galeem*, around his shoulders and the *kamand* lasso rope around his skinny arms. He deposits his protesting wife, Sarsar and son, Chalak, in his zambeel pouch as back-up forces, along with several sacks of gold and jewels, and his instruments of trickery. He sets off to conquer the Tilism-e-Azam. Our Amar walks whistling, puffing his qulcha-bread cheeks, turning his stringy neck. He has a three-feet-long torso and five feet of skinny legs; his stomach is like an earthen pot, head like a coconut, eyes like cumin seeds.

Know all ye souls that Tilism-e-Azam is the grandest of all tilisms and like all tilisms, it is surrounded by *parda-e-zulmat*, the dark regions where oppression, *zulm*, is carried on by djinns, devs and balas – the minions of the sahir. Tareek Jaan was an oppressor of all humble people – the farmers, the warriors, the Pathans, all suffered under his zulm for years and were hypnotised to only see a grand illusory city with magnificient castles, gardens and army.

The main sahirs and sahiras, who administer the city, live in the *Tilism-e-Batin*. Batin – that hides and is hidden. Very much like our Nawab and his ministers with their grand mansions inside the qila. So Tilism-e-Batin is inside this grand fort with impenetrable walls protected by towers reaching the skies, full of armed sahirs and devs that kill anyone who approaches it. Around the Tilism-e-Batin flows *dariya-e-surkh*, the deep red river of blood that can only be crossed by the *pul-e-shamsheer*, the sword bridge. The sahirs and sahiras can cross the bridge by chanting the magic incantation of Samri while others are cut into two pieces, devoured by the white crocodiles of the river, their blood dyeing it a deeper red.

So Amar ayyar reaches parda-e-zulmat, the darkness of Zulmat that surrounds the Tilism-e-Azam. Amar wears his magical galeem – his invisibility wrap, and walks around the city. He sees tall handsome Pathans, turbanless, their proud heads bowed, going about their work. The air is laden with despair, defeat and wretchedness – such are the bazaars and streets of Zulmat.

'Ya Allah! What kind of people are these? *Shakl sey pareshan*, *behis-o-bejaan*, worried, lifeless and spiritless.'

Now you, my knowledgeable audience, already know that Amar ayyar was gifted at birth by the prophets with several tricks and *hunar*. He could take the shape of any person using paints of ayyari. Amar hides in a corner behind a ramshackle shop and quickly takes out his paints of trickery. He paints his face to look like a tall, voluptuous Pathan woman dressed in a red *asharfi*-weave silk skirt, black velvet, star-studded blouse, gold tissue dupatta, *pazeb* tinkling on her feet, teeka enhancing her white brow and *chand bali*s swinging to touch her pink cheeks. So Amar walks *chham-chham*, humming a ghazal.' Mirza Kallan demonstrated the transformation of Amar ayyar, covering his head with a shawl and walking with an exaggerated swing of the hips, singing:

> '*Dekh kar jauban tera kis kis ko hairaani hui*
> *is javani par javani aap divani hui.*[2]
>
> (All are astounded to see my luscious youth
> Youth itself is enamoured with my blossoming youth.)'

The audience goes wild clapping, blowing kisses, commenting suggestively. Kallan amplifies the act, singing on. He smiles as the maulana with a large wart on his forehead from praying five times a day, snorts laughter into his pious white beard and gurgles his hookah.

'But friends, the men of Zulmat were so dead down there that they didn't even look up! Arre, what kind of *sheher* is this? Are they *mard* or *namard*, impotent. Tauba, tauba!' Amar slaps his cheeks in astonishment. Young men, old men, middle-aged men – all sit in shops made of dirty *jholdari* tents, shuffle down streets and work in fields. Suddenly, Amar as Asharfi Bai, realises that she is the only woman walking on the street.

A tonga stops near him thinking he needs a ride. Asharfi gets on to the tonga. The driver, a young handsome boy with dead eyes, asks him, 'Where do you want to go?'

'Take me to the qila.' Asharfi settles her skirts, gives a twitch to her dupatta so that it falls away.

'Bibi, are you new here? Are you not scared?'

'What is there to be afraid of?' Asharfi shrugs with an elegant sway of her shoulders.

'That you are a woman.'

'Hai, hai! So I should be afraid of being a woman. Were you not born of a woman? Where are all the women of this city?'

'Our women live underground, in *tehkhaney* basements inside our homes – *zameen-doz*.'

'And they never come out?'

'Never! Tareek Jaan's minions capture all women for his pleasure. Once they enter Tilism-e-Batin, they never return. I lost my only sister. She was so beautiful. One day she sat in the sun drying her hair, for it was too cold in the tehkhana.' The boy wipes his eyes with his dirty sleeves.

Amar's heart fills with pain, for what can shatter the pride of a man more than seeing his wife, daughter and sister snatched away, living at the mercy of a lustful devil? Of what use are the treasures of the world, warm food in the belly if your women are unsafe? No wonder the brave Rohilla Pathan warriors who had conquered the whole of the *doab*, have lost their spirit and pride, he thinks.'

Mirza Kallan looks at his audience. A profound sadness settles in the gher, there are whispers and murmurs and the older men shake their heads, sighing.

Kallan jumps up suddenly, stares at the darkening sky, raises his arms theatrically:

'Suddenly, the skies grow dark, the sun is overshadowed by black wings of flying *khabbees* devils. Black wings of ten spans, black bodies, red eyes on black hairy faces, horns on their heads – like giant bats. They swoop down on the tonga. The boy screams, jumps down and attempts to run away. A khabbees catches him by his collar with his sharp claws and throws him down on the street. The people on the street are all on their knees, cowering, head lowered, eyes bulging with terror; the shopkeepers crouch behind their wares.

Amar as Asharfi sits calmly, settling her dupatta with great style, takes out a paan from his *batua*, chews it, reddening his lips, enhancing the beauty of his guise.

'Hey woman! Who are you?' A khabbees folds his wings, glaring at Asharfi.

'Asharfi. I have come to visit your town,' Asharfi pouts, leaning forward, her wayward dupatta falling away.

'You are a beauty and the master will be pleased,' one khabbees guffaws, showing his frightening spikey yellow teeth.

'Oh good man, take me to your master. I'm dying to meet the King of Samris!' Asharfi winks.

The khabbees are only too happy to take Asharfi on a takht they conjure. Asharfi picks up her trailing skirts, sits half-reclining on the silken bolsters and tosses a gold piece at the terrified tonga boy. Within moments she is flying over Zulmat, borne by four khabbees, each holding a leg of the takht. Asharfi looks down at the wretched mud-brown Zulmat with its ragged people and thinks of the women living like mice in the tehkhaney.'

Kallan stays long after the dastan session is over, sharing afeem, enjoying the liberating loosening of tongues. Many learned maulvis with their pious beards have become his faithful listeners. Maybe they can intercede with Allah on his behalf and he can ride on their backs to meet his Nigar in paradise.

Notes

1. Sayed Muhammad Husain Jah, *Tilism-e-Hoshruba*, vol. 3.
2. Dagh Dehlvi.

10

Feroza Begum

Sherpur, Spring and Summer of 1897

Man is a creature of myriad faults and Nawab Shams Ali Khan was a man. If youth led him towards ignoble pathways prompted by the devil, he was not the first or the last person to be involved in such amoral activities. The Reich of Germany, Louis XIV of France, the Czars of Russia, the Turkish Sultans – all indulged in debauchery. After listening to these barbaric histories, there is nothing novel in the stories of Indian rulers who populated their harems and indulged in flirtations to enliven their lonely nights.

From the private papers of Zaamin Khan,
Haakim Mahal, Sherpur State

It had been six months since her welcome durbar. The weather had changed to a dry, freezing winter she hated, for the heavy woollens weighed her down. The acceptance of her situation was like a scab – hurting inside, pulling at the skin around with its perpetual awareness. Feroza lived her fate each day, rebelling against it, undefeated and laying down her terms. The Nawab persisted in wooing her with gifts, compliments and verses. After the first night, he never forced himself on her. Huzur Aliya had advised him to be a friend, a brother and a father to her, and curb his youthful passions till she gave in.

Feroza was not a person to hold back her feelings. She would let him see her anger, her hurt and he would listen to her, profess his undying love and great desire for her. She hated herself for the pleasure she derived from the intense hankering in his eyes. He knew there was now a vacuum in her life and guessed her emotional need for passionate love.

Her own reactions to Shams confused her. It was impossible to summon up undiluted hatred for him; he was too complex for that. His passionate lovemaking excited and gratified her. Daroghan Chhamman would inform her of the Nawab's visit and she would be swept into the excitement of preparing for it. It distressed her that her body got used to the physicality of copulation and even yearned for the sexual act. Some days she would be filled with revulsion and plead a headache. He would sit like a besotted lover at her feet, making her feel she had a power over him, that she could withhold or offer him favours. On such days she would give herself to him with something akin to affection.

Feroza was unlike any woman Shams had bedded. She was overpowering, almost brutish in her intensity; her quicksilver temper and moods tired him and tested his patience. She would get annoyed, throw tantrums and sulk for days. She could never reconcile herself to the fact that Shams bedded all kinds of women and she could smell their cheap attar on him. She hated his brandy breath, turning away her face. Alcohol was haram, forbidden for a Muslim.

At times, she would lash out at him, accuse him of murdering her child, cry for her family and beg him to send her back. He would never allow her to go back – the Nawab's women were his possessions forever or till he died. She would shun him and then fret if he didn't come for a few days.

In those early days, when he marvelled at her beauty, even her anger excited him. He would pull her into his arms and profess his love, ask her to hit him, bowing his head to her anger. He was used to simpering, terrified or flirtatious women. It amazed him that Feroza was so unafraid of him. She insisted on calling him by his first name, 'Shams', echoing her mother's desire for an equal marriage. No other woman dared to do so even behind his back. She wanted to encompass him and dominate him like she had Murtaza. At that time, she even believed that he would always desire her and be her smitten lover.

On some mornings, Feroza missed opening her eyes to Murtaza's handsome face snoring gently beside her. She craved for the comfort of another body on the bed at night. Shams left as soon as the act was over and Feroza would lie alone, a hollow, nameless dissatisfaction in the pit of her stomach. Nawabs didn't sleep over. Sometimes he would doze off and she would creep close to that temporary sleep, breathe in his crisp brandy breath, repulsed and excited. Love, hatred, lust, anger and tears in their most primordial forms – their marriage. All other relationships, including Murtaza's tender, hesitant love, were too tame in comparison to the passionate complexity of their marriage.

The days after the welcome durbar, Feroza revelled in her new title. She could feel Sultanat Ara's jealousy whenever she attended the ladies' durbar. Even Huzur Aliya looked at Feroza with such distaste that Feroza would mutter a prayer – a reflex action ingrained in her, to ward off evil.

Sultanat was educated, extremely dignified and conscious of her position as Her Highness. She had set the etiquettes of the harem and the protocol to be observed at various gatherings, which bore the finesse of her father's kingdom of Basoda. She didn't tire telling all the ladies of the durbar that her family was highly educated and she herself had had an English governess. She considered herself a notch above all the women of the harem because of her proficiency in English. Feroza sat glowering as Sultanat entertained the British ladies, wives and daughters of the officials who came to visit and attend her glorious durbar. Sultanat was as servile to the British as her Basoda. At least Shams rarely ever wore English clothes, was proud of his culture and never bowed down to obsequity.

Sultanat spoke courtly Urdu slowly, enunciating each word with perfection, her voice had a light cadence, a sing-song beat, which irritated Feroza. In contrast, Feroza's words would gush out of her mouth the second they took shape in her brain. Once Sultanat said to Feroza, 'Such beauty should not be left wandering around,' within the hearing of a number of Begums, who smiled knowingly. The implication that Feroza had conspired to make herself available to the Nawab, left her seething with anger. She bit back a retort. It was typical of Sultanat to give a compliment with an abrasive insult. Feroza had raged later and Tabu said, 'She feels proud because she can speak the angrez language. Bibi, you are prettier. She's just jealous.'

Feroza asked Shams to employ an English tutor for her because she wanted to learn the language. Shams readily agreed. His own British-style education had been supervised by Captain Colvin, personal minister to the Lt Governor of United Provinces and Mr Bennet, since the age of ten. He had been tutored in the English language and had studied the majesty of the British Empire and its culture. Shams often spoke to Feroza about his grand tour of America and Europe. He was a man of the world and held Feroza enthralled with descriptions of the cities he had visited – New York, London,

Paris. Since he couldn't attend college, tutors from the University of Cambridge accompanied him on his travels to Europe and America at the behest of Queen Victoria. He had even met the Queen and the Duke of Edinburgh in London.

In spite of his exposure to western culture, Shams was a Sherpuri at heart, loved his language and was steeped in Indian music and culture – a quality Feroza greatly admired in him. Like other Indian kings and princes, Shams emulated the ways of the British in superficial ways. The British-style drawing room and dining room, the etiquettes of serving, the use of cutlery and the English kitchen – food, furniture and male clothing were the first cultural transformations. But these changes were limited to the upper classes. The populace of Sherpur regarded English habits with repugnance.

Miss Paul, the English tutor, became a part of Feroza's household. Fuelled by her desire to be equal to Sultanat Ara, Feroza worked hard. She had a quick, though impatient, mind and soon she could grasp the rudimentary words, make sense of what was being said and even manage a few heavily accented, confident sentences. Shams was delighted by Feroza's progress and amused at the battle of egos between his two wives. He wished it were a battle for his heart.

In the spring of 1897, Feroza found herself pregnant. For some months she had stopped dreaming of swimming in blood, but her pregnancy brought back the deep scars of losing her first child. Shams, in spite of his promiscuity, was yet to father a child and Feroza knew that her pregnancy was much-awaited.

Feroza now had a power over him and the desire for revenge in its most elemental form took hold of her. She toyed with the idea of sending word to Dr Wilson and bribing him to abort the child. She could even try the secret portions women took to abort. Shams would not have any child by her. She would kill all his children even if it meant harming herself. Besides, her children might be forced to follow the Shia religion. He had never forced her to convert to his religion but she knew he would expect his children to follow Shiaism.

But before she could try anything, Daroghan Chhamman came with the Hakim.

'I'm well,' Feroza said.

'Begum has missed her period so I brought Hakim Sahib for a diagnosis,' the Daroghan lowered her eyes. She was aware of the menstrual cycles of all the women of the harem, informed no doubt, by Badamiya of their regularity.

A sheet with a fist-sized hole at the centre was held up and the hakim ushered into the drawing room. Feroza put her hand through the hole and the hakim held her pulse for some time.

'Mubarak, the Begum is with child,' he beamed.

Feroza went into her room, caught Laila by her hair and slapped her.

'You whore! You carry tales about me. Get out of my house!'

She pushed a shocked Laila out onto the veranda, screamed for Mahabat Khan to pack her off and make sure that she never showed her face again. Bua looked on, satisfied at the departure.

'I don't want this child, Shams,' Feroza told a flabbergasted Nawab that evening.

'Why, Feroza?' He always found himself on uncertain ground with her. He had thought that Feroza would be as thrilled as he was.

'Because no child of mine would follow your Shia religion!'

'I have allowed you to follow your religion, but this is my child!' he shouted.

'There can be an accident,' Feroza said, enjoying his anguish. 'If I don't want the child, he won't live.'

They fought bitterly over several days. Shams's joy over the pregnancy was sullied by her demand and her prejudiced rants against Shias. Shams's face would darken with anger and he would storm out of her mahal. Fearing she would harm herself, he even promised to make her son the crown prince but Feroza was not appeased. She couldn't abide the thought of her children following Shia practices and (according to her) burning in everlasting hell. For her, life existed in stark extremes – heaven or hell, nothing in between.

Nawab Shams's declaration of his Shia faith at the beginning of his reign was discouraged by the British; but his religious beliefs were deeply entrenched. Indeed, he was able to pull off the controversial move through smart statesmanship. He gave due respect to all the sardars and their religion and chose his ministers from prominent Pathan clans. He married nearly all his children into Sunni Pathan families. I would say that Nawab Shams was particular about his Shia faith but never forced it on his wives or his populace. His children were, of course, another matter.

'Maula Ali is your guardian. Why do you worry? If a lie can save a life, it's not a lie; and you are saving your own flesh and blood! Go, promise her everything and let your crown prince be born.' Huzur Aliya took a deep puff of her hookah. This girl was proving to be too difficult. She was holding them at ransom! With Laila no longer there, they had no information about Feroza. Mahabat Khan seemed to have become loyal to Feroza. She was a generous mistress with a warm affectionate manner towards her servants, though they had to suffer her mercurial temper.

Tabu had taken over Laila's duties and Bua had started cooking for Feroza with the two kaharis helping out. She refused to let Feroza eat food from the royal kitchens, fearing poisoning for there were many who would be jealous of

Feroza. Feroza didn't like the meals they got from the royal kitchens anyway. Shams's kitchen was bare of any form of chillies; the food, though delicious, was too bland for Feroza's taste – good food needed to singe her tongue. Only when the chillies made her nose drip, the fire flaming her senses and she had to shout for water, was she completely sated. Bua used to spice up the food from the royal kitchens with red and yellow chilli powder fried in ghee poured over the *pheeka* curries.

Though there was a dining room, Feroza had her meals on the takht in the veranda, the food spread out in front of her on the dastarkhwan; she missed the chatter of her family. Sometimes a dish would remind her of Gauhar or Nausha and she would find herself unable to eat – as if something had stuck in her throat. Bua would sit fanning her while Tabu served the food. The invisible line between mistress and servant forbade her to ask them to join her. The other Begums had their families staying with them for weeks and months but she had nobody to share her meals with. Sometimes she would pop an odd sweet into Tabu's mouth for Tabu loved sweetmeats.

Finally, Shams promised that all of Feroza's children would be allowed to follow the Sunni faith and her son would be the crown prince. As the news of pregnancy spread, Feroza started getting a lot of importance at the zenana durbar. Huzur Aliya replied to her salam with a toothy smile and blessing, 'May Allah give you a hundred sons; may your husband live long and you never wear widow's white.' She made Feroza sit on her takht and enquired about her health. She even offered a paan from her own pandan – an exceptional favour.

Her Highness Sultanat Begum continued to be aloof and stiff but withheld her curt remarks. Bua would blow prayers on her to keep her safe from the evil eye of the childless Begum. Shams visited her nearly every day and they would walk in the lawns, Feroza trying out her English with him.

He enjoyed her vibrant company, her outspoken opinions and biting humour. Sometimes he would sing to her and his child, putting his face to her belly. She would look back at those months as the closest she came to forgiving him and even loving him. On his insistence, she consented to a new personal maid. She did not like Tabu doing her work.

'Let her inform whoever whatever she wants to,' she said, feeling tired and sweaty as the pregnancy advanced and the unforgiving May sun beat down. She got the carpets removed and filled her bedroom with two inches of water in the sweltering afternoons. A large wood frame encased with cloth, edged with frills, hung across the ceilings in all the rooms and served as fans, pulled by kaharis sitting on the floor outside the door. The kahari would nod off and Feroza would wake up sweaty and irritable. The dry hot wind was cooled and made fragrant by the khus curtains on the veranda arches kept moist with the constant spraying of water.

Shams presented her with a silver cigarette case and taught her to smoke to ward off nausea since she hated paan. After the initial coughing, Feroza got used to smoking, the tobacco smells bringing back memories of Abba. Her appetite had become erratic and Bua catered to her food fetishes with loving care.

Her new maid, Husna, was a lively girl, filling the house with her chatter. Azeezan, the dancing eunuch, came often with gossipy vignettes and dances, twirling in her glittering dress. She had been instructed by Daroghan Chhamman to keep the Begum amused. Dorothy, an Anglo-Indian day nurse, administered her diet and looked after her general well-being. Bua detested her because she often told her that the food wasn't nutritious enough.

'Hai, hai, now this unholy child of an angrez will tell me how to feed my Feroza?' Bua would mutter.

Miss Paul also earned Bua's ire with her early morning lessons, forcing Feroza out of bed when she should be resting. But Feroza loved the lessons and, much to Bua's chagrin, made Tabu sit with her so that they could practise later. Like Miya Jaan Khan and most Sherpuris, Bua believed that the angrez language would slowly take a person away from the true faith and convert them into a *kristaan*.[1] Bua chided Tabu for using angrezi words and the girls would trouble her by speaking gibberish English around her.

'As it is, this girl is not getting proposals after coming here and now she is turning into a kristaan. No one will touch her. She'll become a dirty Englishman's keep,' she told the sympathetic Azeezan.

The month of Muharram came with its sorrowful pallor and all forms of entertainment were banned to mourn the martyrdom of the Prophet's grandson, Hazrat Husain, and his family at the hands of the second Umayyad Caliph. On the eve of Muharram, the Nawab walked with the mourners bearing the *taziya*, the replica of the mausoleum of Hazrat Husain, around the town, followed by the Sherpur army and the infantry. The taziya was displayed in the royal *Imambara* prayer hall in the qila and the ten days of *majlis* congregations began. Narrators and *sozkhwan* singers from all over the country described the tragic death of Hazrat Husain in prose and verse to black-clad mourners. Food and sherbet were distributed every day to all attendees. The Sunni officials, distinct in their white ensembles, also attended the sessions as a mark of respect. They didn't participate in any of the rituals of self-flagellation.

Feroza was two months into her pregnancy, throwing up all day and grouchy with the heat. Huzur Aliya asked her to set up a *zari* for the well-being of her child. The zari was a replica of the mausoleum of Imam Husain and all the Begums had set up zaris in their name at the Imambara. Feroza flatly refused, saying that she and her child were Sunnis and didn't believe in the practice. Huzur Aliya set up a zari for her great-great-grandchild knowing that Feroza would never relent.

A special majlis was held on the seventh day of Muharram in the zenana Imambara.[2] Daroghan Chhamman came with an invite to the majlis. Feroza agreed out of curiosity. Miya Jaan had forbidden all his family from attending majlis.

'I won't wear black or do *maatam*,' she said, feigning great reluctance.[3]

The Daroghan readily agreed and procured a suitable cream-coloured plain dress for her.

On the sweltering June evening, Feroza went for the majlis wearing the plain dress. The Daroghan tried to persuade her to remove all jewellery but she insisted on wearing her earrings and bangles. The zenana Imambara was situated at the far end of the harem and Feroza's palanquin passed through a narrow passageway edged by the imposing red brick qila ramparts on one side and the modest dwellings of the mutah wives on the other. The rough plank doors of the houses were chained and locked as all the Begums were at the Imambara. Khwajasara guards stood in arched alcoves in the ramparts and cannons lined the top.

The Imambara was a white building with three cupolas, much like a mosque with ornate arches. Feroza got down from the palanquin and traversed the courtyard into a large hall with green doors. Silver bannisters and narrow steps led to a raised platform with a silver chair for the speaker, which stood on one end of the hall. All along the wall was a mosaic platform on which the zaris were kept. Feroza walked the length of the displayed zaris, beautifully fashioned out of gold and silver, studded with precious stones and lit with candles.

Daroghan Chhamman pointed out the largest zari, contributed by Huzur Aliya. She bowed deeply before each replica and lighted candles while Feroza stood stiffly, arms by her side. There was a tiny replica of a grave of the six-month-old child-martyr, Ali Asghar – the youngest martyr at the battle of Karbala. On the walls were lined *alams*, the banners of the army of Hazrat Husain, on golden poles topped with the insignia of the hand – encrusted with precious stones. Feroza looked around the empty hall.

'Where are the rest of the Begums?'

'They will come with the *juloos-e-mehdi*, the mehdi procession,' replied the Daroghan ushering her to a black velvet *masnad* on the floor. They could hear the chants of 'Ya Qasim, Ya Husain' interspersed with singing to the rhythmic tattoo of hands beating on numerous chests – the maatam. Feroza had asked Tabu to accompany her. Bua had thrown a fit when Tabu had accompanied Feroza.

'Now they'll think Tabu is a Shia!' she had cried.

The courtyard started filling with women clad in black and green doing maatam. At the head of the procession was Huzur Aliya, walking with a contained wiry agility in spite of her bones, which seemed to have bent with the acrobatics and leaps, both physical and political, she had executed in her life. Behind her the Begums in black churidar dresses, some with green scarves, their faces marked with grief, as a group of *nauha* singers sang of the tragedy of the marriage of Hazrat Qasim with Bibi Kubra, a marriage that lasted for a day and ended with the martyrdom of Hazrat Qasim. A procession of white horses followed, laden with trays of henna, dry fruits, gifts, fruits – offerings sent to the house of the bride before marriage – a poignant representation of a doomed marriage. The banner of Hazrat Qasim, held by a khwajasara, rose above their heads with a green flag garlanded with flowers.

Feroza was shocked to see Sultanat Ara dressed in a green gharara performing the maatam in the procession. She was a Sunni, or at least belonged to a Sunni family like her. Maybe she did it to please Huzur Aliya and Shams. It was good that Feroza had asserted her right to follow her religion and insisted on it for her children.

'The majlis today is hosted by Her Highness,' whispered Daroghan Chhamman.

Feroza stood up as the trays were set down and Huzur Aliya, wiping her tears, took her position facing the raised platform. The ladies settled down on the spotless white sheets on the floor. The narrator, a rotund lady in black, sat on the silver chair and recounted the tragedy of Hazrat Qasim, his brief marriage and martyrdom. Feroza could feel tears pricking her eyes. She was aware of the historic significance of the Battle of Karbala where members of Prophet Muhammad's family were martyred in the most inhuman manner by Yazid, the Caliph. But here the tragedy felt fresh and cataclysmic. She felt emotionally drained. The sweat from bodies packed together mixed with the sharp incense smells was making her nauseous. She got up abruptly, told the Daroghan that she wasn't feeling well and left the majlis before the maatam began.

Notes

1. Christian.

2. On the seventh day of Muharram, the followers of Hazrat Husain were denied water. The day is mourned as the day of the marriage of Hazrat Qasim ibn Hasan, the nephew of Hazrat Husain even though the actual marriage is believed to have been solemnised on the ninth day of Muharram.

3. A mourning practice followed by the Shias of chest-beating in remembrance of the martyrdom of Hazrat Imam Husain, the grandson of Prophet Muhammad.

II

Feroza Begum

Sherpur, Monsoon, 1897

The Nawab performed the skilful 'banna deeni' dance. Puffed batashas were spread on the floor and the Nawab danced with such a light step that the brittle batashas didn't crumble underfoot. He organised a band of musical instrumentalists and trained them to play all Hindustani ragas. He himself could play several instruments with great skill. He had received formal education in music and even the recognised masters touched their ears, paying tribute to his proficiency. The most accomplished tawaifs would tremble singing before him. He was a recognised master beenkaar[1] and his teacher was the world-famous Ustad Wazir Khan from the family of Tansen.

Oral history attributed to Sir Samad Ali Khan,
Chief Minister, Sherpur State[2]

As the pregnancy advanced and her nausea settled, Feroza felt a deep gnawing hunger for something she couldn't identify or put into words. She would often feel depressed, crying for her Abba, missing his cologne and hookah smells. Abba must be missing his late-night baithaks with his friends in the mardana, sharing concerns, old jokes, playing cards and chess – she had taken away all those joys from him. Somewhere, the predictable routine of her old life was being lived without her – the days in five slices interspersed with prayers.

The hakim, after examining her through the perforated sheet again, gave her sweet majun to calm her nerves and give her strength. Shams found her despondent, and almost missed her emotional fluctuations, and their pugnacious sparring. He was still obsessed with Feroza's exquisite beauty; to look upon it and to claim it for himself didn't cease to amaze him. Feroza was unaffected by her looks, and often cursed her beauty as a scourge tempting her fate. Her eyes, vivid and animated, would have shone with the same intensity from any other face. Her beauty was but a backdrop to her spirit.

Shams wanted a certain dependency from Feroza, a craving for his attention and for material things only he could provide; but she hated his entrapment of her with a recurring helpless intensity and was too proud to ask him for anything. She understood the subtle power play – the withdrawal of a privilege would become the core of Shams's power over her. To make her happy, he sent his trusted official, Zaamin Khan, to persuade Miya Jaan Khan to return, but the humiliation was too fresh for the patriarch. Feroza was deeply touched by his gesture even though it came to naught.

They found a common ground in music and poetry. Shams, besides being a highly romantic poet, was also an avid student of classical music and delighted in explaining the nitty-gritty of music to a rapt Feroza. She recited her amateurish ghazals to him. He would appreciate the couplets and suggest a masterful phrase to liberate her tentative thoughts. Poetry writing was an acceptable pastime for Nawab's women. Nawab Yunus Ali Khan's daughter, Umrao Begum, and his wife were renowned poetesses. Most Nawabs wrote poetry and Nawab Ghulam Ali Khan wrote dastans. When Shams sat humming a new todi in his melodious voice, with his eyes closed and a light smile on his face, Feroza could feel a quivering tear in her eyes with the fragile perfection of the notes. She almost forgave him everything – a man of such fine sensibilities could never be cruel.

Coming from a family completely sterile of music where Miya Jaan Khan only permitted singing to the accompaniment of the dhol on festive occasions, Feroza loved the musical atmosphere of the durbar. The zenana durbar at Sheesh Mahal was a vibrant place with its musical soirees and dance performances by renowned singers and dancers. She listened to Gauhar Jaan, Munni Begum and other famous tawaifs.

Initially, she could only appreciate light classical compositions, ghazals and traditional songs but soon her tastes evolved to appreciate the different raags. She had a good ear and could identify a raag she had heard even once. It was as if a new world had opened to her. She would often go to the Rang Mahal to attend performances by great masters like Wazir Khan from the family of Tansen. The male singers could only perform at the Rang Mahal.

As a scholar of music, Shams was passionately involved in restoring the magnificence of the musical tradition of Sherpur, which had its roots in Tansen's classical style. Arbab-e-Nishat, the music department was nurtured by him. He also arranged an orchestra of Indian musical instruments called *roshan chauki*. Feroza used to come out of her mahal every evening to listen to the roshan chauki. It was a mobile orchestra with the musicians and singers borne on a takht and taken around the palaces, performing the evening raags at sunset.

To prop up her spirit, Shams allowed her visitors – Begums distantly related to her family, Shams's relatives and his other wives. The house would buzz with guests from late morning, announced by Mahabat Khan who would pay the palanquin fare, and usher in the Begums. The ladies, with their easy chatter and advice, would stay for hours, showing their familiarity, often staying back for lunch and dinner. Feroza loved company and it was a break from the loneliness, but she would soon tire of entertaining, become impatient with the uninspiring conversations and excuse herself.

Amina Khala visited her with excuses for Asiya's absence. Feroza knew that no respectable Pathan family would bring their daughters to the harem. It was good to see her familiar, loving face and listen to her marvel at the luxuries of the mahal. She brought news of Miya Jaan Khan's family – unhappy in their new circumstances and cramped in their small house in Bareilly, which had never been intended for a prolonged stay. Guilt closed like a tight fist inside her again. Maybe the news of his grandchild might bring Abba back to his ancestral haveli. Gauhar didn't visit her in spite of the many missives sent through Bua. No experience was complete without her sharing it with Gauhar; from a sour tamarind to a remark that hurt. *You try to be happy. That is enough for me.*

Even the mutah wives could visit her now. Bua turned up her nose at them saying they were mostly low-class women – how dare they even speak to Feroza! But Feroza, with her generosity of spirit, soon warmed towards them, listening to their stories, and sharing their concerns. They lived in identical houses, sometimes sharing an accommodation. Each house had two main rooms, a veranda overlooking a courtyard and a small kitchen. There was a back door in all the houses connected to a narrow lane leading to the

Sheesh Mahal and Sher Palace – two places they could be summoned to.

Shams ensured that all the Begums were well looked after by the state department. At that time, Zaamin Khan, a trusted Pathan chieftain of impeccable character was the Haakim Mahal and looked after the harem. Each Begum was provided twelve sets of expensive clothing for the year and jewellery according to their status; food from the royal kitchens was enough to feed their entire family. Most Begums had their female relatives living with them as dependants. The utensils, sent with their daily meals, were never returned and given away as dowry to needy relatives. Their kitchens were well-equipped with chinaware and copper utensils, silver bowls for drinking water, silver pandans, spittoons, etc. For most Begums, their lives had become luxurious. They could now support their impoverished families on their stipends, marry off their sisters and nieces and get employment for their men. They quietly paid the price for the affluence in the form of physical abuse and indignities at the hands of the young Nawab. Their female relatives came and stayed with them for months and amused themselves at the glamorous durbars and singing performances and attended Muharram events. The harem had an aura of enforced gaiety as each season was celebrated with food and songs.

One day, Feroza had an intriguing visitor, the so-called Diwani Begum. She came to visit her with Azeezan, saluted Mahabat Khan and announced, 'I have come to see the new blue-eyed Begum.' Diwani Begum had scratty, short hair and was dressed in tattered clothes. She came up to Feroza, salamed her thrice and recited a Persian couplet. The Begums tittered.

'Diwani Begum!' one Begum said.

'Am I diwani or are you mad?' Diwani Begum cocked an arched eyebrow.

Feroza returned her salam and said, 'Could you please translate the couplet? I know very little Persian.'

Diwani Begum threw back her head and laughed. 'I forgot, the Begums are illiterate!'

'I know Urdu and Arabic.'

'Do you know Hafez and Rumi? Are you even alive? But you're beautiful.' She started singing a charbait quartet and Azeezan joined in.

'Diwani Begum was a tawaif, from Khairpur, Sindh. Nawab Sahib employed her in the music department and fell in love with her. He made her mutahi begum.' Azeezan settled down to narrate the story of Diwani Begum after she had left.

'She was very proud of her learning and often insulted the less-educated Begums. Then one day, Nawab Sahib asked the Begums to attend the zenana durbar to welcome an esteemed guest. All the other Begums dressed up in courtly farshi dresses but Diwani Begum wore an old churidar. Maybe she wanted to show her anger at something. So when she sat down, her churidar tore from her knee. Nawab Sahib was very angry and called her, crooking a finger, and with the same finger, he tore off her churidar!' Azeezan covered her mouth with the edge of her scarf and giggled.

'Diwani Begum also got angry and walked out of the durbar. Nawab Sahib said, "Bring her here and get me a pair of scissors!" He made her sit in the durbar and cut off her hair! And look at this arrogant Begum, she smiled and said, "I would give my life to such a barber." Hai, hai, our Nawab went mad with rage. He wanted to put her in jail and hang her. That night Daroghan Chhamman, she has such a kind heart, went to her house and advised her to pretend madness. So when the guards went to arrest her, they found her in tattered clothes, singing and chasing birds. From that day, she became Diwani

Begum. She comes and goes as she pleases, does whatever she wants. But this is a secret, Begum. If Nawab Sahib even suspects anything, he will surely get her killed!'

Feroza was deeply affected by the story and called Diwani Begum again to her house and started talking to her normally. Diwani Begum clowned around for a while then settled down on the takht. Diwani had an arresting face, a long stem of a neck and incandescent eyes which became alive when she recited couplets. She knew Diwan-e-Hafez and many other diwans[3] by heart. She never smelled bad, so she probably practised some personal hygiene, even though her clothes were muddy like she had dragged them on the floor before wearing them.

She became a regular visitor and Feroza enjoyed her quoting from Hafez and Rumi. She would watch Feroza struggle with the translations like an amused teacher and explain the deeper meaning of the couplet.

'Where is my soulmate with whom I can share my grief?

For aeons my heart lives in separation from him,' she would sigh.[4] 'Begum, you hanker for the perfect love of a human and I long to be united with the Perfect One.'

Feroza felt drawn towards her insight and wisdom – Diwani understood the recesses of her soul. She stayed for hours and Feroza shared her meals with her, much to Bua's disgust. She didn't have to pleasure the Nawab or attend the zenana durbar. Some days her madness was more real to her and she would laugh, curse and sing all day. Then there were days she would talk to Feroza like a dear friend, advise her and comfort her.

She always took her leave saying, 'I have lived in insanity knocking at the door of sanity. But I was knocking on the door I had myself closed.[5] Am I mad or are you mad?'

Now that Feroza had finally settled into her marriage, Bua's worry for Tabu's marriage resurfaced with enhanced desperation. The girl, now in her twenties, was practically unmarriageable and her chances were drastically reduced because of staying in the harem.

Bua was an abandoned wife. Her fault was giving birth to a girl after ten years of marriage. Still, Bua had great faith in marriage. There was no other option for a woman but to bow down to the will of the husband and bear children, as many as possible, to keep the husband occupied. The fault was hers for not having produced children earlier.

Bua visited the matchmakers, assuring them of Tabu's virginity.

'Arre, our Begum keeps her in strict purdah when the Nawab comes.'

Bua saw the doubt in their eyes, and prayed to her most compassionate Allah for deliverance from her burden.

Notes

1. Player of the Indian 'been', a wind instrument.
2. Narrated to his grandson, Tariq Khan.
3. Volumes of poetic works.
4. *Diwan-e-Haf.*
5. Rumi.

12

Feroza Begum

Ramganga, 1897

Bilashuba chashma aab-e-hayat ki koi sot is mein mili hai, khair agar yun bhi hai toh bhai aab-e-hayat umr badhaata hai itna shireen kahan hoga.

(Undoubtedly, a spring from the mythical River of Eternal Life has mixed in the waters of this river; but its waters are sweeter than the waters that give eternal life.)

Mirza Ghalib,
Makateeb-e-Ghalib

It had rained for two days as the monsoons burst upon them with ferocious zeal. Feroza had always loved dramatic weather. She sat watching the rains lash out at the trees and singing barsati songs with Tabu. The rains paused and a picnic was arranged by Shams for Feroza. Dr Wilson feared that her melancholia would affect the growth of the child. The banks of River Ramganga with its swollen waters was decided as the idyllic picnic spot. Feroza wanted to take her friend, Diwani Begum, but it would never be allowed. Though he didn't appreciate his wives getting too close to each other, Shams regarded Diwani's visits as entertaining interludes for Feroza, and turned an indulgent eye.

The morning light was dull with overcast skies and the moist breeze bore the promise of rains. Buggies lined up inside Sher Mahal and the Begums walked out of the lal purdah – the line which circumscribed the harem from freedom – got into their designated buggies, chattering with excitement, their small boxes with a change of clothes held by their maids. Daroghan Chhamman stood checking their attendance and bundling the mutah wives into two buggies. Feroza and Sultanat Ara, as the nikah wives, had their own buggies. Feroza sat with Tabu, her valise strapped at the back, and Bua's sour pickle in a tiny box in case she felt queasy. The carriage doors were closed, the curtains drawn, Zaamin Khan was informed and the massive doors of the DuPont Gate opened up for them. Riding with them was a small contingent of Sherpur lancers on their thoroughbred horses. Mahabat Khan rode alongside Feroza's buggy.

Feroza watched the gates of the palace recede as they rode out of the DuPont Gate named after the French architect of the qila, Mr A.C. DuPont. She was going out of the harem walls after nearly a year. It was still early and the city outside the qila was stirring to life. Curious men stood by the metalled road, keen-eyed under their dusty turbans. Most of them were *lashkar* Pathans with a history of generations of battles fought and martyrs buried.

'The rest of the world is as I left it. If we had turned towards Nasrullah Khan Bazaar, we would have reached my house,' Feroza thought. Her home now lay abandoned, its garden must be overgrown and the white walls streaked grey with moss – lives ruptured because of her.

'Bibi, look at the topkhana gates with the cannons!' Feroza bent over her stomach and watched the carriage go through the three topkhana gates and turn towards the *thandi sadak*, the road leading out of the city. Rice fields that were verdant green spread out on both sides. She leaned back and asked Tabu to open the window and took an earth-scented breath. Feroza remembered the carefree ride to Benazir Palace, their giggles and Ammi's words that she had shrugged off.

Tabu started humming an old charbait barsati song:

'*Nanhi nanhi bundiya re, sawan mein mera jhoolna.*

(Tiny droplets drench me as I play on the swings of sawan.)'

Feroza smiled, humming the song her mother used to sing all those years ago. Amma would stand in the veranda and sing with the drizzle spraying her face. She had forgotten what Amma looked like. They said Gauhar was an exact replica of Amma. She would soon even forget Gauhar's face, unable to incarnate it from memory. Like Amma, she would fade and then Abba would go too. Sawan was a homecoming for married girls, away from the worries of their in-laws. She and the other Nawab's women had no home to go back to.

The clouds were a bulbous dark purple now. A skinny little girl shooed away the cows ambling on the road. She stopped, her hand poised with the stick, head covered with a ragged scarf, her eyes curious and amused. Tabu waved at her and the girl started running along their buggy, laughing, the scarf slipping off her head till the driver shouted at her, showing her the whip.

Feroza could almost taste the moisture in the air as they reached the river and she was gingerly helped down the sandy slope by Mahabat Khan, her feet gritty with the white sand. The picnic area was a mango orchard by the banks of the Ramganga River, cordoned off by canvas walls to preserve the purdah of the Nawab's women. Feroza stood watching the waters lapping at its sandy banks. She had only seen the Ramganga from a distance. The clouds had collapsed in heavy leaden fatigue over the river. She looked at the colourful tents under trees for the begums to rest. The mutah wives were fluttering around in colourful churidar dresses with freshly hand-dyed dupattas in the traditional sawan colours and patterns. Some turned to greet her, touching their forehead in 'adab'. Durries and carpets had been laid out under the trees with takhts, a silver chair for the Nawab. Hookahs stood smouldering and snack trays were set on the tables.

Her Highness was already seated on her takht with a pandan by her side, a silver spittoon on the ground with streaks of fresh red betel juice. This was her durbar in a different setting and she expected all the ladies to pay homage. Feroza went up to Her Highness, salamed, refused paan and sat on the takht near her.

'Begum, the journey must have tired you. Please rest,' said Daroghan Chhamman.

'I'm tired of sitting. I would like to walk around.' Feroza was in no mood for another zenana durbar.

'Rest for a bit. You have to be careful.' Sultanat Ara gave her a thin-lipped, red smile.

'Your Highness, I'll rest after some time.'

Feroza beckoned Tabu and walked towards the distant river, balancing her stomach, holding Tabu's hand, her feet sinking into the moist, cool sand. They walked along the bank, with Mahabat Khan following at a distance. She looked at the iron bridge spanning the river. It now had a train going over it, connecting Sherpur to Bareilly. Right across the Ramganga Bridge was Bareilly where her family now lived, a mere sixty kilometres away. If she rode on her buggy, it would take her about five hours to reach there. Once she crossed the river, she would be in British territory away from the stranglehold of Shams. It was that close.

Suddenly, there was a stir and excited voices rose in surprised exclamations. She turned to see a woman riding on horseback along the bank.

'Bibi, look, angrezan. She is wearing men's clothes.' Tabu covered her open mouth with her palm, giggling.

They watched as a tall, well-built young lady swung off the horse, handed the reins to the syce and took off her sola hat. She made her way to the circle of Begums lolling on the takhts, trying to smooth her wayward blonde hair. She saw Feroza and came towards her smiling.

'Adab, Begum. I'm Sara Small, wife of Colonel Small of the Gurkha regiment stationed at Sherpur,' she said in hesitant Urdu. Her eyes were crinkled with ready laughter and her nose freckled with days in the sun. Tabu suppressed a giggle at her funny accent.

'Adab, I'm Feroza Begum,' Feroza spoke in self-conscious English.

'Ah, the second Her Highness!'

'Welcome, Mrs Small.'

'Please call me Sara. I'm your guest today. The Nawab invited me to the picnic.'

'You came on horseback?'

'Oh, I love riding.'

Feroza sat down on a rock, dipping her feet in the cool water; she bent forward and trailed her hand in the river.

'I have never touched a river.' Tears sprang to her eyes. She blinked, straightened up, smiling. Sara felt her heart melt. She had heard about her.

'Come, let's go into it,' said Sara.

'It's slippery,' Tabu panicked.

'We'll hold you,' said Sara, taking off her boots and rolling up her jodhpurs. Sara held Feroza by the waist and they stepped into the surprisingly cold water. Feroza laughed, relaxing against Sara, the stones slippery and uneven under her feet.

'Come here. It's sandy.' The water lapped around her calves, her churidar wet and clinging. Feroza felt a wetness on her cheek. They sat on a rock, their feet dangling in the water.

'This is the first time I stepped into a river and this is Ramganga, the most important river for us because it gave birth to Sherpur.' Abba used to tell the story of how Sherpur came to be established by the river. She could hear his voice narrating the tale, passed down as an oral memory, between hookah puffs.

'So, Daud Khan, the founder of Rohilla kingdom, came for a hunt with his trained leopards to the banks of River Ramganga. Sherpur was just a small village – a few thatched huts near the Ramganga called Sherpura. He let loose his leopards and waited. They came back badly injured. Daud Khan asked the villagers if there was a tiger in the jungles around. The villagers begged his forgiveness for their dogs, seeing the leopards, had attacked them. It is said that Daud Khan decided to establish a town called Muhammadabad by Ramganga because its waters gave such strength and daring that even dogs could challenge leopards,' Feroza narrated in a mixture of Urdu and English.

'Such a wonderful story!'

'That's why we Pathans are so bold,' laughed Feroza, her fingers trailing the silky water.

They sat with the hesitant sun warm on their backs and Sara spoke of her twin sons Kevin and John who were in a boarding school at Nainital. She missed them and their pranks and surprises.

'When you become a mother, it's like a part of you is always out there. You want to cling and cling.'

'I feel nothing right now.'

'Ah you will, when you hold the little one.' Sara patted her arm.

'Begum, Nawab Sahib is calling you and Sara Memsahib for the *tarbooz ladai*, watermelon fight,' a kahari announced breathlessly. Feroza got up quickly and started walking to the bank, holding Sara.

'Nawab Sahib was asking for you, Begum,' the kahari tried to convey the urgency.

He is angry. Feroza felt her heart thudding with apprehension.

He might shout at her or embarrass her in front of Sara.

'What did you tell him?'

'That you had gone with Sara Memsahib to see the river.'

He was so unpredictable. Maybe he would take offence at her for not waiting for him at the camp or for sitting with Sara. Feroza started walking with short, panicked steps and Sara, sensing her anxiety, quickly scrambled into her boots, and caught up with her.

They walked up the bank and Sara could see the Nawab on his silver chair, surrounded by his wives. He looked up immediately as they approached, alert, seeking the remains of their conversation on their faces, and noting Feroza's wet, muddy churidar. Sara paid her respects to the Nawab and Her Highness. Feroza touched her forehead formally and took her seat to his left. Two kaharis hauled a huge tub of watermelon slices and placed it in front of the Nawab.

'My Begums love watermelon fights. I get watermelons from Rajasthan all year,' he laughed, taking a large piece from the Daroghan's platter. He thrust his fingers into the cut, wrenched out a handful and smeared it on Feroza's face roughly, smiling all the time. Only she could feel the bite of his fingers and the black, sharp-edged seeds grazing her cheeks. He turned and laid a smeared, soft finger on

Sultanat's cheek. Daroghan Chhamman handed a piece each to the two Begums. Feroza rubbed her melon hands on Shams's forehead and hair, her eyes challenging. Shams laughingly cringed away, caught her hand and said, '*Aap ne to hamein sharabor kar diya*, you have drenched me through!' A sensuous spark lit his eyes.

The rest of the Begums joined in, rushing forward, hands diving into the melon pieces, slathering each other amidst squealing laughter. Sara put some juice on Feroza's forehead and she reciprocated by rubbing Sara's ruddy cheeks. The other Begums went wild with the play, the Nawab standing in their midst, his hands touching them and the women growing bolder. He felt like a god, like Krishna surrounded by adoring, amorous women. Some Begums had cast off their dupattas, their kurtas were light pink and flecked with seeds, and their hair stuck to their faces. Usually the fight culminated in the Nawab's tent with one or two Begums. Today, he was trying to rein in the revelry because of Sara.

Choti Begum, an erstwhile singer, started singing a rather bawdy song and dancing. The voluptuous Shaukat Begum lunged forward and smeared juice on the Nawab's chest and tore his thin mulmul kurta. Feroza felt embarrassed for them with their crude play, got up and told the Daroghan that she wasn't feeling well. Some Begums had cornered Sara who was playing with them good-naturedly.

Feroza went to her tent. Her change of clothes and a pail of water with a basin were already there. The abrasions were raw and stinging as she washed her face, changed and lay down on the simple bed. She refused to join the festive lunch under the trees. What would Sara be thinking?

Sara visited her new friend frequently, requesting permission from Shams, and Feroza found great comfort in the warmth of her friendship. Shams found that she kept Feroza in good spirits and often invited her over. Huzur

Aliya made a kahari sit outside on the veranda to report on the meeting – how long it lasted, what was being said, were they laughing or crying, etc. Since most of the conversation was in English, the kahari couldn't report much.

Sara brought English magazines and they would spend hours poring over them. Feroza was hungry for knowledge of the outside world and Sara would speak of England and her own time in a boarding school. Feroza dressed her up in a farshi even though the kurta didn't fit Sara's muscular frame.

Sara loved the glamour of Feroza's life though she wouldn't trade her freedom for anything. Soon Feroza had narrated the story of her kidnapping, the abortion and how she had brought ruin to her family. Listening to the oft-told story first-hand was shocking, but there was little Sara could do to help her friend. Sometimes Diwani Begum would join them, participating in the conversation and asking Feroza to translate for her. Sara guessed that Diwani Begum wasn't mad and always addressed her by her name – Akhtar Begum. Diwani never let Feroza call her Akhtar. She dropped her act when she was with them. They were a strange trio, chatting in a mixture of tongues, laughing and smoking. Diwani had become quite a smoker and Feroza would tease her about her addiction.

Bua would grumble, 'Angrez are all liars and deceivers. They took away our Mughal *badshah*. These women don't bathe even after going to their husbands, not even after going to the toilet. They just wipe with a piece of paper. How can you sit and eat with her? Tauba, tauba. At least think of your child!'

13

Ameera

Sherpur, 2016

They have started exams at school. I haven't been to school since that day. I'm trapped in the house. Totally sympathise with Feroza Begum now. I lie for hours in my room and can feel the dark wood ceiling of my room press down upon me. The lime paint on the walls has puffed up with the damp and I scrape it off, just to have something to do.

I barely go out anyway, except for some occasional shopping in Nasrullah Khan Bazaar with Ammi. There are cafés and restaurants in Civil Lines, some even have ladies' sections but we almost never eat out. Ammi says that sitting in cafés with friends only happens in the movies. Ammi doesn't even like my visiting Sonia who lives quite close by. Sometimes I feel like walking out of the gates and taking a rickshaw – just going anywhere. If I did that, Meel would run after me, calling out. It would become an embarrassing scene. Where would I go, anyway? But it's not as bad as the lal purdah. At least I can go to school, or used to, anyway.

Sonia had called after I missed the first exam and offered again to ask her Dad to lend money for the fees. I told her I hadn't prepared for the exams and would fail anyway. I lied to Ammi saying that there were hardly any classes, attendance was low, and she just accepted it! The suspicious Ammi who checked our bags and kept a tab on us had simply vanished. Ammi just wants to surround herself with grief, news of slain Kashmiri boys, lynchings – the gruesomeness of the world gives her comfort. The world is suffering and so are we.

I listen to Dadi's stories at night. I live in a time warp. I haven't charged my phone. By now the batteries must have completely died – battery coma.

'What did Feroza Begum do all day?' I ask Dadi.

'Oh, the Begums sat and chatted, attended mehfils, dressed up and waited for their husband. Every season was celebrated. New dishes were tried out and sent from the kitchens.'

'How could Feroza Begum live with the man she hated?'

'There are different kinds of loving. Persian has eighty words for love. The Nawab loved Feroza Begum in his own way. He could be cruel at times, like most husbands, but he really cared for her when she was ill. That was important in those times. They say when she shouted at him, he would often just stand and listen. Wasn't that love?'

'Did you love Dada?'

'Of course. If you only get to eat dal all your life, wouldn't you love dal?' she winks.

If I drop out of school, they might arrange my marriage too. Maybe I would marry Sami. He took the punishment just to be with me. He's cute and I feel comfortable talking to him – it's like sipping warm coffee. The idea of going to bed with a stranger makes my flesh crawl. I don't understand how they did it in those days. It's still quite common. Naved Chacha hadn't seen Samiya Chachi till their marriage.

Abba fell in love with Ammi. She was the girl next door and I like to imagine him slinking off to meet her. Dadi had sold off a part of the house to Sayed Sahib, Ammi's father. I find their romance so sweet. But they fight nearly all the time these days – money, tepid gravy, Dadi's medicine, anything can become a flashpoint. It keeps Samiya Chachi glued to the upstairs window. They used to fight earlier too – little squabbles where one of them would back down. Ammi was always the calm one, bowing out and getting back to normal life. Abba is known for his typical Pathan raging temper. Dadi says it's hereditary. I feel they will never get back to being normal again.

It's all because of Jugnu. Ammi feels Jugnu is suffering because Abba had decided to file a case against the minister to save his measly shops and land. She blames him for not going on bent knees to save their only son. Abba's shops are in the middle of the proposed Mahatma Mall project and he had received notice along with others for acquisition. Naved Chacha and the other shopowners and landowners had decided to sell off or had been 'persuaded' to do so and had received compensation. The new Land Acquisition Act made the compensation handsome. Naved Chacha says the minister is so powerful that he will get our land in the end.

The minister wants to build a grand plaza around Gandhi Memorial. He has already demolished the old topkhana gates and the rest of the gates to the city and made ugly new ones.

Naved Chacha keeps asking Abba to sell off the shops but Abba shrugs him off. He was pretty hurt that Naved Chacha decided to partition the house. Dadi is upset too. She says it's all because of Samiya Chachi. First, she called him back from his high-paying Dubai job and then took him away from his family. I think Naved Chacha wanted to come back. He is laid-back and loves Sherpur's leisurely lifestyle.

'If you're brought up with the idea that you belong to royalty, it rusts your hands and feet. How long can you survive selling off land? Only this house will be left at the end. You must become a doctorni and work,' Dadi tells me. She talks about members of the royal family who were reduced to begging on the streets after selling off their lands. I know she is right. Abba doesn't work or anything. He keeps selling off land.

I wish I could drum up my old ambition again. Maybe it was Dadi's desire ingrained in my mind. She keeps saying that I have so many opportunities and should make use of them. No one except Dadi takes my career goals seriously. Being a doctor or a gynae is an acceptable profession for a girl. The other option is teaching – no way. Teachers aren't paid much, and most of them are so nasty. Actually I'm not even sure if I want to be a doc. Suppose, I wanted to become a beautician, a model or a pilot? Shit would hit the fan.

I just want to become someone important and earn a lot of money for the family. Doctors earn a lot. Feroza Begum wanted to become a poetess. At least, she loved writing poetry but her father told her that tawaifs wrote poetry. Dadi says many of the Nawab's women were poetesses. Maybe she wrote poetry after she entered the harem but it never got published. Or she got too bogged down by all that had happened to her to write.

Dadi is worried about me because I'm too quiet and listless. She makes me drink weird strength-giving hakim medicines. She cooks them herself and says they are old family remedies passed down through generations. Maybe I could be a lady hakim and recreate all those old medicines – indigenous medicines are all the rage in the West. She doesn't believe that there are no classes going on at school and tries to get the truth out of me. What is the point of telling her – it will lead to more fights. I wish the focus was not on me. I'm not used to it. I wish Jugnu would get all right and come home. Then maybe things would get back to normal.

14

Feroza Begum

Sherpur, 1898–99

> On 4 January 1898 at 10 p.m., Sarkar Aliya, daughter of Sahibzada Sayed Altaf Ali Khan alias Miya Jaan Khan, was blessed with a daughter. His Highness gave gifts to all the mounted army, the infantry and the Ali Ghol bodyguards present at the time and a state holiday was declared. On 6 January, His Highness addressed the durbar for all nobility and prominent families. On 9 January, the 'chhati' ceremony was celebrated with great pomp. The courtiers presented 'kurta topi' for the child; singers and dancers from Delhi, Lucknow and Calcutta gave stellar performances. The Nawab named his daughter 'Sikandar Jahan Begum' and purchased gems worth rupees 5,00,000 for her.
>
> *Sherpur Gazette* (1898–99)

For twelve hours, Feroza writhed in pain, screamed and cried for her mother and Gauhar in a little side room sanitised for the delivery, with Dr Wilson and Nurse Dorothy attending to her and Bua muttering prayers by her side. In the final hours of the labour, Shams paced the drawing room where Huzur Aliya, rosary in hand, sat with Her Highness Sultanat Ara.

'A healthy girl,' the nurse informed, smiling.

'Never mind, there'll be boys later,' sighed Huzur Aliya, tucking her rosary back into her pouch.

Shams went into the labour room where Feroza lay with her hair streaming on the pillow; sweat still glistened on her flushed face as she smiled at the tiny pink face wrapped in the soft mulmul from the kurta of the late Nawab. Shams picked up his daughter, helped by Dorothy.

'She is as beautiful as you, but has dark eyes,' he said and walked out of the room cradling the baby.

'Where is he taking her?'

'Huzur Aliya is waiting in the drawing room with Her Highness.'

'It is after all her first great-great-grandchild, even if it's a girl,' Bua smoothed Feroza's hair.

'Arre Bibi, I prayed she looks like you or at least not be *kaali* like me,' laughed Tabu.

'Then she would be her foster-khala's daughter. Ah, how Miya Jaan would have rejoiced,' smiled Bua.

The Nawab put the baby on Huzur Aliya's lap, who took out a pouch with silver coins, circled it around the baby seven times and handed it to Daroghan Chhamman to distribute among the servants as sadqa. She then placed the child in Sultanat's lap.

'You have the first right over the child. Bring her up as your own.'

Her role over, she got up slowly and summoned the palanquin. The Nawab sent coins for the waiting army and bodyguards.

Sultanat Ara kissed the downy forehead of the sleeping child. It had been secretly decided that she would bring up the baby and a wet nurse had been hired. Babies in the royal palace were handed around freely like awards and medals; so Huzur Aliya, the most powerful of Nawab Yunus Ali Khan's wives, had been given Shams to bring up and train as the future crown prince. She was a widow at that time but her hold over the harem was as strong as ever.

Tabu rushed to Feroza with the news. Feroza, pale from shock, sat up, calling desperately for the Nawab. Shams came, learning of Feroza's state from Dorothy.

'You'll bear more children, Feroza. Think of Sultanat Begum. She can never be a mother and she deserved...'

'It's that childless crone, that bitch you call your grandmother, who has done this to cause me pain,' Feroza screamed, struggling to get out of bed. Bua and Dorothy held her back.

'Be quiet! I won't hear another word!'

'That woman will turn my daughter into a Shia! That's what she wants. You had promised...' Suddenly, Feroza fell back, her face waxen; blackness engulfed her as blood soaked into the sheets.

'Nawab Sahib, don't agitate her! She'll bleed to death,' Dr Wilson pleaded.

Shams turned and left the room.

Blood, milk and tears. Her body opened up and flowed endlessly; her breasts engorged and Bua tried to expel the useless milk, putting warm compresses to ease the pain. The hakim gave her medicines to dry up the milk. Feroza threw them away, screaming for her daughter.

Shams didn't visit her. He could be oblivious to her pain – yes, he had that indifference. She had convinced herself that he cared for her. All the wooing was probably orchestrated by Huzur Aliya. Her sense of betrayal intensified when she heard of celebratory mehfils and the special durbar to announce the birth of Sikandar Jahan Begum. If it were a boy, cannons would have been fired and sweets distributed to the whole populace. He would come to her again for a boy.

Daroghan Chhamman came often and listened to Feroza's in-absentia arguments with the Nawab. Feroza, her kurta wet with milk, would plead for her daughter, argue and finally curse the royal line. Shams had not faced her since the delivery. Huzur Aliya had advised him to stay away till Feroza got used to the new situation.

'Begum, your daughter is doing well. Preparations are going on for *chhati* celebrations. You'll see her there. Now you rest and gain strength.'

'Bibi, you will wear your jhoomar teeka and sit with your baby in your lap,' Bua said.

Daroghan had told a terrified Bua to make sure that Feroza was well-behaved at the chhati – the Nawab might never let her see her daughter or even imprison her.

Azeezan visited Sultanat Ara's rooms with her songs and demands. She would bring news of the baby every day.

'Mashallah, I have never seen such a *noorani* child, smiling all the time; hardly cries. Her complexion is like rose petals and her eyes are exactly like yours, though not blue.' Azeezan would burst into the congratulatory song she was preparing for the chhati ceremony and chatter about the preparations. She had demanded gold earrings from Her Highness.

Feroza would listen agog and ask a hundred questions – what was the baby wearing, who fed her, where did she sleep, how good was the wet nurse. She came to know that Sultanat slept with the child next to her on her bed, waking up when she cried, summoning the wet nurse for the feed. The Nawab visited them every morning before going to the durbar, playing with his 'Nanhi' on his lap. All that should have been hers, her baby curled up next to her, smelling of her milk. Her daughter had not even opened her eyes to see her mother. She felt hollowed out once again.

'Feroza, Hafez says the world is a lunatic's sphere. Don't agree it's real even with your feet upon it,'[1] Diwani Begum said. She had not left Feroza's side since the birth, smoking incessantly and curling up on the sofa in her room at night.

Daroghan Chhamman brought Feroza's gift from the Nawab – a farshi gharara in the palest of green with intricate gold work, matched with an emerald and diamond set complete with teeka and jhoomar. Daroghan Chhamman spoke about the guests who had come from all the princely states, the singers and dancers who would perform and the gifts Feroza would receive with little Nanhi in her lap. Bua was happy to see the colour return to Feroza's cheeks and promised to persuade Gauhar to come for a little while.

The Sheesh Mahal was lit with hundreds of candles fighting the gloom of a foggy winter night. Feroza alighted from the palanquin. The chhati durbar was in her honour – the mother. On another day, she would have marvelled at the decorations, the many-hued lights from the chandeliers, felt proud at the women standing at the door to welcome and congratulate her; those closest to the Nawab in the hierarchy of relatives, even daring to hold her hand. The Daroghan escorted her to Huzur Aliya's takht. Feroza's pulse quickened with anger but she lowered her eyes and touched her forehead; she moved on and greeted Her Highness Sultanat Ara in a similar way, her eyes searching. She sat down on her designated takht next to the Nawab's silver chair.

Sultanat Ara rose and presented her with a ruby set.

'Where is my daughter?' Feroza whispered.

Sultanat's heart suddenly clenched.

'May you have many sons,' she said and motioned to a huge, dark woman standing to one side with a bundle in her arms. The woman, probably the wet nurse, stepped forward and Sultanat put the baby in Feroza's lap. Feroza sat still, a tear splashed on the sleeping child's face. Nanhi looked up at her mother with black, unfocused eyes, her pink mouth forming an 'o'. Feroza laughed, her heart expanding with painful happiness, and touched the soft cheek, making her smile. She kissed the forehead with the diamond band, inhaling the earthy milk smells.

The women, jealously guarding their closeness to the royal line, presented gifts for the princess in order of precedence. Gold coins, clothes and toys started piling up as Feroza touched her forehead and accepted the gifts. Daroghan Chhamman, in the role of Nanhi's foster grandmother, gave *chhochak*[2] baby clothes and a cradle. Amina Khala presented a gold bracelet for the baby from Zubeida Begum, probably sent secretly. Feroza felt a pang for Abba, Gauhar and her family.

Gauhar, she has your tiny dimple.

The Nawab came in with the usual announcements and courtesies, kissed Nanhi, avoiding Feroza's eyes and settled down on his throne. She watched his turned shoulder, the turning away observed by all. The mirasans and domnis started singing the congratulatory songs. Feroza caressed Nanhi's face and she immediately turned towards her finger.

'She's hungry,' thought Feroza. She turned her back towards the singers, raised her kurta and fed Nanhi for the first time, feeling her warm milk flow into the hungry mouth. The wet nurse got up sloppily and offered to feed. She was a strong, stocky woman with dark brows, her lips black with old paan stains; a dirty cloth-encased *taweez* talisman was stuck at the base of her thick neck. She didn't seem very clean and moved with a casual laziness more due to her attitude than her weight. Feroza hated her immediately. Her only merit was that she was from Huzur Aliya's village.

Nanhi's mouth slackened after energetic suckling and she dozed close to Feroza's heart. Huzur Aliya's eyes were fixed on Feroza's back and she whispered something to the Daroghan.

'Begum, the stars are out. We'll start the chhati ceremony,' Daroghan Chhamman said. Feroza rose with the child in her arms and walked out of the Sheesh Mahal flanked by Shams and a young male cousin holding their swords over her head. A silver chauki was set in the middle of the garden. Feroza sat down with her daughter. The swords were held over their heads with the promise of eternal protection. As per the custom, she started counting the stars aloud.

They don't celebrate chhati anymore. It dates back to the tribal life of the Rohilla Pathans. So on the sixth day of the birth, the mother and child are taken out of the house under the night skies. The mother counts the stars out loud. If it were a boy, women would call out the ancient Pashtun cry '*raaey khorey*' ('Come sisters, a son is born') – a warning to the enemies of the birth of a new protector and avenger. Sons made dynasties stronger and men proud and brave. In the highlands of Afghanistan, they still announce the birth of a boy.

The Nawab left to attend the durbar where the courtiers walking in a procession would present a topi-kurta ensemble for the baby. There would be an all-night dance and song mehfil at the Rang Mahal. Feroza sat playing with the baby, memorising her face, touching the folds of her neck and admiring her long fingers. She refused to eat. The guests left and the Daroghan asked her to give the child to the wet nurse. Feroza looked up, a desperate plea in her eyes.

'I'll send her to you every day, Feroza. She's your daughter,' said Sultanat and Feroza let her take the sleeping infant.

True to her word, Sultanat sent little Nanhi every day with Nazuk. Nazuk, meaning delicate, was a ludicrous name for the lumbering wet nurse. Feroza could smell her sweat and grimy odour on Nanhi and carefully examined the baby to see if she was clean. Feroza and Tabu would play with Nanhi as they used to play with dolls. She loved to feed Nanhi, the baby recognising her and demanding to be fed as soon as she came.

'She remembers the smell and voice of her mother,' Bua would say. Bua was instructed to occupy Nazuk with food, paan and talk to squeeze out more time. Nazuk would flop on the floor, gossip and eat, complaining that she could barely get any sleep. As Huzur Aliya had predicted, Feroza got used to her new life, rising early and getting ready to receive Nanhi. The evenings were lonely. The Nawab rarely came to meet her, avoiding her accusations and frustrated anger. She could see her importance at the durbar wane. She had given birth to a daughter and the Nawab's affections had predictably diminished.

The other Begums who had thronged her mahal during the pregnancy stopped visiting her. Diwani Begum came as usual; her madness had liberated her from zenana politics and her movements were never reported. If she didn't come for a few days, Feroza would send Mahabat Khan to call her. Diwani suffered from blinding headaches and would scream in agony. Feroza got medicines for her from her hakim; they helped in alleviating her suffering. She would emerge out of the episodes with enhanced, almost visionary lucidity.

Feroza had sensed it from the restlessness of Shams's dark eyes and his indifference to her acidic remarks before Azeezan told her. There had always been faceless rivals and shadows who lurked to satisfy his lust but now one of them had a name – Miss Flora. She was an Anglo-Indian singer who entertained the Nawab with *hazilat* or vulgar poetry.

'Begum, you cannot even imagine the bawdy things she writes! Tauba, tauba. My tongue would burn to utter her words. And our Nawab loves her indecent poetry. Her father was angrez and she is as white as you,' whispered Azeezan.

Diwani laughed at Feroza's annoyance and said, 'We are fireflies sparkling for a night in his harem. How dare you believe that you were different? I thought I was superior to all the women of the harem. I would surely become a queen. Now I have understood the truth of this world, and they call me diwani.'

The acquisition of Miya Jaan Khan's mardana baithak by the Nawab emphasized Feroza's declining importance at the durbar. The haveli was situated at the edge of the qila walls and Shams extended the boundary to completely enclose it.

'Your father never gave any dowry. So this is his *salaami* gift to his son-in-law,' he told the enraged Feroza.

'No, Shams. This is robbery!'

'When we make choices, we should be ready for repercussions.' He walked out, disregarding her scathing reply.

The haveli was a place of pride for Feroza's family, dating back to her great-great-grandfather. Feroza was heartbroken and could imagine the devastation Abba must have felt when the news reached him. Convinced that Shams's action was a precursor to his taking over all their lands and houses, she sent word to Amina Khala to somehow convince Miya Jaan Khan to return. Finally, Miya Jaan was persuaded by his friends and family to come back to Sherpur and protect his ancestral property. Shams was happy at the return of the refugees even though Miya Jaan stayed away from the durbar. It reflected badly on him that his father-in-law lived in self-imposed exile like his other estranged relatives.

Feroza felt that the centre of her life was back in its place. She immediately sent Bua to convey her regards.

'You should see how the boys have grown! Ruqayya wanted to come along with me. Gauhar was there, too,' Bua paused, looking at Feroza's expectant eyes.

'Miya Jaan Khan said that you had disobeyed and humiliated him; that because of you they lost their ancestral haveli. So no one from the family will ever have anything to do with you. That is his *vasiyat* for his descendants.' Miya Jaan's will would be followed by his children and probably theirs. It was a covenant of honour they would keep.

Shams had not visited Feroza's bed even for a night since the delivery almost six months ago, feigning consideration for her state. A woman was supposed to be away from her husband for at least forty days till she was completely 'pure' and had stopped bleeding. When he resumed his visits, they were so rare that her surprise bordered on gratification. He was probably tired of her tantrums and snide remarks. Maybe, he preferred Flora and his pliant concubines. She tried to swallow the torridity of their marriage but it would spurt out, feral, from her mouth. She could feel him tether his anger and just about stop short of hitting her before storming out. All she wanted was a turning back to the way they were, for him to profess his desire and love for her – but he had never been hers even for those brief months. She was prepared to put away all the negativities into a dark well to survive the marriage. He would come back to her out of pity or obligation. Then there were just acts that men and women did – *zina*, if consummated out of wedlock, and *hambistari*, in marriage.

She thrived on her confrontations with Shams, venting out her unhappiness and spewing out her desperate hatred for him. She craved his passionate reaction and felt invigorated like a fighter returning with satisfied wounds after a skirmish against a powerful adversary. She waited for his face to darken with anger, his fists to clench and his bellowing fury. Most fights ended with him storming out of her mahal and not returning for days. Feroza felt a measure of triumph – what could he do to her?

Shams was glad that Miya Jaan Khan had refused to meet Feroza; she was totally in his power. He also got Colonel

Small transferred out of Sherpur. Colonel Small's transfer was a blow to Feroza who argued with Shams, pleaded and then accused him of engineering the separation from her friend. Sara came to bid farewell. She had no forwarding address that she could give to Feroza, knowing that her letters could never breach the harem, but promised to somehow get in touch. She brought a 'Dutch cap' for Feroza – a female diaphragm made of soft leather.

'Feroza, you're an educated woman; you should be in charge of your body. You might not want children right now.' Sara explained the use of the cervical cap to a blushing Feroza.

'Take care of yourself, my darling,' she kissed Feroza, hugged Bua and Tabu, bidding farewell in Urdu.

'I'll send one for you as a wedding present,' she said to Tabu, who sat examining the cap, readying her many questions for Feroza.

Notes

1. *Diwan-e-Hafez.*

2. Chhochak are baby clothes and gifts given by the maternal grandmother to the newborn.

15

Amar in the Tilism-e-Azam and the Unfortunate Princess Lalarukh

'The greatest of dastangos, the narrators of the tale of Tilism-e-Azam, the cup-bearers of divine inspiration describe the Tilism-e-Batin and the dariya-e-surkh thus: that a river of blood teeming with white crocodiles guards the qila of the Tilism-e-Batin, the hidden part of Tilism-e-Azam. It flows as our River Ramganga, on which Daud Khan established the greatest of cities, Sherpur.

For more than a hundred years the brave Rohilla Pathans have lived by the Ramganga and in their veins flows *aab-e-Ramganga*, the Ramganga waters, making them ferocious and unconquered. So the dariya-e-surkh flows between Zulmat and Tilism-e-Batin. It has the property of making the people of Zulmat brave, but the Pathans are forbidden to drink from it.

Amar as Asharfi Bai flies to the river, which can only be crossed by pul-e-shamsheer, the sword bridge that cuts into two all trespassers to be eaten by the crocodiles and djinns, the water deep red with their blood. Asharfi peers down at the crocodiles crushing the bones of men in their massive jaws and trembles, but the khabbees fly the takht over the river. Suddenly, there is a black cloud, billowing green fumes. Two suns race across the skies and collide, bursting with an earth-shaking explosion. Asharfi falls back on the takht and screams, 'Hai Allah!' in a high-pitched female voice. A khabbees laughs.

'That is Huzur Afat Char Chashm, the great-grandmother of Tareek Jaan, the most powerful sorceress, practising her magic.'

Amar thinks, 'Ya Allah, where have I come? I must run away or I will be fried and my *boties* will be served as kababs to these wretched khabbees. Hai, hai!'

They are flying over deep gorges and mountains, a now-terrified Amar hanging on, ready for more explosions, tears streaming down his cheeks. He looks down and what does he see? A baradari of pearls and marbles, its arches studded with thousands of precious stones glistening in the setting sun, set in a garden of silver grass blades.

The khabbees set down the takht on the garden and fly off. Amar walks towards the baradari, the arches embellished with golden curtains, takhts covered with embroidered masnads, pandans with fresh paans, *guldans* filled with flowers and *ughaldans* shining by the side of the takhts. Kaharis are running around laying down Persian carpets, placing pitchers of wine and bowls of fruits. Khwajasaras are laughing at bawdy jokes, teasing the kaharis, pinching their cheeks and bottoms.

Two maids run towards him. 'Oho, who is this new *shikar*?' says one, finger on her plump cheek.

'Maybe caught from a brothel,' giggles another, covering her mouth.

'Keep your mouth shut, you girls!' shouts a stout woman dressed completely in white.

'Come here! What is your name?' she says, hands on her waist, looking at Asharfi with the air of one in charge.

Asharfi bows and touches her forehead, smiling. 'You can call me by any name that pleases you, but people call me "Asharfi".'

'*Khoob*! Can you sing?'

'Like a pari. Give me an occasion to please the great King of Samris.'

And so Asharfi is assigned a place with the musicians.

The mehfil of *raag-o-rang* has been readied and the ladies of Tareek Jaan's harem are in attendance. There are women and paries of all shapes and sizes, tall, short, fat, reedy, ugly, beautiful, for the King has strange tastes; a dark kahari can please him and find place in his harem as a concubine or if he is in the mood, he has a mutah performed.

There are only two permanent nikah wives, the great sorceress, Chief Queen Malika Husnara Jadu, and Begum Mahpara, a famous singer Tareek Jaan had bestowed the place of a nikah wife – so enraptured was he by her voice. The Begums and concubines take their positions around the throne according to their ranks, Husnara to his right, as she is the chief queen, and Mahpara, the number two queen, to the left. Amar notices that Lalarukh is not among the women.

Tareek Jaan enters the baradari, announced by the chobdar. He is dressed in a bright red and gold shervani, his stomach protruding, face twisted with devilish thoughts. He wears a green velvet topi with a sarpech of emerald and diamonds glistening on his evil head. He looks around at all his women. This is his harem guarded by eunuchs and castrated parizads where no man can even think of entering.

All prostrate to the ground and Tareek Jaan takes his place.

'Who is the new woman the khabbees have brought?'

Asharfi comes forward, bows low, salams deeply, kisses the fat, black toes of the King of Samris and says, '*Khuda tumharey bagh mein kabhi khizan na laye*, may God make your garden blossom forever! I'm your maidservant, Asharfi Bai.'

Asharfi arrays herself on the carpet, picks up the tanpura and tunes it. The players of the tabla, sarangi and sitar sit around her, ready for her to commence singing. Now, my friends, you know that after his birth the prophets had blessed Amar ayyar with the sweetest voice ever heard in the seven skies and he could sing both as a man and a woman. Soon everyone in the audience is swaying to his song; Tareek Jaan is exulting, 'Wah! Wah! *Subhan Allah*!'

Asharfi stands up, dances a little step, takes the goblet of wine from a girl, singing and dancing she moves forward, pirouettes daintily, quickly sprinkles the *sufoof-e-behoshi*, the anaesthetic powder, in the goblet and puts it to Tareek's lips with a flirtatious smile. Tareek looks into the eyes of the ravishing Asharfi and drinks from the goblet. He rises to grab her twirling form and falls down unconscious.

The khwajasaras rush forward, the Begums and concubines stand up exclaiming; there is confusion, cries and shouted orders as they try to revive Tareek Jaan. Amar quickly disappears into his galeem and walks out of the garden in search of Princess Lalarukh.

Ah, how can I describe the harem, the mahalsara, of Tareek Jaan – *gali dar gali*, paths within secret paths; palaces and gardens beyond imagination for the willing Begums and concubines, and hovels, dark and dreary, for the unwilling and damned. From some rooms float the notes of the songs being practised and from others, the screams of tortured souls. There are gardens where sorceresses are performing their rituals, praying to Samri and practising their magic. Flames shoot up and ashes float down.

Amar moves around, filled with wonder, pity and fear till he comes to the Palace of Crystal. In the Bagh-e-Panj-Hiss, the Garden of Five Senses, sits a despondent Lalarukh, her delicate pink colour now pale yellow, her body languishing, at death's door. Several beautiful maidens are trying to distract and amuse her. One maiden has started narrating her escapade with an old man in great detail amidst giggles and vulgar remarks.

Amar quickly changes into a toothless crone, dons ragged white garments and with a thick stick in hand, bends double and hobbles her way into the garden. She grunts and bows in salam.

'Quiet, you hussy. Can't you see that Princess Lalarukh is unwell?'

'Oho, and who are you, old woman?' says a bold one.

'You don't know me? Looks like you haven't been married and never will be, by the looks of it.' Amar settles down on a stool, a hand on her aching back.

'No, *badi bi*, she is unmarried still,' says another, smiling.

'Hah! With such escapades who will marry this *harrafah*.' Amar adjusts his crushed cotton dupatta on his head, his toothless gums working on an old paan.

'Ah, your parents will come to me soon enough. I'm Phapha Kutni, the matchmaker.'

'More likely the match-destroyer,' mutters the bold maiden.

'*Hain*? You chatty, irritating *jhanpal* bird, watch out!' Amar picks up the knobbly cane menacingly. The girls cluster together giggling, whispering. Phapha Kutni was known all over for visiting homes, striking matches and destroying marriages with her malicious gossip and chatter. Many a Pathan had pronounced talaq on his wife after hearing unconfirmed gossip from her.

'Now begone you all! The princess needs to rest. Can't you see she's upset? Run away before I dredge up your secrets and spread gossip. You will all end up as old maids!' The girls go away, whispering.

Amar edges close to Lalarukh and whispers, 'Princess Lalarukh, it's me, Amar ayyar!' Lalarukh looks up, startled and Amar shows her a miniature painting of her wedding. Eyes brimming, she touches the picture.

'Aah! I will never see him again. How is my beloved husband? I have lost his gift to me, my child!' She clutches the picture to her heart.

'He is well, but worried about you.'

'Alas! I cannot leave this Tilism-e-Azam unless it's destroyed.'

'Don't be disheartened. When a tilism is created by a sorcerer, it has a time period mentioned in the *lauh-e-tilism*, the magic tablet of tilism, that has all the secrets, including the name of the Tilism *Kusha*, the destroyer of tilism. If we find the lauh-e-tilism and give it to the destroyer, he will become invincible on realising his power. Then, he can decimate the Tilism-e-Azam and kill Tareek Jaan.'

'But where is it hidden and how can we find it?'

'Keep your eyes and ears open, princess and I will seek information about it too.'

While Amar as Phapha Kutni and Lalarukh are talking, a golden *putli*, puppet-spy, belonging to Huzur Afat Char Chashm, the four-eyed great-grandmother of Tareek Jaan, flies into the garden and hears the exchange.

Now putlis are created from lentil flour and given powers by the sorcerers and sorceresses. They fly around and spy, reporting everything to their owners. They can even spy on thoughts and the secrets of the heart. The putli flies to Huzur Afat Char Chashm, who is reciting magical chants from her sorcerer's book and shrieks, 'Amar ayyar has come, Amar is with the princess of Koh Kaaf in the Bagh-e-Panj-Hiss.'

'*Hain, kya kaha*? What did you just say?' Huzur Afat catches the putli and listens to the whole story. She snaps her finger and two golden claws – the *panjas* – appear.

'Go, catch that Amar ayyar and bring him to me,' she commands. The panjas flies to the garden. But by this time, Amar, who knows that there are spies everywhere in the harem, disappears into his galeem and the panjas returns empty-handed to an enraged Huzur Afat. She immediately flies to Tareek Jaan's baradari on her throne and finds Tareek Jaan sprawled on the floor, khwajasaras spraying his face with rose water while the queens and concubines sit around chatting and sipping wine. The chief queen, Husnara, is hurling abuses at Queen Mahpara, the pretender to her position.

'You whores, you sit around drinking wine while your King lies unconscious! And you queens are fighting for the crown when the enemy is at your door!' Huzur Afat shrieks, the rope-like tendons of her throat swelling with her abuses. She cradles Tareek Jaan's head on her bony lap and sprays the *aab-e-Jamshedi*, the magical waters of King Jamshed.

Tareek Jaan sits up, looking around.

'Aah, grandson, you have been tricked by Amar, the great ayyar. He has infiltrated your tilism. This is the beginning of the end!' Tareek Jaan raises his hand and a wall of fire appears; he reaches in and takes out the Book of Samri, opens a page, staring at it.

'What does it say?' Huzur Afat's four eyes are bulging out.

'It says Amar will start destroying my Tilism-e-Azam!' Tareek Jaan's black belly trembles.

So Tareek Jaan marches in wrath to the Garden of Five Senses where Lalarukh sits lost in thought, a ray of hope tingeing her face with colour.

'*Manaam* Tareek Jaan!' he bellows and Lalarukh's breath catches in her throat. Tareek Jaan strides forward and catching her delicate shoulders with his bear-like hands, roars, 'You have betrayed my trust! You have gone back on your promise. You shall pay!' His eyes are bloodshot with anger and his revolting body shakes with frenzied rage as he drags Lalarukh into the room and flings her on the bed. Then he spreads his shaking arms wide, raising them towards the sky and chants, 'Ya Laat! Ya Mannaat! Ya Samri!'

Lalarukh cowers on the bed, transfixed with terror. The *Ism-e-Azam*, the Great Name, that can protect her, flees from her mind. A long needle appears in Tareek Jaan's hand, he bends down, catches Lalarukh by her throat, pulls out her tongue and pierces the needle through, rendering her speechless, unable to take the Great Name. She lies frozen with magic, eyes bulging, knowing that this is the end of her life and that she might never see her Saad and her father again.

With one swoop of his hand, Tareek Jaan conjures a curved dagger and plunges it into her thigh. A bloodied fountain sprouts and Lala's soul flies out of her open mouth; quick as lightning, Tareek takes out a dead bird from his cloak and puts its open beak to Lalarukh's mouth. The soul is caught in the bird's body and Lalarukh's lifeless body slumps back on the bed as if in deep sleep. Tareek Jaan puts the pretty green and lilac bird into an iron cage and strides out of the palace, cage in hand.

'Aaseb bin Afreet!' he calls out.

Aaseb, the son of Afreet djinn, materialises before him in his grotesque form – head of a ram, with curved black horns, a third red eye glowing on his forehead, body of a man with hooves for hands and feet. He is about twenty feet tall with snakes hanging from his neck and coiling around his body.

'Take this *rooh* of Princess Lalarukh into the Dungeons of Zulmat,' commands Tareek Jaan, handing the iron cage to Aaseb. Amar ayyar decides to follow Aaseb to the Dungeons of Zulmat and attempt to rescue Lalarukh's rooh.

Aaseb is in charge of the Zulmat Dungeons deep inside the dark regions of Zulmat, beyond the Desert of the Dead. The dungeons are deep inside the barren black mountain where thousands of rebellious djinns, men, women, kings, sorcerers and parizads live in agonising captivity. Aaseb flies to the dungeons followed by the invisible Amar over the Desert of the Dead. Amar pauses at the mouth of the cave. It is guarded by two fire-spewing giant snakes. As Aaseb trots into the cave, opening its stone door by a magical chant, the snakes sense Amar's presence and rear their heads, spitting at him. He has to retreat or his guise would be revealed.

Now, listen to the story of Lalarukh's body in the harem. Amar runs back with the speed of light to the harem in Tilism-e-Batin. His heart is on fire with grief over the loss of Lalarukh's soul. Amar reaches the Crystal Palace and what does he see? Princess Lalarukh is sitting on her crystal bed, attended by fair maidens, dressing up in bright red *fora-e-uroosi*, the bridal dress! She's laughing and chatting happily.

'Ah Princess Lalarukh, how soon you have forgotten my master, your husband!' thinks Amar.

Such are the vagaries of youth. The power of wealth always defeats the power of love. This is the law of human nature. So, Amar dejectedly watches the nikah ceremony as Lalarukh happily accepts the black-hearted Tareek Jaan as her new husband. *Khatam Shud*, the end!' Mirza Kallan rises.

'Arey, Mirza Sahib, how can the dastan end here? How did Tilism-e-Azam end? How was Lalarukh rescued?'

'The Tilism-e-Azam will never end. It will remain and you and I, with our captive souls will live on. There is happiness in living inside an illusion, who needs a soul? *Rooh ki parwaaz ho gayi, yeh jism hai jo jeeye jaa raha hai*, the soul has flown away and this stubborn body lives on.' Mirza Kallan sighs, takes his bowl and lota, collects the coins from his host, touches his forehead in salam and leaves, ignoring the murmuring and protesting audience.

'Arre, Mirza has started having too much afeem now,' says one.

'*Gham bhi afeem hai*, sorrow is also afeem,' sighs another.

16

Feroza Begum and Nanhi

Sherpur, 1900–04

Famous writers have written about Nawab Shams and his harems. These writers were either rebuffed at the court or wanted to earn a living by salacious gossip. One renowned writer from Awadh wrote a very successful novel filled with fantastic exaggerations. He was convinced that Miss Flora, the daughter of his mistress, was confined in the harem by Nawab Shams. All this has blighted the Nawab's reputation.

Darbar-e-Sherpur,
Bilquis Begum

The year 1900 saw the death of the matriarch Huzur Aliya and the birth of the much-awaited crown prince, Hasan Ali Khan. Cannons were fired in celebration and the town witnessed grand festivities for days. Achhi Begum, the mother of the crown prince, a quiet and humble tawaif from the family of Biggan Jaan, shot into prominence at the Sheesh Mahal zenana durbar. The durbar was now the undisputed domain of Sultanat Ara. Feroza's relationship with Sultanat was never warm. She would often be seized with jealousy when Nanhi called Sultanat 'Ammi' while Feroza was 'Chhoti Ammi', a secondary mother. She got angry when Nanhi's visit was cut short with some excuse or if she wasn't sent. Feroza cursed the childless Sultanat loudly for exerting control over the child.

Initially, Feroza tried to call her Fatima in her house but 'Nanhi' seemed to slide off everyone's tongue easily and Feroza gave up the attempt. She was 'Nanhi' to her parents and 'Nanhi Begum' to everyone else. Feroza loved her prattle, taught her new words and laughed at her antics. She lived for those hours with her Nanhi, comparing Nanhi's little hands and face to her own – 'See your eyes are like mine, this nose is mine.' It was a game that amused Nanhi and reinforced her identification with Chhoti Ammi. Feroza would ask, '*Kiski beti?* Whose daughter are you?' She taught Nanhi to say, 'Chhoti Ammi *ki*.' It was a familiar question for Nanhi and she was 'Ammi *ki beti*' or 'Daddy *ki beti*' when the occasion rose.

As soon as the child could understand, Feroza told her of the time that Nanhi was growing in her womb. Her love for Nanhi was expressed loudly and vehemently – 'You are my *jaan*, the core of my being, my world.' She was hugged, kissed, and the household revolved around her desires and needs.

Nanhi felt the difference between the love of her two mothers. Sultanat was loving in quiet ways, never proclaiming her devotion like Feroza; she smelt of comforting paan and Feroza, a heavy smoker, had the sharper tobacco smells. But then Feroza didn't hold back her anger and her eyes bulged out in a way that terrified little Nanhi. Feroza would sometimes slap Nanhi and Tabu would rush to rescue her. But when the anger evaporated, the love would return with greater force. Diwani told Feroza that she wanted too much from all her relationships – an all-overarching love which she never got.

'Feroza, only my ishq for you is selfless – deep like the roots of a tree, demanding nothing in return,' Diwani proclaimed.

When she was two, Nanhi was joined in the nursery by her half-brother Hasan, the crown prince, given away to Sultanat Ara. She was the Begum of Sherpur and it was befitting that she should raise the crown prince with her education and royal upbringing. Sultanat, after years of abject servility towards Huzur Aliya, who always maintained that Sultanat owed her status to the matriarch, now found herself ruling over the zenana, the stigma of her childlessness forgotten.

Feroza knew from Azeezan that the Nawab visited Sultanat every day to play with Nanhi and little Hasan, though he never slept with Sultanat. Except for the early years when Shams came to Sultanat duty-bound, they had barely slept together. It was unreasonable of her to expect him to waste his seed on her now when she had been declared infertile. At least she had children whom she loved dearly.

Feroza developed a deep bond with Achhi Begum after Hasan was given away like her Nanhi. Achhi Begum would often visit her and speak of her son, the miraculous event of giving birth to the crown prince and her golden future beyond her ordinary birth. She was plain-looking, petite with a muscular column of neck developed by hours of singing practice as a young girl. Feroza had heard of her ill-treatment by the other wives but she never complained against anyone. Sometimes she sang soulful ghazals for Feroza, her throat swelling, birthing immaculate notes – in those moments she was remarkable.

When Nanhi was four years and four months old, a *bismillah* ceremony was organised at Sultanat's palace – the first reading of the Arabic alphabet. To Feroza's intense anger, a Shia mullani had been engaged to teach Nanhi.

The little girl sat solemn in a red gharara, her pudgy fingers tracing the lines on the Quran, repeating the first words of the holy book. Though it tore her heart to miss the most important milestone in Nanhi's life, Feroza refused to attend the ceremony, berating the Nawab for going back on his word. Shams, as usual, avoided her for many days after the ceremony. When he finally came over, Feroza's fury, contained for days, blew up.

'You had promised that my children would be Sunni! She is not even your crown prince. At least let her be Sunni.'

'She's my daughter and she is Shia!'

'You lied to me…'

'I lied to save her life! You were ready to kill my Nanhi.'

Shia, Sunni – they were condemned to battle each other relentlessly on the issue till the breath went out of one of their bodies. Their faces would twist with hatred and they would circle each other, striking at the weakest point. Shams's visits had become even more rare and they saw each other at the durbar more often than at the mahal. Feroza vowed to get back at Shams for going back on his word by never bearing him any more children. She thought of secretly engaging a Sunni mullani for her Nanhi but such a step would mean defiance. It would incite the Nawab's infamous *ataab* (rage). She cared little about what he could do to her but knowing Shams, he would stop Nanhi from visiting her. She decided to teach Nanhi the Sunni way of praying, herself.

As always, Diwani Begum quoted Hafez when she heard of the Shia-Sunni fights.

'How can you define God with mere words? Can the universe pass through your lips?'

'Oh, you would never understand.'

'Because I don't have children or because you think I'm not a Muslim? All my thoughts are about God. All this Shia-Sunni is a mad illusion.'

'You talk like a Sufi.' Feroza shrugged away Diwani Begum's advice and religion remained a festering wound in her relationship with Shams.

As Nanhi stepped into the world of learning, Sultanat started supervising her education with great zeal. She made sure that Nanhi was taught English along with Arabic, Urdu and Persian. Though Feroza cribbed about such a great burden on the little child, she delighted in Nanhi's sharp mind. Diwani started teaching her Hafez's compositions which, she felt, were an essential part of every education.

Nanhi wandered between grown-ups, doing as she was asked – learning, reciting, amusing. She was a pleaser and delighted her parents with her recitation of English nursery rhymes, parroting them as many times as demanded. Growing up with two volatile parents gave her a hesitant air, charming in young girls. She shrank from Shams's and Feroza's vociferous emotions and curbed her own spontaneity.

Though she was pampered and loved by all three parents, she felt that their love depended on her obeying their wishes. Feroza was amused at her little lies to keep peace – assuring Feroza that she loved her most of all, that she wanted to live with her Chhoti Ammi forever. Feroza was sure Nanhi would give similar assurances to her other parents. She tried not to fight with Shams when Nanhi was around, sensing the child's tension. Nanhi would know immediately that Shams was expected to visit her from the preparations, and grow apprehensive. By now it was nearly impossible for them to be in each other's company without needling each other and lashing out. Nanhi would stop her play and her face would cloud with anxiety. She was beset with guilt because most of the time the fight somehow involved her.

As little Hasan took up more of Sultanat's time, Nanhi turned to Feroza with her little stories and confidences. She never demanded anything of Feroza or of her Daddy, or threw tantrums like normal children. If she needed or desired anything, she would ask the placid Sultanat – never persisting with the demand if she was denied. Nanhi was Shams's great love. He looked forward to meeting her and listening to her artless chatter. She waited for his late morning visit at Sultanat's mahal, eager to entertain him with a rhyme she had learnt, hoping for an unexpected surprise gift. He sent for toys and clothes for her from all over the world and loved to watch her eyes widen with delight.

Nanhi told Feroza about her secret friendship with Rani. Around the same age as Nanhi, Rani was the kahari Lata's niece who lived in a tiny hut in the orchard. It was their secret because Nanhi knew Sultanat would definitely forbid her from meeting her only friend. Feroza would understand because she was friends with Tabu Khala and Diwani Khala. Chhoti Ammi was happiest when she sat smoking and talking to Diwani Khala.

Feroza chuckled over her encounters with her rustic friend. Rani had to stay with her aunt because her mother had run away with the coachman's son and had a baby by him. Rani's father had remarried and abandoned her. Her stepmother didn't want Rani.

'Rani says if you're fair you should marry someone fair and if you're dark then you should marry a dark person. Chhoti Ammi, leave Daddy and marry a fair person,' Nanhi came to Feroza with the newfound wisdom from Rani to crack the enigma of the lives of grown-ups. Rani believed that her mother ran away because she was unhappy with her dark-complexioned husband.

'Oho, you find a black man for your Tabu Khala,' laughed Tabu.

'You can marry Daddy!'

Feroza loved to hear Nanhi's Rani stories – her mud chulha on which she made tea, the stale roti and vegetables Nanhi ate sitting on the cool mud floor, putting the vegetables at the centre of the roti, breaking off the edges of the roti to scoop at the vegetables till the last and the most delicious bit at the centre was left. Rani became Nanhi's guide in all things fine – how to create fire from embers, make sweet chai, pull out earthworms and make *papeeya* out of mango seeds, which made a rough 'pay-pay' sound when blown into. Nanhi showed Feroza the papeeya as evidence of Rani's skill.

'You have to wake up the gods by ringing a bell and only then can they listen to your prayers. Rani says her gods are really powerful.'

'No, our Allah Mian is the most powerful and you should only pray to him or you will burn in hell.'

Nanhi looked at Feroza, her forehead crinkled with doubt. Rani had five gods – Laxmi for wealth, Ganesha for good luck, Shiva to have a husband and Ram and Sita. Nanhi loved to gather flowers for them and light the diya in front of the little figurines – then you could ask for anything. It was more fun than reading incomprehensible Arabic prayers with the mullani. Feroza would ask Nanhi to pray with her, hoping she would learn the Sunni way of prayer. Nanhi, who found very little difference between Shia and Sunni prayers, would get confused and cry when Feroza scolded her. She loved Rani's gods who were happy with just flowers and light. Then Diwani Khala told her that there was no Hell after death, the world was Heaven and Hell. It was all very complicated.

It was around this time that Feroza became pregnant again. The unplanned pregnancy brought back the old insecurities. Shams was ecstatic but the same issues and the inevitable fights ensued. Feroza had no ambitions of birthing a crown prince and replacing Hasan. She hoped for a baby girl who would belong only to her. She told Nanhi about her little sister. Nanhi could play with her when she visited them.

'You will love her more because she will live with you.' Like her Ammi, even Chhoti Ammi would get busy with the baby and ignore her. But Feroza lost the baby in the fourth month after a particularly vehement Shia-Sunni fight with Shams. He slapped her full in the face and she fell, clutching vainly at the edge of the bed to break her fall.

She had screamed curses and insults at him and her anguish flowed out for days; her face and womb took many days to recover. Violence was a great leveller. Her lineage couldn't protect her. How could she have thought that she was different? She was like all those poor abused women of the harem. Her hatred for Shams became a constant acid choking her, unmitigated by memories of his earlier devotion.

'Where did she go, my sister? Did she go into Tabu Khala's stomach?' Nanhi stood looking at her swollen face, her brow tense with anxiety. Feroza kissed her tiny hands with a watery smile.

'No, she went back to Allah Mian's house in paradise,' said Diwani.

'She died?'

'Yes.'

Nanhi burst out crying. 'I killed my sister! I told Rani's gods to take her and put her into Tabu Khala's stomach.'

'How could she come to me, Nanhi Begum? I'm not married,' Tabu laughed and wiped away Nanhi's tears.

'Rani told me to be careful. Her gods are very powerful,' hiccupped a distraught Nanhi.

'You pray to all gods, okay? There are as many gods as there are creations,' said Diwani.

Nanhi nodded. This was the wisest thing to do, and Nanhi decided to please all gods. She even kissed the sad little man who hung around her English teacher's neck.

17

Feroza Begum and Nanhi

Sherpur, 1905–07

> When Nawab Shams rages, his face becomes *qaharnaak* (apocalyptic) and those who are in his presence feel their lives ebbing away from their bodies. When he smiles, his face is very attractive. His complexion at the height of his youth was wheatish but now he looks pale with a yellowish pallor as if recovering from an illness. His height is not less than five feet nine inches and he has always been quite slim.
>
> From the private papers of Zaamin Khan,
> Haakim Mahal, Sherpur State

It seemed to Feroza that the years flew by and Nanhi was already eight. She was growing up, getting taller nearly every day. Feroza made her wear pyjamas under the frocks Shams got for her from England. For the first time, Nanhi protested.

'It's looking horrible. Everyone was laughing at me at Naila's birthday party!'

She had attended a birthday party at the chief minister's residence. All his daughters were so prettily dressed in British frocks – and no pyjamas.

'You're now a young girl. You have to cover your legs and wear a scarf.'

Both the mothers were adamant about the hated pyjamas, impressing upon her that she was growing up. Rani was happy with Nanhi's shalwar dress because it meant less mosquito bites on her legs and she could sit on the ground easily.

The year 1906 saw the birth of two more sons – Rafi Ali Khan, born prematurely, beat his brother Zafar Ali Khan by a month to become the second in line to the throne. Rafi's mother was Farida Begum, a widow from a genteel Pathan family and Zafar's mother was a singer who used to work at the Arbab-e-Nishat. Both the women became nikah wives of the Nawab. Hasan, the crown prince, too old at six to live inside the zenana, was shifted out of Sultanat's mahal to the Angrezi Kothi outside the qila for more intensive training. The kothi, built in the turreted British architectural style, was surrounded by fields and riding tracks suitable for training. Hasan had the best English, Urdu and Persian teachers and was being instructed in riding and warfare by a British colonel. Nanhi missed her brother and hated that he had become all puffed up with his own importance. Still, she listened rapt as he told her about his daily regimen, the horses he rode and the tough exercises he had to do. She laughed at his imitations of his tutors. Hasan worked diligently at his lessons, accumulating all skills for future use as the king. His tutors were impressed and sent glowing reports to the Nawab.

Every evening, Hasan came to pay his respects to his foster mother and his biological mother. Two years younger than Nanhi, he would measure himself against her. Nanhi, with her mother's lanky frame, would always triumph.

It annoyed him that his height did not keep up with his exalted status.

'When I become Nawab, I'll give you lots of jewellery and a house,' he impressed upon her.

'My Daddy will give me a lot, don't worry.' Nanhi made a scornful face. She was jealous of his new life. If she were a boy, she could go riding and be the crown prince. But she knew Daddy loved her more than Hasan. He hugged her, brought her toys and sat talking to her. With Hasan, he was challenging, asking him questions while the boy stood with hands behind his back. Hasan would get upset if he didn't know the answers – meanings of words, couplets, breeds of horses. He made sure he had the answer for his father the next day.

'I'll also stay in Angrezi Kothi with Hasan,' she told the Nawab one day, her chin quivering, ready to be thwarted.

'You'll have a kothi for yourself because you are going to get married soon,' Shams kissed her brow.

'Is he white like me?' Nanhi frowned.

'Yes, he is as white as you, my little one.'

'But I won't sleep with him because I don't want to have a baby.' Shams hugged her, laughing.

Those were good days: the Nawab's line was secure with three sons, the fields lush green with the ripening rice, the bones of his ancestors rested peacefully in the soil and the stories of battles fought and won sung by charbait singers in the mohallas. Shams smoothed his perfectly shaped moustaches the barber worked on nightly, under blazing chandeliers. He had made his ancestors proud and built a model state, prospering under the benign gaze of the British.

Tabu received a marriage proposal from a widower, Ameeruddin Haya, the famous dastango. Bua was beyond ecstatic, ready to throw Tabu into the arms of Mirza Kallan, as he was popularly called.

'Bibi, Tabu is so lucky. They are Mughals from the family of the Mughal emperor who was killed by these angrez bastards. They don't want any dowry – just the girl in her set of clothes. The boy has a house of his own in Katra mohalla and earns good money telling dastans,' Bua said.

'I want Tabu to see the man she is going to marry,' Feroza said, stubbing out her cigarette.

'Ya Allah! What has happened to you, Bibi? Do girls meet their husbands before marriage? It's that Sara angrezan who has put such thoughts into your head.'

'She can at least see him wherever he goes to tell his dastan. Right, Tabu? You go and see your dulha and only if you like him, we will marry you,' Feroza pinched a blushing Tabu's cheek. Bua went away, muttering about the influence of the angrezan and how Tabu would never get married if she would go around seeing boys. By Bua's calculation, Feroza and Tabu, born a month apart, were nearly thirty now. Tabu looked young because of her petite frame.

Feroza ignored Bua and sent off Tabu wrapped in a burqa with Mahabat Khan to Gher Mardan Khan where Mirza Kallan was telling his tale that Thursday. Mahabat Khan led Tabu through a tiny door to a house overlooking the common gher courtyard. The house belonged to a family known to Mahabat Khan and he had requested them to allow the Begum's foster sister to listen to the dastan. There was a gallery with arches overlooking the courtyard with split bamboo curtains where the women sat secretly listening to the dastan.

'Sit and listen to your Prince Gulfam,' whispered Mahabat Khan with a smile.

So Tabu sat with three fat women on a creaking takht and watched the gher fill up with men settling down on durries with their hookahs, talking in their deep voices amidst the overhanging smoke as they waited for the dastango.

Tabu liked his kind face, the dreamy smile and the powerful voice that enveloped the courtyard with its warmth; his laughter when he narrated a comic scene and the intensity of his eyes lost in the emotion of love and longing.

'So Tabu Begum, did you like him?'

Tabu hugged Feroza, blushing. 'He's a kind man,' she whispered.

'That's a rare quality in a man. So should I say yes?'

Tabu nodded and ran off to her room.

18

Ameera

Sherpur, 2016

There were no mangoes this year. The mango trees peep at us from over Naved Chacha's walls. Dadi says she knew things would go wrong when their mango trees didn't flower this year. It had happened only once before – the year Dada passed away. Dadi's existence is filled with mystical signs and prophetic dreams. She is convinced that the evil djinns have taken over the house, edging out the good djinns who had lived in our house forever.

Everyone has given up on Jugnu but maybe he would come back reformed, finish school and then go to college. Maybe Abba is right, Ammi really did spoil Jugnu. He used to go off on his new bike instead of going for tuitions. He even spent all the tuition fees he was supposed to give to the teacher. When the teacher called up Ammi, he said he had spent it on the bike; since Abba was so against the bike in the first place, Ammi gave him the fees again. And it went on and on. Ammi protected Jugnu from Abba. She didn't tell Abba that Jugnu was suspended for misbehaving with Rita ma'am and wasn't going to school. Rita ma'am had called him 'a dirty Pathan from the gutter'. I would have shouted back at her too.

Jugnu had treated his suspension like a holiday from school. But why should only Ammi be responsible for what happened? God! Patriarchy has become a part of my mindset. Blame mothers for anything that goes wrong. Abba never met his teachers or looked into what he was up to. Fathers are supposed to keep an eye on what goes on outside.

I knew everything of course – secret keeper. I knew he was going to Benazir Palace with Hureira that day. They used to practice parkour there – climbing up the ruins, doing somersaults and stunts. Hureira used to shoot Jugnu's feats and upload them on Insta. Jugnu had quite a following. I should have known they were also doing drugs. That's what Hureira and his gang are famous for. I feel terribly guilty at times.

Perhaps Jugnu was the only one who saw me clearly. He gave me importance, told me his secrets and that's why I didn't tell on him. I was insanely jealous of him though I love him, of course. Once I even punctured his bike tyres. Jugnu had his bike, parkour and I had nothing. I still don't have anything and I'm stuck in this house forever, like Feroza Begum.

They caught him with Hureira and another boy taking drugs at Benazir Palace. Luckily, they didn't find any drugs on him. The lawyer asked Jugnu to plead guilty and requested the judge to send him to the rehab centre at Bareilly. The other boys had drugs in their pockets, so they're in Juvenile Jail for a long time. Ammi believes if Abba had got him out of Juvenile Jail with the minister's help, he would be with us instead of the rehab centre. Ammi doesn't believe that Jugnu was into drugs. She tells her friends and family that he got caught with some bad boys. I feel so embarrassed for her. No one believes her.

'Zainab had no idea how to bring up a son. I brought up my boys without a father and they never got into any wrong things. Adil didn't study much. He had to manage the lands and he sent Naved for his engineering degree,' Dadi said. Naved Chacha was supposed to support the whole family with his Dubai job. Now he is jobless and his business isn't doing so well.

I think Ammi will die if she doesn't meet Jugnu. She wants to visit him at the rehab but Abba has forbidden her. In our house, no one can move without Abba's permission or knowledge. Ammi cries for hours when Jugnu calls once a week. Abba says Jugnu should know that they are angry and humiliated by his behaviour. He feels Jugnu needs tough treatment to get over his filthy habit. This is his last chance to reform himself. Uggh! Fathers can be so heartless. Miya Jaan Khan and mine. They just need to show they're powerful, in control or something. I think Jugnu needs our support to get over his addiction. We need to address his issues rather than turn away from him.

Today, they had a major face-off. Ammi threatened to go to Bareilly on her own. I don't think she can manage it. She would have to borrow money, hire a taxi or board a bus. She has never travelled on her own.

'If you go to meet that wastrel, I shall give you talaq!' Abba had shouted.

It seems everything went still after that. You say the word thrice and the marriage is over. Where would Ammi go if they divorce? Where would I live? It's easy to end a marriage – a fit of rage and it's all over. Even though they have laws against triple talaq, this is the reality.

We walk around the word all the time now. Abba and Ammi don't even talk. If Ammi needs money for household stuff, she asks Dadi to get it from Abba. I feel like taking Ammi to Bareilly. It's just a two-hour journey and there are so many buses. Abba can't throw both of us out. I have never walked out of the house alone. Meel always accompanies me.

Marriage is fragile – that's what Dadi's story tells me. Feroza Begum was divorced by Murtaza. Her mother had also gotten divorced for calling her husband by his name – so crazy. You're married one moment and then, poof – it's over! Or it can be an everlasting hell with no escape.

19

Amar and the Secrets of Lauh-e-tilism

'If we were to die with the dead, the world would come to an end, beta. For the sake of my milk that I have nurtured you with, Kallan, agree to the marriage,' Amma wept, her thickly veined, rough hands holding his. She could feel Kallan slipping deep into addiction. He had stopped going for dastan sessions and Wali was worried. Her late husband, like most dastangos, had afeem during his sessions to pep himself up. Kallan had afeem first thing in the morning, something he never did earlier. Only a wife and responsibilities could cure him.

Kallan, overcome with tenderness, opened her palm, touched the tiny black lines on the tip of her thumb and forefinger and observed the pinch-yellow from turmeric and the brown *katha* stain from her paan. It was not right that she should cook for him and look after his house in her old age. She should rest at her eldest son, Aleemuddin's house, who was a prosperous court dastango. Kallan envied him. If only he earned as much as Aleemuddin, he wouldn't have ignored Nigar's raging fever, which ultimately killed her.

He agreed to marry Tabu, the girl who smiled from the shadows, whom he had once followed down the alley in his intoxicated state, because he was sure she was Nigar. He had called out and she had half-turned in the dark, her silhouette and profile with that smile making his heart ache for Nigar.

'She looks a lot like Nigar, only darker. But she will become fair after marriage and children,' said Amma.

Amma was marrying him below their station. Tabu was just a maid's daughter but who would marry a widower, a poor dastango, even if he had a Mughal lineage? The girl lived in the palace and knew the *tehzeeb* of genteel households. She had very little prospects because of her stay inside the harem, but seemed like a decent, sensible girl. A bit old, but she would do. The Begum would give her a good dowry because she was her milk sister. There were no males in her family to trouble Kallan later.

Mirza Kallan was deeply exhausted with the claims on his body and mind. Waliuddin wanted him to complete the story and his mother wanted him to marry so that she would be free of his responsibility. But he had already died with his Nigar. Sometimes, he would wake up in the middle of the night, sure that he lay under mounds of earth with Nigar, their hands joined together, facing each other – the way they had slept together for thirteen years every night since their marriage.

'My body is yours, Amma. Do as you wish,' he murmured.

Later, he would remember nothing of his marriage or its consummation. Afeem had dulled his consciousness as his listless body obeyed the diktats of society. In the days following the marriage, Tabu settled in, taking over the reins from Amma; Kallan started taking even larger doses of afeem to dull the pain and guilt of having betrayed Nigar. She used to say that men carry on with their lives, remarry and forget their wives, such is their *mitti*. He cried out her name in anguished stupor, the shocked face of Tabu floating in his haze.

'Don't expect *wafa*, faithfulness, from me, Nigar,' he would tell Tabu as she wept her silent tears.

Mirza Waliuddin came a few days after the marriage, with his *pothi* notebook and pen, hoping to feed on his brain, urging him to complete the story. Kallan still hadn't started to go for his dastan sessions.

Mirza Kallan sighed and shook his head. 'Even Nigar's memories have left me now,' he said.

'Look around you, Bhai, your new wife has turned your house into a garden. She's so innocent. What is her fault in life? You have to provide for her. For her sake, let's complete the dastan and we shall be rewarded by the Nawab.'

'Bhai Sahib, please have tea.' Tabu stood behind the split bamboo curtain. Mirza Waliuddin got up and took the tray from her hands with its fading red henna patterns, peeping out of the side of the curtain.

He settled down with the tea. Mirza Kallan sipped his afeem.

'Kallan Bhai, you must start going back to the dastan sessions from this Thursday or you will lose your following. People waited for you last Thursday and I told them that you had just gotten married and narrated a *qissa*.'

Tabu listened in from behind the curtain as Waliuddin counselled Kallan. Amma had told her to serve her husband's every need, obey him and be patient. At least Kallan was a gentle person, never forcing himself on her or laying a violent hand – her expectation of a normal marriage. In their deepest of shared moments, he would call out to Nigar, sometimes he would call her Nigar, and she accepted her new name.

Tabu became his Scheherazade, attempting to catch his attention and create a relationship with stories from the harem and of Feroza Begum's predicament. The tales and gossip he had heard in the bazaar melded into sharp images;

Kallan would lie awake along after the tale was over, his blood curdling at the plight of the harem women. He told Wali that he would continue the dastan.

That evening he dressed neatly, his clothes washed by Tabu and left for Gher Mardan Khan.

'Mirza Sahib, for you,' Tabu handed Kallan a cream-coloured sleeveless cardigan she had knitted for the March evening chill.

'Ah Nigar, how much you care for me and I give you nothing in return. I have even taken away your name.' He stroked the soft cardigan.

'I like my new name,' Tabu smiled and came forward, helping him ease the cardigan over his head, smoothing it over his skinny frame.

Waliuddin would be waiting for him, writing down as he spoke. He had to pick up the lost threads of the dastan. He felt a dismal hope – maybe he could tell people the truth.

Asman Pari had given the teeka-e-yaqut to Lalarukh to know the truth. Though knowing, she'd said, never gave happiness.

'Teeka-e-yaqut; I'm the teeka-e-yaqut and I shall reveal the truth,' Kallan murmured, taking his seat.

'The great Ravi narrated the dastan of Tilism-e-Azam and its destruction thus:

So Amar ayyar, disheartened and heartbroken, comes out of the palace where the grand wedding of Tareek Jaan and Princess Lalarukh is being celebrated.

He disguises himself as a Pathan, wearing a shalwar kameez and a proud *pagri* on his head and moves around in the bazaars of the town hoping to get some clues about the lauh-e-tilism and the way to destroy the Tilism-e-Azam. He made his way to a *chaikhana* – the best place to get all the gossip.

As earlier, he found the Pathans going about their work with their turban-less heads lowered. There was none of the blustering liveliness in their conversation and no one sang tales of valour in traditional charbait compositions typical of bazaars. He walked the bazaars with shops of gold, silver, silk, all types of fruit, kababs sizzling on skewers and beggars sitting by the roadside. People bought and sold with little joy. No women in black and blue burqas bargained in loud voices, emboldened by anonymity, rifling through the wares and being coaxed by the shopkeepers.

Amar, realising that he would get no information from the scared people, sits down under a banyan tree some distance from the bazaar. A face suddenly appears on the trunk of the tree – a face with the sharp features of a Pathan with a long white beard.

'Who are you?' Amar asks, fearing the djinns and evil spirits of Zulmat.

'I'm a Pathan warrior. My ancestors came from the mountains of Roh and we conquered the doab region between the Ganga and Yamuna rivers. Even the British and the Marathas trembled before our lascar.'

'Why are you here in this tree?'

'Look around!' Amar looks and finds that all the branches of the tree and all its roots hanging to the ground have faces of old Pathans with long white beards and razor-sharp eyes.

'We are the *buzurgs*, the ancestors of the Rohillas, the last ones with the daring to challenge Tareek Jaan. And he has trapped us in this state – neither dead nor alive. Tareek Jaan has destroyed the spirit of the Pathans.' The Pathan sighs and the leaves shiver with sorrow.

'We were told that Amar ayyar will come and help the Tilism Kusha, the destroyer of the Tilism-e-Azam,' says one old Pathan.

'But who is the Tilism Kusha? Speak, for I'm Amar ayyar!'

As Amar takes off the paints of trickery and shows them his true form, the faces light up with joy. Amar quickly changes back into the guise of a Pathan.

'Now tell me, who is the Tilism Kusha and where is the lauh-e-tilism?'

'We only know that the Tilism Kusha is the chief queen of this evil-hearted monster, Tareek Jaan. But she's not aware of it,' says the Pathan in the tree trunk.

'Knowledge is power, Amar ayyar. You have to persuade Malika Husnara to take up arms against Tareek Jaan,' says a hanging root.

Amar ponders the words of the buzurg Pathans. He has to somehow get back into the Tilism-e-Batin and meet Malika Husnara, tell her that she, as the Tilism Kusha, has the power to destroy the Tilism-e-Azam. She would need the lauh-e-tilism to fortify herself and he had to help her find it. That was the only way to rescue Princess Lalarukh and get back her soul.

Amar wears his galeem and disappears from sight. He rides a horse of a sahir going into the Tilism-e-Batin. He reaches the Turquoise Palace of Malika Husnara and goes inside.

Husnara sits in front of her dressing table, her hourie-face bearing signs of distress. She is an extremely powerful sorceress and with her magic she had acquired the face of the most beautiful woman on earth. She is dressed in her red robe, for she only wears red and her long tresses are being perfumed by her trusted maid, Malti. Amar stands quietly to hear their talk.

'Malika Husnara, you are so beautiful yet the King of Samris spent last night with that whore, Sahiba domni. I don't know what he sees in her, dark as she is.' Malti spreads Husnara's hair over a basket from which grey wisps of incense rise and envelope the golden strands.

Sahiba is a singer who has enraptured Tareek Jaan's heart. Tareek Jaan had kidnapped her. It was said she agreed to marry Tareek if he would make her the chief queen and teach her the secrets of dark magic.

Husnara picks up a large gilt-edged mirror – the *Sheesha-e-Jamshedi* that told her of the future.

'Sahiba domni will be crowned as the chief queen!' frowns Husnara.

'But she is just a nautch girl! O Begum, why do you fret? He will tire of her,' said Malti, massaging her head.

'The mirror of Jamshed never lies. I have wasted my life with Tareek Jaan!' Husnara stands up, anger igniting a flame in her hands. She throws a ball of fire at the curtains. Husnara is known to burn everything down in anger.

Ah, only hellfire is more destructive than the fire of the wrath of a humiliated woman. Men beware, if they catch you, they will destroy you. Hang on to your pyjamas!' Mirza Kallan laughs with his audience.

'Malika! Malika! Stop!' pleads Malti.

Amar shouts from under the galeem, 'I can help you, O beautiful Malika!'

Husnara quickly looks into the Sheesha-e-Jamshedi. 'Amar ayyar is here!' she breathes.

'Yes, Malika Husnara. I'm Amar ayyar. I can help you if you help me rescue Princess Lalarukh.'

Husnara hates the daily degradation of Tareek Jaan's temporary weddings, his revelries, the kidnapping of young girls and now this danger of being ousted from her position of the chief queen. She can be as powerful as Tareek and create a tilism of her own once she is free of him.

'I bring you great news, Malika. You are the Tilism Kusha, the destroyer of this tilism! I learnt this from the buzurg Rohilla chieftains,' says Amar.

Husnara quickly looks into the Sheesha-e-Jamshedi.

'It says that Tilism-e-Azam will be destroyed and Tareek Jaan killed by me! I'm the Tilism Kusha!' Blood rushes to Husnara's face, excitement and power making her head swim. She is fated to destroy Tilism-e-Azam and kill that hateful, fornicating wretch, Tareek! She understands now that Tareek married her, practically forced her father to give her away with promises of keeping her as the chief queen, to keep her enslaved to himself, so that her powers never fully developed. She was never to discover that she was the destroyer of the tilism!

'The forces of Koh Kaaf and Saad bin Ameer Hamza will stand beside you to challenge the might of Tareek Jaan!' Amar removes his galeem. Malti rushes around to close all the doors and windows for fear of spies and Husnara casts a spell to burn the magical putlis of Huzur Afat.

Amar narrates the story of Princess Lalarukh and how her soul lay trapped in the Zulmat Dungeons.

'There are ten thousand sahirs with their armies who will bow to my command. When I married Tareek, they swore allegiance to him. Now I must quietly call them back and get ready for battle.' She had to start awakening her powers with prayers and chants.

'But first we have to get the lauh-e-tilism,' says Amar.

Friends, you already know that the lauh-e-tilism, the magical tablet, has all the secrets of the tilism inscribed on it. When the Tilism Kusha wears the magical lauh-e-tilism on his or her neck and goes to war, he or she gets the power to destroy the tilism. So when the tilism is created, the Samri keeps the lauh-e-tilism, bearing the seeds of its destruction, in a safe place.

'I only know that the lauh-e-tilism is kept with Huzur Afat. I don't know where she has hidden it.'

Amar wears his galeem and goes in search of Huzur Afat. He finds Tareek talking to Huzur Afat in her chamber, 'Grandmother, I have come for your help. I know Amar is in Tilism-e-Batin but we are unable to find him. I have sent out sorcerers and putlis all over. Have you kept the lauh-e-tilism carefully?'

'Ha, I'm not as careless as you. The lauh-e-tilism is kept in a place that is beyond your imagination but the curse of your tilism is that the Tilism Kusha lives inside the Tilism-e-Azam. If she turns against you, you are finished. You have to kill her!'

'I cannot. She is too powerful. Maybe more powerful than you and me. But if she doesn't have the lauh-e-tilism, she cannot do anything.'

Afat calms down a little and offers Tareek Jaan some wine. 'My son, why do you have this madness for women? Because of Lalarukh, Amar is creating havoc. This lust for women will ruin you! You should take boys. Your astrological chart says that you will be killed by a woman.'

Tareek suddenly gets up angrily, 'I shall not be killed. I was born of the dust from Samri's grave – not from a man. No man can kill me. Now give me the lauh-e-tilism and I will feel safe. Where is it?'

'It is safer where I have put it – in the belly of Rohu Mahipusht, the fish-man! Even he has no idea about it.'

Tareek Jaan smiled, 'You have done well! Now I will rest easy.'

And now, the night has fallen on us, as on our fates, and on our beloved Amar; I take your leave.' Mirza Kallan took out the clay *chillum* of his hookah, blowing on the ashen coals.

'*Lo hamara huqqa bhi raakh hua. Hum khamakhah gud-gudae faa rahe hain.* (My hookah has turned to ashes but I continue to gurgle it.)'

'Kallan Bhai! What kind of a story is this? How can a woman be the Tilism Kusha?' Waliuddin confronted him once they reached home.

'Why not? It is the women who are suffering the most. Look around you. Nigar tells me such things of the Nawab's harem that my blood boils. What kind of men are these who let their women be kidnapped and raped? They call themselves Pathans!'

Kallan sat up on his charpai, his eyes glittering with anger. The frustration and grief of Tabu's narratives had become a sore canker in his sensitive heart.

'There is no Tilism Kusha to break the tilism of Nawab Shams Ali Khan. We shall die under this tyrant,' he sighed and reclined back on the bolster.

'Bhai, what about Amir Hamza and Saad bin Ameer Hamza? Won't they do anything to rescue Lalarukh?'

'Ah, Saad never came for Feroza Begum. He divorced her.'

'Who is Feroza Begum?'

'Tareek Jaan has taken away her soul, her body is being abused,' Kallan closed his eyes.

'Kallan Bhai, you are taking too much afeem. Your mind is getting confused. Tilism Kusha has to be from among the descendants of the prophets in the Amir Hamza tale. He has to be a follower of Islam. Not a heathen sorceress! Besides, your story is too rebellious. If the Nawab gets to hear about it, he will destroy the dastan and you will be put in the stinking jailkhana and your nails pulled out.'

'The dastan remains the same all through the ages. Names and faces change. Didn't you see how many people came to hear my dastan yesterday? They love it because they hate the Nawab. In times of great stress, people turn to storytellers and poets to give them words.'

'You are courting disaster for all of us.'

'It's just a dastan. You write it down. I wish I could.'

'But who would buy it, Kallan Bhai? The Nawab?'

'It would be such a tale that the Nawab would not be able to guess,' smiled Kallan, stirring his afeem.

20

Feroza Begum and Nanhi

Sherpur, 1907–10

> There is a long-established custom in our families that not only the Nawab, but the other well-to-do members of the family, often keep their daughters at their houses after marriage. The son-in-law, in such a case, has to live with his father-in-law so that the parents of the girl may watch over the couple until the time harmony is well established between them and they can live independently.
>
> Nawab Shams Ali Khan,
> Letter to British Agent dated 1912

Feroza wanted Nanhi to marry a royal prince from another state, even if such a match meant parting from her. It was the only way Nanhi could live her own life beyond her father's control. The issue had once again been hotly contested between them, almost eclipsing the constant Shia-Sunni scraps. As always, she had no say in her child's life.

The Nawabs of Sherpur traditionally wed their daughters to the sons of their Rohilla sardars – the familial ties a surety for their loyalty. Nawab Shams asked his trusted official, Husain Raza Khan, to present his two sons to him. Nawab Shams leaned forward, his eyes peeling off the layers and observing every detail. The younger son, Mehdi Raza Khan, a lad of twelve with the first burst of moustache, stood boldly, unaffected by the presence of the sovereign. The elder son, Mohsin, looked away or looked down at his restless toes.

'Give him to me.' He nodded towards Mehdi.

'Sarkar, he is yours,' said Husain, touching his forehead, knowing that his reply would change the course of the boy's life.

Husain Raza Khan could not dare refuse his sovereign to 'give away' his son Mehdi in *farzandi*, as a foster son, to be brought up by the Nawab, even if it meant turning the boy into a Shia – an important prerequisite to the marriage. Feroza felt suffocated. There was no escape for Nanhi. The only positive aspect of the match was that Mehdi was distantly related to her family.

Mehdi's mother, Sumayya, was not in favour of the match, which was practically forced on them. She decided to marry her elder son, Mohsin, to her niece, Farhat, who belonged to a rather impoverished family. Sumayya Begum pushed this alliance saying, 'One daughter-in-law is a princess. How can I expect her to press my feet? Farhat will look after me and keep the house.' It was an age-old logic to marry the son into a family a rung lower, to be able to dominate the daughter-in-law. Husain Raza gave in.

Preparations for Nanhi's wedding began and Sultanat, with great magnanimity, decided that Feroza should have the pleasure of preparing the nine-year-old bride. So Nanhi came to stay with Feroza for a month. For the first time, she didn't have to share her daughter's days with others. She slept clutching Nanhi to her heart. It was a bitter-sweet time for Feroza who still missed her family deeply.

'There is no one from my *maika* to share my happiness.'

She spoke to Nanhi about Abba, Nausha and Gauhar, projecting their happiness, imagining how they would have celebrated the occasion with her.

Nanhi was made to sit in a corner of Feroza's room for the period of seclusion before the wedding. She enjoyed all the attention she received, gorging on special laddoos made for the *manjha* ceremony and the traditional bridal breakfast of jalebis and milk to sweeten her disposition. Everyone called her *nanhi dulhan* – the little bride. She only missed playing with Rani.

Tabu caught fireflies for her in her scarf. She would fill the jar with the glowing insects to keep Nanhi company at night. But Diwani didn't like the captive fireflies and made her release them saying, 'Captivity is not the way to live, jaan. God's creatures should be free.'

The only thing Nanhi detested was the slathering of flower-scented *ubtan* all over her body – the oatmeal chafed her skin. Shams, seeing the reddish patches on her arms, forbade its application. He also didn't let Feroza get Nanhi's nose pierced and got a special clip-on nath for his darling. It was unheard of that the bride have an unpierced nose and the two mothers scoffed at the mollycoddling.

'Huh, how much can you protect your daughter? A woman's existence is filled with grief and pain.' Feroza was secretly pleased that at least through Nanhi he could feel a woman's agony.

Shams would join the singing sessions in the bride's room after the *dhol chhapai*,[1] often singing bridal songs for Nanhi with moist eyes.

Gauhar couldn't attend the wedding but sent a ruby set for Nanhi through Amina Khala. It was originally their mother's and Feroza remembered her wearing it for weddings. She was very touched, especially because Gauhar had defied her father's ban with the secret gesture.

The nikah was performed on 21 March 1907 with the exuberance of the first wedding of the generation. The bazaars were lit with electric lights and fireworks welcomed the grand baarat on horses and elephants from Gher Mardan Khan to the qila.

Nanhi sat wearing an elaborate farshi skirt and her head covered; the tassels from the scarf irritated her nose. She scrunched and wriggled her nose, not daring to scratch for fear of pulling at the heavy nose ring. The embroidered kurta seemed to have pins pricking her torso. She fidgeted as she sat between her two mothers, trying to find a comfortable position.

The maulvi was speaking from the other side of the purdah – a long-winding speech in which she could only make out her name – Sikandar Jahan Begum, the conqueror of the world. Daddy said that was the meaning of her name. What worlds would she conquer after she was reduced to being the diminutive 'Nanhi'? The maulvi stopped speaking and Feroza nudged Nanhi. It was her turn.

'*Qubool hai*! Qubool hai!' Nanhi piped loudly in her childish voice. She had forgotten to be shy and soft. Feroza chuckled and hugged her as everyone burst into laughter.

'Qubool hai,' she whispered, to compensate.

Sultanat congratulated Feroza and the two women sniffed and hugged. The domnis started singing the special song composed for Nanhi.

Feroza had dressed up Diwani in new clothes. She looked sweet with her short hair covered with the pink tinsel dupatta.

She sat quietly in a corner. Even Sultanat didn't recognise her. Faces faded from memory in the zenana.

Mehdi Raza came to see his bride flanked by his cousin sisters; the corner of their scarves covered his head to ward off the ever-present evil eye.

'See, your dulha is as fair as you,' whispered Feroza and Nanhi looked up at him and smiled through the veil covering her face.

Mehdi bowed his head and touched his forehead to greet his mothers-in-law. Shams escorted him to Nanhi's takht and made him sit next to her with a jovial laugh. Nanhi was enjoying herself in spite of feeling a bit hungry. She needed to use the washroom. She whispered to Sultanat who asked her to wait for a bit.

The bride and the groom were asked to sit facing each other and a copy of the Quran and a mirror was put between them in accordance with the Persian *arsi mus'haf* tradition.

'Now look in the mirror and see your bride's face,' said Sultanat.

'But he can see me!' said Nanhi, mystified.

Everyone laughed, and Feroza asked her to be quiet and look at Mehdi in the mirror.

Nanhi obediently leaned forward and looked at Mehdi's self-conscious face reflected in the mirror under the tent of a red dupatta covering their heads to give them a private moment. With the *arsi* (mirror) and *mus'haf* (Quran) between them, the now-married couple had their first official glimpse of each other. Mehdi was looking uncomfortable, so she smiled reassuringly at him.

'Are you hungry?' she whispered to the mirror image.

He contemplated her face and said nothing. He was a disciplined boy. What would the women say if he started chatting with his bride? He had seen many brides and they were bent double like glittering sacks. But this bride was a princess. His brother and cousins had warned him – 'Be careful, your bride speaks English. You won't know what to say to her *ghit pit*.' But she was speaking in Urdu, so it was all fine.

He was asked to read a Quranic verse and blow on his wife's face, which he did.

'Now say, *tum sher main bhedh* (you are a lioness, I'm a lamb)!' said Tabu.

Mehdi was prepared for this. '*Main sher tum bhedh* (I'm a lion and you are a lamb),' he said loudly. Shams laughed and said he was a true Pathan. The women came for the salami – gifts and coins for the couple. Nanhi was now squirming in her seat as the urgency to relieve herself grew.

'I had asked you to go before putting on the gharara. Now sit still!' hissed Feroza.

Finally, to the relief of the two children, the ceremonies and salams were over and Nanhi rushed to her washroom and took off the skirt. She was asked to wear it again because her in-laws had come to see her.

'I'm hungry!' The bride stood bare-legged in her tiny kurta with jewels covering her head and torso, on the verge of tears. It was past her dinner time; she had barely had lunch because her hands were covered with henna. Feroza instead of scolding her, kissed her and took off her nose ring. Tabu fed her pulao mixed with gravy, the meat pieces broken into tiny bits just the way she liked. She also told her a story she had heard from her husband. Thus mollified and fed, Nanhi wore her gharara again, covered her head and went back to her takht to greet another series of glitzy women.

'I'll never get married again,' said the exhausted bride after it was all over. It was way past her bedtime.

After all the excitement of the wedding, Nanhi went back to living with Sultanat till the nebulous time that she would 'grow up'. She entertained Rani with stories about her wedding and answered her many thoughtful questions. Rani's wedding would be different; she would walk around the fire seven times with her groom.

Sultanat now began training Nanhi in the nitty-gritty of running a household, managing servants and laying out meals for guests. But Nanhi's favourite meal was with Rani – the thick rotis they cooked together and the chutney or leftover vegetables washed down with sweet tea. She was by now adept at making rotis and tea – skills she would never require.

The Shia mullani redoubled her efforts at teaching her the deeper philosophy of the religion, its history and the various prayers. Feroza in turn made her recite all Sunni prayers, and gave her all the justification for not following the Shia tenets.

'Your husband is a Sunni too. Both of you can just pretend to be Shias and ask for Allah's mercy. Allah understands your predicament,' Feroza sighed. Nanhi had by now learnt to tread both the worlds with the ease of a trapeze artiste and barely gave religion thought.

The Nawab was getting a grand palace prepared for her and Mehdi inside the qila where he could see her every day and she could live away from her husband's bustling extended family. Mehdi would be given a position at the court. Nanhi was excited and apprehensive at the change in her life that everyone kept talking about.

21

Ameera

Sherpur, 2016

Dadi took a drag of her hookah, 'Mehdi, my grandfather, was a very simple boy and the glitter of the court didn't impress him. It wasn't easy for him to adjust to his new life as a son-in-law of the Nawab. He had entered the farzandi of the Nawab and was now housed with the crown prince, Hasan, at the Angrezi Kothi, attending lessons with him. Most importantly, he was learning to be a Shia. Knowledgeable Shia clerics were appointed for Mehdi but the boy didn't learn his lessons properly and seemed indifferent. He was homesick for the gullies of Gher Mardan Khan where he played with his brother and cousins, where all houses were interconnected with ties of blood. You could traverse all the houses through tiny doors. Some houses in our gher still have those doors. So poor Mehdi was mercilessly teased by his cousins for becoming the Nawab's *ghar jamai*, for putting on airs and for having an English-speaking princess bride. He felt alienated. Once a week, he was allowed to go home to meet his parents and elders. They found him quiet and withdrawn. He felt a deep anger and sense of betrayal towards his father for giving him away. He had become a stranger among his own people.'

Dadi used the word '*ghairiyat*' – to become *ghair*, a stranger. It has been so long since I went to school that I was feeling far removed from the bustle of that life. Even Sonia had become ghair. I switch on the phone to speak to her.

Hi. Why did you miss your exams?

Sami's message flashed on Whatsapp. Seriously, dude. It's none of your business, I want to say. We're not even friends – unless you call one chat during punishment, friendship. I call Sonia.

'So, should I reply?'

'Seriously? Just ignore. Unless you want to chat.'

'It seems rude.'

'He's being rude. He knows it's about the fees. But your call. You decide.'

I do get to decide who I want to hook up with, though hooking up is barely possible in Sherpur and Abba-Ammi would freak out. Feroza Begum and even Nanhi had no choice. In Feroza's case, the guy she married, dumped her. Things happened to her and she dealt with them as best as she could. Nanhi was married off in childhood.

I do have choices. Maybe.

'Exams were horrible. I'll fail Chem.'

'I don't think I'll ever go to school.'

Maybe I'll stay in this house forever. Or till I'm married off, because if you aren't studying, you might as well get married and be of some use.

'Are you mad? Come after Dussehra break with a medical certificate. It'll all be okay. These were only term exams. Just pay up before the finals.'

'Are you sure? What if Abba can't pay up even then? I'll have to drop out.'

'Everything is pretty casual here. Shiv sir was asking me if I had Uncle's number.'

I had given my personal number for the class register. Everyone does that to escape complaints. I had switched on my phone after a long time. Sonia tells me to bring up the fee issue with Ammi and Abba. It's true they are dealing with a lot, but my problems are real too.

I lie on my bed listening to her familiar voice. She talks about her crush, Ahmad, and how they sneaked off to the Nursery wing. She is so bold and free. I wish I could be like her. I wish I could *be* her, in her skin, living her life. She doesn't have a mother and lives with her father and a younger sister. They are so cool, they wear anything they like at home and really chill. Sonia says whatever comes to her mind. She is like Diwani in Dadi's story – a free spirit. Her Dad is very ambitious for the girls and wants them to go abroad for their studies.

Shit, Abba and Ammi are fighting again. Why do they have to do it in the veranda for everyone to see? I tell Sonia I got to go, and peep out. Dadi is smoking a cigarette – her quick fix for stress.

'How many lives will you destroy, Zainab? First Jugnu, and now Ameera. Stay away from my children!'

'Ameera couldn't appear for her exams because *you* didn't pay her fees. Because those shops and the case is more important to you than your children. They took Jugnu away because *you* were too proud to beg the minister...'

'That two-bit teacher, Shiv, comes up to me on his scooter and asks me why Ameera missed her exams; and I didn't even know about it!'

'So I'm the only one responsible for my children's education? It's all my fault?'

'You didn't even tell me Jugnu was suspended. Who gave him money for drugs? You! What kind of a mother are you?'

'And you can't even pay your daughter's school fees. What kind of a father are you? She'll drop out of school and marry a high-school pass like you!'

I come out into the veranda. This fight is about me, I've got to be there. I can feel the beginning of a fireball of rage, spinning, gathering momentum and choking me.

'Ameera, why didn't you tell me about the exams?' Abba pounces on me.

'I told you about the fees.'

'But I didn't know… I would have done something.'

'You would have done nothing. You don't care, no one cares. It's better I go away somewhere,' I burst out.

'Yes go, and become a druggie like your brother!'

'I wish I could. It would help me deal with all this!'

'What are you saying, Ameera?!' Ammi starts crying.

'Ammi, you only care about Jugnu and you want to give up everything to meet him. What about me? My school, exams and career? Abba won't even allow me to go for tuitions and Jugnu got a new bike to attend tuitions.'

Once I start, it just flows out – all the unhappiness, grief, guilt – to their utter silence. They are finally listening.

Sherpur State,
9 September 1911

My dearest Sara,

I hope my letter finds you in good health and spirits. You must be surprised to hear from me after such a long time. I had no idea where to reach you. It was therefore a happy coincidence to meet Judith Hart, the wife of Colonel Hart, who has been posted here. She spoke of you and your family posted at Allahabad and I immediately pressed her to give me your address.

I miss you, my dearest friend. The boys, I hear, are all grown up and out of school. John, following his father's footsteps in the military and the scholar, Kevin, I hear, is at Oxford. You must be so proud of them. My Nanhi is married now and living with her husband, Mehdi Raza Khan, in the qila. We marry our children early and the 'going away' ceremony is performed when they attain maturity. Nanhi has a happy disposition unlike her parents and has settled down well. Mehdi is a kind, dignified boy and visits me every day. He is distantly related to me on my mother's side. Staying in the qila has its disadvantages and the boy is completely under Shams's control. He is even made to pray the Shia way, which he hates. He confides in me and I feel so helpless.

These past few months I have been ill. The doctor says it's my lungs and I will recover. They are trying out all kinds of injections and I stayed for some time in Nainital. The pure air of the hills, they said, will do me good.

I feel all the unhappiness and grief has settled into me and diseased my body. Shams is so kind to me now. It is as if he is atoning for all that happened earlier. I cannot forgive him for killing two of my children (yes, there was another after Nanhi), though he tries to keep me happy so that I can fight the disease. There are his sudden kindnesses, the unexpected tenderness that stops me from hating him completely.

I feel so old now. My hair is greying. Bua tells me that Tabu and I are both thirty-three years old. She ties a knot for every year of our lives on my birthday by the lunar calendar. It's called 'saal-girah'. Abba used to celebrate my birthday.

I suffer because I was the cause of anguish and humiliation for my father. He shall never forgive me. I'm the cause of his disgrace. He also lost his haveli, his mardana baithak, the pride of his ancestors, because of me. One day, my little sister, Ruqayya, visited me. She is married now, and secretly defied Abba to meet me! You cannot imagine my happiness that day. I had to hide her and make her wear Tabu's clothes, wrap her in a poor cotton chadar because she is so beautiful and I was afraid for her. Shams visits me unannounced.

I secretly read *Husn ka Daku* by a famous Awadh writer. It's banned here, of course, but Tabu's husband sent me a copy. He told Tabu that the plot was inspired by my abduction. I believe, the book has become quite popular and has brought ill-repute to Shams. It is about a debauched ruler who kidnapped newly wedded brides.

They say the author believed that the Nawab had forcibly detained Miss Flora in the harem. Now Flora was the daughter of the writer's mistress. I do know Flora lives in Sherpur and writes vulgar poetry to entertain Shams. I can only guess at her relationship with Shams. Enough of gossip now. Diwani sends her love. She has become quite addicted to my cigarettes in spite of all her Sufi thoughts. She curls up on my sofa smoking, talking and singing. She is a source of great solace for me.

I know you might never reply to this letter. There is no way to reach me. But at least I can unburden my heart. Tabu will post this letter and I hope she doesn't get caught. I won't be able to write very often. You know why.

I miss you, and will forever remain,

Your unfortunate friend,
Feroza

22

Feroza Begum and Nanhi

Sherpur, 1911–12

A painting of the crown prince, Hasan Ali Khan, hung in the *farrashkhana*, the furnishings department. It showed a young Hasan, a bit tall for his twelve years, proudly astride a horse, a light smile on his perfect aquiline features. The grace and beauty of that painting still haunts me.

From the private papers of Zaamin Khan,
Haakim Mahal, Sherpur State

Nanhi's rukhsati ceremony was performed at Feroza's mahalsara. She tried to soothe the apprehensive thirteen-year-old on the threshold of married life saying, 'Mehdi will make a kind husband, God willing. Besides, you are the Nawab's daughter. He dare not trouble you; but there are things he would do to you which you must accept as a part of married life.' Feroza prayed that her daughter gets all the joys of a happy marriage that she had been denied.

As the young couple settled down into their new home, they would visit Feroza every day for the formal salam. Feroza could see Nanhi's sparkling happiness and her delight in her new home. They took Feroza to see the mahal Shams had got constructed and furnished by a French decorator with all the modern facilities.

'We eat together every day on this dining table; unless Daddy asks Mehdi to dine with him.'

Eating together, getting meals made for Mehdi was Nanhi's greatest delight. Shams never dined with any of his wives and Nanhi loved the intimacy of shared meals. Often, she would send novel dishes from her angrezi kitchen for Feroza and Sultanat – cutlets, puddings, roasts, cakes and ice creams. Feroza found the English fare rather bland but loved the sweetmeats and ice creams.

Nanhi had brought Rani to her mahal and promptly arranged her marriage to the coachman, much to her Buaji's relief. Rani remained her closest friend and confidante, dispensing her wisdom in matters of the household and marriage in general.

On a wintry morning in 1911, Sherpur woke up to the tragic news that the crown prince, Hasan Ali Khan, had passed away after a brief illness at Angrezi Kothi. A state mourning was declared.

Hasan's death brought on Nanhi's first asthmatic attack, the shock clutching at her heart and squeezing the air from her lungs. Mehdi tried to console Nanhi and sent for the doctor. He was himself quite shaken at the loss of a dear friend. He had lived and studied with Hasan for several years. The Nawab rushed to Nanhi and she clung to him gasping, saying that she had killed Hasan. She was not allowed to attend the funeral and lay choking with grief, an oxygen mask helping her to breathe. A devastated

Sultanat went for the funeral and Feroza came to take care of Nanhi.

'Chhoti Ammi, he died because I cursed him. One day, I wanted to go to Rani because she had roasted sweet potatoes on the chulha for me and Hasan wouldn't let me go. He said I shouldn't be friends with poor people or visit their huts. So I said, "May you never become Nawab!"' Nanhi narrated between gasps.

Hasan had blocked her way, refusing to let her meet Rani. Nanhi had slapped him, pushed him and made him stumble. But he had held the doorknob till, frustrated, Nanhi had uttered the fateful words. Feroza had told her that each day there is a time, a mere heartbeat of time, when a prayer is answered – *qubuliyat ka waqt*. This was another prayer she should never have uttered. She had lost her brother, the only person with whom she could lay bare her emotions, laugh with, fight, and even use the cuss words she had overheard.

'It was his destiny, Nanhi. He had been given only a short life,' Feroza sighed.

After the funeral, Nanhi went to live with Sultanat for some time, the two grieving together. She didn't know who whispered it to her first, but somewhere in the corner of her nascent adult mind, the doubt calcified. She knew Daddy was cruel. She remembered little things buried in her subconscious – signs of his cruelty on her mothers, stories half-heard, Chhoti Ammi's swollen face when she lost her child. As Nanhi sat holding Achhi Begum, Hasan's mother, silent in her swathes of white mulmul, she realised with a shock that Achhi Begum's hair had been shaved off. Her scalp was rough with tiny hair sticking out from under the scarf.

Rumours and stories circulated with increasing ugliness and even today echo on the tongues of people. Achhi Begum was often the butt of snide and jealous remarks by the other wives. They would often speak to the Nawab about Achhi Begum's increasing hauteur. They even said that Hasan had told his mother that once he became the Nawab, he would set everything right for her. It is said that Hasan was upset by the ill-treatment of his mother at the hands of the Nawab and the other wives.

'That son of a domni singer is plotting my death!' the Nawab had raged. 'I have two more sons and I can change my crown prince while I live.'

Achhi Begum swore that Hasan was innocent.

'May my son die in forty days if I lie! I swear on the life of my Hasan.'

Forty days after this incident, Hasan was alive and had received honours and recommendations. He was selected to be the Page Boy to His Imperial Majesty at the forthcoming Delhi Durbar in 1911. It was a rare honour. Then Achhi Begum committed a fatal error. She attended the zenana durbar wearing her teeka-jhoomar with aplomb, bowed low before the Nawab and touched her forehead seven times instead of the usual three. Her over-elaborate salam implied that she stood vindicated.

The Nawab was livid at her audacity. He commanded that Achhi Begum be turned into a *kawwa hakni* – a living scarecrow. That very day her hair was shorn and she was dressed in torn clothes. All her jewels and finery were confiscated. The female guards dragged her out of her mahalsara, crying, begging forgiveness, and threw her into a dark room reserved for the lowliest of maidservants. The clothes on her back and an enamel bowl were her only possessions now.

When Feroza came to know of the Nawab's ataab and Achhi Begum's punishment, she implored him for mercy, but the Nawab would not listen. He was seething at the impudence of a mere singer whom he had elevated to the position of a temporary wife and at the scum of a son who was plotting to overthrow him. Feroza had virtually no hold over him. Their marriage was now a festering hell that both wanted to avoid.

Then Hasan took ill. There were whispers in the prayer meetings held at the Imambara for Hasan's health. The women with feverishly circulating rosaries in their fingers, gossiped between prayers that they knew couldn't save the prince.

It is said that the royal physician, Dr Abdurraheem Khan, was called to administer the poison. Also present at the secret meeting was the Nawab's cousin and trusted friend, Mujtaba Khan. Both the gentlemen implored the Nawab to change his mind. The unspeakable deed was not going to be easily overlooked by the British. That very night, Dr Khan fled to Bareilly, leaving his family in Sherpur. He set up his practice there. Mujtaba Khan also fled the same night with his family and settled in Nainital. Their refusal and flight didn't change the fate of the young boy.

Feroza, dressed in simple clothes, her face half-obscured by Tabu's chadar, sneaked out of her mahal one night to Achhi Begum's hovel with Tabu. Only Mahabat Khan knew of this forbidden excursion.

Achhi Begum sat on a jute mat in a dank, windowless room with a small hurricane lamp burning in the alcove. The brick floor was uneven, full of holes and probably home to rats. An enamel tub filled with stale-smelling excretions was placed in one corner. Achhi Begum, already petite, had shrunk to a skeletal state for she was fed only rice water. Her eyes protruded out of the bony sockets as she looked at the visitors uncomprehendingly. She placed her feeding bowl in front of herself. Feroza uncovered her face and said, 'Adab Achhi Begum, it's me, Feroza.'

'Is he dead, my Hasan?'

'No, no. We are praying. May Allah grant him a long life!' Feroza sat down beside her and gathered Achhi Begum into her arms; the stubble on her head grazed Feroza's wet cheeks. Tabu put two parathas and a laddoo in her bowl.

'You eat, Begum. All will be well.' Tabu broke a piece of paratha and put it in Achhi Begum's mouth.

'Begum, please save my son. It's my fault, they can kill me. He's just a child!' she sobbed, the morsel falling out of her mouth. They sat with her for some time, coaxing her to eat and trying to comfort her.

'Feroza Begum, I lied! Hasan said he would make me live like a queen once he became the Nawab. My oath was a lie… and now my son will die.'

As she made her way back to her mahal through the narrow brick lanes with claustrophobic houses for concubines and mutah wives, Feroza knew that Hasan would not live. They all treaded a thin line every day with every word and action.

The prince never lived to perform his illustrious role at the Delhi Durbar.

They brought the *janaza* to the women's quarters for the mothers. The boy with the promise of incipient masculinity on his face lay on the ornate bier. Achhi Begum got reprieve from her hell to witness a greater hell. She was sent back to her mahalsara and her punishment revoked.

Achhi Begum outlived the Nawab. It is said she became blind crying for her son.

The month of Muharram that year echoed with the lament of Hasan's tragic death. Mehdi felt sickened at the Nawab's loud demonstrations of grief for his son at the Muharram meetings. 'Ah, my son, my Hasan!' He moaned, wept and beat his chest. The tragedy of the Karbala massacre of the Prophet's family mingled with his grief over losing his son. Those close to Shams knew his core of religiosity and his desire to do what he deemed was right. In his most violent acts, he believed that he was an instrument of God's will. God wanted him to remove the threat to his life – his crown prince.

As was his practice, the Nawab fasted for all ten days of Muharram. On the tenth day, he led the taziya procession to the burial ground near the Ramganga River. He marched barefoot holding the alam banner of the martyr Hazrat Husain, his back bent, and his face twisted with anguish.

The taziya or *naql* was a resplendent replica of Hazrat Imam Husain's coffin, about twelve feet high, made of wood, gold and silver tissue, carried on the shoulders of the mourners. This was the grand finale to ten days of mourning. Mehdi accompanied the procession barefoot and bareheaded as the rest of the mourners. The nauha singers sang Meer Anees's heart-rending compositions to the hollow beating of hundreds of chests and the firing of infantry guns.

Mehdi detested every step he took, weak from the *faqa*, the essential starvation customary for the mourners. His bare feet were numb and his turban-less head felt frozen with the January evening chill. He flinched at the bite of the occasional pebble. Though it was bitterly cold, his throat was parched and his lips cracked. His rejection of the Shia faith was a reflection of the turmoil between the Shia Nawab and his Sunni subjects. The sense of isolation became more acute during the Muharram rituals as he stood away from the Sunni Pathans in their light-coloured shervanis and felt their eyes on him, his black clothes and his performance of the rituals they rejected.

Sarkar, he is yours.

The ground of the graveyard was frozen wet, with dark trees huddling around, wrapped in a ghostly white mist. It had become deathly dark. The moon hid behind purple clouds, black silhouettes of people with candles and lanterns stood and the sozkhwans' voices cracked with the lamenting marsiya:

'Is waqt sab jahan meri aankhon mein hai siyah,
Logon Khuda ke wastey mujhko batao raah;
Sayyed kidhar tadapta hai, amma kidhar hain aah?
Kis simat hai nabi ke nawasey ki qatalgah?[1]

(Now the whole world lies dark before me,
Oh people! For the sake of Allah, show me the way;
Whence lies the Sayyed (Hazrat Husain) writhing?
Where was the grandson of the Prophet slaughtered?)'

Mehdi's chest constricted. He walked away from the close knot around the Nawab and stood at the edge of the crowd. There would be many more Muharrams, many taziya processions and taziya burials in his life. Someone handed him a glass of sherbet to break his fast.

Mehdi had not visited Nanhi in the zenana for the period of mourning as separation of the spouses was mandatory. He missed his wife, who had turned out to be a simple person bent on making him happy rather than the haughty princess his brothers had warned him about. He loved her little inward gasp of air before she spoke and the hesitant smile that played on her face while gauging his mood. He had often burdened her with his frustrated angst at his situation and she had dealt with it all calmly.

'Nanhi, I can never be a Shia. I tried, but…' They had had the same conversation last year. Nanhi laid her hand on his.

'It doesn't matter. Chhoti Ammi never became a Shia and Ammi just follows all the rituals because she has to as Her Highness. At heart, she is a Sunni too.'

Feroza and Mehdi had assumed that Nanhi was a Sunni, but she identified herself as a Shia and felt the mourning rituals of Muharram justified. Nanhi sympathised with the deep dejection felt by the Shia community. The Shias were friends of Hazrat Ali, cousin and son-in-law of the Prophet, and stood against the mistreatment of the Prophet

Muhammad's family and the usurpation of the Caliphate. She believed that the differences between the two communities were superficial. She tried to reason with Mehdi, but his illogical aversion was too deeply ingrained. It was the same with Chhoti Ammi.

She looked at his body slumped in the chair and longed to pull him back into their life together.

'It's just a few days in a year. Ammi says just pretend and do what is required. Anyway, now Muharram is over. Come, I've made pancakes for you. I learnt to make them from the English cook.' She smiled and pulled at his hand. He took her in his arms and breathed out his anger.

Mehdi often visited Feroza and unburdened his young heart. She understood the root of his anguish. He couldn't reconcile his official duties with his religious conscience. Feroza was deeply sympathetic, but felt helpless. His mind was a battleground raging against his father. He had stopped visiting his parents, barely speaking to his father when he saw him at the court. Feroza tried to persuade him to visit his mother Sumayya Begum and his other relatives.

'They should have thought about it before giving me away. Khala, I have become a joke among my own people. I'm a kept man. I have no family now!'

Another reason for Mehdi not visiting his home was that he couldn't deal with the typical brand of Sherpuri humour at his expense – tongue-in-cheek, snidely critical at the same time. He was no longer their own and felt the estrangement in the way they looked at him.

Every time Nanhi brought up the topic, Mehdi would say, 'Why do they want me now? I don't want to go to Gher Mardan Khan. You go if you want.'

Nanhi tried to compensate by visiting her in-laws often with gifts for everyone, including the servants. Her arrival would be announced in advance and her mother-in-law would busy herself in preparations to receive the princess in a proper manner. Farhat, her sister-in-law, would welcome her loudly and later complain to Sumayya Begum that they loved Nanhi more even though she slaved all day to keep everyone happy. Nanhi's gifts were interpreted as the flaunting of her wealth and position. She remained an outsider, a princess to be attended to with great deference.

Nanhi could feel Mehdi receding from her physically and emotionally as the stresses of court life battered his soul. She would try to cajole him to recapture the first few months of their marriage and their discovery of each other. He would often be preoccupied and irritable but rarely ever raised his voice in anger. Nanhi had expected worse from a husband, as the natural order of things. Bua would often say, 'If your husband won't beat you, whom will he beat? The neighbour's wife?'

Mehdi would relent, come back to her after days of blackness and she would wonder if he did so because she was a princess. The servants reported daily on their conjugal life and Daddy would scan her face asking if she was happy and if Mehdi was kind to her. She was after all his Nanhi, the little one, condemned to diminutiveness.

Notes

1. Meer Anees, *Marsiya*.

A Photograph of the Coronation Durbar (1911)

Two months after Hasan's death, the Grand Coronation Durbar of Emperor George V was held in Delhi on 12 December 1911. A photograph of the coronation procession shows Nawab Shams, seated on a ceremonial elephant with the British Agent. The Nawab, in elaborate robes with his gold *kalghi* on his cap, looks around with his habitual stance of alert surveillance. The gold and silver hauda bears the Sherpur crest, a *chattar* umbrella shields him and the British Agent. Their elephant is caparisoned with gold jewellery – a teeka and gold mesh on its forehead and *goshwaras* hang down his ears; the intricately worked saddle is kept in place by a gold bar at the bottom. Two elephant boys walk along the sides.

At the durbar, where the King Emperor wearing the Imperial crown received homage from native princes, Nawab Shams Ali Khan was awarded the title of the Knight Grand Commander of the Order of the Star of India.

23

Husnara, the Tilism Kusha, Rallies Her Forces

'The wise Ravi and the cup-bearers of wine narrate the grand tale of Tilism-e-Azam and the dastardly Tareek Jaan thus:

Husnara Jadu – the sahira of unsurpassed beauty, wit and sagacity – seeks out allies to defeat Tareek Jaan. She decides to take the help of her cousin sisters, Sadaf and Gulistan.

Princess Sadaf possesses the powerful *Akhtar Marwarid*, the star pearl that could render the most potent spell invalid, heal life-threatening wounds and even produce magical slaves. Sadaf was Husnara's cousin and the mutah wife of Tareek Jaan. She had been forced into marriage by him.

Ah, Gulistan Jadu, what can I say of her, friends. Ten times more beautiful than her aunt Bahar; she had learnt sorcery from Bahar who had laid down her life in the great fight against Afrasiyab. Gulistan Jadu has created an ever-blossoming garden with flowers from all over the universe – *gul daudi*, *gul andaleeb*, *gul-e-rana*, *babuk*, *benafsha*, *gulab*, *gul-e-nargis*, *gul-e-niloufar*, *gul-e-sumbul*; but this was no ordinary garden for the flowers had deadly powers to kill, maim, stun or hypnotise. Like her aunt Bahar, her sorcery lay in the blooming, innocent flowers.

Husnara sends Malti with *sufoof-e-khwab*, the dream powder, to the two sorceresses and that night the three sisters meet in their dreams.

Husnara bursts out, 'Sadaf, Gulistan, I'm the Tilism Kusha! Amar ayyar told me, and Sheesha-e-Jamshedi has confirmed that I will destroy the Tilism-e-Azam and kill Tareek Jaan!'

'What? You, a woman, the Tilism Kusha? I thought only Amir Hamza or his descendants could be the Tilism Kusha,' says Sadaf.

'Maybe the gods have taken pity on us. I'll destroy Tareek Jaan as he has blighted our lives,' Husnara laughs.

'Have you become a Muslim?' asks Gulistan.

'No. But I'm ready to fight alongside the forces of Islam to end this Tilism-e-Azam. Don't you understand, my sweet sisters, that if it is fated that this Tilism-e-Azam will be destroyed by me, I'll go to war and I cannot fight you? You must join me in this fight. Don't you hate Tareek Jaan as much as I do?'

Sadaf's pearl brow is steeped in thought. The battle will shake the nadir of the earth and the zenith of the skies; it could lay waste her father's kingdom and spell her doom. But she had the Akhtar Marwarid which, if used well, might incapacitate the King of Samris. She also desired the destruction of Tilism-e-Azam and to be liberated of her faithless, ignoble husband. It made more sense to be on the side of the Tilism Kusha who was fated to destroy the tilism. So, Sadaf of the pearl power promises her support.

Now hear of Gulistan's predicament. Husnara knows Gulistan is desperately in love with Haroon, a Muslim chieftain in Saad bin Ameer Hamza's army, whom she had met only once in the battle against Afrasiyab. Her father and Tareek Jaan would do everything in their power – even take her life – to prevent the match.

'Gulistan, my darling, only I know of your heart's desire. If you can throw off this yoke of slavery, your father can be persuaded to wed you to Haroon!' Even in her sleep Gulistan blushes like a new flower and agrees to support Husnara.

'Sisters, I'm proud of your daring. Know that you would be called on to make tremendous sacrifices and face untold hardships.'

Tareek Jaan is terrified when his spies and magical mirror tell him that Husnara knows she is the Tilism Kusha and has teamed up with Sadaf and Gulistan. Husnara has conjured up a powerful spell around her palace that even Tareek cannot break.

Amar, meanwhile, takes out his wife Sarsar and their son, Chalak bin Amar from his zambeel. Their son Chalak is also an ayyar trained by his parents. Sarsar is very angry and screams at Amar.

'You want all the glory for yourself. Now you remember us when you nearly got killed!' she fumes.

'Be quiet, woman! Let us think of how to help destroy this tilism,' says Amar, sitting down on a tree trunk.

Chalak stretches out, looking around. He is short and fat – in contrast to his father.

'I'm hungry. I can't think without food. Please get some out from your zambeel, Father,' he pleads.

Amar gives him a slap, and he falls back whining, hand on his cheek.

'*Namurad*! You are thinking of food now. Here take your ayyari weapons and go to the Zulmat Dungeons to rescue all the prisoners there and get Princess Lalarukh's rooh. You will find food there if you like snakes!' Amar hands Chalak the pouch of trickery and magical snare ropes.

'And you, Sarsar, go to the mahalsara of Lalarukh and see what havoc you can create there.'

'Huh! And you, my handsome husband?'

'I'll go to Husnara and get the lauh-e-tilism for her.' Amar blows the whistle and within moments, the slave boys of Husnara led by her maid appear and fly him off to the Feroza Palace of Husnara.

So, our Amar ayyar is in the mehman khana, the guest house of Husnara. He drinks wine from a golden cup and quickly deposits it in his zambeel. Husnara sweeps into the mehman khana, and waves the handmaidens and khwajasara to leave.

Amar stands up and touches his forehead, bowing.

'I learnt the place of the lauh-e-tilism. It is in the stomach of Rohu Mahipusht who lives in the River of Silver Hues. I must get it before they change its place!'

'Ah, that is the only thing I need to destroy this tilism!'

'One more thing – Tareek Jaan is not Afrasiyab's son. He was born out of dust from the grave of Jamshed. And being born of no man he cannot be killed by a man.'

'I knew it! It was whispered that Afrasiyab could not father any child. This confirms that Tareek Jaan will die at my hands – the hands of a woman!'

'I take your leave, Malika, to go on the quest for the lauh-e-tilism,' says Amar bowing.'

Back home, Mirza Kallan rolled into his chador assuming a foetal position on the takht and dozed off in his opium stupor. Waliuddin sat looking at his brother in disgust. The way he was going, there was little prospect of the story being completed. Moreover, there were whispers that Mirza Kallan incited rebellion against the Nawab. But he couldn't leave Kallan at this point in the story. Kallan's grip over the story and its characters was still very strong in spite of his addiction. He remembered all the characters, their backstories, took the dastan into unexpected twists and turns, often injecting couplets in the appropriate places.

Tabu stood behind the bamboo curtain, a worried silhouette, watching as Waliuddin left after keeping the day's earnings on the table and calling out to her. She was just as anxious about the increasing doses of afeem, persuading Kallan with great difficulty to go for the dastan sessions on Thursdays so that they wouldn't starve. Kallan ate very little and most of the time lay in a daze muttering to himself, his dastan fusing into reality.

'Go tell your Feroza Begum that she is the Tilism Kusha. But what can she do? Her soul has been taken away,' he kept saying to Tabu with great urgency.

Tabu sometimes felt that the only thing that was real for him was his dastan. He didn't even care for his unborn child nestling in Tabu's womb, gnawing at her frail frame with pangs of hunger. He had been delighted when she had told him of her pregnancy and talked about his plans for his son's future. But that was just a moment of clarity before the all-numbing afeem. It was after five years of childlessness, prayers and Hakim's medicines that Tabu had finally got pregnant. Bua had advocated the pregnancy in the hope that a child would draw Kallan out of his addiction. She was alarmed at Tabu's scrawny state, often bringing her food and money.

'At least he doesn't beat you. Look at the so-called Begums. They go on foot to his palace and are brought back on stretchers. Even our Feroza lost her child.'

When Tabu was in her seventh month, Bua took her to Feroza's palace for her confinement, knowing that there would never be enough money to feed Tabu who had become skeletal with a huge protruding stomach. Feroza and Bua made her eat ghee, dry fruits and drink strength-giving mixtures from the hakim. Feroza even called the doctor to examine her, much to Bua's consternation.

'Tauba, tauba. A male examining a veiled girl.'

Tabu worried about Kallan. 'He doesn't eat anything till I put roti in his mouth. He's like a child himself,' she would say tearfully, looking at the spread before her.

'You eat! Don't punish your child for that wretch. How will you answer in Allah's court? Eat and rest. Get ready to become a mother,' Feroza told her. Waliuddin had promised to send food for Kallan every day. Their mother was too ill to do anything for him.

Bua would send Mahabat Khan. 'Go and see if that *afeemkhor* is dead or alive,' she would say.

Though he assured Nigar in his dreams that Tabu would never take her place, Kallan missed her quiet sadness, the tinkling of her bangles and her nightly tales of the harem. She had become his cup-bearer, his saqi. The weather was still cold and he longed for her warm body next to him, their child nestling between them, his hand on their hope, delighting at each restless movement in the womb. He wore the sweater Tabu had knitted for him. 'Nigar, you still sit on my head,' he laughed, putting on the cap knitted by Nigar. He had to complete the dastan to earn money for his child and to bring back Tabu. He also needed money for his afeem.

Sherpur State,
30 August 1913

My dearest Sara,

I hope you and your family are in good health. I also hope you are receiving my letters of which I can never be sure. I write with the good news that my Nanhi has been blessed with a son. I long to hold my grandson in my arms, but I'm not so blessed. The very air I breathe has turned poisonous and the doctors have prohibited anyone from entering my room. Nanhi comes every day with the baby in her arms and sits by the door. My only wish is to clasp my darlings in my arms; but I cannot touch my own grandchildren for the disease eating my body.

Mehdi is a very fine boy. He confessed to me that the future religion of his children is a cause of worry. I don't know how to help them. I can't bear it that my grandchildren shall be Shias. I feel so angry just thinking about it. The fever burns me. It seems that my whole life has been a futile struggle.

Diwani keeps telling me, 'Laugh because it's the purest sound; Sing because it's the food the world needs.'[1] Even in this state she makes me sing and it does make me feel better.

Bua attends to me saying she is old anyway and Tabu visits me often even though I scold her. Diwani, of course, refuses to leave her place in my room on the sofa and often sleeps over. She says her body longs to die every day. I'm blessed by their love and devotion for me.

A tragic news – my beloved Abba passed away. He had been ailing for some time and I had sent Bua to beg him to forgive me and to somehow meet me. But he said that I had disobeyed him and had chosen to leave him. Now I will meet him only in death. I have requested Shams to bury me in my family graveyard as per Sunni customs. My sisters and brothers will at least see my dead face. Abba had forbidden them to meet me in life and they feel themselves bound to his will even after his death.

You must have heard about the crown prince's marriage to the daughter of the chief minister, Sir Samad Ghani Khan. It was a forced marriage. Samad Khan never agreed. The Nawab's army surrounded his house while he was out of station for some work and the nikah was performed. Samad Khan is married to the slain regent's daughter, so now the royal bloodline is mixed with the regent's blood. Abba used to say that the royal family has the regent's blood on its hands. He was shot at a few feet from our house. The marriage is designed to wash off the blame and to rally the Pathans behind the bloodline.

My father was also related to the regent. Abba's rejection of our marriage and his flight to Bareilly spoilt the gain it could have brought to Shams. All that is history now. I often think how it would have been if I were an obedient daughter or an amenable wife. Did I tempt fate, or was this always my fate?

The powerful get more glory in this world and their misdeeds go unpunished. But I think they do get caught in the hereafter. I have lost a lot of weight and my body seems to accelerate towards old age. I rarely go to the zenana durbar. The glamour of the court life that I loved so much holds no delight for me.

I hear that Shams grows more unreasonable in his anger. They say it's the heat of the hakim's *kushtas* he eats to increase his virility. Fortunately, he fears my acid tongue and the poisonous air around me. He rarely visits me but enquires about my health daily from the doctor. His fear of darkness and death is such that bulbs are lit all night in his palace. There is no question of an electrical breakdown. Heads would roll, as they say.

Please convey my regards to the Colonel and love to the boys.

I hope we shall meet some day.

I remain forever,
Your friend,
Feroza

Notes

1. Hafez Shirazi

24

Feroza Begum and Nanhi

Sherpur, 1913–17

The Nawab married Babbo Jaan, placed a crown on her head and made the other Begums give 'nazar' to her. She was given the title of Shahana Dulhan. She was not attractive but the star of her fate was in ascendance. She was acquired after a lot of stratagems. The Governor of United Provinces was hand in glove with the Nawab in this kidnapping. Such was the Nawab's power that the British government gave her the title of Her Highness and dethroned Sultanat Ara Begum.

From the private papers of Zaamin Khan,
Haakim Mahal, Sherpur State

Azeezan rushed into Feroza's mahal, pushing aside Mahabat Khan with both hands.

'Hai, hai! Don't stop me today. I have to meet the Begum right now!'

She ran into the veranda with a flurry of her skirts and sat down on the floor with an exhausted thud, clutching her heart.

'Go away, you gossipmonger. The Begum is asleep,' said Bua, getting up from the takht where she was dozing in the pleasant wind from the electric fan – a guilty pleasure.

'May your daughter birth many sons. Give me some water and paan. Hai, hai, I had to come as soon as I heard…' Azeezan settled her scarf with the dull tinsels on her head.

Her deep, rasping voice woke up Feroza.

'Arre Bua, give her some water and send her in,' she called out, raising herself out of bed. She must have come with some important news. Feroza paid her extra to keep track of all that was going on in the zenana. Bua muttered dire threats, called Azeezan some jovial names to which she guffawed, and gave her water. She then opened the silver pandan and busied herself making a basic betel leaf concoction with tobacco.

'Begum, adab! May you birth a hundred sons and grandsons,' Azeezan entered the room, the paan safely tucked into her cheek.

'Hmm, what news?' Feroza propped her face on her palm, turning sideways.

'Arre Begum, our Nawab Sahib is getting married! May my tongue blacken and fall out if I lie.' Azeezan squatted down on the carpet, waving her hands dramatically.

'So what? He does mutah all the time,' Feroza sighed, still lethargic from her mid-afternoon nap.

'Ah, you are too simple, Begum. Nawab Sahib is doing nikah with that woman who sings on your *bhopuu tava*!' All the servants called the newly invented gramophone, bhopuu tava – 'bhopuu', the horn-shaped brass amplifier and 'tava' the black, flat record that looked like an iron skillet.

Feroza sat up. 'Babbo Jaan. That's her name – from Meerut!' Azeezan gave a triumphant clap. At that time the singers announced their names at the end of each record as the recording was done in India but the records were manufactured in Germany.

'Begum, do you remember she came for the Nawab's birthday celebrations? Our Nawab lost his heart. He would have caught her then, but she ran away. When the Nawab sent an invitation to her to sing at Sherpur again, she said – "I will not go to that *murghikhana* (hen coop)!"' Azeezan bit her red-stained tongue, grinning. Bua had also joined them, easing herself on a stool.

'Now you know our Nawab. Whatever he desires he has to get it, and by Allah's grace, he is so intelligent. So he arranged for a soiree at Governor Sahib's place at Moradabad and called many singers. Arre, even the Governor conspired with our Nawab. You know all the angrez respect him so much. So this *haramzadi* (hai, she will be a Begum soon), she came and sang there – such a woman she is. O Bua, give me one more paan. My heart is sinking and my throat is full of thorns.' Bua had come prepared and took out a paan wrapped in the edge of her dupatta. Azeezan carried on, chewing the paan.

'So when the mehfil ended, it was early morning and she was asked to sit in the motor car. It was the Nawab's car. Now look at that witch – she went off to sleep and when she woke up, she was in Sherpur! Our Nawab, may he live a hundred years, had fulfilled his desire!' Azeezan guffawed, her dark eyes dancing with merriment.

Feroza sat up. The Nawab had kidnapped many women and girls but Babbo Jaan was a singer of national fame.

'And listen Begum, this woman is such a shameless, unscrupulous bitch, she said: "I won't get down from the motor till you fulfil my conditions,"' Azeezan paused dramatically, pursing her reddened lips.

'What conditions? Arre, speak up!'

'That the Nawab will make her his nikah wife, crown her as the chief queen and all prisoners be released!' Azeezan counted off the three conditions on her fingers.

'What?'

'And Nawab Sahib has agreed! Hai, hai, now tawaifs will sit with Begums and Begums will bow down and present nazar to the tawaif! Tauba, tauba.' Azeezan beat her cheeks with her palms.

'Oh, you should see her. Allah be my witness – she is blacker than me. Nose and eyes are so-so. She is so short, no bigger than a dwarf and as thin as Tabu. What does the Nawab see in her? I saw her going into Rang Mahal with my own eyes!'

'Put away the bhopuu now, Bibi. We can listen to your Babbo Jaan all the time,' laughed Bua.

'*Main hoon Babbo Jaan, Meerut wali*,' Azeezan imitated in a shrill voice.

Feroza sent off Azeezan with a few coins, her head pounding with the beginning of a headache. She shouted for tea and sent a kahari to call Badamiya. Badamiya confirmed the news and added that the nikah would be performed in the evening. Then there would be a zenana durbar where the new Begum would be crowned. A crown of diamonds was being prepared for her and another ordered for her from the angrez country.

Shahana Begum alias Babbo Jaan, entered the zenana durbar, announced by two female chobdarnis holding silver staffs that they struck on the floor. Chobdarnis were only assigned to the Begum Sherpur and the Nawab. All the Begums stood up, their conditioned response to the chobdarnis' announcement. Sultanat and Feroza remained seated in their assigned places to the right and left of the royal throne. They stood up when the Nawab was announced, watching his triumphant grin as he accompanied his new wife. Feroza, though ill and mostly confined to her mahal, had decided to attend the durbar out of curiosity rather than compulsion.

To say Babbo Jaan was ordinary-looking would be an understatement. She was petite, as Azeezan had said, and dark in a world where light complexion was an important claim to beauty; her only claim to any measure of attractiveness were her dark arched brows over a pair of glittering coal-black eyes and a generous mouth which could twist into a disapproving sneer or a sensuous pout.

She wore several necklaces, the teeka and jhoomar struggled to find a place on her small head; a large nath circled her cheek, and earrings hung down to her shoulders. The maid holding her farshi skirt revealed heavy anklets, weighing about two sers on each foot, impeding movement. She walked slowly, her defiant eyes sweeping the scene, taking in the Begums touching their foreheads, seeking out and gauging the importance of each person.

The salam done, the Begums straightened up, not daring to whisper, pinned by the Nawab's eyes. The mirasans struck their congratulatory song as the Nawab reached his throne. He paused in front of Sultanat Ara standing to the right of his throne and said curtly, 'Begum, you take your seat there.' He pointed towards the left of the throne where Feroza stood. 'Next to Feroza Begum.'

Sultanat Ara stood rooted to the spot. It seemed as though everyone had stopped breathing. Daroghan Chhamman stepped forward quickly and escorted the dispossessed Begum Sherpur to the left of the throne. A power shift had taken place as Shahana Begum sat down, making sure that every pleat of her skirt was in place. Two maids fussed around her, settling her on her takht.

Sultanat walked towards Feroza, stony-faced, her head high. Feroza thought of moving away, giving up her seat; Sultanat looked at her and gave her head an imperceptible shake. She didn't want pity. The humiliation was hers to suffer at every single durbar. Kindness would make it worse. She sat next to Feroza, third in the pecking order now.

The Nawab sat down under his canopied throne and asked the Daroghan to begin the proceedings. Daroghan

Chhamman proffered a diamond-encrusted crown which he put on the head of the new queen where it sat large and incongruous.

'Shahana Dulhan is Her Highness Begum Sherpur now. All the Begums will give nazar to her,' declared the Daroghan.

The Nawab smiled and took his seat. Sultanat Ara was handed a gold coin to present as nazar to the new Begum Sherpur. Sultanat performed the task with great dignity. Feroza followed her. The Daroghan noted down the amounts in a register as all the Begums in order of precedence and other relatives paid their respects.

Sultanat Ara Begum had suffered much, followed the expected patterns and had been rewarded with children from other wives. After all these tribulations, she was unceremoniously divested of her position. She could not sleep for days as every durbar brought fresh indignity to the proud Begum. Shahana Begum took over the zenana durbar and the Imambara. She was a staunch Shia and Muharram majlis at the Imambara was now even more resplendent. She sang the nauha with such painful beauty that Feroza attended the majlis just to hear her melodious lament.

The Nawab's new Begum and the heartbreak it caused to Sultanat, emphasised the limits of Nanhi's relationship with her father. After Nanhi's marriage, there was a distancing in her relationship with her Daddy. She had never been open and frank with Daddy anyway. She was always gauging his moods, choosing her words to please him and seeking his approbation. His raging temper towards others had always petrified her yet she craved for the grandeur of his love.

Now there were new boundaries in spite of the deep love they shared. She was terrified of the power Shahana Begum had over her father and was disturbed by her own helplessness at the humiliation faced by her mothers. As was her nature, Nanhi avoided trouble and treaded around

Shahana Begum with great care and courtesy. The insincerity of her words and her disloyalty towards Sultanat filled her with anxious guilt. Nanhi was rarely herself – she was always bound by the relationships and decorum of court life.

Nanhi listened daily to Mehdi's accounts of injustices meted out to the people and became aware of the excessive cruelty of the Nawab's despotic rule. Mehdi said that the Nawab could get away with anything because he had supported the British Empire by sending troops, horses and the Sherpur Lancers contingent to Egypt during the World War. Moreover, he was helping the British in reining in the nationalist movement among Muslims.

The Nawab, according to him, cared little for Rohilla sardars. He had changed the Nawabi covenant in 1917 to give more powers to the crown, curtailing the rights of the Sardars. The stipends to family members were subject to the pleasure of the Nawab. A spate of letters to the British Agent protesting against the withdrawal of pensions were disregarded by the British Agent. Mehdi riled about the offhanded way the Nawab spoke to him at times and lived in daily fear of public humiliation. He was bound to the court because of his marriage and the position granted to his father and brother. At times, it took everything to quell the urge to storm out of the durbar. The withheld rage would then burst out at home and poison his family life.

Nanhi kept herself busy with her two sons, the expanding household and her official duties. In the quiet afternoons, she would speak her mind to Rani and ponder over her advice. She felt she was balanced over a precipice.

25

Chalak bin Amar in the Zulmat Dungeons and the Grand Battle with Afreet Djinn

'Bahar, I'll call her Bahar,' Mirza Kallan smiled.

'Mashallah, what a fortunate name. I hope Bahar brings good fortune to your home,' Waliuddin hugged Kallan.

'It was a very difficult labour and we thought we would lose the mother and the child. But Feroza Begum sent for the angrez doctor. Allah be praised, they are fine now, though Tabu is weak and the child is very tiny. She looks like your Nigar,' Amma smiled.

'Kallan Bhai, how about some mithai?' said Waliuddin.

'I will send mithai. Tabu's mother sent some with me when I went to see Bahar. Now Kallan, Tabu has to rest and will come after her *chilla* bath forty days later. Only then you can hold your daughter to your chest.'

Amma was happy even though she had hoped for a son who'd have been a support for Kallan. More children would come, though looking at Tabu's pale face she feared for her.

'Now you have the responsibility of a daughter on you, mend your ways, Kallan. If Maula wishes, you will have sons too. Give up your bad habit and start earning; you have to provide for Bahar,' said Amma before leaving.

Kallan and Waliuddin distributed sweets at the dastan session in the gher that day. Kallan glowed with the felicitations from the host and listeners. He felt a surge of energy, a great desire to hold his little family close. As usual, there was a good gathering at the dastan session and Waliuddin was happy that the story was drawing to a close.

The weather had become warm and the courtyard had been sprayed with water to cool it down. A new *ghara* with a garland of fresh mogra flowers around its neck was kept at one side of the takht, the fragrance of the flowers lending a sweetness to the air. The white sheet on the takht also bore a basketful of mogra flowers. Mirza Kallan was filled with deep thankfulness and hope as he stirred his afeem and began the dastan with a *hamd* in praise of Allah instead of the usual saqinama:

'*Karoon hamd khallaq-e-aasman, khuda-e-tilismat ku-o-makan;*
Wo ek kalima-e-kun mein bandha tilism, har ek shakl ko de diya usne jism;
Nahin koi duniya mein uska nazeer, muheet-e-aala kulley shae qadeer.[1]

(I praise thee, O Lord of the universes, the devisor of magical cities;
With one word he created the magic of life and bestowed us faces and bodies;

There is none that can compare with him, he encompasses
and rules all.)'

Our Chalak, Amar's son, sets off whistling, plodding along with the mission of feeding himself. In the bazaar of Tilism-e-Azam, he sits down to eat two tandoori murgh, one plate of fish curry, two *bater* birds, twenty kababs, ten nans, one big *matka* of kheer, one bowl of carrot halwa, one bowl of habshi halwa, twelve laddoos and twelve gulab jamuns. Then, patting his huge belly and burping ten times, he starts thinking about getting to the Zulmat Dungeons to recover Lalarukh's rooh. Listening to the bazaar talk he comes to know that Tareek Jaan is looking desperately for Amar. So Chalak quickly hides in an alley and using the paints of trickery, changes himself into an image of his father. As he creeps out of the alley, pretending to hide behind a shop, a hovering putli sees him and flies screeching, 'Amar ayyar is here! Catch Amar ayyar!'

Two magical claws swoop down, catch him by his forearms and he is flying off over the red river and pul-e-shamsheer to the castle of Tareek Jaan.

Tareek Jaan is delighted. 'Ha, Amar ayyar, you thought you could escape so easily. Bind him in chains and put him in the iron cage! Now, you will taste the ecstasy of the Zulmat Dungeons before I execute you!'

He claps his hands and twelve khabbeeses fly into the palace and Chalak is taken to the blackest of black mountains of the Zulmat Dungeons. The great pythons guard the mouth of the cave, hissing and raring their heads.

Aaseb bin Afreet, the son of Afreet and the keeper of the dungeons, steps out and brays, 'Wait till you go in, you scoundrel!' His ram head with curved horns and elongated yellow pupils dance with delight. He claps and the stone door of the dungeon opens up.

Aaseb hangs the cage on one hoof-like hand, effortlessly swinging and banging it on the blood-drenched walls as he walks into the dungeons, his other hand bearing a lamp to light up the horrors of the dark dungeons.

'None can escape my dungeons alive! Even death is scared of coming here. See all these cages. They were sorcerers who dared defy Khudawand Tareek Jaan.' There are hundreds of sorcerers, djinns and humans hanging in cages. Aaseb hangs Chalak's cage with snakes coiling beneath, their hoods spread out, ready to strike.

Chalak wails, 'I'm not Amar, I promise, by my god. I've been tricked. Release me and my seven generations will serve Tareek Jaan, I swear!'

Aaseb bleats with laughter, his eyes glowing red in the semi-darkness and throws a scorpion at Chalak. 'You will pray for death and death will not come.' Chalak screeches and tries to catch the scorpion.

Aaseb laughs and leaves and the dungeon is dark as the grave.

May Allah save us from the torments of the grave! Snakes are slithering over Chalak's body, tiny leeches cover his face, sucking his blood. He feels them with his hands, tries to get up screaming and falls back from the shackles on his hands and feet.

'Keep still and the snakes won't bite,' says a guttural voice. Chalak stops screaming, sits still, not breathing till the snakes slither away. Sitting before him in another cage is a bent, skeletal old man, dressed in tattered robes and his eyes shining with a strange light in the dark gloom.

'I'm Chalak bin Amar,' says Chalak, picking leeches from his cheeks.

'Chalak bin Amar!' The old man stands up in his cage, his shackles jangling.

'He has come! Chalak is here!' screams the other man. The old man starts sobbing tearlessly for his tears have dried up. Soon there are more voices echoing in the darkness, 'Chalak bin Amar has come!'

'Chalak, it is destined that you release us from this dungeon. I read that in the Book of Samri before I was imprisoned. I'm Rafey, the chief magician at Tareek Jaan's court. I dared to defy him when he asked me to submit my daughter and bow before him.'

'But what can I do?'

'Have courage, you'll find a way.'

The news spreads in the dungeons.

'Don't forget the souls of harem-dwellers,' a young girl in a cage whispers.

'Where are they?'

'The souls are trapped in parrots, *mynahs*, *bulbuls*, kept in the deepest parts of the Zulmat Dungeons. They are the women, djinns and paries who were kidnapped and kept in the harem of Tareek Jaan. Their bodies are enslaved to him,' she says.

A huge dev, his face ugly and mottled with a rough beard, dressed in a rhinoceros hide, lumbers in bearing a tray with a stack of rotis and a bowl.

'He is the feeder. He gives us food when we are half-dead,' says Rafey.

The dev stops near Chalak's cage and says, 'Ah, Amar ayyar, eat all you want because your execution is tomorrow.' He sets down the tray and opens Chalak's cage with a bunch of keys.

'Hai, hai, my seven generations will serve Tareek Jaan. Please forgive this stupid slave. I will die,' he cries, beating his breast theatrically.

'Enough now! I have brought some salan and roti. Don't die or faint; it will spoil the fun.'

Chalak sniffs, eyes the shorba and says, 'How can I eat? You have chained my hands.'

'Okay, I'll remove the chains for some time. You calm down.' The dev takes another key from the bunch, bends and with his torso half in the cage, opens Chalak's handcuffs, patting him almost affectionately. Chalak smiles, takes out a vial of sufoof-e-behoshi, the anaesthetic powder, and throws the powder on the dev's face. The dev staggers back, sneezes and falls down like a large tree, unconscious.

Chalak quickly climbs out of the cage, takes the bunch of keys and unlocks Rafey's cage and shackles. Rafey embraces Chalak, and they start opening other cages. Men, women, parizads, sorcerers, sorceresses tumble out of the cages embracing and laughing. Ah, what a sight it is!

Chalak goes to the deepest end of the cave where he sees several birds in cages hanging from the roof. He looks around in confusion.

'Where is Lalarukh?'

Chalak goes from cage to cage asking for Lalarukh till they find a green and purple bird sitting with her feathers puffed up, eyes closed, beak buried in her chest.

'Lalarukh?' asks Chalak and the bird opens her glazed eyes. Chalak knows he has found Lalarukh.

Chalak carries the cage and Rafey tells him, 'You have to hurry and put the soul of Lalarukh back in her body before the bird dies. Then her soul will go away forever. Only Zaroon knows the magic of soul transfer here. He will help you.'

'It can be done but we have little time and we need to fly. Let's free the djinns now,' says Zaroon. And they mutter the chants to free the djinns.

Rafey holds up his arms and addresses them. '*Ya djinn o djinns*! Take heed that Afreet will be here with his offsprings, Aaseb and Tez Chashm and thousands of his clans and their armies. Are you ready to fight for your freedom?'

'We are yours to command,' says the most terrible of the djinns.

Rafey throws an enchanted iron ball that blows open the rock door and they are blinded by the scorching sun of the desert. Standing there is the army of Afreet djinn!

Ah, what can I say of the terrible battle that raged for days, the flaming thunderstorms that lit up the skies, the lakhs of sorcerers, sorceresses, parizads and djinns that died. Rafey and the sorcerers had little at their command, their magic was weak, their instruments – globes, staffs and swords – had been taken away from them. Husnara sends Sadaf with her Akhtar Marwarid pearl to heal Rafey and his army.

Then Afreet flies up to Sadaf, his terrible third eye red with anger and Sadaf shines the pearl on his eye. His scream shakes the seven heavens as his most potent eye burns and he falls down covering his jackal face with hoof hands, red and purple flames erupting all over his body. Afreet, the greatest of djinns, the favourite of *shaitan*, dies a terrible death. The lascar of Afreet led by Aaseb is now in flight as their leader burns in everlasting hell.

A roar of 'Ya Samri! Ya Laat!' rises in the air as the sorcerers celebrate their hard-won freedom.

Sadaf cries, 'Join hands with the Tilism Kusha, Husnara Jadu, to destroy the oppression of Tilism-e-Azam!' And so the cry of rebellion grows stronger.

We leave the sorcerers to their preparations and now a few words about Lalarukh and her rooh. Chalak, bearing the cage of Lalarukh's soul, flies on the back of a djinn accompanied by Zaroon on his djinn. Meanwhile, Sarsar had entered the harem of Tareek Jaan. 'I'm Sarsar, wife of Amar ayyar. Don't worry, help is near,' Sarsar whispers to Lalarukh.

Suddenly, a powerful gust of wind blows around Lalarukh's palace as Zaroon swoops down to put a spell on all the inhabitants. The maids and the khwajasaras fall down in a dead faint. Even the spy birds doze off on the branches. Even Huzur Afat and Tez Chashm fall asleep – so powerful was the spell. Sarsar's paints of trickery dissolve and she faints at Lalarukh's feet. Chalak and Zaroon descend into the garden and make their way to the bedchamber.

Chalak tells Zaroon that the lady lying at the feet of Lalarukh is his mother, Sarsar. Zaroon snaps his fingers and Sarsar wakes up. He then asks Sarsar to uncover Lalarukh's right thigh and plunges a dagger into it. Blood, red and blue, sprouts out of the pearl-white thigh and Zaroon, taking out the dying bird, bathes it in the blood. He then takes the bird to Lalarukh's lips and squeezes its neck. A pure white whiff of smoke flies out of its beak and Zaroon quickly prises open Lalarukh's mouth and the smoke wafts in.

Lalarukh opens her eyes with a cry and sits up, looking around, disoriented. She touches the glowing teeka-e-yaqut on her forehead and is stunned. She now remembers every day, every event that took place in the vile harem of Tareek Jaan. She is filled with revulsion and shame at the way her body had been abused and traumatised. She had even forgotten her beloved Saad.

'Ah! Of what use is this body that has shamed me, lain wanton in the arms of Tareek?'

Sarsar says, 'Princess, you had no soul and your body was controlled by powers beyond you. Your soul is as pure as snow. Allah knows all and is most merciful.'

'We now have to return the souls of other harem-dwellers in the secrecy of the night before the birds die; or these women would be left soulless all their lives,' says Zaroon, flying away with Chalak. Zaroon goes from room to room where the women and paries lived in pathetic conditions, at the bidding of Tareek, going to him when they were summoned. He restores their souls with the help of Sarsar. They are all strictly warned to not exhibit any suspicious behaviour and to go about their work as they did before. Only now they had hope of deliverance.

Tareek, hearing of the death of Afreet in the great battle, immediately crowns Sahiba domni as his chief queen with great pomp and show to humiliate Husnara. He makes all his wives bow before Sahiba and present nazar to her. Ah, such is fate that the unworthy enjoy crowns and high status and the daughters with noble Pathan blood are treated like chattel!'

Kallan drains the dregs of the afeem. He sits long after the dastan is over, talking, smoking with his host, not wanting to leave the warmth of the assembly for his dismal home.

Notes

1. Abul Faiz Faizi, *Laal Nama*, vol. 2.

26

Ameera

Sherpur, 2016

Maybe they felt guilty, but when I asked for permission to visit Sonia on Diwali, they agreed to let me go there for the whole day. I suspect Dadi counselled them to be a bit relaxed. I was beyond happy. I hadn't met Sonia in ages. She had just shifted to her new house in Civil Lines.

I fall in love with Sonia's compact little duplex flat with the huge windows letting in the winter sun and the bedrooms leading out into plant-filled balconies. Sonia and Chhoti, her little sister, have their own rooms on the first floor – so cosy and private. Her father lives on the ground floor. Sonia lost her mother when she was six and her father takes care of the girls with great devotion, even cooking their favourite dishes. I can't imagine Abba in the kitchen. If Ammi is ill, he merely tells Bua what to cook – that's the extent of his home duties.

The Hindu neighbourhood in Civil Lines is cleaner, the drains are covered up. There are no offensive butcher shops with swarms of flies and naked pieces of meat hanging like banners. Sonia's dad has prepared a feast in my honour – paneer and veg pulao. We decide to walk to Café Coffee Day (CCD) for cold coffee and brownies. They have only recently opened a CCD there. A number of swanky food joints have come up at what used to be Shahbad Gate – Pizza Place, Food Plaza, Baker's Hut. We only used to have Rainbow Biscuits a few years ago. The owners of Rainbow Biscuits claimed that Nawab Shams had sent their grandfather, Irshad Khansama, to Paris to learn baking.

The old Shahbad Gate has been replaced by a new arched gateway made in a pretend-old style. It ends up looking like an incongruous backdrop to the smart shops. I relish each step on the pedestrian path in the mild winter sun. There is no Meel trailing behind me on his rickety cycle.

'They are breaking down the old Sherpur Club. Do you want to watch?' Sonia says as we sit sipping cold coffee with ice cream. I know that Sherpur Club had been fenced off and put behind a turquoise blue metal sheet purdah before the final destruction. What you cannot see is soon forgotten. Dadi told me that the Sherpur Club had been built by Nawab Shams around the time he had married Feroza Begum. It was one of the first buildings he had constructed to entertain British officials and Indian princes. Dadi says Dada used to go every evening to play poker and billiards. At the end, right before the veiling, there were four old fogies with one lone bulb charged by a battery hanging over the card table; the electricity had been cut off due to non-payment of dues. I have a vague memory of a new year party in the lawns and climbing over the twin lion statues standing guard on either sides of the staircase.

There is a gap in the metal sheets and we watch two yellow cranes gash at the club's triangular capital. It was a very Roman-looking building. The walls are still painted salmon pink and white. There is debris all over the front lawns. I can see the front hall now where the old men used to sit bent over their cards.

'What will they do with the lions?' I look at the two lions painted in bright yellow enamel paint by some eager bureaucrat.

'Probably they will be taken to the minister's house and stand guard there.'

'Nisaar main teri galiyon ke ae watan, ke jahan,
Chali hai rasm ke koi na sar utha ke chaley,
Jo koi chahne waala tawaaf ko nikley,
Nazar chura ke chaley, jism o jaan bacha ke chaley.[1]

(I sacrifice my life to your alleys, beloved nation where,
Custom now dictates that none walk with head held high,
And if at all a lover walks a pilgrimage of love,
He needs to lower his eyes, guard his body and life.)'

Dadi recites when I tell her about the club.

Things speeded up after they brought down the club. Part of the club garden was used as a sort of recreation area of the Mahatma Mall. A few days later, Abba's case was dismissed after the first hearing and his land was acquired by the government. At least my fees for the whole year was paid up from the handsome compensation – three times the market price. I watched Abba's shops being broken down on the way home from school; swallowed up by the sprouting double-storeyed Mahatma Mall; the glass windows glinted in victory. The tenants had wrapped up their wares in cartons and taken them away on carts and rickshaws. The statue of Mahatma Gandhi was taken away from the Gandhi Memorial. It looked too diminutive there.

Money put a happy sheen on everything, including the lichen-streaked walls. Abba bought Pakistani chiffon suits for Ammi and me. I chose the green one because I know

Abba wanted Ammi to wear pink. Naved Chacha persuaded Abba to let Ammi visit Jugnu with him. Ammi was calmer after the visit and spoke of sending Jugnu to Aligarh Muslim University for a course in the polytechnic department.

Though my performance at the half-yearlies was dismal, Abba refused to send me for tuitions to prepare for the finals. Ammi and Dadi tried to persuade him. Maybe he will agree next year. I'll definitely need help for the Boards. Shiv Sir is helping me out during school hours and Sonia gives me her tuition notes. Sonia says they promote nearly everyone to Class XII. Okay, even if I get there, how will I ever get through the entrance tests for med schools without tuitions? I don't even know if I want to be a doc. Actually, I don't know what I want to become, or if I would be allowed a 'becoming'. Most of the motivational articles I read talk of imagining success in your mind and creating your own realities. I feel caught in the realities around me. They can never change or give way to my version.

Notes

1. Faiz Ahmad Faiz, *Nuskha Hai Wafa*, p. 161.

Bhowali Sanatorium,
25 May 1918

My dearest Sara,

I hope and pray that your family is in good health and abundance. I write to congratulate you on the marriage of John and Elizabeth. Please convey my best wishes to the young couple. May they be happy in the union and be blessed with many children.

My Nanhi is now a mother of three sons and happy in her life. I watch the boys play in the courtyard and hear them laughing. Right now, I'm at the Bhowali Sanatorium, for a month of treatment. My disease is progressing and I know that I don't have much time. I do feel better with the medicines and the cough has improved. The medicines and care will only prolong a meaningless life. You will hardly recognise me. I look so old and thin - Allah wants me to suffer old age in my thirties.

Tabu is having trouble in her marriage. Her husband, though a talented dastango from a respectable family, is an opium addict. He cannot provide for her and their daughter. I have given her employment in my mahalsara and she has come with me to Bhowali. Both of us sisters are cursed with unhappy marriages.

Shams is spending the summer at his palace in Nainital with Shahana Begum. You must have heard about her elevation as 'Her Highness'. The British Government has recognised her as Her Highness Begum Sherpur, dethroning Sultanat Ara. Sultanat Ara's stepbrother, Nawab Ibrahim of Basoda, appealed against the decision but was rejected.

Shahana Begum who was Babbo Jaan, a mere tawaif, rules over us. She makes the Begums, even Sultanat Ara, stand in front of her waiting for her acknowledgement of their salam. This only reveals her mean birth. She holds the zenana durbar with such arrogance that I can't bear to attend. I often excuse myself pleading ill-health. Allah has his way of punishing the haughty. Azeezan tells me that the hakim has declared that she will never bear children. But Shams continues to be besotted by her.

My heart goes out to Sultanat Ara. She was a wonderful mother to my Nanhi, though I was so jealous of her. It is because of her influence that Nanhi has turned out to be a very dignified and balanced woman. Nanhi tells me that Sultanat Ara barely sleeps or eats because of the daily insults heaped on her. She's a proud, quiet person and this is hard on her.

Shahana Begum is a staunch Shia and she holds majlis (prayer meetings) for forty days during Muharram. Her voice, when she sings the mournful songs, is so beautiful that I can't help crying. May Allah forgive me. I go just to hear her sing.

Nanhi has to attend all sessions and so does Mehdi. I tell them to seek atonement from Allah later. Diwani starts chanting Hafez's lines when she sees Nanhi – 'Run, my dear, from anything that may not strengthen your precious budding wings.' Maybe her recitation is prophetic. I pray that in some way my children can escape this place and live their lives practising the true faith. Only this desire of somehow delivering them from this hell keeps me alive.

Sometimes I think things would have been different if I had pretended to accept the Shia faith, given birth to a crown prince or if I had been a tolerant wife. Shams did love me initially. My life was destined to be as brief as a firefly's – that's what, Diwani says, the life of a harem woman is like. I didn't even enjoy my shining and now I await darkness.

I get tired easily now and this is a long letter. These things close to my heart I can share with you. Your letters are a source of great comfort for me even though they are rare. You can write to me at the Sanatorium. I'm here for a month and then another two months at Rose Cottage nearby. Please pray for Nanhi and her family.

I remain your ever-loving friend,
Feroza

27

Feroza Begum

Sherpur, 1920

> I examined Begum Sahiba for the first time on the 11th with Dr Rahman and found symptoms and signs indicating advanced tuberculosis disease in both lungs. As far as I can judge, there is hardly any chance of her recovery. Her disease is far too gone.
>
> Dr R.K. Kakkar,
> 27 April 1920, Bhowali Sanatorium

Lying in her deathbed, Feroza scrapes at her old wounds, drums up the anger and the humiliation when he first hit her. Her mouth filled with blood like it does so often now. She had lost the baby and her pride. Her sense of self had started unravelling then, the fabric had worn out with the onslaughts over the years, but she had gathered it all to herself with her characteristic stubbornness. She had kept alive the memories of the molestation of her body and soul, lining them up, reliving them and preserving their freshness over the years. She felt free and fearless like Diwani Begum – there was nothing more he could do to her. Finally, her illness banished him from her bed and later, her home.

Though he took good care of her, providing her the best medical care, she could never forget or forgive. Shams was moved by pity at her state and lavished all the care on her that his money could provide. He delighted in her dependence and weakness, loved to be the all-powerful benefactor searching for a grateful look in her eyes. Sometimes he missed their fiery sparring and the occasional lovemaking. She has lost the battle and he would go on living.

Feroza could feel the life ebbing out of her as she stayed up the night coughing blood and losing weight steadily. The doctor had advised another trip to Bhowali Sanatorium and arrangements were being made for the journey. The fire of anger, her greatest scourge, now kept her alive and her fevered brain was ignited with unrealistic stratagems. She owed it to her daughter's family, trapped in this unholy hell, to somehow engineer their deliverance. Like her father, she could never let go of justified anger or a sense of betrayal.

The world, according to her, was balanced on the premise of fate as a result of actions and humans as instruments of justice. Allah would punish Shams in the hereafter but he should feel the pain of losing a treasured child in this life. Diwani had emerged from one of her shattering headaches and told her that she had a vision – Nanhi was travelling in a hilly region with her family. Maybe it was oracular.

She sent word through Azeezan that she wanted to meet Sultanat Ara before leaving for Bhowali. They hadn't met for a long time. Feroza rarely attended the zenana durbar. Her ego forbade her to stand before a tawaif and wait for her to accept her salam. She spent her time reading dastans from the State Library. She particularly liked Kallan Mirza's dastans. As usual, her day flowed around Nanhi's visit with her boys. Nanhi, seated at her bedroom door, would talk to her for hours. It was not expected that Sultanat Ara with her higher position would take the short walk to Feroza's mahal to enquire about her health. She sent polite enquiries through Nanhi.

Feroza sat at a distance from Sultanat Ara after bowing with courtly courtesy. Both were aware that the private meeting would be reported. It might be overlooked, for it was permissible to visit a dying invalid at least once. Bua and Tabu guarded the door.

'Your Highness…' began Feroza.

'I'm no longer that.'

'For me, you will always be Her Highness, Begum Sherpur. I don't have much time left. I can't thank you enough for your many kindnesses. You are such a wonderful mother to Nanhi and I will leave the world content in the knowledge that you will always be with her.' Feroza paused and Sultanat could hear her wheezing breath.

'May Allah grant you health and life,' she murmured.

'My greatest concern is Nanhi and her happiness. She can never be happy with Mehdi if she lives here. She has to go away,' Feroza's voice was a rasp.

'Feroza Begum, how is this ever possible? The Nawab would never allow it.'

'Mehdi will leave her. He said so. He is too proud to continue living like this.'

'What can we do? I also suffer every day.'

Her words were spiritless whispers in the opulent drawing room, her eyes darted around fearful, lest the words take life and escape the room.

'How can you tolerate it? You are the Princess of Basoda. That woman is not even dust beneath your feet!' Feroza collapsed back into the sofa, coughing.

'Feroza Begum, don't agitate yourself. Allah will find a way,' Sultanat handed her a glass of water.

Feroza gulped the water and said, 'Allah will only help you if you try. Or you will die in humiliation here.' Sultanat Ara sat silent.

'Why don't you write to your brother? Tell him of your suffering and maybe he can find a way...'

'I'm not free to write to my brother. Besides, I have barely met him a few times since my marriage.'

'Yet he cares for you and tried to fight your case when the government took away your title. I can send the letter from Bhowali. He can call you to Basoda on some pretext and you can take Nanhi and Mehdi with you.' Feroza was ablaze and Sultanat was propelled into her mission.

The idea of taking Sultanat's help was playing on her mind ever since Tabu had narrated the episode of Husnara teaming up with the other wives of Tareek Jaan. Diwani had also advised her to take Sultanat Ara into confidence. Feroza truly believed that Diwani was imbued with prescient wisdom after her headaches – she was a pure soul. Maybe her vision would become a reality and Nanhi would escape.

Sultanat returned to her palace thoughtful. The dethroning was a deep wound that was wrenched open every time she was forced to attend the durbar, every fresh humiliation widening its serrated edges. If Mehdi had threatened to leave Nanhi, he would. He wasn't the kind to issue idle threats.

Nawab Iftikhar of Basoda was her stepbrother. He was around her age and they had been pretty close as children. Though she was the daughter from a 'secondary wife' Sagheeran Bai, Iftikhar had always been kind to her. Her marriage and position had elevated her status. Moreover, Iftikhar was a typically proud Pathan who would answer her plea. He had tried to save her. She wrote to her brother.

Feroza went for a long stay at the Bhowali Sanatorium in April 1920 to get some relief from her persistent cough and fever. Nadira, her stepdaughter from Munni Begum, went with her along with Tabu and Bua. Nadira was very fond of Feroza and had been drawn into her orbit of love since childhood. She looked after Feroza and wrote to her father in detail about Feroza's condition. Nawab Shams had stationed the revenue minister at Bhowali to send a daily telegram reporting her condition – temperature, food intake, cough and sleep pattern. Shams sent his personal doctor, Dr Ansari, with injections imported from England to make the Begum better.

In a handwritten note, the Nawab wrote to the revenue minister:

'*Very pleased to hear from Dr Ansari about the marked improvement in the patient's condition. Please tell her from my side that she should stay in Bhowali for the whole season… Good ghee will be sent from here twice a week. If the cook cannot make sweets, another can be sent… You can take Rose Cottage for hire.*'

Feroza saw her father in her dream. Then he became a constant presence in her room, often sitting in the armchair or on her bed near her feet bowed over his walking stick, waiting. Feroza had heard from old people that when a person is nearing death, he starts seeing visions of his dead ancestors.

She was comforted by his presence and spoke to him of her worries for Nanhi and how she had to ensure her escape before she died. Abba never replied, just looked at her thoughtfully. His expression only softened into a smile when she told him of Nanhi's sons. She knew he had forgiven her but was too proud to say so.

Feroza's condition became critical in May and she insisted on returning to Sherpur to live out her last days with Nanhi and her grandchildren. She also craved Diwani's songs and quotes. Shams made the arrangements for her return. They awaited her death and she awaited news from Basoda. If only she could be reassured that Nanhi had a future.

Nanhi moved to the room next to hers with Najaf, her youngest, leaving the older sons with Rani. Rani brought them every day to say salams; Haider, the eldest, enquiring about her health in a very proper way. Nanhi sat at the door, longing to hold her mother through the restless nights. She watched the nurse and Bua trying to ease Feroza's pain as though a drama was unfolding in front of her.

She recited all the prayers she knew – Shia, Sunni, Christian and to Rani's powerful Hindu gods. All night she lay listening to her mother's cough, the wheezy drone of her snores when she fell into exhausted sleep, her delirious talks to Abba and her cries for Gauhar. Was it good to pray for death and deliverance? The slow lingering death in the house had taken its toll on everyone. Even the boys didn't play in the courtyard, but sat quietly biding time till they were allowed to go.

Nanhi sent word to Gauhar, imploring her to come and see Feroza for the last time. But Gauhar, a dependent widow, living with her brothers and bound by the common will of their father, was helpless.

'*Main bulata to hoon usko magar ae jazba-e-dil*
Uspey ban jaye kuch aisi ke bin aaye na bane.[1]

(I call out to her with longing but what can I say,
May her heart struck with desperation, compel her to come.)'

Feroza sighed and shook her head – Gauhar would now only see her in death.

Sometimes, Feroza was seized with terror at the thought of the grave, remembering *azaab-e-qabr*, the torments of the grave narrated by Abba – the creatures with long nails gashing at the sinners, the worms eating her flesh and the fire of hell scalding her remains.

'Ya Allah, forgive my sins; Abba, forgive your daughter!' she would chant, begging forgiveness from all who came to visit her. Shams came to see her from afar, a handkerchief held to his nose.

Feroza looked at him for a long while and said, 'Shams, I forgive you.'

She severed the last tie with the man who had ruled her destiny.

Preparing for death, she turned back to the rigid religious practices advocated by Miya Jaan Khan. The prayers at specified times and the ablutions calmed her; the world classified into pure and impure, the faithful and heathen, made things simpler. She tried to keep herself pure, *paak*, but the incessant cough would cause the urine to dribble out. She would wash and change with Tabu's assistance. The daily business of living exhausted her. She worried if she would be bathed properly after her death – made paak for the hereafter.

Diwani laughed at her worries and terrors, telling her she was returning to her real home, promising to follow her there soon. She barely left Feroza's room and spent the days inscribing poems on the bedroom walls with a pencil. Her scribbling and singing relaxed Feroza. Tabu told her that the walls of Diwani Begum's hovel were covered with verses inscribed with charcoal. Diwani feared that she would forget these immortal lines as her 'madness' overcame her sanity.

Feroza gave Nanhi the box of jewels and mehr money which had been handed to her at the time of her divorce by her father-in-law. Most of Nanhi's jewellery was kept at the state treasury to be worn on state occasions. Only certain pieces given by her mothers and in-laws were kept with her. Feroza hoped that Nanhi would make her bid to freedom by leaving with Sultanat Ara. She would require the jewellery to deal with the circumstances that she might confront.

Feroza was confident that Sultanat and her brother would look after Nanhi and her family. Maybe Mehdi would get employment at Basoda. Mother and daughter spoke about the possibilities on good days. It was all Feroza could think and desperately pray for. In the throes of fever, she screamed at Nanhi to run away. She clung to life, hoping for some news till death seized her.

Feroza's dying wish was to kiss the hand of her daughter. The doctor spread a handkerchief on Nanhi's hand, asked her to wrap her scarf around her nose and mouth and led her into Feroza's room. Feroza placed her fevered lips on Nanhi's covered hand; even through the cold cloth she could feel the warm pulse of the life she had created.

Feroza passed away as the monsoon burst with its first showers in Sherpur. She was surrounded by the women who loved her – Nanhi, Tabu, Bua and Diwani. Shams, paranoid about disease and death, didn't want Nanhi to go anywhere near the contagion-riddled corpse. But Nanhi defied her father for the first time in her life and prepared her mother for burial. She bathed Feroza, assisted by Tabu with instructions from Bua. It was customary for holy Sayyidanis, the descendants of Prophet Muhammad, to bathe the dead. Feroza had always shunned them saying that they made a living out of death. Nanhi knew that Feroza would have wanted her to bathe her body even though she never said so.

Shams informed the three brothers who vaguely remembered Feroza as a person and more as a lament to waywardness. They were reluctant pallbearers, taking her directly to the family burial ground; the women of the family could not see her even in death. How could Feroza's body enter a house she had been forbidden to enter while she was alive? How could the women pay their respects to Feroza and disrespect Miya Jaan's last will?

Mehdi wanted them to wait out the rain and conferred with Nausha, the only brother whose face showed some grief. There was a bare tin shed at one side where they sometimes bathed the male dead bodies. It was the only place they could keep the body till the burial. A hasty funeral prayer was performed, attended by a few kinsmen drenched in the monsoon deluge.

The grave was wet and soft with rain and they feared that the edges would fall in even before they could lower her in. Nausha stood inside the grave with Mehdi when they handed her down. Wet mud was thrown in quickly over the white shroud. Within a month, the monsoon grass covered the unmarked grave.

'*Jeetey jee hamein beghar kiya aur mar ke hamarey kandhey tudwaye* (While she lived, she rendered us homeless, and in death, she broke our shoulders),' muttered one of the brothers, a comment that survived and concluded the telling of Feroza Begum's story in the oral family history.

Nanhi and Sultanat grieved together and awaited their rescue. Tenacious and inexorable even in death, Feroza Begum would have her revenge from the other side of the grave.

Notes

1. Mirza Ghalib.

28

Opening of Hujra of the Goshtkhor and Tareek Jaan's Supreme Sacrifice

'*Naya phir rang layi sham-e-jadu*
Bura aya nazar anjam-e-jadu.[1]

(New hues dye the evening of enchantment
Harbingers of its imminent destruction.)'

Jadu, tilism surrounds us and we are blind, or choose to close our eyes to its imminent destruction – this illusion, we live in, will one day turn to ashes. We shall return to dust. So the great souls who have knowledge of the unseen, narrate the destruction of Tilism-e-Azam thus:

The King of Samris gets the news of the demolition of the prison of Zulmat and the death of the great Afreet at the hands of Sadaf. He rages, cries in despair for if Afreet can die at the hands of the rebels, his own death looms large before him. Sahiba domni, his new chief queen, serves him a strength-giving kushta and promises to lay down her life to protect him. Huzur Afat appears, splitting the ground and rising up before him.

'Beta, don't lose heart. Be brave. Defeat the enemies with your wit and magic. The time has come to open the hujra of Goshtkhor,' she says.

Now friends, the hujra is a sequestered place in the desert of Zulmat. A magic crystal dome wherein resides one of the most powerful magicians, Goshtkhor. He was half-djinn and half-human. For forty years, he had isolated himself, living in the magic dome and performing powerful rituals to please Samri, Laat and Mannat – the dark gods of magic. He had given up what he loved most – *gosht*, human and pari flesh. Goshtkhor had dug up the skulls from the graves of great Pathan warriors and burnt them for his prayers. Abstinence and forty years of prayers without a wink of sleep has made his magic very potent.

'I have requested Goshtkhor to help us defeat the rebels. He will join us if you feed him the blood of your crown prince,' says Huzur Afat.

Ahh, which father can kill his son with his own hands? The pride of his heart, his successor, Prince Bemisal, was as unique as his name. Tareek trembles in anguish for the Samri was a loving father. From the time of his birth, he had doted on the prince, showered him with all luxuries and trained him in the dark arts himself. Bemisal's was the first face he saw every morning and the boy was a dutiful son, worshipping the ground beneath Tareek's feet. But friends, the fear of death is such. Who wouldn't exchange his death for another's?

Huzur Afat says, 'Listen, my son. May your life be long, you will have other sons. This prince was born to be sacrificed to save you. And who are we to question fate?

His mother, Queen Harah, is so proud of having produced an heir and waits for your death.' Indeed, Afat's putli had reported a conversation between Bemisal and his mother. The simple boy had remarked that he would give his mother all the riches in the universe when he became king. The other women of the harem also hated Harah and said that she, a mere concubine who had become queen after she was blessed with Bemisal, had put on airs since her elevation. A woman's greatest enemy is a jealous woman, my friends.

Tareek Jaan returns with a heavy heart. Perhaps Huzur Afat was right – Bemisal was fated to save his life. Tareek's heart breaks looking into Bemisal's trusting eyes as he asks him to bathe and change for they had to go on a long journey.

'Son, our Tilism-e-Azam is in danger and we have to make sacrifices to protect it,' he says, holding the bony shoulders of the lad, moved by the sight of the downy beginnings of the first moustache on Bemisal's fair face.

'Abba huzoor, my magic and I are at your command,' says Bemisal with childlike seriousness.

Ah, his loving words are like several piercing arrows! Tareek Jaan bids Bemisal to get ready in his formal princely robes. Bemisal returns after bathing, dressed in a resplendent golden shervani. He looks as radiant as the morning sun with the promise of youth. A sigh escapes Tareek's lips; he calls him near and kissing him tenderly on his brow, clasps him to his bosom for one last time. Then, taking off his jewelled turban with the fist-sized emerald stone, places it on the young head. It's too big for the boy's head and Bemisal laughs.

'Abba huzoor, I cannot wear this! It's too big and it's yours.'

Tareek makes him sit on his crystal throne borne by the crimson cloud. Ahh, at least this once let him taste the experience of sitting on the great throne of Samris, thinks the grieving father. The boy is surprised and delighted at this unexpected favour. Every second, Tareek's heart urges him to command the prince to go back but the arrow of fate once released cannot return and the father and son fly willy-nilly towards their fate.

The looming crystal dome of the hujra glints in the merciless sun of the Zulmat desert. Tareek Jaan puts his hand on the dome, recites a spell and it splits open.

'I have brought Bemisal with me, O Goshtkhor,' says Tareek Jaan, his voice quivering.

'Enter!' comes the sorcerer's voice and they enter a hall under the dome, its mud floor smeared with dung, splattered with sindoor, piles of skulls lining the walls. At the centre of the hall, on a tiger skin with a skull-headed staff standing on one end, sits the emaciated Goshtkhor dressed in a black loincloth, his body covered with white ashes, face reddened with sindoor and thick lines of kohl around his blazing eyes. His lips drool at the sight of the strapping young prince.

The boy feels a lurch of fear. 'Who is he, Abba huzoor?' he whispers.

'A sahir who will help us,' says Tareek Jaan, not meeting his terrified eyes.

Goshtkhor wipes his mouth and utters a spell and gives Tareek a little box.

'Put the samri sindoor on the boy's face,' he tells Tareek Jaan.

Tareek takes the sindoor and with trembling hands smears it on Bemisal's forehead and face. Bemisal stands stunned, shudders and a change comes over him. His eyes roll up, the whites showing and he starts swaying like a possessed being.

'Kill me, kill me for Samri,' he screams, his frenzied eyes flitting from side to side. He then takes out Tareek's dagger, hands it to him and kneels down before him, his eyes pleading. Tareek hesitates, his eyes flowing with tears, for how can a father kill his only son?

Friends, it was faith that prompted Prophet Ibrahim to attempt to take his son's life and it is the greatest fear – the fear of death – that makes Tareek kill his son.

Bemisal takes Tareek's hand and presses the blade of the dagger on his own neck, an ecstatic grin on his face. With one swipe the King of Samris cuts his jugular vein, catching Bemisal as he falls back, and his young blood sprouts and flows on the mud, mixes with the sindoor and eclipses the glowing face.

Goshtkhor rushes forward with his bowl to collect the manna of blood to break his forty-year fast, a look of greedy delight on his wrinkled face. Bemisal lies on his side, an ethereal smile on his bloodied face. Tareek Jaan closes his eyes and turns away from the lifeless body.

Goshtkhor slurps the blood noisily from his bowl; then crawls on all fours licking the ground with his lusting tongue, his lips turning red.

'Ya Samri, let my son's sacrifice not be in vain. Save my tilism,' Tareek says, covering his face to stop the shuddering sobs shaking his grand frame.

Goshtkhor's face glows pink, his veins fuse into his flesh and he sits down on the tiger skin, closes his eyes.

'There will be a battle, a bloody battle. You did well to take my help. Now, leave the sacrificial body and go!'

Tareek takes one last look at his prince and flies out of the dome, trying not to think of what Goshtkhor would do to his dead son's body.

'Ahh, I'm the most unfortunate father, I can't even bury my dead son,' he howls in anguish and beats his breast as he flies back to the Tilism-e-Azam. Huzur Afat calls the zenana durbar in the Sheesh Mahal.

'I have summoned you here to inform you that our beloved crown prince, Bemisal, has made the supreme sacrifice to open the hujra of Goshtkhor…'

There is an anguished scream as the unfortunate Queen Harah falls down in a dead faint. Huzur Afat gestures at the Daroghan to remove the woman.

'The hujra is now open,' continues Huzur Afat. 'Tareek Jaan, the King of Samris, is preparing for the great battle to crush the haramzadis Husnara, Sadaf and Gulistan. No one will remain even to take their names! And any woman or pari helping the rebels in any way will be fed to Goshtkhor along with her maids and guards.'

She storms out and Lalarukh and the other women and paries with souls sit immobile with blank faces.

Now two words about Amar ayyar and the lauh-e-tilism. My listeners already know that the lauh-e-tilism is the talisman which the Tilism Kusha needs to destroy the tilism.

So our Amar ayyar sets off with all his instruments of ayyari secure in his zambeel to acquire the lauh-e-tilism from Rohu Mahipusht, who lives in the River Ramganga with the lauh-e-tilism secure in his belly. It is said that as long as the River Ramganga flowed, the Tilism-e-Azam would exist on its banks and Rohu Mahipusht was the keeper of the River Ramganga and of the lauh-e-tilism.'

'Ramganga?' interjected a maulana.

'Yes, Ramganga, the life-giving river of Sherpur. That's where our lauh-e-tilism resides,' Kallan's eyes twinkle. His audience is familiar with his interposing of the real and the fantastic. It adds an edge to his tale.

'Amar reaches the edge of the Ramganga, changes himself into the beautiful Princess Zehra dressed in durbar ceremonial clothes. He lounges on the takht like a young princess at a picnic with her entourage and starts singing a ghazal in the most melodious voice known to man.

The ripples of music reach the Ramganga and the waves are stilled with the melody. Look, what do we see? A head emerges from the river, the face of a man with silver scales glistening on his cheeks, eyes flat, white, unblinking and mouth, a lipless slit – Rohu Mahipusht. He rises out of the Ramganga – a full-grown, tall, slim man with grey and silver fish scales down his back. He sits at her feet, swaying with delirious ecstasy.

Princess Zehra takes the ghazal to its climax, keeps the rubab aside and gives him a cup of roseate wine mixed with the sufoof-e-behoshi. Rohu Mahipusht drinks it in a single gulp and falls down unconscious. Now Amar jumps up and cuts Rohu's bloated stomach and there, glowing in the blood, is the lauh-e-tilism! Amar takes it out, cleans it and wears it around his neck. The lauh-e-tilism is but a two-inch-long tablet made of jade with the secret of the Tilism-e-Azam inscribed on it.

As soon as Rohu Mahipusht dies, the Ramganga starts boiling, and thousands of fishes and tens of crocodiles jump out to lie on the sand, flipping in agony. The first manzil of the destruction of Tilism-e-Azam is reached.

The sheesha-e-Samri glows red and informs Tareek Jaan that the lauh-e-tilism has been stolen by Amar ayyar on the banks of the Ramganga. It is the beginning of the end.

'Don't worry, King of Samris, Husnara has to first awaken the lauh-e-tilism and acquire the *Tegha Noorafshani* sword. All this is impossible for that spoilt, ease-loving Husnara,' Queen Sahiba comforts a terrified Tareek Jaan.

Now two words about Husnara. She is ecstatic when Amar ayyar brings her the lauh-e-tilism but she knows that awakening its magic would require all her strength.

'Only Qutub Pir can tell me how to revive the lauh-e-tilism,' she says.

Husnara, whose power can shake the very heavens and who rules over a hundred sahirs, sits in the blazing desert of Vadi-e-Marg, the Valley of Death, with parched lips and festering wounds on her feet, to pray to Qutub Pir. Qutub

Pir appears before her, afloat on a celestial takht and says, 'Only the blood of an unborn killed and sacrificed willingly by the mother can kindle the lauh-e-tilism and reveal its secrets. But you must answer the question – can you justify the destruction of a life that is young and promising? It is fated that you will kill Tareek Jaan and you will destroy his tilism. Be courageous and true!'

She summons her putlis and commands, 'Go this lamha to the women of the harem who have got back their rooh and put the sufoof-e-khwab in their drink and tell them that tonight I have summoned them to my dream!'

So that night all the hundred and seventy-two women and paries who had secretly got back their souls find themselves facing the Tilism Kusha Husnara in their dream.

Husnara raises her arms and proclaims, 'Sisters, we are together and we shall fight the greatest evil; he whose name I shall not take for fear of alerting him to this secret meeting. The destruction of this shaitan requires the greatest sacrifice that a woman can make!'

Husnara looks at all the faces floating in the magma of her dream, listening with rapt attention.

'Be prepared, sisters! Some of you will lose your life and your youth in this battle, but remember, we cannot be defeated for I am the Tilism Kusha and it is fated that he shall die at my hands.'

Husnara takes off the lauh-e-tilism from her neck and shows it to the women and paries.

'This is the lauh-e-tilism which will destroy him and his tilism, but to realise its magical powers I need a woman or pari to make the greatest sacrifice. I need the blood of an unborn child. But it is not easy for a mother to destroy a life growing within her, however conceived.'

'I will kill my unborn child!' Lalarukh steps forward, the teeka-e-yaqut glowing with truth on her forehead. On the day she got back her soul, she realised that she was with child from Tareek Jaan.

'My teeka-e-yaqut tells me that the child in my womb, if he lives, will be more powerful and evil, than this shaitan. He will live for five hundred years and perpetrate unimagined terror on djinns, humans and paries. The core of the earth would tremble at his power and the heavens doubt the Great Name of the Creator. No Tilism Kusha will ever be born to vanquish him. The universe will near qayamat!'

Husnara nods, for Lalarukh has answered the question of Qutub Pir – what can justify the death of an unborn full of promise?

'You will find the means to kill your unborn and rid your body and the earth of this terrible burden,' she says and dismisses the dream.

The next day, when Lalarukh opens her hair to take her bath, a tiny teardrop of a diamond falls to the floor. She picks it up and knows it contains magic and is the means of her deliverance. She swallows it and within a moment, blood flows out of her. Sarsar in the guise of a dai scrapes out the unborn scourge who is determined to cling to the womb and fulfil its destiny. She collects the foetus and blood and rushes to Husnara.

Husnara performs the prayers and chanting to Samri, dips the lauh-e-tilism in the blood of the unborn chanting, 'Ya Samri, Ya Jamshed.'

Ah friends, such is the magic of the lauh-e-tilism that it glows orange like the rising sun and ancient words appear on it that Husnara reads and chants. The date for the end of the tilism is revealed.

Cities and forts are created by man and become ruins. *Har urooj ko zawaal hai* – for every rise there is a fall, friends.'

Mirza Kallan raises his hand in salam and smiles, '*Yaar zinda mehfil baqi, gar diya zindagi ne saath to mulaqat hogi.*

Till friends live, gatherings endure. If life is faithful, we shall meet again.'

Notes

1. Ahmad Husain Qamar, *Tilism-e-Hoshruba*, vol. 6.

29

Nanhi Begum

Sherpur, 1920

An invitation from the state of Basoda arrived in August that year, requesting the Nawab and his Begums to grace the occasion of the *aqeeqa* ceremony of the crown prince at Basoda. There was a separate invitation for Nanhi and her family. The Nawab conveyed his congratulations and expressed his inability to attend the function due to pressing commitments.

Sultanat Ara tried to persuade him to allow her to visit her homeland after twenty-four years. She was old now, she said, and hadn't even attended her father's funeral; now her mother was ailing. There was no precedent of Nawab Shams's Begums visiting their homes in their lifetime. The Nawab finally allowed her to go with her entourage but refused to allow his favourite daughter to leave on account of Muharram. She was in mourning and it didn't look good that she go to attend a celebration. Perhaps he feared that Sultanat wouldn't return and Nanhi – with Feroza dead, she had no ties to Sherpur. Mehdi was always withdrawn, aloof, and the Nawab could sense his resentment. After much deliberation and Nanhi's insistence, Sultanat left Sherpur never to return.

Nanhi felt as if she had emerged fragile and unsure from the womb once again, casting around for comfort and sustenance. There were pieces of herself that only her mothers knew, the feelings they could assuage and the problems that would lighten just by telling them. If Hasan were alive, she could share with him how everything seemed different now, how she felt adrift and even the pull of her children chafed at her. Mehdi had retreated behind an irascible wall as Muharram approached. Already, to appease him and to avoid confrontations, she had started praying the Sunni way. They couldn't engage a Sunni maulvi for the boys, which was a matter of great unhappiness for Mehdi.

'Abba, today I'll ride beside Dhuldhul,' young Haider beamed.

'What new drama is this?' Mehdi frowned.

Dhuldhul, the horse of Imam Husain, led the procession of Muharram.

'Daddy wants Haider to be the faqir of Imam Husain,' Nanhi sent the children away with Tabu and closed the door. Had she hoped that Mehdi won't notice? He would have lashed out at her after the procession. By then it would have been over.

'What does that mean?'

'He'll ride beside Dhuldhul in the procession and beg for alms in the name of Imam Husain.'

'What! The great-grandson of Mardan Khan will not go begging for alms!' Mehdi's voice rose and he gripped the back of the chair.

'It's only symbolic. Remember last year when he had the fever? Daddy made a *mannat* prayer at the Imambara that if he recovered, he would be a faqir for Imam Husain. It's only for a day.'

'Isn't it enough for you people that I have lost my religion? That I'm ridiculed by my family? And now the world will see my son…' Something had snapped in Mehdi and Nanhi rushed to close the windows. There was always some maid listening in. What if Daddy came to know that Mehdi had refused to send his son? She also secretly feared that if the mannat wasn't fulfilled, Haider would fall ill again. She couldn't share this fear with Mehdi who would lecture her on being superstitious.

'It's better that I die or go away instead of bearing this humiliation!' Mehdi stormed out of the room and shut himself up in his study.

The Nawab noted Mehdi's absence as they gathered for the procession. He was told that Mehdi was unwell. The Nawab signalled for the procession to start and sent Dr Ansari to Nanhi's mahal.

From his study window, Mehdi saw the mourners accompanying the taziya to the Imambara. His Haider sat on a white horse; the reins were held by the syce. He held on to the saddle with a solemn air, balancing himself and beating his chest intermittently. A small cloth bag was slung across his chest to collect alms. Mehdi buried his face in his hands. They were all in the Nawab's power. He would know that Mehdi had pretended to be ill because he objected to his son's role.

That night he went to the zenana and confronted Nanhi.

'Nanhi if you want a palace life, stay here; or else come with me!'

'Where?' Nanhi's voice choked with terror.

'Wherever. Live in a hut with me. I'm leaving with my sons. I can't bear to see them like this.'

'You'll leave me?' Her whisper was half to herself.

'You're leaving us by not coming with us.'

'I can't live here alone.' The decision was made. Mehdi held her in his arms.

'Come with me to Bareilly.'

'Daddy will…' Fear fluttered once again.

'It's dangerous. So we shall keep it a secret,' Mehdi kissed her forehead.

Till the final day, he didn't disclose his plans to Nanhi fearing that in her terrified love for her father, she might blurt out the truth. Nanhi felt strong with the belief that she was finally fulfilling Feroza's wish. Her Chhoti Ammi had known that she would only be happy away from Sherpur's claustrophobic court life. She would take Bua, Tabu, Mahabat Khan and Rani with her. Feroza's household had all come to live with her after her death and Nanhi felt responsible for them.

Tabu had already started staying at Nanhi's house most of the time, going back only to cook something for Kallan and tidy up the house. Accusations of being unfaithful and of fornicating with the Nawab had worn her down. They hadn't had a semblance of marriage since the time Tabu had taken up employment with Feroza. She knew Wali would look after his brother. Kallan probably wouldn't even notice that she had left him. If she chose to stay back, she would definitely be imprisoned or persecuted. Kallan was incapable of looking after their daughter. He was convinced that the Nawab had fathered their daughter and that he had been tricked into marrying the Nawab's whore.

There was no way Mehdi could persuade her to abandon these women and their children – they would suffer at the Nawab's hands if left behind. Bua protested, saying she would go back to her old house but Nanhi refused to go without her. Mehdi gave in, admiring Nanhi's loyalty and asked her to pack a small suitcase with just a few clothes and her jewels. He took Mahabat Khan and Rani's husband into confidence. Bareilly was the chosen destination for the flight because of its proximity and Mehdi's ancestral haveli at Gher Saeed

Khan. From there, they would proceed to Basoda and seek to rebuild their life.

Nanhi regretted that she couldn't take Diwani Begum with her. Diwani had shut herself in her hovel after Feroza passed away, barely eating. She finally succumbed to her crippling anxiety and the alternate reality of her visions. Whenever Nanhi visited her, she would scream, 'Run, run my dear!' She only asked for pencils or charcoal to write and rewrite the verses on her walls.

Mehdi set himself to the task of planning their escape. The most probable route would be to cross the Ramganga by the rail-cum-traffic bridge on the road to Bareilly. The Ramganga flowed closest to Sherpur's boundary there and two miles after crossing the Ramganga, they would be in the safe precincts of the British domains. It also had the highest probability of discovery. Their vehicles could be stopped and searched at the bridge.

Finally, he decided to take a longer route through Swar tehsil, crossing the Ramganga at a British-built bridge on the road connecting Bareilly to Nainital. It would take about two hours to reach the bridge and another two hours to enter Bareilly – every minute a risk. If an alarm was raised, the army would fan out in all directions.

Sleeping alone, as Mehdi slept in the mardana throughout Muharram, Nanhi would be seized with panic and wake up drenched in sweat. Mehdi sent notes in English through Rani to reassure her – this was the closest she had ever felt to him.

The majlis on the seventh of Muharram was very popular. Shias and Sunnis from nearby villages flooded the town, watching the processions and the *churi maatam*.[1] The children clamoured for the sweets distributed after the majlis. Nanhi returned from the majlis exhausted. Tabu, Rani and Bua were at home while the other maids were still standing in jostling lines. An ordinary tonga hired by Mahabat Khan stood at the zenana back entrance of the palace, shaded by the mango trees. Tabu had already loaded the suitcases on it.

Nanhi was expecting the flight every day. She quickly put on her burqa and took the sleeping Najaf in her arms. Mehdi led Haider and Asghar to the tonga, quietening their questions with stories. They settled down on their seats and the tonga creaked out towards the DuPont Gate where many similar tongas were lined up, impeded by groups of mourners crowding around the guards handing out the sweet *tabarruq* – four laddoos wrapped in a silk kerchief.

The driver got down and collected the sweets for the Begums, requesting the guards to clear the way. There were a number of tongas bearing ladies and the driver, already briefed, gave the names of Begums belonging to a known family from Milak tehsil. The guards noted down the names. Nanhi looked back through the window. A second tonga bearing Bua, Tabu and Rani with their children driven by Rani's husband was now being interrogated.

Nanhi watched the qila walls receding; the magnificent cupola of the durbar hall was the last to leave. Tabu glanced towards the gully where Kallan Mirza lived, spinning tales in his opium haze, deep in his magical tilism world. The kaharis would return late at night and raise the alarm. They had to reach Bareilly before that.

The road to Swar was a pathway paved with stones. They jostled along with increasing anxiety for two hours till they reached the bridge. Cars awaited them on the other side. They still had some way to go till the Bareilly border where the power of the Nawab ended and the British dominions began, but the road was better. Since speed was paramount, Mehdi had arranged for the cars, taking the help of disgruntled members of another branch of the royal line whose pension had been stopped by the Nawab. Nanhi only relaxed when they entered their haveli in Bareilly, giving way to tears of relief and loss.

It was only the next morning that the Nawab was informed. The maids returning to an empty house had waited for Nanhi to return for some time and then ran to the Daroghan. It was late but the home minister had immediately sent guards towards the two routes that fugitives from Sherpur usually took – Bareilly or Badayun. The train station was checked and the stationmaster quizzed about a large family boarding the night train.

The Nawab was beside himself with rage and immediately rushed to Nanhi's house. He walked through the rooms, looking at a cradle, an abandoned toy, his anger giving way to disbelief. How could his beloved Nanhi abandon him even if Mehdi wished to leave?

When the guards returned empty-handed, the Nawab correctly surmised that Mehdi must have taken refuge in his ancestral haveli at Bareilly. He was powerless against them there and vented his anger on Mehdi's family. He put his father, Husain, and brother, Mohsin, under house arrest, threatening to lay the whole Gher Mardan Khan waste. He would demolish the houses and put the ancient settlement under the plough.

At least three of his top officials belonged to Gher Mardan Khan. Mehdi's father was the Naib Sadar, the deputy minister. The other officials pleaded with him, promising to persuade the family to return. Mohsin meanwhile dug a hole in a back wall and fled with his family to Bareilly. The Nawab sold off all of Mohsin's belongings and wanted to auction the haveli of Husain Raza Khan. Once again, the intervention of the other sardar families pleading the many contributions of the family of Mardan Khan to Sherpur, stopped the juggernaut that would have destroyed one of the oldest mohallas of Sherpur.

Notes

1. Self-flagellation by the mourners with tiny knives strung on chains.

30

The Grand Battle and the Destruction of Tilism-e-Azam

Mirza Kallan lay on a rough hemp rope cot in his veranda, dressed only in pyjamas rolled up to his knees. His bare back and half of his face was marked by the criss-cross pattern of the bed ropes as he lay in a deep opiate sleep, oblivious to the fierce heat of the day and the dry *loo* wind that shook the bamboo curtains. The sole *khus* curtain leaning against a veranda arch had provided some relief when it was damp from the water splashed by Tabu; but now it was bone dry and the still-blazing evening sun was making its way into the veranda, burning the soles of his feet and his wasted calves. He stirred. The clanging of the iron door chain, persistent and patient, had penetrated his insensate sleep. Tabu was at the mahalsara as usual. Cursing under his breath, Kallan got up slowly.

'*Kaun saab*, who's it, sir?'

'Kallan Bhai!' It was Waliuddin.

'*Aao*, *aao*, come in,' Mirza Kallan opened the door, smiling sheepishly, scratching his chest and stifling a yawn.

He went back into the cover of the veranda with quick steps, mildly irritated at the courtyard burning under his bare feet. Somewhat belatedly thinking of making himself decent, he struggled into a semi-transparent, old mulmul kurta.

'Where's Bhabhi?' Waliuddin looked around as if the walls reported her absence.

'They have gone to Nanhi Begum's,' yawned Mirza Kallan, stretching his arms above his head.

'Bhai, are you well? You didn't attend the dastan session yesterday. Last week you were not well. I tried to cover up by telling the tale of Toti Begum to keep your audience engaged. That poet Jalal is also telling the dastan of *Tilism-e-Hoshruba* and they will all drift there,' Waliuddin dusted the takht and sat down.

'I'm well. Just didn't feel like telling the dastan,' Kallan sat back on the cot, resisting the urge to lie down again.

'I wanted to speak to you about your dastan,' Waliuddin smoothed the crinkles of the sheet which bore yellow spots from turmeric and a brownish halo from a child's urine. He shifted away from it and leaned back against the bolster.

'In your dastan, first you made a kafir sorceress the Tilism Kusha and I warned you about it. Now she is going to destroy the Tilism-e-Azam. Where is the grand war? The great warriors of Islam led by Saad bin Ameer Hamza?'

'They never came. There will be no war! Look around you. Can the tilism of this tyrant be destroyed? So how can Tilism-e-Azam be demolished? The oppressors will continue to rule and abuse our women and we Pathans and Mughals will cower in our homes and submit our women to his whoring!' Kallan's eyes were red with anger and the remnants of intoxication.

'Bhai, we are dastangos, not warriors. We tell the story, earn money and that's our first duty towards our listeners and families. I know Bhabhi goes to work in the qila and takes Bahar with her. These things are never hidden. It's shameful that she has to feed you all. Our father, a Mughal, and Bhabhi earns for your afeem!'

Wali paused, looking at Kallan's stony face. 'I would rather starve than send my wife to the qila. And things are not good for me too. If we finish the dastan, we can sell it, earn commission from the Nawab and the debtors can be kept at bay.' Suddenly, he understood Kallan's frustration and his abortion of the dastan before its logical end.

Kallan turned his face away from him, lay flat on his back and flung an arm over his face. His Nigar was going to the qila, fornicating with the ignominious Nawab. How could the Begum hide her and for how long? In fact, he was sure that Nigar was no longer his. She had changed in so many ways. He had shouted at her, called her a slut, the Nawab's whore, but she continued with her employment. She didn't come home for days, especially after their fights.

'Have you eaten? Did Bhabhi cook something for you?'

'Yes,' Kallan lied. Tabu had kept food for him in the *neymatkhana*, the tiny cupboard with wire mesh sides where food could last for a few hours in the heat. Was it today or yesterday that she had come? He tried to eat as little as possible from the tainted money she used to buy them food. He had no desire to touch her, or even speak to her. He did steal some money for his afeem, hating himself.

'What happens to the story now?' Waliuddin persisted.

'Husnara, Gulistan and Sadaf are arrested and sent to the dungeons of Zulmat, their eyes gouged out, their bodies maimed, suffering from the bites of snakes and guarded by the djinns. All the rebel women of the harem are executed and new women take their place.' Kallan moved his arm from his face and kept looking at a cobweb swaying on the ceiling.

'And what became of Lalarukh?'

'She is beheaded and her body is sent back to Koh Kaaf.'

'And there is no war?'

'Saad cried till he became blind.'

'Kallan Bhai, you are making the story too complicated and tragic. The audience won't like it. We were so near the destruction of Tareek Jaan and his tilism!'

'Then you finish the story. You know how to. My story only has despair.'

Kallan turned his back towards him, pulled a chadar over his head and pretended to sleep. Waliuddin sat for some time. Kallan did not stir. The story had to be completed and though he was not a great dastango like his brother, he had to do it. He set to work reading the old dastans, writing notes – all this came so naturally to Kallan.

Waliuddin Mirza took Mirza Kallan's place next Thursday and continued the tale to its climax. He began by singing a hamd in praise of the Almighty.

'So the honey-tongued witnesses of this great tale and the cup-bearers of great knowledge and wisdom narrate the dastan of Tilism-e-Azam thus:

On both sides, the preparation for the Great Battle commence and all creation watches with bated breath for the final showdown, trembling at the destruction that would follow. Tareek Jaan uses all his magic and iron from the cosmic realm of Samri to create iron balls of such fearsome power as to destroy the earth and burn the heavens. Saad bin Ameer Hamza is marching from Koh Kaaf with the largest army of men and parizads ever assembled and 1,800 ayyars trained by Amar ayyar himself.

Tegha Noorafshani, the ancient sword of Jamshed preserved by the kingdom of Noorafshan, has come into

Husnara's possession as the King of Noorafshan agrees to fight by her side.

So friends, the day of commencement of the battle dawns, the bugle of war is blown and all great sorcerers from Tilism-e-Zubeiri, Tilism-e-Neelum, Tilism-e-Toran etcetera, arrive with their armies of lakhs, their flying steeds and fire-breathing dragons. Black flags with 'Samri', 'Jamshed' and 'Pheron' flutter above all ranks. Tareek Jaan flies in on his ruby throne, a crimson cloud hovers above him, shading his majestic head and thousands of fire-breathing anacondas fly behind.

The billowing dust rises in the eastern horizon, eclipsing the sun. Lashkar-e-Islam is led by Saad bin Ameer Hamza astride his white steed, dressed in the armour of Imam Husain and bearing the sword of Ameer Hamza and alams. Suddenly, a dark red cloud rises from the north as Husnara joins the army of Islam.'

Waliuddin paused. He couldn't change the Tilism Kusha now though his heart rebelled at the very idea of having a woman sorceress, a heathen at that, as the destroyer of tilism. He wiped his forehead, took a sip of tea (he abhorred the afeem that had destroyed his brother), saw the restlessness on the faces of his audience and decided to continue as best as he could.

'Husnara Tilism Kusha's army is flanked on the right by Sadaf, her powerful pearl – Akhtar Marwarid – shining in her hand and Gulistan Jadu on her left with her army of floating, deadly flowers which could torture, kill and drive armies mad. Following Husnara are armies of the sorcerers Rafey and Zaroon, rescued by Chalak, who have thrown in their lot with her. Saad enquires about his beloved Lalarukh from Husnara and is filled with vengeful anger.

Tareek Jaan motions for the kettledrums of war to be sounded.

The armies face each other, make formations and Tareek Jaan challenges, 'Saad bin Ameer Hamza, you who could not keep your wife, now take the help of my wives! Where is your shame? And you whores, I still give you one chance to come back to me!'

Saad cries in anger and his horse lunges forward with his sword flashing like lightning. Tareek Jaan hovers on his flying steed and throws an iron ball at Saad's contingent, killing thousands instantly.

Suddenly Tareek Jaan sees Husnara flying towards him, the lauh-e-tilism gleaming around her neck. Tareek opens the hujra of Goshtkhor. The earth splits open and from the womb of the earth rises Goshtkhor, his head like a dome, his chest as broad as a span of a desert; his body fed by thousands of cattle heads has become colossal. His eyes bulge at the sight of the rebel army, his giant shark jaws open, drooling for the meat of men and paries. Tareek Jaan yells, 'Kill and eat as many as you can!'

Goshtkhor steps forward and with the swipe of one giant hand, grabs a hundred soldiers and devours them in one mouthful, grinning with his needle-sharp teeth reddened by their blood. Saad, analysing the situation, orders a full retreat.

Tareek Jaan yelps with laughter, rises higher on his flying throne and caws, 'Where is the great soldier of Islam, the grandson of Ameer Hamza, who had challenged the might of Khudawand? And where are your whores hiding?'

'Stop! We cannot fight his physical power, we have to fight his magic,' says Husnara.

Husnara blows a smoke that renders Goshtkhor momentarily blind. Gulistan releases her most tantalising perfume and Husnara flashes the lauh-e-tilism. The rays of lauh-e-tilism make him forget his magic and the hypnotic effect of the fragrance takes hold of him. Goshtkhor starts beating his chest and screaming in frenzy, 'Gulistan!

Gulistan!' He tears off his chains and kneels before Gulistan who sits smiling on her white peacock.

'O Goshtkhor, khanakharab, you dare kill my army?' she says with a petulant pout.

'Command me, I'm your slave!'

'Then go, turn around and kill all of Tareek Jaan's army! Kill all his sorcerers, devs and djinns. Eat them!'

Goshtkhor stands up and rushes at Tareek Jaan's army like a mad ogre, crushing, eating and killing. Tareek Jaan stands shocked. The battle is reversed!

'We are doomed!' Tareek Jaan trembles.

Huzur Afat knows that there is only one way. She flies on her throne high above the towering Goshtkhor and calls out to him, 'I, the slave of Samri, will give the supreme sacrifice for your death!'

Goshtkhor looks up and Huzur Afat takes out her dagger and slashes her own throat. Blood gushes down like black acid over Goshtkhor's face and body. With a scream that shakes the core of the earth, Goshtkhor falls and explodes into a mass of simmering black coal. The sky goes purple-black and shooting stars fall burning to the earth, his magical spirit in the shape of a huge green bird rises out of his cracked skull, screeching, 'Alas! Alas! You have killed me. I was Goshtkhor!'

Tareek Jaan rushes out of the pavilion as Huzur Afat collapses, her skull cracking open on the dust of the battlefield. The sky grows blacker than ever and a hail of burning coals rains down as the great sorceress dies. A black bird, her jaan, flies out of Huzur Afat's skull and screams, 'Alas! Alas! I gave my life, I accomplished my mission. I was Huzur Afat, slave of Samri!'

Tareek Jaan kneels down, beating his breast in anguish, mourning his great-grandmother's death; all his sahirs bow down in honour of her grand sacrifice. The lauh-e-tilism shines suddenly on Husnara's neck and she knows this is the right time to kill Tareek Jaan. Husnara then conjures up a thick magic cloud that surrounds Tareek Jaan till he cannot see and shines the lauh-e-tilism on him and he forgets all his magic.

Tareek Jaan trembles, unable to fly. He turns his back and tries to flee back into the tent but Husnara stands before him, her sword raised, blocking his way.

'Fight with me face to face, you coward!' she screams and brings down her sword on his head. Tareek Jaan saves himself and swords clang between man and wife for five days. Blood dripping down their faces, clothes torn, they fight the last battle as all the sorcerers and rebels surround them. On the fifth day, Husnara is fatally wounded in her stomach; but before Tareek Jaan could pull out his sword, Husnara thrusts the instrument of his death, the Tegha Noorafshani sword through his heart. With a deep growl, Tareek Jaan falls and the earth trembles with his weight, his body erupts in flames, his skull cracks open and tens of bird spirits fly out of his skull, wailing, 'Alas! You killed me! I was Tareek Jaan, the King of Samris!'

Husnara rises up, catches the birds with both her hands, opens her mouth like a deep cave and swallows all the captive magical spirits of Tareek Jaan, thus becoming the most powerful sorceress of all time! A joyous cheer goes up in the camp of the rebels. Sadaf flies down and places her pearl on Husnara's bleeding stomach, which heals immediately. The sisters embrace; Saad and the soldiers of Islam bow in sajda to the Great Creator in thanksgiving.

The Tilism-e-Azam, the grand illusion of Tareek Jaan that took a hundred years to create, crumples like paper, the grand palaces and durbars reduce to ashes, the rivers evaporate like fog and the real sun rises over the horizon. It was all an illusion created out of cosmic power. The Pathans of Tilism-e-Zahir, the Zulmat region, raise their hands in thanksgiving, put on their proud turbans; sounds of *daff* and charbait songs of valour can be heard once again in the gullies of the town.

The harem-dwellers rush out with cries and tears of happiness. Lalarukh, with the teeka gleaming red on her forehead, walks out and stands at the edge of the Ramganga River, now gushing with water from the mountains, and looks at Saad on his white steed galloping across the bridge no longer guarded by the ogre guards. It is a joyous meeting of lovers and soulmates.

Amar ayyar embraces his wife Sarsar who had guarded the harem women and paries from harm. The Pathan women, kaharis and other captive women rush back to their husbands and homes. The nikah of Saad bin Ameer Hamza and Princess Lalarukh is celebrated with a grand feast, their free town illuminated with thousands of lights.

I thank the Lord that this humble tongue could narrate the dastan of Ameer Hamza, which has been narrated in thousands of tongues since time before time itself, written in several daftars and volumes and will continue on the tongues of greater men and live in the hearts of all till *qayamat*.'

The audience burst out with 'wah wahs' of appreciation, sweets were handed out and Waliuddin bowed low, touching his forehead, accepting praise from the old Pathans. The host gave him two boxes of sohan halwa, for him and Kallan, with wishes for speedy recovery of the latter.

Waliuddin, thrilled at the accolades and happy at the success of the finale that he had himself created, went to Kallan's house. It was dark and the door opened at his touch.

'Kallan Bhai?' he called.

'Come in, Wali.' Kallan was sitting on the veranda floor, hugging his knees to his chest. The house was pitch-dark. Waliuddin rushed forward.

'What happened, Bhai? Are you ill?' he sat down beside Kallan.

'Nigar has left me again,' said Kallan, his voice flat.

'Where is she? And Bahar?'

'Mahabat Khan's brother told me that they… all of them have left… my Nigar, she died again.' Suddenly, he hugged Waliuddin and broke out in dry, cracked sobs.

Kallan narrated and wrote, with the help of Waliuddin, nine volumes of *Tilism-e-Nairang-e-Khayal*. He passed away in 1939 in Peepulwala Gher and was buried there.

31

Nanhi Begum

Bareilly and Basoda, 1920–30

Mehdi Raza Khan was so influenced by Sultanat Begum that he fled with his wife and family to Basoda. But a shock awaited the beleaguered family. The Nawab of Basoda had found the perfect means to avenge the humiliation suffered by his sister at the hands of Nawab Shams.

Sir Samad Ali Khan,
Chief Minister, Sherpur State

The haveli in Gher Saeed Khan was a huge, rundown place with just the bare necessities, guarded by an old retainer. Tabu and Rani set to work, cleaning up the place and setting some sort of order to the black-walled, sooty kitchen. The news of Mehdi's flight was received by his relatives in Gher Saeed Khan with amazement; soon the house was filled with crowds of close and distant relatives.

They brought food and helped them settle in. The story of the escapade and the reasons for it were narrated over and over and Mehdi applauded for his daring. Older men patted his back and told him he was a true Pathan. Nanhi was introduced to the extended family and explained the relationships and the complex intermarriages. As they were also related to Feroza, the women paid condolence visits. Nanhi wrote to Sultanat Ara, seeking asylum in Basoda.

Nanhi believed that her Daddy would rend the earth and the skies to bring her back, that the world would fall apart, at least in Sherpur, but everything was in its old equilibrium, or seemed to be so. She could barely sleep, terrified that at any hour the guards would break down their door, arrest Mehdi and drag them back to Sherpur. Daddy was close enough to the British that he could ask them to hand over the runaways.

At times she was racked with guilt at leaving Daddy, remembering his great love for her and her sons. She knew he would be devastated beyond words but Chhoti Ammi's soul would be at peace now. At least Mehdi was with her in a way he never was earlier – relaxed, attentive and loving. She had found her husband and heard his guffawing laughter for the first time. They could be happy again.

Haider had a hundred questions; his chief concern was to get back in time for the procession on the tenth day of Muharram. His grandfather had promised that this year Haider would walk all the way to Karbala for the taziya burial. Haider, with the discerning wisdom of a child, directed his questions to Nanhi while Asghar stood beside him, his face mirroring the confusion. Nanhi hugged them and said nothing. How could she explain to them what her mind refused to accept, that they would never see her Daddy again.

Mohsin and a murderously angry Farhat joined them at the haveli with their brood. Farhat ranted at their selfishness and blamed them for their uprooting. She was very upset at the selling of all their possessions for no fault of theirs. She sat cursing the Nawab, invoking Allah's wrath on him and his future generations till Nanhi could bear it no more.

'You owe all you have, and all your children will ever have to Daddy. Don't you dare curse him in my presence!' she said, surprising Farhat. She carried on to say that if Farhat wished to share a roof with her, she should curb her tongue. Farhat was quiet after that and kept away from Nanhi.

Mohsin was supportive of their flight. He was sure things would calm down and they would go back once Mehdi was safely in Basoda. The Nawab would realise that they had no role to play in Nanhi's escape.

The emissaries from the Nawab of Basoda arrived after about ten days of suspense and constant prayers. Nanhi secretly prayed for atonement for not observing the Muharram rituals, as always trying to please all gods. The idea that fate and its workings was a delicate balance was deeply embedded in her psyche even though she considered herself broad-minded and educated.

Mehdi asked Mohsin to come along with them but he refused, unwilling to abandon his parents and Sherpur. With a heavy heart, Mehdi bade farewell to his brother whom he would probably never meet again.

Nanhi and her family left for Agra by car. There, they boarded a train to Bhopal. The boys were excited at the new sights and sounds and their first train ride; Bua cried all the way for leaving Feroza and the graves of her ancestors. They were received at the Bhopal station by the Nawab of Basoda's cars. Though they were offered to stay the night, Nanhi refused because the Nawab of Bhopal was a close friend of Nawab Shams. Nawab Shams might have anticipated their final destination and warned his friend. After a five-hour drive, they finally arrived at Basoda to an ecstatic welcome by Sultanat Ara.

Mehdi, along with Haider and Asghar, were housed in the male section and Nanhi and little Najaf stayed in the zenana. She missed the boys and Mehdi. Her room was a little away from Sultanat Ara's quarters and she visited her daily, revelling in the warmth of her love. She met the wives and mothers of the Nawab, attended the zenana durbar, much along the lines of Sherpur. Nanhi enjoyed the Rajasthani dance and song programmes and watching the women in colourful lehengas.

It was a hilly town, lush after the rains and the weather pleasant with the onset of winters. The havelis housing the Begums were beautifully constructed in Rajasthani and Mughal styles and laid out with sprawling gardens. The maids spoke a strange Malwi dialect, which Nanhi couldn't understand but Rani could manage after some time. All her needs were taken care of. Sultanat Ara comforted her saying that Nawab Iftikhar would surely find a place for Mehdi and they would soon get a house to themselves. She could live here and bring up her children.

A devastating shock awaited the beleaguered family for Nawab Iftikhar had found the perfect instrument to avenge his sister's insult at the court of Sherpur.

At first, it wasn't clear to Nanhi that she was a virtual prisoner. One day, Rani was restrained from going with a message to Sultanat Ara. The Daroghan of the zenana informed her that they could not move out of their quarters and all their needs would be provided for. Nanhi's questions about the length of their imprisonment went unanswered. She demanded to meet her husband and children and was informed by the Chief Eunuch that they had been sent back to Bareilly! She was refused an audience with the Begum of Basoda or Nawab Iftikhar to plead her case.

Sultanat Ara requested her brother to have mercy on Nanhi and her family. Nanhi was like a daughter to her, but Nawab Iftikhar was as vengeful as Nawab Shams. Even if he was less awarded than Nawab Shams and Basoda was a smaller, thirteen-gun salute state to Sherpur's fifteen-gun salute, they were Rohilla Pathans too.

Abdul Ghani Khan, Qila Captaan and head of Ali Ghol,[1] was sent by Nawab Shams to get Sultanat Begum back. It is probable that the Nawab was aware that Nanhi and her family were now at Basoda. Sultanat Ara had already made up her mind. She received the maids sent with the entourage and sent word to Abdul Ghani Khan that she considered him her brother and as a brother he should respect her wishes and not force her to return.

The kaharis returning from Basoda told the Nawab the harrowing tale of the princess. She was a prisoner in the harems and the son-in-law had been sent away with his beloved grandsons. Even more atrocious was their whispered news that Sultanat Ara was planning to serve notice of talaq!'

'Talaq? But wasn't that accepted in those days? Feroza Begum was divorced too and so was her mother,' Ameera sat up.

'Yes, but imagine a woman of the harem giving talaq to the Nawab! It was a matter of great humiliation for the Nawab. He was already heartbroken at the loss of his daughter and grandsons. So Sultanat Ara applied for divorce, which was finalised in 1922. In fact, Nawab alleged that Sultanat Ara was having an affair with Mehdi so she should not be given mehr! He appealed to the British and Lord Reading interceded on his behalf and ruled that the mehr money not be paid to Sultanat Ara. The substantial amount would have granted some independence and dignity to Sultanat Ara. She lived in Basoda for the rest of her life and died in 1925.'

'And Nanhi Begum?'

'Sultanat Ara finally prevailed on her brother and Nanhi Begum was reunited with Mehdi and her sons at Bareilly. Nawab Shams granted pardon to Mohsin Raza, who returned to Sherpur to an empty house, glad that at least he still had the haveli of his ancestors to live in.

Nawab Shams pined for Nanhi and his beloved grandsons for the rest of his life. When he came to know that Nanhi had returned to Bareilly, he sent his chief minister, Sir Samad Ali Khan, thrice to Nanhi entreating her to return, that all was forgiven and he just wanted to see her before he died. Mehdi had made it clear that he would never step into Sherpur till Nawab Shams lived, but he wouldn't stop Nanhi from meeting her father. Nanhi feared that her Daddy might not allow her to go back to Mehdi, so she refused to go to Sherpur. So, this was Feroza Begum's revenge. It is said the Nawab could never recover from the heartbreak of losing his beloved Nanhi and died soon after. He was only fifty-five.

Nanhi Begum returned to Sherpur after Nawab Shams's death in 1930 and met her brother, Nawab Rafi Ali Khan. Mehdi was reunited with his family.

Nawab Rafi Ali Khan persuaded her to live in Sherpur and gave her a mahalsara in the qila. Her sons were given high positions in the administration. I dimly remember those years of living in the qila. She died right before the merger of Sherpur State into the Indian Union in 1949. The qila was given by the Nawab to the Government of India and we came to live here in Gher Mardan Khan – our ancestral haveli.

So this is the story of Feroza Begum and our family. Sometimes I wonder if Nanhi should have stayed at Bareilly and let her sons struggle instead of going back to the clutches of royalty. But the power of the name – being called a "Sahibzada" or "Sahibzadi" defines you and your fate.'

Notes

1. Personal bodyguard of the Nawab.

Lord Curzons Visit to Sherpur, 1927

A later picture of Nawab Shams in his fifties, on the visit of Lord Curzon, three years before his death, shows a prematurely old, hunched, weak-looking figure, the body curling into itself, the shoulders curved in and the chest proudly bearing the weight of his many medals.

32

Ameera

Sherpur, 2017

We are going to the Benazir Palace ruins. Dadi had promised to take me after the final exams. Getting there isn't easy. We hire a battery-operated rickshaw. It's a secret – Ammi and Abba would never understand. Dadi told Ammi that she was going to Civil Lines to visit an old friend. Chanda Bua had quietly packed last night's shami kababs and *parathey*. Dadi barely ventures out of the house and hates the battery rickshaws because they are too bumpy. I love her even more for doing this for me. Chanda Bua hides the tiffin in her burqa and we set off.

I imagine the ride Feroza Begum must have taken more than a century ago – the clip-clop of hooves and all those lovely clothes. But they were closed up in a box while we enjoy the fresh air. The three topkhana gates that lead into the city are now replaced by shiny, Mughal-style gateways with the name of the minister on the foundation stone. Dadi is shocked. She knew about the gates, but seeing them really gone must be terrible. I put my arm around her.

'Every new Nawab wants to build forts and buildings to show his power,' she sighs.

We go through the gateways and turn towards the ring road that encircles the city. The minister has broadened the road into a four-lane highway bifurcated by an iron grill. Dadi points out the *banda* embankment made by the Nawab to contain the Ramganga during the monsoons. This is a favourite road for speed bikers. Jugnu used to bunk tuitions and race his bike here. So cool. I wish I were a boy. At least in Sherpur.

The mango trees in the Benazir orchard are in full bloom like ours at home. I inhale the sweet raw-mango aroma. It's going to be a good year with lots of mangoes. We cross a little bridge and Dadi points at the now dry artificial stream going around the palace. Feroza Begum must have taken the boat ride on this stream. We get down at the palace. It's a colossal ruin.

'Now you look around. You're as wilful as Feroza Begum!' Dadi smiles and goes for a stroll around the grounds with Chanda Bua.

I climb the staircase going up to the hall. The iron bannister has rusted and the droopy lamps along the stairs are without bulbs. I can't step on the portico; the floor is all cracked now. The stables were under the portico. The grand hall, where Nawab Shams recited his ghazal for Feroza Begum, is roofless and completely choked with a jungle of trees reaching out to the skies. I can't even enter it. I find a piece of turquoise blue tile and run down to show it to Dadi.

'They used to have Freemason meetings here. Your Dada was a member. At that time, the roof of the main hall was inlaid with blue tiles with stars. It used to look like a starry sky. Is there anything left of the zenana? They called it the

Badr-e-Muneer Palace. Just go and have a look.' Dadi points at a path which used to go to the female quarters and sits down in the rickshaw, looking very tired.

I walk on the mud path between the trees. There are remains of a massive gateway with a broken wall on the sides. Nothing is left of the palace now. It's just a mound of bricks and pillaging bushes.

It was somewhere here that they had found Jugnu with Hureira and another boy. I remember how Jugnu's face used to light up when he spoke of parkour – running and climbing over the old structures, doing flips in the air. He had shown me videos shot by Hureira. He called himself 'Javed Raza Khan Pathan' on social media and had a good following.

Jugnu used to say that even if he died, the videos would stand evidence to his bravery. He was just a young boy trying to prove himself. Maybe he had an identity crisis. He had even started wearing that typical Pathan-style cap.

On the way back, I tell Dadi about Jugnu's parkour and show her a video.

'If he wanted to fight like a Pathan warrior, he should have fought to protect the gates and our heritage. What's the use of jumping all over the ruins?'

Dadi starts humming an old charbait song,

'*Kaan dabake bitiya-batiya chal mere bhaiyya.*

(Keep quiet, and tread your way, o brother.)'

I barely made it to Class XII – conditional promotion, which means they can dump me back into Class XI if I fail the term exams. Sonia says that is highly unlikely – there are too many conditional promotees and Class XI is already overcrowded. Maybe they will have a separate section for the failures.

I have to go for tuitions. It's just the first day of the session and I can feel the anxieties clustering at the back of my neck. Sonia is coming back home with me to speak to Ammi about tuitions. I don't want her to, but she is adamant. Knowing Sonia, she will bully me into speaking to Ammi right away. I'm too exhausted to negotiate a hard 'no' from Abba. I don't know if Ammi can persuade him.

Sami comes up to me as we settle into our bus seats.

'For you,' he hands me a glass jar of black insects.

'Jugnus. They'll survive only for a day in the jar.' I quickly stuff it into my bag, murmuring a surprised thanks. Sonia clears her throat and bites back a naughty smile. There are some giggles and suppressed coughs; Sami goes red, retreats and jumps down from the bus.

We are still talking about Sami and fireflies when our bus is stopped near the Mahatma Mall. They need more students waving flags when the minister inaugurates the mall. It's hardly a mall. Just a semicircular building around the Gandhi Memorial. Nawab Rafi had brought Gandhiji's slippers and enshrined them here.

I don't want to get down from the bus. What if someone took away the jar. Rita ma'am is running around, shouting at the children to get down, so I take the tiny party flag from the teacher and line up. There are those flowery arches, red carpets and posters with pictures of the minister. Sonia assures me that it won't take too long. The little girl with the scissor-bearing thali is already standing near the ribbon. The school band is playing old Bapu songs. The minister is on his way on a buggy especially imported from England. His party lost the state elections but he managed to hold on to his seat.

Gandhi Memorial now has a new marble slab and conch shells to make up for the missing Mahatma Gandhi statue. I look at the massive statue of the minister at the centre of the hub, a little way off the memorial.

'Sonia, the statue – isn't it like our Nawab's statue?'

'You mad? The face is different; the clothes are different…'

'But the base is the same – six-sided with the floral pattern!' We crane our necks.

The stance is similar – the legs slightly apart, the arm on the non-existent sword.

Back at home, I await their shining. When we had the lawn, there were masses of fireflies twinkling in the monsoon nights. They are early this year, maybe because of the April showers. In the evening they ignite with a plaintive glow, crawl around the base of the jar, reconciled to their captive state. I let them out under the mehdi tree in the deepening gloom, watch them stumble and spread their tentative wings. One by one, they fly off in lighted streaks till the last one remains. I pick it up. It sits on my finger, watching me, then crawls up to my fingertip. I hold it up high. It arches a blaze across the dark sky.

Author's Note

Murshid, meaning guide, is a peculiar name for a graveyard – its inhabitants are beyond guidance. It opens up suddenly, a vast open space in the middle of clustered old houses. That's where they probably buried her. I couldn't find her. I don't think there was ever a headstone. She would have processed the prosaic surroundings of her eternal home as an insult.

Her story was among the many *aap beeti-jag beeti* stories narrated in the water-sprayed courtyards during the nights of inevitable power cuts which filtered through the mosquito nets. The voices of the narrators echoed through the narrow gullies between conjoined houses, passed down the generations, the sequence of events jumbled and resolved, everyone participating and contributing with the shreds they remembered. Her life was a cautionary tale of the vagaries of willfulness and rejection of guidance. It caught my youthful imagination, stayed with me for years and took me on a journey to the grand old houses and the humble gullies, demanding a retelling of oral histories and vocalising a forgotten name. The names of women disappear from the pages of history; some names are banished from lips and hearts.

People scoffed at my questions and my desire to tell her story – what was there to tell anyway. The history books mentioned her in passing because she had birthed a child. She lived in our family history after we had abandoned her in life and death. It was not just a story; it was a world I wanted to recreate in all its glorious brutality. What was her world like? What defined her days? What were her aspirations, her thoughts? How did she die? I chased and sifted through stories of reliable and unreliable narrators, official histories preserved in the Raza Library, letters, secret diaries and the dusty shelves of regional archives. While cementing the pieces of her story and reincarnating her, I unwittingly superimposed my thoughts and views upon her persona. Surely she shared my outrage at the indignities heaped upon her. Maybe I was just filling in the blank spaces of her life, looking at her from a modern lens, vocalising her feelings with a vocabulary which she didn't have. I knew instinctively that she never accepted her fate. I could clearly see her passion, her anger rebelling each day as fate closed around her. They all said her temper was ungovernable. Even the Nawab would stand and listen to her rage against him.

I was straddling the fault lines of history and fiction, meandering one way, then the other. Finally, I decided to place her story in the realm of fiction and take artistic liberties like a dastango, to embellish and weave the strands of my tale around the evanescent kernel, hoping that my audience would return to my dastangoi session and read on.

I'm thankful to Isbah Khan, the librarian, as well as the staff members and scholars at the Raza Library, for their help and guidance in accessing archives and text. To Azhar Inayati sahab for permitting me to use his lyrical lines, which so aptly described the Nawab's passion. I'm especially indebted to Jahanara Begum for her work, *Remembrance of Days Past* – a first-person account of the world my characters inhabited. To Princess Mehrunnisa for her writings on growing up in Rampur and to several members of the royal family for their oral accounts that crystallized the contours of my book. To Tariq Khan for his stories and anecdotes, his accurate delineation of relationships and royal lineage. To Bilquis Jahan Begum for her diary, *Darbar-e-Rampur*, which vividly describes the life in the harems and to Raza Library for sharing the manuscript. To all the relatives and friends who narrated their family oral history.

I turned to Anuradha Roy, who with her tremendous generosity offered to read my work and painstakingly helped me with the language and structure. I can't thank her enough for that. I thank Namita Gokhale for endorsing my work with such unaffected kindness. I'm deeply indebted to Amitav Ghosh, Rana Safvi, Musharraf Ali Farooqi, Anjum Hasan and Manu Pillai for taking out time to read the novel, for their encouragement and words of support.

My mother, for her descriptions of textures, tastes and the sense of Rampur, her great belief in my ability and her impatience with the endless rounds of edits. Iqbal Ghani Khan, my uncle, who first narrated the grand sweep of Rohilla history on long drives and for teaching me to read and read well.

To Taran, my cousin, for donning the mantle of my literary mentor and for her to-be-taken-with-fistful-of-salt comments which made me kill my darlings remorselessly. The book became a much better book because of Taran, Zulfia, my aunt, Irmeen, my sister and my friends Uttaran and Priyanka. To Mariam for getting into Ameera's skin and helping me rewrite her. My brother, Saleem, for always extrapolating my career beyond my expectation. Asad for giving an unforeseen dimension to my characters. To my extended family at Saman Zaar for their loving warmth and laughter. To Mamu Jan for family lore.

My Rampur Book Club friends for treating me like a writer while I was still struggling with introducing myself as one, and for keeping me sane through the lonely writing years.

A special thanks to my literary agent Kanishka Gupta, for his faith in me, his no-holds-barred comments and his friendship. To Karthik Venkatesh, my editor at Westland, for the edits and the Westland team for their support in its first publication. To Hachette India and Thomas Abraham, for taking up *The Begum and the Dastan* for republication, and to Abhivyakti, Sini and the Hachette team for putting in painstaking efforts over it. To Adrija Ghosh for the fabulous cover design, which captures the essence of my feelings while writing the story. To Manmohan Kumar for the elegant typesetting.

Finally, and as always, my husband for walking patiently by my side throughout my search, for opening doors to gather memories and exploring places with me. My children Nadir and Gaeti for their faith in me, for helping mere in vent myself, and for their love. To my father, Afsar Husain, for teaching me optimistic perseverance. This book is for him.